In memory of
Mrs. Newell Spangler
by
Jim and Bonnie Cooper
through Friends of the Library Matching Gift Program 2003

A Feast of Carrion

A Feast of Carrion

Keith McCarthy

CARROLL & GRAF PUBLISHERS
New York

Carroll & Graf Publishers
An imprint of Avalon Publishing Group, Inc
161 William Street
NY 10038-2607
www.carrollandgraf.com

First Carroll & Graf edition 2003

First published in the UK by Constable,
an imprint of Constable & Robinson Ltd 2003

Copyright © Keith McCarthy 2003

ISBN 0-7867-1222-8

Printed and bound in the EU

This is dedicated to my wife, Judy, and my three daughters,
Isobel, Laura and Bethany. They had the grace never
to laugh at my literary ambitions
(at least not when I was in the room).

Foreword

This is a work of pure fiction. It represents the police in a not particularly favourable light and it is only fair that I should say now that it is in no way intended to be a portrait of those who serve in the Gloucestershire Constabulary, for whom I have the highest regard.

Prologue

He could have turned on a light, but he knew that there was a mirror in that cold, bleak place and it would have been too much to see himself and thereby know who he was and what he was doing. The darkness gave him anonymity. It smothered him as a lover might, allowing him to do what he wanted without shame. It urged him on even, whispered silently that though others might not understand, the night at least would not condemn. After all, it suggested, who will be hurt? This was not rape or theft or murder that he did.

This was love.

He knew the layout of the room well. He knew the starkness, the formality that stood erect all around him. He knew that, entering by the double doors, the large book that held the names of his lovers would be on a shelf to his right-hand side, and beyond it there was a large mirror fixed to the wall.

He kept the torch beam low so that it only skirted the base of the mirror as he sought the book. It was open, as it always was, the several different styles of writing – some neat, most untidy or illegible – and the wide variety of inks creating a patchwork effect.

His lovers.

The word made him shiver. He hardly dared think it, certainly never uttered it.

Who would it be tonight?

Counting them all, there were twenty-six to choose from. Not that many, although probably enough to allow a reasonable selection. Usually there were at least thirty, and once the place had been full and he had had the pick of forty-eight.

Of course, not all were eligible.

No men, for instance. He wasn't homosexual, after all. The thought of all that sodomy and prick sucking made him feel sick.

And the women needed careful weeding out. No one over sixty, and no one under sixteen. He had strong opinions on such matters.

Greedily he moved the light down the page, then turned to the next. Not good. Not good at all.

He retraced his path more slowly, all the way to the beginning, paused and sighed, then started again, stopping this time about half-way.

Deirdre Wegener, aged 56 years.

She had come off the ward. That was possibly good, because she would most likely not be fully dressed, but, depending on the reason for her admission, it might be very bad. Sometimes they were post-op, sprouting tubes and drains, wounds dehiscing, even suppurating and smelling. He didn't want that kind of thing.

Not entirely satisfied with his choice but seeing nothing better, he noted the number in the last column – forty-three – and turned away from the ledger in search of Deirdre Wegener. The light moved around the large, empty coldness and on to the wall opposite him. Twelve white metal doors stood in an impassive but commanding row before him. A vibrating hum came from deep within them as if they passed the time in murmuring softly to themselves. It was a satisfied, welcoming sort of sound, and it made him think that perhaps they at least did not disapprove.

Number forty-three was behind the third door from his right. It would be second from the bottom in the line of four. He pulled the metal lever at the left-hand side of the door, the click sounding sickeningly loud. He paused instinctively to listen, afraid that the humming, louder now, hid someone's breathing. Nothing. He opened the door, the torchlight falling on tray forty-three and the white nylon bag that lay upon it.

There was a hydraulic lift tucked away in an alcove and this he pushed over so that it lined up with the opening, then raised it slightly so that it was level with number forty-three. As he touched the tray to pull it forward on to the lift, for the first time he began to feel sexually aroused. He locked the tray into position by a peg, then let the lift fall to its lowest limit and pulled the tray into the centre of the room.

The excitement was starting to make him feel sick. Pulling the white zip down, he heard his heart thumping and there was a tremor in his hands.

In life she had not been beautiful, and death had done little for her, but she was large-breasted and big-hipped. She was also naked.

He stood astride her for long, long seconds, aware suddenly that he was in a mortuary, that it was the middle of the night and that he had an erection. He began to unzip his trousers, his mouth dry and ready almost to vomit.

He leaned forward, touching the coldness of her breasts, stroking the white, rubbery flesh of her belly. Somewhere inside his head he could hear a voice pleading with him to stop, but it was a voice that had no power now. He could feel his erection stretching his flesh and, as he moved his hands down to her hips and thighs, he was suddenly lost in something that was voracious and would not be stopped.

He stood up straight, his legs shaking so much that he thought he would fall, practically ripping his trousers open, pulling his underpants down. He started to weep silently. Why, he could not say, but it was not going to stop him. With one last look to the ceiling, perhaps to God, he began to crouch down astride the naked corpse . . .

It was then that the lights flicked on and he jumped as if electrocuted.

Part One

A fluorescent light had been left on in one of the small study cubicles that were dotted around the high, spacious room. Grouped into fours, each facing at right angles to its neighbour, the cubicles were perhaps intended to be crosses of learning, or swastikas of academic achievement. The graffiti scratched into the wooden veneer, now illumined by this solitary bulb, spoke more of boredom, lust and distraction than a thirst for scholarly accomplishment.

Further out from the cubicle, the glow quickly became yellow and feeble but it was far stronger than the gentle radiance of city light pollution that breathed on the tall windows and skylights. It caught a woman's face, impossibly passive as it erupted into ugly, red impetiginous boils, yet thankfully casting half into darkness. The plaque beneath told those who cared that this was Geraldine Darier, who had died in 1924, aged a mere twenty-nine years.

It caught full face, however, the twisted upper body of Martin Vagus (1881–1938), the head turned on the neck to expose the right side of the neck, and this itself stripped of skin and subcutis to reveal for study that which lay beneath. Small labels, written in neat black ink but illegible in the poor illumination, had been attached to each structure. Above this Martin Vagus stared with seeming unconcern through preternaturally blue eyes.

Next to him, in a case of its own, there was a tongue, from its buccal womb untimely ripp'd, held now within an oblong Perspex case, although the reader was told that once it had talked for Jonathan Koplik, born in 1834, dying, presumably in silence, some seventy-three years later. A neat wedge had been cut out of the right side, to expose the muscle stiffened by amyloidosis, a by-product of his myeloma.

Just a metre further back was a long glass and wood display case in which there were sixty foetuses, each labelled and explained, each alone in its nakedness and each pathetically unnamed; the story of the first trimester.

To right and left of this were two more heads. Truly one quarter of the face of Francis Merkel (1861–1911) had been eaten away by a tumour, his sole remaining eye hooded and sad as it stared across at his companion, Fanny Lewis.

Fanny had been a prostitute who had lived from 1900 until 1941, but it is doubtful if her latter years had been happy. Syphilis had caught her young, and it had stayed with her. It had allowed her to pursue her unchosen career, lying quietly with her in her dirty bed at night, happy to be the passive partner. Only rarely had she been aware of her burden, yet it had never left her, had never stopped its whispering work. Little had she known of it until, years later, a small sore had appeared upon the bridge of her nose. A sore that had grown until it had eaten a hole in her face.

Not many clients after that.

Nearly at the limits of its empire, the light took a gentle and uncloying grasp on two upright figures, separated by about two metres and standing back to back, one a woman, the other a man. They looked for all the world as if they had just ended an acrimonious argument, as if they had walked away from each other and now stood in silent disregard and contempt.

What the light did not reveal, what indeed it cast into darkness, was that these were no normal actors, and that their variance from normality was altogether more strange than the mere fact that both were naked. Bipedal motion was beyond them, for both were unipeds; more than that they were one-eyed, one-armed and one-eared, for each had been sawn in half, longitudinally. Their innermost beauty, that to which most of humanity is blind, was revealed.

The light barely reached the wall beyond, with its crammed bookshelves. Certainly no titles could be read, and it would only have been someone with the acutest eyesight who would have made out the shadow that was spread upon the spines.

The shadow of a rope.

Eisenmenger had noticed the Dean's smile before, how it was used sometimes to encourage, sometimes to placate, sometimes to patronize and almost always to deceive but, in all instances, always *used*. Mind you, as smiles go, he had to admit that it was a good one. Technically there was much to recommend it: it was symmetrical, it was broad and it was adorned with small creases in the skin of the cheeks, two either side, that were parallel and slightly curved. The only trouble was that somewhere between the mouth and the eyes, the smile faded, perhaps defeated by the austerity of the long climb up the steep, Roman nose, or perhaps by the frigidity in the pale blue eyes. Thus when Dean Schlemm smiled there was no humour in it, only cruelty.

And now he smiled at Eisenmenger. No words, no sigh, no movement, even, of the grey-flecked eyebrows. Merely the technical representation of a smile.

In the hush, Eisenmenger could not help reflecting that the Dean was perfectly suited to his environment. Darwin could have found all his answers here, in the depths of one of the oldest medical schools in Europe. He could have observed a race of creatures who, finding themselves in a new and hostile environment, had undergone radical but effective variation. Thus human beings had become academics, and they had thereby lost all trace of compassion, empathy, insight and conscience.

"So you cannot be sure that all the specimens in the museum are above reproach?"

The voice was quiet, almost sorrowful, but the sorrow issued from his awareness of his power and his duty. It was sorrow that he would have to sacrifice Eisenmenger if obligations were not fulfilled, and it was sorrow that would not wring from him a single tear.

While he was trying to frame a reply that gave no hint of irritation, Eisenmenger was thinking that even the Dean's colouring was protective, his face a ruddy brown that blended perfectly with the panelling and marquetry around him. Too many university lunches, too much port and brandy, no doubt.

"You must understand that I have only had responsibility for the museum for the past three and a half years . . . "

Even Eisenmenger could hear that the pathos had been overdone.

"Quite."

What did that mean? For a long moment, he had no idea what Dean Schlemm was talking about. It was nothing but a small percussive device, planted and detonated to disrupt thought processes.

" . . . but I can assure you that in that time no specimen has been accepted by the museum that has not had the appropriate informed consent."

If this satisfied the Dean, he showed not a flicker of it.

The Dean's office was literally palatial. Once this room had been the drawing room of a medieval palace and the decoration – not

7

original but the victim of Victorian restoration – reflected this. The ceiling was high enough to have its own minor meteorological system, the walls were wood-panelled and dotted with coats of arms, and the windows were bow-fronted and leaded. All of this made Eisenmenger feel, despite the lack of clerical purple, that he was the subject of a religious inquisition.

The Dean turned to his companion.

"Alexander?"

His companion was Alexander Hamilton-Bailey, the Asherman Professor of Anatomy. It was a distinguished post and, academically at least, Hamilton-Bailey was eminently suited to fill it, but physically he was less obviously a candidate for such eminence. Diminutive, retiring, almost shy, he did not so much fill the post as allow it to contract down around him. That said, Eisenmenger quite liked him. He was unfailingly courteous and did not show the same degree of contemptuous animosity towards him as most of the senior academics did.

There was a pause before Hamilton-Bailey responded. It was as though this small, delicate man was trying to drag his attention into the room from a far distant place. He looked pale and Eisenmenger wondered if he were hungover or incubating a virus. When he returned the other's smile it was brief and manufactured, as if all he was doing was returning a secret sign like a mason's handshake.

Eisenmenger reflected that being interviewed by these two was a bit like being interviewed by two animals that were clearly of the same species but, equally clearly, were of completely different breeds. The Dean was a sporting hound, lean, athletic and graceful, one eye forever on those who might be looking at him: the Professor of Anatomy was something less kind to the eye – perhaps a Pekinese – and considerably less inclined to physical prowess. To see them sitting side by side was to see a scene that appeared unnatural.

"Well, whilst I am sure that Dr Eisenmenger has nothing for which to reproach himself personally, we have to consider earlier contributions."

So they were contributions, were they? Hamilton-Bailey spoke of them as if they were charitable gifts, small change thoughtlessly taken from the fluff of the back pocket.

"I don't see that I can be held in any way responsible for what occurred before I was appointed," he pointed out. Quite reasonably, too, he thought.

The Dean paused and gave the impression that he was waiting for the Professor of Anatomy to say something. When nothing was forthcoming from the pallid, thin lips, Schlemm himself had to point out, "Be that as it may, but I am sure that you will appreciate that your inaction in the matter, now that it has been drawn to your attention, would be difficult to defend."

Schlemm looked again to his professorial colleague for some sign of his support, but he found himself alone. His frown, like all his other facial gestures, was exquisite, and it was by no means ineffective as a weapon. Generally it served to silence, humble and frighten, yet on his colleague it now proved useless. Hamilton-Bailey may physically have been sitting on his right-hand side at the end of the long conference table, but his spirit was too obviously wandering in other places. In fact he was regarding the highly polished wood of the table as if it wove mesmeric patterns in the grain. Actually, Eisenmenger was developing the suspicion that Hamilton-Bailey hadn't washed, that the tailored suit, brightly white shirt and silk, crested tie were inappropriate vestments covering a slightly vaporous core.

Eisenmenger didn't know much about the Professor of Anatomy, even less about his home life, but the rumours concerning his wife had a virility and persistence that even he could not miss. There was even the juiciest of juicy ones that Dean Schlemm had once been amongst the dramatis personae, although their present matiness seemed to suggest otherwise. In view of Hamilton-Bailey's present malaise, Eisenmenger wondered whether his domestic situation had relapsed.

At least his obvious distraction helped to lessen the unpleasant material that was being lobbed in his direction, lobbed with an action that was balletic in its execution but no less accurate for that.

"Do you know how many pathological exhibits there are in the museum?" he asked and, just in case the Dean should try to ignore this enquiry, he added, "Over ten thousand. And that's only the ones we know about. The museum's been in existence for over three hundred years. There are store rooms that I don't think have been opened for decades."

Schlemm sighed, showing how reasonable he was, how he understood the implications of what he wanted.

"We are all well aware of the age and . . . " Searching for the *mot juste* he turned briefly to the Professor of Anatomy, but didn't wait long enough for the other to stir himself before continuing, "eminence of the museum. There is nothing like it in the country, and little to compare with it in Europe."

Somehow, amidst all this reasonableness, the Dean gave him the impression that something huge, uncomfortable and immensely shitty was coming his way.

"And clearly," he went on, "you have gained much in being associated with it."

It didn't require night vision binoculars to spot the nasty little predator in the deep shadows of the Dean's oratory.

"It would be a shame, therefore, if a *difficulty*," he emphasized the word to underline its euphemistic context, "were to arise because you had not had the foresight to ensure that there is nothing within the museum that is less than exemplary."

For a moment he had been lost by the Dean's verbosity. It was in this lacuna that Professor Hamilton-Bailey found within himself enough strength to enter the discussion again.

"Just as all the anatomical exhibits have a complete provenance, with fully informed and documented consent for their use in the museum, we must ensure that the pathological items cannot be faulted."

Dean Schlemm, clearly delighted that he was no longer fighting a lone battle, smiled at his colleague.

"Precisely," he said.

"And in order to start the process of verification, I will ensure that all the relevant documentation on the anatomical exhibits is with your office in four weeks' time."

How the Dean beamed upon the Professor of Anatomy! And how this radiant pleasure was reflected by the small, refined features of Hamilton-Bailey!

Inevitably the moment ended and they turned to Eisenmenger, their junior colleague, the Dean's expression one of anticipation.

It was not, of course, fair and they knew it just as well as he did. The anatomical part of the museum constituted less than twenty-five per cent in terms of number of items, and many of those were models. In any case, every single body that was dissected by the Department of Anatomy was offered with full documentation under the guidance of the Anatomy Act. The specimens that were provided by the Pathology Department had tended to adopt considerably more diverse routes into the museum. Being quite honest with himself, Eisenmenger didn't want to know how the majority of the grotesqueries had found themselves in glass jars on its shelves.

"It's going to be very difficult . . . " he began. If he had wanted either of the two men on the opposite side of the table to help him out following this start, disillusionment was his immediate reward.

"Quite," remarked the Dean, while the Professor of Anatomy only smiled.

10

Nobody could say that he didn't persevere, so he tried again, but this time with even less success.

" . . . and it may take some considerable time . . . "

Now there was nothing but silent expectation coming from them, a gulf that he was being pushed relentlessly to fill.

Then the Dean asked softly, "So you will want to start at once?"

For a moment an explosion of impotent indignation threatened to spark, expand and consume him, but it had gone before it reached his face, his eyes or his voice. What was the point? He could not win.

In the vast, arcane and intricate hierarchy that was the medical school's structure of management and organization, he was an organism that was small, delicate and easy to tread on, whether accidentally or otherwise. It was because he was easily destroyed that he needed the patronage of men such as these, men who would not have been in his top ten list for desert island companionship: men who would not have been in the top five billion, probably.

He was being mugged, and everyone in the room knew it.

The anger blossomed and peaked, then, unable to make its mark upon the world, it seeped away. He sighed.

"Of course," he said softly.

They didn't, he noticed, exactly shake hands and clap each other on the shoulders, but the air of mutual satisfaction was plain.

"Splendid," murmured the Dean.

There came a knock upon the door. The Dean's secretary, a small, middle-aged woman who never smiled, put her head into the room.

"I'm sorry to interrupt, Dean."

The Dean turned to her expectantly. "What is it?"

"There's been some sort of incident in the museum. I am told that Dr Eisenmenger is urgently required."

She spoke if she didn't believe it. What could be so urgent that the Dean of the medical school was to be interrupted? The Dean also greeted this with astonishment. He frowned and there was a significant moment when Eisenmenger thought that he was going to be prevented from going.

"Well," said the Dean slowly, "I suppose we have all but finished . . . "

He looked to Hamilton-Bailey who shrugged.

Eisenmenger stood awkwardly. He began to make his way to the door as the Dean called to him, "We will review the situation in three months."

Being in no position to negotiate he merely turned, nodded agreement, and hurried out, wondering what could possibly have happened in the museum. He had noticed a tray at the Dean's elbow: Jamaican Blue Mountain or some such, served in bright silverware, and accompanied by a plate of macaroons. He had not been offered a chance to partake and as the door closed behind him he heard the fine china chink. He had just enough humour left to smile.

The Dean's secretary bore a striking resemblance to her employer both in looks and attitude. She could almost have been his older, slightly more desiccated sister. Perhaps there was a family of creatures such as these, who cloaked themselves in near-human disguise, but were of an older, far more intelligent and cultured race. Thin and austere, disapproval woven into her flesh, she had eyes that saw the world and liked not a thing about it. Certainly her gaze as it sliced through Eisenmenger was not the look of someone thinking up adjectives in praise of him.

"One of your secretaries apparently needs to talk with you urgently."

He noted the 'apparently'. Noted too the tone, an ounce of which could almost have broken his back so heavy was the distaste.

It was Gloria. Gloria was joyously common, bright and gaudy: a bit like a crested duck. Had about the same mental ability as well.

"Dr Eisenmenger?"

"What is it, Gloria?"

"Something's happened in the museum. We've just had Stephan on the phone and he sounded hysterical, as if he'd lost it completely."

Gloria was incapable of sounding anything other than cheerful. She had enough drive and personality for ten people. Misfortune bounced off her, badly shaken by the encounter: she wasn't interested in the concept. The loss of her legs would have been her chance to take things easy: blindness would have been an opportunity for lower electricity bills.

Not that bad luck didn't stop trying. Her husband had left her for an exotic dancer, come back three years later, beaten her up and taken her savings; her daughter had been nearly killed in a road traffic accident, and she had inflammatory bowel disease that prompted frequent hospitalizations.

"Did he say what was wrong?"

"Something about a dead body."

She said it slyly, as if making a joke.

"A dead body?"

"That's what he said."

He sighed.

"I'll come straight over."

The Dean's secretary had been listening of course. He pondered whether to wipe the telephone receiver with his handkerchief but thought she'd do it herself anyway.

"Thanks."

The sniff was faint but far from inaudible.

Schlemm and Hamilton-Bailey had talked of administrative matters over their coffee and biscuits, but it had been chit-chat, nothing more; small talk meant to camouflage and obfuscate rather than communicate.

At last, Schlemm said, "You look tired, Alexander."

The Professor of Anatomy was momentarily flustered.

"Not sleeping well?" enquired the Dean, employing a solicitous expression.

"Oh, you know," and then because that sounded rather lame he went on, "There's a lot going on in Anatomy at the moment. Three papers in preparation, the Anatomy prize, and then there's my book – you know, the new edition of *Gray's*."

That he had been chosen to edit the new *Gray's Anatomy* was for Hamilton-Bailey something worth trumpeting, and trumpet it he did on every occasion that came his way.

Strangely the Dean missed the significance of this.

"How's Irene? I haven't seen her for ages."

The question seemed to cause a momentary pain in Hamilton-Bailey for he rushed to hide discomfort by saying at once, "She's fine." Then, as if the assurance might not be entirely convincing, "Fine."

The Dean evinced relief.

"We must have you round for dinner. Sally would so like to see you and Irene again."

The prospect of this engagement, strangely, abstracted no great joy from the Professor of Anatomy, a fact that did not evade the Dean's notice.

"Wonderful," was the little man's sole response, uttered in a tone tinged with melancholy.

After Hamilton-Bailey had gone, Schlemm sat and pondered.

Irene Hamilton-Bailey was wandering again, that much was plain. He wondered who was the recipient of her sexual favours this time. The marriage had long ago become one of convenience, at least on her part. For her, whatever love she had once possessed for her spouse had withered into dry contempt. Hamilton-Bailey clearly still loved her, but that meant nothing to her. She was independently wealthy. Independent full stop. That her independence – the Dean thought, spoke and even ate in euphemisms – caused Hamilton-Bailey constant, unending agony had always been plain to all his colleagues.

Once, Schlemm had asked her why she didn't leave him, and she had looked surprised.

"Why on earth would I want to do that? The marriage is perfect. I contribute my wealth and all that wealth brings, he contributes his academic position."

And he allows you to indulge yourself, he had thought.

"But are you not afraid that he will leave you?" he had asked then.

She had laughed. "Good grief no! Alex loves his creature comforts too much. He could never survive on his professorial salary alone."

It wasn't a situation he would want to find himself in, he had decided. He much preferred his peccadilloes discreet.

"Does he . . . *indulge* himself?" He made it sound like masturbation rather than adultery.

Irene Hamilton-Bailey looked shocked. "Good God, no!" After a pause, she added, "What an absurd thought!" Then, more reflectively, she added, "I'd cut him off without a penny if he ever did . . . "

The hypocrisy of this caused Schlemm silent amusement, but further consideration of Alexander Hamilton-Bailey's circumstances was at that moment precluded by Irene Hamilton-Bailey's assault on his erect penis.

The Dean's office was in the Administration building, across the road from the bulk of the medical school. Eisenmenger dodged the morning traffic and entered the museum through the back doors, using his key. The sole illumination in this small entrance hall was from a bare light bulb hanging from a short length of brown flex. Such was the lack of radiance you could see the filament through the melancholic dimness that it exuded. The only exit was a flight of wooden stairs that led up to a door on which was a sign proclaiming the privacy of the recesses beyond. On either side of the stairs were empty boxes and cigarette ends.

He climbed the stairs and pushed the door, expecting it to be unlocked, but it wasn't. That was odd, since Goodpasture was always first in and always put the self-locking door on the latch. It took him a moment to locate the key in his jacket pocket.

"Stephan?"

14

He ought to have been in his room, the first on the right, but he wasn't. Bowman wasn't there either, but that was to be expected. Tim Bowman's internal clock wasn't set to GMT, but then, since he spent most of his time in another space-time continuum altogether, that wasn't entirely without surprise.

He moved along the corridor to Goodpasture's office, found that bereft of human company too. Where was everybody?

His eyes flicked across the window on to the museum. From where he was standing in the doorway, the view was towards the eastern end of the southern hall. He could see little of the central area that joined the northern and southern halls and nothing of the floor area there. Later he remembered how cold and frail was the winter morning light, how the academic hues of the book-lined upper gallery were muted by it.

It felt wrong, even then. Goodpasture should have been at work in his office, while his assistants (Stephan, at least) made busy with whatever tasks he had assigned them. Even without Stephan's peculiar telephone call this silence was wrong. Some things were immutable, whatever their intrinsic worth, and the early morning workings of the museum were amongst them.

He went further along the corridor to the door on his left that led into the large workroom. It was here that the models were prepared or repaired, where new exhibits were mounted and labelled, where the practicalities were addressed. This too was locked; this too was wrong.

He had no choice now but to descend the stairs at the end and enter the museum. These stairs were carpeted and he had never understood why. Nowhere else behind the scenes was accorded this extravagance.

The door at the bottom was unlocked and he pushed it open. It creaked, but then it always did.

The Museum of Anatomy and Pathology was housed in a huge H-shaped building. It was nearly three storeys high and had at the centre of its roof a glass dome. Beneath the dome, in the crossbar that joined the two long rectangular halls, there was a magnificent round wooden table, fully five metres in diameter, made of polished oak. Around this were arrayed twenty-four chairs.

The two parallel halls ran precisely east to west. They provided the main floorspace for the large number of pathological and anatomical exhibits, although those on display were only a small selection of the total number. Large store rooms, accessible from an alcove in the middle of the southern wall of the southern hall, held the rest. At each corner of each hall there were spiral staircases that were steep and made of iron that was smooth and black. These were joined at the top by a gallery that followed the outline of the whole museum and gave access to the upper bookshelves. Bookshelves covered all the walls where there were no doors. There were nearly thirty thousand books. The only windows, aside from Goodpasture's, were in the dome or set high in the ceiling.

It was a magnificent building, perfect for its function. Enhancing its function, really. Goodpasture, who had studied its history, made its spirit part of his, would waste no opportunity to wax to anyone who would listen (or at least anyone who he imagined was listening, although most people's attention withered like a disused limb when he got going) about the academic atmosphere, the feeling of history, the men (and even the odd woman) good and great who had sat and studied in the halls . . . etc, etc, etc.

Goodpasture, though, was like that. A man who had been constructed from nerve roots all pointing in the same direction, sinews that were unbendable, principles that were unbreakable beyond the strength of man, and a world view that was telescopic in its magnification and just as tunnel-bound and focused. All these and what good did it do him? None in Eisenmenger's view, since the Good Lord (or whichever Supreme Being had been responsible for the construction of this small man in a small world) had omitted a sense of humour, the unguent without which he was constantly irritating those around him. Of all the things that might profitably have been left on the floor of the biology laboratory where God's minions had toiled to construct him (the moustache, the dandruff, the hopeless fashion sense and the dry, leathery skin that no amount of cosmetic could have saved from *sallowness*, for instance) it had been decided that he should possess no consciousness of irony. It ruined him, and it made Eisenmenger feel guilty that he could feel no sorrow for him.

Indeed, the main emotion Goodpasture induced was either irritation or amusement, depending on one's viewpoint. That Goodpasture had never learned to address Basil Russell, august and hated head of Histopathology, by his appropriate title of 'Professor' was a purulent abscess in Russell's side but a source of joy ascending to Eisenmenger.

Yet there was no doubt that he was an excellent curator of this curious place, for he loved it. If Goodpasture had been allowed, he would have had one of the smaller store rooms converted into a bedroom for himself and his wife, there to spend the remaining

16

years of his perfectly confined life surrounded by all that he loved and all, it was perfectly clear, that loved him.

It was hard to believe from observing and talking to Goodpasture that there existed deeper strata, although a single incident had led Eisenmenger to suspect their existence. This had been the time when Goodpasture's wife, a dumpy woman with broken false teeth and a womb that had obviously gone to live in the deep south and taken much of her pelvic floor with it, had suddenly appeared in the museum. Greatly agitated, Goodpasture had taken her to his office where they had remained incarcerated for over an hour. When they had emerged, Goodpasture had requested the rest of the day off, citing a crisis concerning his stepson. Eisenmenger – who had been ignorant of the existence of this relative – enquired if it was serious and had been told by an extremely upset Mrs Goodpasture that it was, exceedingly so. Could he help? They had looked at each other then, but Goodpasture had shaken his head firmly. They had left, and when Goodpasture had returned the next day he would speak no more of it, no matter how hard he was pressed. Eisenmenger found this frustrating. He had fleetingly seen that the man was not a mere sketch but was possessed of a third dimension, yet almost at once he insisted that it should be forgotten.

Thus within the week, Goodpasture had become flattened into his more familiar two dimensions, once again immersed in the museum, and it was difficult not to believe that his whole life was in that one building. True, to look around at the individual parts was to gaze upon some strange and shocking things but nonetheless it was plain that Goodpasture saw them with different eyes. Even the unadorned organs on display – and there were hundreds of those – with their tumours, haematomas, congenital abnormalities and abscesses attracted from most either prurient or studious attention, yet from Goodpasture they elicited a sense of companionship.

If anything that lived and breathed came close to embodying the museum and all that it represented, then that thing was Goodpasture.

But where was he now? And where, moreover, was Stephan?

And then he saw it.

What was it that he noticed first? In his recollection all the senses were synchronous, yet he doubted that it was as simple during the reality of it. Memory, he suspected, had ordered, reordered and tailored the experience to make of it a smooth progression in time.

17

Was it the smell? The faint yet slightly acrid tang of drying and dried blood that is as much as anything else the smell of death? A subtle smell but one that somehow forges a link with the deepest centre of emotion, the curled and swirled horse's head that lies nestled in the safest, warmest part of the temporal lobe.

Perhaps it was the feel of coldness on his face, the coolness of an empty space, the frigidity of a morgue, carrying with it the insistence that this was no human place.

And then there were the faint whimpers, heard from a far distant place, echoing so faintly that the sound's twin was little more than a distortion at the dying fall of every sound.

Whichever was first or second, third or fourth, whatever the order in which these things came to him and begged for attention, none could compete with the enormity of that which his eyes brought him then. As soon as his mind had registered what was displayed before him, all else seemed to go, fading instantaneously into transparency, as if before the angry breath of God.

And yet . . .

And yet, later, he came to believe that the first thought in his head as he turned to face the beautiful round of the oak conference table was something peripheral, something that did not appear to be of immediate relevance.

She's beautiful . . .

She was perhaps a metre-sixty tall, with short, bobbed hair that had been hennaed. Her eyes were open and they were deep, dark brown. They were the eyes of the dead, already filmed, but they were still striking and they were still beautiful.

He could not get over the fact that even in death, even in a death such as this, she retained her beauty.

And familiarity.

He remembered thinking that he had seen her before, but it was a thought soon gone, too delicate and natal to last in the crush of overwhelming perceptions, emotions and reactions that rushed in upon it. Certainly there was no time then to consider where or when he might have looked upon her in life, not with her death before him.

And such a death as that.

She was unclothed and hanging above the round conference table almost, as far as he could see from the angle at which he stood, above its exact centre. Around her neck was a pale red rope. It looked as if it was made of nylon, although he could not be certain from that distance, but the colour – a gentle pink in the weak winter's light – seemed almost to have been chosen for its implications of femininity and grace. The knot was behind her left ear and therefore on his side. It caused her head to twist to the right, jutting her jaw forward and up.

His eyes followed the rope upwards. He had no recollection that he willed them upwards, merely that they followed the natural path from body to knot and thence to its point of origin.

Yet the rope was impossibly long. It rose up past the tops of the display cabinets, past the great spherical lights, great white glass globes themselves suspended on impressively long chains to varying heights, past the balcony that ran along the upper half of the building, and yet still ever up, to pass beyond the limit of his gaze.

It was then that he realized it came down from the highest point of the building, the great glass dome, and not only could he not see its beginning, he could not even see how it could be fixed there.

Very gingerly he moved forward, careful to avoid the splashes on the carpet.

Her face was faintly congested, and he thought then that it was the congestion of the asphyxiated. He could see that her eyes were slightly bloodshot.

Just a metre closer, but the detail became clearer, the horror magnified.

She had been sliced open. Someone had quite deliberately incised her from larynx to pubis, pulling the flesh back from the ribcage, grasping skin, fat and muscle, like belly pork, and pulling hard and long. Her breasts were large and heavy, and now they hung down, distorting the line of the hide, as if it was a jacket with overfilled pockets. The ribs grinned whitely beneath, unaccustomed to such exhibition.

But then, as if the access had proved too restricted, a horizontal cut had been made, perpendicular to the first and running just above the level of the umbilicus, around her flanks and on to her back. Thus a cross was formed, with two lower flaps that flopped down exposing the abdominal cavity, exposing the green-grey curls and coils of the small intestine.

And even there the abomination did not end.

The intestines may appear unruly, writhing and ill disciplined in their close-packed confines, but they are in fact constrained. Some of their length is closely invested with membrane, tied to the back of the abdominal cavity, but their greater part has more freedom, restrained by a membrane – the mesentery – that fans out from the retroperitoneum, a short leash upon which they can play but not escape.

The mesentery had been cut, for nothing else would explain why coil within coil hung forward, grasping air and space. But this was not a neat, surgical incision. This had been hacked as if hurried, and in the urgency and poor precision, the blade must have nicked some other structure – the aorta or inferior vena cava perhaps, maybe even the kidney.

So the gut rolled out and down, and blood had streamed out with them, trickling down the dully glistening surface like a water feature in the courtyard of the region of the damned. Some of it had run down her legs, but most of it had dripped, then splashed on to the oak table. A large pool had collected there, dark red, viscous, outgrowing the table's confines and dropping thence to the floor.

As he looked at this, at this attractive young girl, perhaps twenty, at this desecration that was gothic in its conception, theatrical in its enaction, he knew, despite the ordering and reordering, analysis, dismantling and rebuilding that went on in his mind later, that for long minutes there was nothing else in the museum, the world, anywhere.

This was all.

He must have stood looking at the bloodied mess, nothing else impinging on his awareness, for long, long minutes before the whimpering cries turned his head and he saw the almost foetal form at the end of the hall. Its eyes looked bright in the gloom, as if it were some creature from the imagination, and the noises were soft, meant not for attention, perhaps for comfort. It took him a moment to recognize who it was.

Libman had been completely overwhelmed by the sight, backed against a bookcase, staring at the atrocity from the distance of half the hall's length. It was a wonder he had been able to make the phone call to the Pathology General Office.

"Stephan?"

He had to skirt around the periphery of the slaughter. Taking his eyes away from it had seemed to require almost sacrilegious purpose, as if nothing else should be allowed to distract from this thing that had been constructed at the focal point of the museum.

"Stephan?"

The boy did not respond. Not even with his eyes.

He walked up to him and then stood directly before him. Even then he felt invisible, Libman's eyes just staring at the memory of the thing.

"Stephan?"

Still no reaction to this third attempt, and so he tried yet again, only louder, actually shouting. Still nothing. If this had been a film he would have slapped him, but he didn't feel particularly inclined to cinematic cliché at that moment. He took the boy by the shoulders and at once felt a fine tremor.

"Stephan?" Softer now, but directly into his face, and squeezing gently the young man's shoulders, feeling the rough fabric of the faded blue rugby shirt. The stare came round to him and within a second Libman was focusing on Eisenmenger's stubbled beard.

"Can you hear me, Stephan?"

There was a nod. For a moment he glanced in the direction of the bloodied thing, then back to Eisenmenger.

"I suggest we go upstairs and sit down. Okay?"

But it wasn't okay. Most definitely not. The tremor had coarsened and the eyes had widened as they had flicked to the thing at Eisenmenger's back. No way was Stephan going to walk towards it. The whimpering returned and he began to shake his head vigorously, his feet pushing his back against the bookcase.

"All right, all right."

He tried to sound reassuring, maybe even succeeded. He looked around. A metal spiral staircase on his right led up to the balcony.

"We'll go up to the balcony. Go past it that way. You can shut your eyes and I'll hold on to you, okay?"

For a minute, he thought that even this was going to prove too unpalatable, that he would just have to leave Libman to his terrors while he phoned for the police, but there was a small nod amidst all the shaking.

He took him by the upper arm and more or less pushed him up the stairs and then along the clanking balcony. It was like walking a half-sentient android, one without full awareness of what was required. Libman kept his eyes shut the whole time, one hand on the rail, the other stiffly at his side.

When they drew more or less level with the rope Eisenmenger found his gaze dragged irresistibly towards it. From up here, above the atrocity, the perspective gained added even more to the awfulness. The full extent of the dreadful grandeur, the symmetry of the blood splayed out in deep red splashes upon the table and far beyond, the theatricality of it all, the consideration of the design, all became much more apparent. Had it been anything other than a human being down there, it would have been art.

Suddenly Stephan stopped and drew away from the metal rail, his body flattening itself against the glass and wood of Goodpasture's panoramic window. The whimpering began again. He must have caught a glimpse of it, whether through accident or design. It was only with great force that Eisenmenger managed to propel him forward and past it. As soon as it was behind them, the boy relaxed and progress became easier. All the while Eisenmenger talked to him under his breath, reassuring him that he need fear nothing.

They then had to descend another spiral staircase but thankfully this was just out of sight, in an alcove that contained a connecting door to the rest of the Pathology Department.

"Are you okay, Stephan?"

He nodded, a jerky movement that was more spastic than it should have been.

"We'll go upstairs to your room and then phone the police."

They made the trip with little difficulty. Eisenmenger sat him down in his untidy, poky office and breathed relief, but if he had hoped that by removing him from the vicinity of the object there would be some return to normality, his disappointment was not long delayed.

"Stephan?"

Nothing. He seemed to have relapsed for he just shivered once and began to cry, his face in his hands.

"Stephan?" The instinct was to raise his voice, but he ignored it. "Stephan? Did you tell anyone else?"

He put his hand out to the boy's shoulder.

"Does anyone else know about this?"

At long last there was a reaction and Libman's eyes found him. The head shook slowly.

There was a phone in the room. It was dirty and chipped, a telephone sanitizer's delight, but it worked. He dialled 999.

The woman's voice was almost bored as he reported a murder.

"A murder," she repeated and there was no questioning rise in pitch as there ought to have been. A pause then, "Are you sure?"

Gosh, perhaps it was suicide after all . . .

But presumably they were trained to do this. No point in sending squad cars screaming around the countryside if granny's demise had been by galloping dandruff and not the hand of a desperate ruffian.

"Yes, I'm certain. I'm a pathologist."

If he expected this nugget to crack the façade, he was wrong.

"Your name, please."

"Eisenmenger. Dr Eisenmenger."

"And the location of the body?"

"The Museum of Anatomy and Pathology. St Benjamin's Medical School."

"Don't touch anything. Please wait at the scene until the police arrive."

And with that she was gone. What's another murder?

Libman was still shaking but he had stopped weeping. It occurred to Eisenmenger that he should be making him something to drink, but the domestic arrangements of the two assistant curators consisted of half a jar of coffee creamer, an empty kettle and three mugs that had enough detritus crusted on the inside and the outside to have nurtured primordial life. He filled the kettle from the sink by the door and set it to boil.

"Is there anything to drink in here?"

No answer.

"Stephan?"

He gave up asking.

"I'm going to get some teabags."

He knew that Goodpasture would have some and he didn't want to leave Libman too long. And that, of course, set him wondering again. Where was Goodpasture? Only once had he known Goodpasture to be late since had he started at the medical school, and that had been when his wife had nearly died from acute peritonitis secondary to a perforated appendix. He had spent the next three weeks apologizing every time Eisenmenger saw him, as if the lapse were unforgivable.

In Goodpasture's office the temptation to go to the window, to stand transfixed at the glass, was almost beyond endurance. Like an alcoholic in front of a litre bottle of scotch he had to concentrate on turning away, force himself to cast the image behind him.

He thought that he knew where the old man kept his tea and coffee. The kettle was there, on a low chest of drawers just inside the doorway on the right. It was accompanied by two cups, complete with saucers, together with two spoons and a bowl of sugar: all were cleaned to a standard that would have brought a smile to a sergeant-major's face. Had he spent some time in the army?

Yet despite all this apparatus, beverages for the brewing of, he could find no trace of anything to make with them. It was while he was searching through the myriad drawers, cupboards and crannies that he had heard someone knock on the side door that led in from the street.

When he had made his way back down the stairs, he opened the door cautiously to two policemen.

Eisenmenger had seen too many bodies during his life. He had been there at the discovery of young men, old men, wives, aunts, mothers and daughters, children and adolescents. Some were fresh, some were rotted close to anonymity yet all retained their ability to force tears from the men who moved softly around them. Some had been hardly touched by death, their features and imperfect bodies almost as God had wanted; others had been mutilated – shotgunned, burned, hacked, tortured, flayed – their humanity left only in the eyes of the beholders, and thereby heightened, multiplied by memory's tricks and the mind's comparisons and empathies.

He had been present once when the body of a woman, killed by a jealous lover, had been found in the cupboard under the stairs of her mother's house. The murderer, a young accountant with shiny eyes and a smile that lifted the heart, had called that morning, taking with him a twenty-centimetre kitchen knife in place of flowers. The door had been opened by the mother and she, in turn, had been opened by this charming suitor.

It was late afternoon by the time the father arrived home, falling over his wife's corpse as he opened his newly painted blue front door. Everyone had assumed that the daughter was at work, until one of the constables had, in the course of his duties, checked this poky place full of meters, mops, brooms and polish, only to discover the accountant's second victim, slumped over amongst the dusters. The knife was still at her side and the head was nearly separated from the torso. She had looked not scared, merely puzzled, as if perplexed perhaps by this oddity of behaviour, this breach of etiquette.

Then there had been the time when he had been called to a mass grave, seven men tortured with cattle prods, executed by shotgun and buried in a Surrey wood, on the wrong side in a feud over cocaine. The lime had had little time to delete their faces, to wipe away their varied looks of fear and pain, and none, he had noticed, had been puzzled. It was plain that here was not broken etiquette, for their world held rules that dictated different codes, different expectations. They held no perplexity that this was being done for they understood all too well the thoughts and motivations of their antagonists. Perhaps because of this, their deaths were somehow less painful because they comprehended the reasons for all the physical agony they endured.

And the worst?

The worst was the last. The worst was the one that was not only the worst but the one that was different. The worst was one where he could not play the clinician, where he could not merely make his entry after Act One to pontificate and ruminate upon the finer sides to death. The worst was when a trick was played by fate and he found himself there at the time, there when he had no right to be there.

She was a six-year-old child, a brown-eyed girl called Tamsin Bright who had died in his arms.

He had cadged a lift with a policeman he knew vaguely, Constable Bob Johnson, because his car was in for a service. After a day spent in the County Court, defending his findings against some smart-alec barrister with money, accent and even some brains, he had felt ready for a rest and a drink. He hadn't listened to the radio messages, could never understand them anyway.

"Sorry," said his companion and Eisenmenger hadn't twigged what he was talking about until the lights and the siren had gone on and Johnson had started to drive too fast too easily. For a while he remembered feeling slightly elated, excited in a kind of puerile way at the manner in which they moved around the traffic, even driving on the wrong side of the road, to reach their destination.

The house was a bungalow, decayed and dirtied into a hovel, the garden filled with black plastic sacks and oil patches. There was smoke coming from a living-room window that had been broken and ineptly boarded up, and from the cracked glass of the front door. They were the first police to arrive. A small crowd had collected, a cross-section of middle-aged men, young mothers and older women, none apparently brave enough or concerned enough to do anything other than spectate.

"Is there anyone in there?"

It was as though he was asking them to confess to arson or to point a finger of accusation. No one knew.

"Who lives here?"

A mother and her little girl. This datum given as if passing secrets to the enemy.

Johnson had turned to him.

"You'd better stay here."

If only he had, but he hadn't. He had ideas. Stupid ideas that he was a hero.

So Eisenmenger had followed him and Johnson didn't argue: perhaps he was secretly glad not to be alone. When he reached the door he had already raised his baton. He stood to one side of the rotting doorframe, pushing Eisenmenger to the other. With his head turned away he smacked the glass and it shattered. Only more smoke came out, no flame. He put his hand in and turned the handle. He was gone into the smoke before Eisenmenger knew it.

Eisenmenger had hesitated then, but had to follow, had to be the hero.

The relief he felt when at once he realized that there was no raging inferno, that the smoke and smell were emanating from dirty rags piled on the living-room floor. The carpet had burned but it had not caught and not spread to anything else. Johnson had picked up a stained blanket from the armchair and thrown it over the smouldering heap. Then they heard the fire tender arrive and Johnson had gone to meet it, leaving Eisenmenger alone.

Leaving him to wander out of the living room and into the back room, the kitchen-diner. The door had been closed, but there had been a cacophony. Music playing, a scramble of talking and shouting, the wood of the door meshing it all together, although it was clearly very loud. The television, he thought, but then he heard something else. Something that was not tinny and recorded.

A small crying.

Then . . .

Eisenmenger knew at once what the next noise was. A sort of inverted sigh, air rushing together to fill a vacuum, and then a clap as two curtains of atmosphere met.

At once there was a scream like no other scream could ever be.

He shoved the door open.

What he saw then became petrified within him, a moment of such total horror that he knew not even death would expunge it, that it would live eternally, made incarnate by its awfulness.

In the centre of the room, while a woman stood back against the wall and idly flicked a cigarette lighter and looked dreamily into space with a smile, was a mass of smoky flame.

And in the centre of that mass was a little girl.

The dining table was laid, the television was on and playing loudly. The radio was on too, just out of tune, Radio Three fading and crescendoing through something classical. The room was filling with smoke now, the grey clouds collecting below the ceiling, wreathed around a pink, stained lampshade.

The girl was writhing on the floor, screaming, screaming, screaming.

There was nothing to throw on to her, and all he could do was wrench off his jacket and rush forward with it held in front of him. He had fallen on top of her, banging down upon the flames, feeling the heat and the hurt but not the pain. It had taken perhaps twenty seconds to put out the flame, but it had been a billion days too long.

Burned to cracked blackness, oozing redness from jagged flakes, naked save for a few tatters of nylon that had melded to her flesh, half her face had gone, and both arms, her torso and one leg were charred. He thought she was dead then.

He had had to pick her up in order to make sure that all the fire was gone. Now he looked up at the woman, but she hadn't even turned in his direction.

He had opened his mouth and shouted for Johnson. Shouted as he had never shouted before.

It must have brought the little girl back to consciousness, for she looked up at him then, and the dreadfulness began anew.

She was dying, that much was clear. As he had held her, she had twitched and he had felt her flesh crack in his grasp. He could only hope that she was beyond pain, that the fire had destroyed her capacity to feel agony. Someone had come in behind him and he had heard a gasp and some profanity, but Eisenmenger's world was the small girl and nothing more. At least she had stopped screaming. Her one remaining eye had found his face and he had seen within it not fear, not pain, not even distress, but merely a question.

The last words she had said were in his head at all times, lying there and occasionally sounding him out, asking a question that he could never answer, that filled him with dread, hope and wonder all at once.

A question that proved that there is a God and simultaneously proved that He is a cruel God.

"Where's my mummy?"

And then she slipped away from him, leaving behind her only the stink of burned human grease in his nostrils and a fatty, rose-coloured stain on his white shirt.

They had taken the woman away, still uninterested in the small bundle on the floor in the middle of the room, still seeing something in the distance, while Eisenmenger had stood and looked out of the window at a small and untended garden. It was only then that he had recognized the music.

Ravel's Pavane.

Walking finally out of that house, he had walked out of the whole of his previous life.

"Oh, shit."

Johnson had breathed the word, but Lockwood articulated it. Johnson glanced across at his fellow officer, a shrewd idea what was coming next. Lockwood was blond, fresh-faced and stupid, all

27

qualities for which he compensated by being overbearing, arrogant and aggressive. He desperately wanted to get out of the uniformed branch and thus tended to despise everything but the CID. In his attempts to leap the great divide he had volunteered to help out with a surveillance operation and it was from this that he and Johnson were returning when the call had been broadcast.

Lockwood had spent most of the last four hours firmly stuck up Johnson's nose and Johnson had taken to praying for something to detumesce the cocky little bugger. Now it looked as if this hanging monstrosity was about to have the desired effect. A pause of perhaps three seconds, a choking noise and then Lockwood had turned rapidly away, his hand to his mouth, his eyes watering.

"Not on the crime scene," Johnson murmured as Lockwood pushed past him and headed for a wastepaper bin. It was then that he had looked across at Eisenmenger who had come with them after letting them in. Then that he had seen again the look of bewilderment in his eyes.

Why me?

Over the months after the death of Tamsin Bright, Johnson got to know Eisenmenger quite well. When Eisenmenger had resigned his position as Senior Lecturer in Forensic Pathology, taking a year's sabbatical, most of Johnson's colleagues had been unable to understand. For people who were forced to tread through human slime and depravity every day, what was another death, even if it was a six-year-old girl, even if she was burned to death by her own mother?

Johnson, though, Johnson had been there. He had seen what it had done to Eisenmenger, in the space of a few minutes. Johnson had witnessed a man who had suddenly been forced to look at things in a very different way. The light of bewilderment had been strong in Eisenmenger's eye then: it had taken a good few months to fade.

And now this.

He had looked long and hard at Eisenmenger while Lockwood was using the nearest wastepaper basket for unauthorized purposes, had tried to force a smile or something from him, but all he got was a twitch of the lips and a frown. What he saw was a man who wanted to remain apart. His blue eyes were still seeing but were not going to react, his mouth was slightly turned down at the corners as if disapproving. Johnson couldn't see that he had lost any of his grey hair since last he had seen him, but now it was cropped severely and he thus looked almost penitent.

Lockwood came up for air, perhaps caught sight of a stray loop of intestine, then found some more breakfast.

"Just you and the boy, is it? No one else knows?"

Eisenmenger had nodded.

"Do you know who she is?"

And Eisenmenger had then paused for a long time before replying slowly, "I don't know. Maybe, maybe not."

For a second Johnson had wondered if he was being told a lie, but if he was, it was a good one.

"What are the exits?"

"The main one from the medical school, across the courtyard, the one from the street that you came in by and the one from the Department of Pathology."

"Are they all locked?"

"They should be."

"We'd better check." He looked across at Lockwood. "When you've finished, Lockwood, perhaps you could check that all the entrances are secured."

From a kneeling position, Lockwood, looking pink and broiled, nodded in between grasped breaths.

"You haven't touched anything?"

Eisenmenger smiled then, although it was tired and weak.

"No," he confirmed, "I haven't touched a thing."

And that's when it started in earnest. Gone was the peace, gone was the air of stillness. Suddenly the museum became not a place of solitude, reading and memorizing but a background against which an invasion took place. Johnson reported in by radio what he had found, another line of communication with the outside was thrown, and another small breach was made in the walls of quiet.

Johnson went back with Eisenmenger to Libman. "Is he all right?"

Eisenmenger shrugged. "Shock, I'd say."

"Bit extreme, isn't it?"

Eisenmenger frowned. "Is it? I can't honestly say, Johnson. Anyway, who am I to judge? Perhaps his reaction is the proper one, mine and yours the aberrant one. We look at what's been done to that girl and we might wince or draw a deep breath, but is that normal?"

Johnson remained unconvinced. He would have fancied having a go at interrogating Libman, but he had many other things to attend to.

"I'm afraid I'm going to have to ask you to stay in here with him, Doctor."

For a moment Eisenmenger didn't understand why Johnson sounded so apologetic, then he realized. He was a suspect, just like Libman. He smiled and pointed at the door.

"That doesn't lock. We'd be better off waiting in the curator's office next door. With the curtain closed."

Johnson's job now was to preserve the scene. He had requested help and this arrived some minutes later in the form of two more patrol officers, Caplan and Bellini. The contrast between their cocksure world-weariness as they walked in, and the look of stunned mind-lessness that swamped them as they saw the body struck Johnson as curiously comical. Their language had been profane, but that pro-fanity had been a curious tribute to the enormity of this act.

He assigned Bellini to keep an eye on the curator's office, while sending Caplan to guard the door to the street, Lockwood the door to the medical school courtyard. He had returned then to stand again before the oak table in the centre of the museum. There was something about it that caught in his mind, something vague . . .

The next to arrive had in fact not been an official member of the cast. This upstart, this insurgent, had been the Professor of Pathology and he had burst upon the scene in something of a temper. Johnson's error had arisen because he had supposed that locked doors would keep the unwanted elements out. However he had reckoned without two things possessed by the aforementioned Professor. One was a key, the other was a superabundance of ego that dictated he wasn't about to be told what to do by a Detective Sergeant of Police.

His approach was signalled when Johnson became aware of a noisy banging and rattling coming from the door to the Department of Pathology. Johnson ignored it, not willing to leave his post until his superiors arrived. Unfortunately he was compelled to aban-don this plan when a key was inserted into the lock. Johnson had hurried over just as the Professor, an immensely obese man with dyed hair and a round plethoric face, came into the main part of the room.

Clearly extremely angry he had demanded first of Lockwood and then of Johnson what was going on. Then he had seen the body. His face had gone slack, although his eyes had seemed stiff, and his skin had settled into a sort of greasy greyness. He had said, "My God," several times then looked to Johnson perhaps for some form of support. That he had failed to respond to their initial enquiries as to his name and status was not surprising, although they had eventually discovered his name (Russell) and his position

(Head of Histopathology). Johnson had politely but firmly insisted that he should join Eisenmenger and the assistant curator in the curator's office. It had taken a considerable amount of persuasion but eventually he consented.

The arrival of Ben Alport, the Coroner's Officer for the district, had swiftly followed. Johnson and Ben were old friends, but he was relatively new to this job. The first glance, the adhesive stare, the mouth opening, all had followed their usual course. His contribution to the debate had been an awed, "Bloody hell," before turning away and looking too pale to be healthy.

"There's a chunder bucket over there, if you think you need it."

Alport opened his mouth, but said nothing. Shaking his head, he turned again, as if to face his demons.

"Bloody hell," he said again, squinting at the sight as if to filter out some of the horror. He turned to Johnson with a question, but before he could vocalize it, Johnson looked at him steadily and said quietly, "No. I've never seen anything like it before. Nothing even approaching it."

And they had stood side by side and stared at the thing before them.

It was then that the sun, previously obscured by thick off-white cloud, broke through and suddenly the glass dome was bright and beams of light struck down, highlighting shadows and giving red life to the crimson blood patches. The light, too, shone down upon the girl, flamed her hair brightly, haloed her head.

Johnson saw it at once.

"Jesus Christ," he breathed, and no one was there to get the joke.

Alport looked at him.

"What is it?"

But Johnson was thinking. It couldn't be a coincidence. It all fitted.

Everyone who had entered this room had paused (as if before an altar), had stared at the centrepiece (a fair imitation of the death of Christ on the Cross, mixed with a good measure of the Madonna) and had proceeded to talk in whispers. Even the building, thought Johnson, his eyes moving along the high ceiling and considering the overall structure, had features in common with a cathedral . . .

Russell and Eisenmenger had not really got on from the first day they had met. Eisenmenger always considered himself a reasonable human being, able to tolerate most people who would tolerate him, but he had soon discovered that Russell did not belong to this large group, the set of people who behaved in a pleasant way. In fact it had rapidly become apparent that the set of which Russell was a member, of which he was ruler supreme, was the set of complete and utter, pure and unalloyed bastards.

Eisenmenger had heard the rumours, of course. Russell had a reputation that was like rancid skunks' secretions, and pathology was such a small pond that such a pungent thing was inevitably going to set the nostrils twitching of everyone in it, assuming they were still sane. Charming to your face, a complete shite as soon as you left the room. Unable to accept criticism, unable even to accept that anyone else's opinion was worth considering. Paranoid, small-minded, arrogant and scheming. They said that he bugged the phones, that he had sued several of his colleagues for supposed defamation, even, horror of horrors (and this was the killer) that he occasionally pinched private work.

As if all that wasn't enough, he had no particularly attractive physical features, at least none of which Eisenmenger was aware. He was tall, slightly above average, yet managed to appear impressively obese, with lank black hair and greasy skin stretched across a chubby face. He wore the finest tailored clothes but somehow made them look shabby. He had never married and thus had no offspring, for which Eisenmenger, having no desire to meet the spawn of Satan on this side of the ethereal curtain, thanked God daily.

Eisenmenger had known all this and more, but several things had conspired to make him take the job in Russell's department. He had to go somewhere, and having resigned as a forensic pathologist following his sabbatical, he had found himself curiously unemployable. Three jobs had been applied for; three jobs had gone elsewhere. No one, it seemed, wanted a pathologist with a conscience.

Then there was the divorce. No children but messy. Lots of deeply embedded contempt running in a seam with irritation, frustration and, he was surprised to find, greed. She took him for a lot and somehow he hadn't really cared. The process had become one of catharsis and he had found himself enjoying the feeling of Puritanism and asceticism as she had stripped him of a large percentage of goods worldly and material.

The only problem then being that he needed a regular income.

The advertisement of the job in Russell's department had come along just then. It was, in fact, a readvertisement – for the third time – and so his success at the interview had not been difficult. Eisenmenger was wise enough to recognize that they would probably have given the job to a walking, talking parsnip if one had turned up who was a member of the Royal College of Pathologists.

And so he was here, fighting continual, covert battles with Russell on every front, while maintaining a studied, flawed politeness whenever they were forced into each other's company.

Russell was looking out of the window, the curtain pulled back, and he was agitated. Eisenmenger had never seen him like this before. He was completely absorbed by the scene and it occurred to Eisenmenger that he was in effect obsessed by it. He was sweating, a phenomenon far from unknown in relation to Russell, but he carried also a worried look that was unusual. Had it been anyone else, Eisenmenger might have made enquiries, but he knew better than to attempt such human contact with Russell.

From where he was standing, Eisenmenger could see Russell's insubstantial reflection in the thick glass, a hovering immaterial wraith that Russell seemed to see right through, despite its presence immediately before him. He wondered if Russell ever really saw himself, even when looking in a mirror. Certainly, he guessed, Russell wouldn't see what others saw – an articulate and intelligent slime mould with a severe personality defect – but did he actually possess any insight at all? Did he go home at night and weep away the small hours in remorse for all the acts of bastardy he had committed in the daylight hours? Did he even think that they were acts of bastardy?

That, Eisenmenger suspected, was where the truth lurked. He strongly suspected that Russell could justify in his mind every single word and act, no matter how calumnious.

Russell it was who broke the silence, saying as much to himself as anyone else, "I can't believe this. What the hell has happened here? This is terrible, truly terrible."

Anything that Eisenmenger might have said seemed to him to be superfluous and it was left to Russell to continue, "Who is she?"

He demanded this in a louder voice, as if Eisenmenger ought to know.

"Who knows? A nurse? A medical student? A complete outsider? Could be anyone, couldn't it?"

Russell seemed perplexed, at a total loss.

"But to do that . . . It's madness, sheer madness."

For the first time he looked at Eisenmenger and there was in his eyes a look almost of fear.

"What is? The murder itself, or the manner of it?"

Russell seemed hardly to comprehend Eisenmenger's words.

"The butchery, of course," he said incredulously.

Eisenmenger wasn't so sure. "Maybe," he muttered. He didn't feel in the mood to enter into debate about the psychiatry of murder.

When Russell looked away again it occurred to him that the good Professor was actually shaking with nerves.

More silence.

"What the fuck are they doing?" Russell said this under his breath, a frown adding to the picture of anxiety. "They're just standing around. Why doesn't someone do something?"

Russell had made his name in surgical pathology and Eisenmenger was forced to admit that for all his character defects, it was a very good name. About forensic pathology, however, he knew nothing, not that his ego would allow him to admit as much.

"A senior officer has yet to arrive. Nobody does anything until he gets here, and nobody will touch the body until a forensic pathologist has seen it."

Russell looked across at him clearly thinking of making some offensive remark, but his eye caught Stephan. He was sitting against the wall, his head back, his mouth half open, his eyes half closed.

"What is the matter with that boy?" he asked.

"He's in deep shock," said Eisenmenger, but there was a hint of anger in the words.

"Shock?" Russell's tone implied this was an unreasonable reaction, beyond belief.

"He's not used to atrocities like this."

Eisenmenger didn't bother filtering the sarcasm from his voice. He turned away at once, as if in disgust, as if the thing beyond the window made a more palatable sight than Basil Russell did.

Russell snorted but declined to engage in combat. Instead he turned his attention to the fourth occupant of the room, Constable Bellini, who was unable to keep his orbs from staring at the sundry items displayed.

"How long is this going to take? I have a great deal of work to do."

Eisenmenger watched Bellini's timing with admiration. For perhaps two seconds it was as if he hadn't heard, then he turned his head and said in a voice that suggested absolute power wielded with total boredom, "I am afraid that it'll take as long as it takes." He capped this with five hundred milliseconds of pause before adding, "Sir."

Russell's eyes told of a brief spasm of anger, but the remainder of his face was passive.

"I fail to see why I am even being detained here. I arrived after the discovery of the body . . . "

Bellini didn't actually sigh, but everything was there save for the noise.

34

"I'm sorry, sir. I'm only carrying out my orders."

"And who is in charge?"

"At the moment, Sergeant Johnson, sir."

Russell's smile was an exercise in muscle stretching, no more. When he uttered a formal "Thank you," before turning back to the scene below, Eisenmenger knew that Johnson was in for trouble: it was a scenario he had witnessed before.

Bellini returned to his wandering scrutiny of the things around him, while Eisenmenger and Russell resumed their vigil upon the scene below, but Russell could only manage a minute's more silence before muttering, "God knows what the Dean will say about this."

"I should imagine he'll be mighty pissed off," observed Eisenmenger in a tired voice, and couldn't stop himself from continuing, "but probably not quite as pissed off as she was."

Castle leaned back in the car, his head against the seat, his eyes looking at a dark mark on the interior of the roof that was shaped like a crescent. Surely that wasn't a heel mark, he pondered, as much to take his mind from the disjointed, erratic motion as out of any great interest. He felt sick and his head ached.

There were thoughts in his head that felt as if they didn't belong there, that had been implanted there, but no matter how much he tried they wouldn't budge.

Didn't that mean he was going mad?

Perhaps he was, perhaps the thoughts were lies, perhaps he wasn't really hungover from a night spent with a vodka bottle, close to weeping but never quite able to produce proper fucking tears.

The car swerved violently, turning right at a speed that made Castle suddenly aware that he had a stomach and that it was not a happy stomach.

"Do be bloody careful," he sighed, his eyes now closed.

The driver, Detective Constable Wilson, kept his eyes on the road, but his voice held a small smile as he murmured, "Sorry, sir."

Castle missed the undertone of insolence, the world in his head more important to him. He wasn't mad, worse luck. He wasn't that fortunate.

After a while he asked, "Where are we going?"

In the front passenger seat, Beverley Wharton sighed too quietly to be heard. The stupid old fucker's incompetence was becoming impossible to bear. She had told him once, not fifteen minutes before. She felt as if she were charged with shepherding an old uncle around, making sure that he didn't knock anything over or get his willy out in public. How was she supposed to do her job properly and look after this old has-been?

"St Benjamin's, sir."

Castle grunted. In the time between asking the question and receiving an answer, his mind had gone back to the previous night.

"A body, wasn't it?"

"That's right, sir."

Wilson grinned broadly, so that had Castle been looking he would have seen the ears move symmetrically up and back on the side of his head. Wharton saw this and shot him a warning look. He dropped the grin, compensating himself with snatched glances at her legs. These rapid, passive looks were enough to give him a hard-on, what with the shortness of the skirt and her reputation . . .

There was another pause. They got stuck in some traffic and when Castle turned his head to look out of the window he saw a porn shop. What, he wondered, were the odds on looking out at random from a car and seeing a porn shop? Probably as high as fifty-fifty.

"In the hospital?"

"The medical school."

They moved off. With a small spurt on the siren, they forced an opening in the queue and shot forward.

"Do we have any idea how he died?"

Wharton could have laughed, knew better than to bother.

"She, sir. And she was found hanging, apparently."

"How do we know it's not suicide?"

To Castle this was a reasonable question. After all, if it was in the medical school, he could imagine some distraught teenager, upset over exam results. It had been only a month ago that he'd been pulled from his bed at four o'clock in the morning, to bring his investigatorial talents to bear upon a sixty-two-year-old drunk found in his neighbour's sideway. Yes, his flies were undone, yes, he had been there all night and yes, he had a head wound but, what with a blood alcohol high enough to clean paint brushes, not to mention fifty pounds of cash unremoved from his pockets, even Inspector Lestrade could have figured out that the Met's finest were not required to tax their brains for too long.

To Wharton however the enquiry was laughable, but then she knew the details, details she had neglected to pass on to her superior. As soon as Johnson had given her a brief description, she had known that this was *her* case. This was the one that would make

36

the person who solved it. The publicity alone was worth instant promotion.

And who else was there to solve it? Certainly not an old has-been crock of shit like Castle. She would bring him along because she had to, but he would be merely the passenger. She would make damned sure who got the credit, that everyone knew that he had been of no use at all.

Not that anyone needed reminding.

"Oh, I don't think there's much doubt, sir," she said softly.

Castle didn't pick up on the irony. His mind was back on the night before.

Johnson was so struck with the imagery he now saw all about him that when he became aware of the commotion from above and to his left, it seemed for a moment to be almost sacrilegious. He moved forward from his post near the main doors in front of the foyer, into the main body of the museum. It was coming from somewhere near the curator's office. If Caplan had let someone in off the street, he would be the one to take the brown stuff. Concerned he began to make his way to the small door that led up to the corridor from the street door.

Before he got there, the door was opened and Wharton came through it. She stopped abruptly in front of him. Her eyes hardly caught him before they had gone, jerked away and, although she was looking over his left shoulder, he knew at once what she was seeing. The widening of the eyes told him.

Then she broadened her appreciation, first to the right, then the left. Her eyes remained wide as the array of macabre exhibits came into focus. She finished by looking all around her, even up the tall, book-lined walls behind her.

But it was the centrepiece that drew her back, as it did with all of them.

He didn't like Wharton, never had. No one, save his wife, had been privy to Johnson's opinion of Wharton – and he was determined that no one ever would be – but he thought that he knew the kind of person she was, and it was the kind of person he detested.

She had a career to make and it wasn't easy for women, but Johnson had known plenty of women who had risen in the Police Service without being bitches. Johnson didn't often use language like that, but he felt strongly about Wharton, having seen the way she worked. He had had to pick up the debris after she had cruelly destroyed her colleagues and, on one occasion, when he was convinced (although he couldn't prove) that she taken a bribe and allowed another woman police officer to take the blame. All this would have sufficed to render her contemptible in Johnson's eyes, but there was the business of sexual favours as well, and that placed her completely beyond the bounds of acceptability. He knew (for they had joked about it during smoky, drunken evenings in the pub) that she had slept with three out of the four chief inspectors at the station, and the knowing grins on the faces of some of their superiors had told him that it hadn't stopped there.

And now she had recently become a Detective Inspector, his superior. All on the back of the Eaton-Lambert case, in which she had suddenly come to prominence, such that they couldn't ignore at the Promotion Board.

But Johnson had been on the Eaton-Lambert case too . . .

Presumably they had given her to Castle either as a dare (*go on, see if you can raise the dead!*) or as a punishment for upsetting someone in authority.

Johnson was forced to admit that she was not unattractive, but he felt that it was not handled well. In his view, elegance was the quality that softened and synergized with beauty; without it, attractiveness was an animal, passionless thing.

Her eyes were back on him. They both knew that there was dislike, and more, between them, although never once had it been spoken. Then Castle appeared. Johnson had known him a long time, had seen the decline from bright and lustrous to failing and fading, but this morning he was shocked by the look of the man.

"Morning, sir," he said to him, ignoring Wharton. Castle did not hear him. His face, already pallid, had become grey-white and his mouth had become slightly open. He too was staring at the thing in the centre of the museum. Johnson wondered if he was going to faint.

"Your report, please." Wharton didn't exactly sound arrogant. Not *exactly*. Once they had been equals, and thus he knew that there was much pleasure to be tasted in being his superior. There was no point in letting it annoy him.

From his notebook he read out the words he had hastily scribbled while waiting for their arrival. If Castle was paying attention, he was doing it without visible sign.

"Where is this office?" Wharton asked, referring to the curator's office where Eisenmenger, Russell and Libman were corralled.

"Up there. You passed it. I sent Bellini up there to keep an eye on them."

She nodded reluctantly, not wanting to be too generous with the praise.

The Scenes of Crime Officer arrived. He wandered over smelling of smoke and, somewhat peculiarly, garlic as if he feared a vampiric presence.

"All right if I start?" he asked. The question had been addressed to Castle, but it was Wharton who gave permission. He trotted away, happily taking pictures that under any other circumstances would have been obscene. Wharton took one glance at her senior colleague and could almost be seen to be sighing in disdain. She turned back to Johnson.

"Get that bloody area ringed off, will you?"

Johnson knew better than to force a smile at Wharton's unintended wordplay. Plastic posts were produced, yellow tape slung between them, a circle of about seven metres diameter around the table.

Standing side by side Wharton and Johnson peered upwards.

"It looks as though it's tied off on that strut," said Wharton.

"But how do you get up there? And it must have taken the strength of Samson to heave the body up from down here."

Wharton screwed her eyes against the daylight that came in through the dome. "Is that a pulley or something? That might explain a few things."

Johnson couldn't say. Wharton lost interest. "Do we know who she is yet?"

Johnson had to report failure, as far as his enquiries had taken him. Wharton said nothing, but said it with overwhelming contempt.

"Who's doing the autopsy?"

It was the turn of Ben Alport to act his part. Stepping forward at his cue, the Coroner's Officer said, "Dr Sydenham."

Unfortunately, he too failed to make the grade, as this news was not greeted with anything approaching euphoria. Indeed, the look, the sigh and the considerably audible "Oh, Christ" told him not only that here was unwelcome information, but that he was being held responsible for it.

Before he could explain or justify anything, Wharton had turned away and was asking loudly, but of no one obvious, "Where are Forensics?"

The questions were being struck from hard authority much enjoyed. Johnson's dislike of Wharton's style did not preclude his admiration for her abilities. He had seen her take command before, filling the lacuna that Castle could not help but leave.

Yet today, even for a man well known for his laid-back, not to say moribund, manner, Castle was excelling himself. His first glance at the body had been long but Johnson felt that it had been less than analytical; it had been the stare of a layman, only seeing the shock of death and the crimson despair splattered around, not the underlying currents that had created and animated the monster.

Yet it was Castle, for all his distraction, who first articulated it. Johnson had had the thought in the recess of his mind, but something had stopped it from stepping forward, something that had about it fear, dread even. True, it was not his place to stand and proclaim theories and hypotheses, but this deference to his position had never before stopped his brain from considering, contemplating and connecting. Only on this one occasion had he not been able to step back and take a wider, more contextual look.

To all the others the sheer, bloody gruesomeness of it had cloaked its symbolism. Who looks for meaning when clearing up massacre?

But perhaps out of his seeming detachment came a perspective that the others missed.

Whatever the cause it was indeed Castle, moving in a listless state from exhibit to exhibit as if on a holiday trip to one of the great city museums, who suddenly stopped in front of one of the less gruesome displays, shuddered and closed his eyes. It was as though something had brought him forth from his reverie, for his glance jerked, first to Wharton, then to the body, thence up the long, long rope.

He didn't say anything, but Johnson had the impression that at last there was some cerebration occurring beneath the skin and the skull.

He moved forward and stood directly in front of the yellow tape, intent upon the girl's face.

Wharton, despite herself, stopped and waited.

Castle's voice was full of tears as he half whispered, half cried, "She's been hung, drawn and quartered."

Everyone's eyes turned again to the girl, to what had been done to her.

Suddenly the atmosphere in the museum became very cold.

Jamie Fournier didn't wake until after ten that day. He was not hungover, and the cannabis had left no discernible trace, but he was tired.

He smiled.

Pleasurably tired.

He lay on his bed looking up at the ceiling, recalling the events of the previous night, enjoying the resultant erection for a few minutes.

He looked at his watch, saw the time and tried to recall which lecture he had missed, which he was missing at that moment and which he was about to miss. Various aspects of renal physiology, he suspected. The delights of counter-current mechanisms, the mysteries of what the kidney did with uric acid, and the arcane inscrutability of the juxtaglomerular apparatus.

He reckoned he could live without such enlightenment. At least until closer to the end of year exams.

Yawning, he finally made enough effort to rise from his bed, place his feet on the floor and think about a shower. One good thing about rising late was that there was no queue for the bathroom.

In the shower his mind wandered into memory once more and again he experienced priapic pleasures. God, he could hardly believe how lucky he was. As soon as he had seen Nikki on that first confused morning of his career as a medical student, he had wanted her. She had stood out from the crowd, instantly attractive both of face and figure. Yet he had never really thought that she would want him.

Not that it had been instantaneously mutual. In fact she had gone through men at a rate that even most of the other medical students found astonishing, that some found sordid. To the best of his knowledge over the following twelve months she had gone through five boyfriends before finding him, and that was discounting the scurrilous rumours that persistently circulated about her liaisons with lecturers and other members of the teaching staff . . .

Nikki denied them, that was the important thing. Jealousy, she opined with a certainty that Jamie found entirely believable. And she gave them a lot to be jealous about; no one ever denied that. She had begged him not to take heed, had even cried once about how horrible people were. He had held her and told her not to worry, and for a long time they had just talked and laughed softly, a secret and private time that Jamie knew was special. Certainly more special than the brief relationships she had enjoyed before finding Jamie.

Not that they had ever talked about marriage or anything like that, but Jamie could see that it might not in time be an unimaginable fate.

And as their relationship had strengthened and deepened over the weeks, Jamie had discovered that not only was Nikki a remarkably attractive young woman, she was also a quite aston-ishingly good lover.

Quite astonishingly good . . .

He slipped into the lecture through the doors at the back of the the-atre. There was an average attendance, perhaps seventy per cent of the two hundred second-year students were there, all in varying states of boredom as Dr Shrapnel droned on in front of ten-year-old diagrams depicting electrolyte movements in the renal tubule. Jamie wasn't noticed, except by a few of the other students, and all was as it should be.

Except he soon realized that it wasn't.

Nikki wasn't there, for one thing. Not that such an absence was unheard of. Nikki spent much time shopping in department stores, and when she wasn't unmercilessly bludgeoning her credit card to death in that way, she was torturing it by having her hair done or spending an hour at the gym.

Nikki was well off, far more so than Jamie, although she didn't use it against him. She came from a wealthy Surrey family (it was entirely possible that she had decided to make a spontaneous visit home) and she was therefore forever in funds. That was how she could afford the drugs.

But the absence of Nikki wasn't all. He couldn't say precisely what, but he felt an air of solemnity, almost of sombreness about the audience around him. Shrapnel seemed his usual self – dishevelled, unexcited and unexciting – as he completely failed to hide the fact that he had given this lecture at least twenty times before. Whatever it was, Jamie decided, it wasn't something that Shrapnel had said.

It was only when the lecture had finished and they were queuing for coffee that he discovered the reason. They were just rumours, of course, but few of the people who spoke to him doubted that they had basis in fact.

And it was then that his world did not so much fall apart as dis-solve, rotting into putrescence in the space of a few dreadful seconds.

The rumours, of course, were wild. They said that a body had been discovered in the museum, that the body was that of a young woman. Some said that she had been beheaded, others that she had been raped and strangled; all contained an element of atrocious-ness in the act. Some knew that she was a nurse, some that she was a physiotherapist: one had even heard, with absolute authority, that she was a prostitute and that the creepy curator was being held on suspicion.

The one point in common that they all contained, however, a pivot around which they all circled, about which these embroidered creations were tethered to the earth of reality, was that the body was in the museum. The police had sealed it off, the entrance adorned by a constable.

Of that there could be no question.

And it was that fact that sickened Jamie with fear.

Sydenham arrived then, carrying with him not only a fat brown briefcase but also an air of superiority and expectation of deference, all items that punctured the hush and the chill that had come over the assembled company. From where he stood in Goodpasture's office, Eisenmenger could see that he was developing a bald patch, something he had never before appreciated.

"That's Sydenham, isn't it?" enquired Russell, the question veneered with a modicum of sneer. When Eisenmenger didn't reply, he went on, "They don't stand a bloody chance of catching the killer now."

There was an automatic reflex to take up a contrary position on everything that Russell said, but it was tempered by an unwilling urge to agree with him on this particular point. Anyway, surely even Sydenham couldn't cock this one up, could he?

As usual, Eisenmenger found the wisest course to be one of silence.

Charles Sydenham had been a forensic pathologist for over thirty years, time in which the subspecialty had changed considerably, time in which he had changed not one iota. It was said that he had developed a sudden interest in forensic pathology when he had been discovered by his wife taking his secretary across his desk, the subsequent divorce settlement requiring an immediate increase in income.

In those far-distant, much-recalled days when what doctors said was what people believed, an ordinary Coroner's post-mortem took only ten minutes (requiring not even the removal of the organs from the body) and a full forensic post-mortem only twenty minutes. As long as you were happy to stand up in court and declaim your findings with sufficient bravado, no one had a mind to argue.

Now, however, life was a little more complex for the forensic pathologist. People argued, they refused to accept things merely because some fat loudmouth with a medical degree and enough arrogance to float an oil tanker said so. Thus forensic post-mortems took three, four, even six hours; long hours in which every detail was explored, in which every bruise, blemish and zit was noted, measured and dissected, every possibility considered, every sample imaginable taken. Now some had even taken to videotaping the whole affair, so that there was proof of chain of evidence and, perhaps more importantly, proof that they had worked as hard as they could to reach their conclusions, thereby justifying the fee.

All this, however, was not for Sydenham. He preferred the more holistic approach to the subject, in which details were squashed into the broader picture, in which it was unnecessary to investigate every blemish 'just because those lawyer-buggers in the CPS can't do their jobs properly.' In the witness box he fell heavily upon bluster, bullshit and towering arrogance: if he said it was so, then it was so. Few defending barristers could shift him, although there had been one or two notable exemptions from this record.

Sydenham proceeded to his task. He forsook the disposable protective overalls that the forensics officer held out for him with a disdainful, "I don't want those bloody things, they make you look like Andy Pandy."

"Fibres, sir," pointed out the officer.

Sydenham curled his lip at one end. It was a theatrical gesture but on the face of such a theatrician it worked perfectly.

"My dear boy, I am not a bloody Alsatian."

He stood defiantly and the forensics officer looked over to Castle, who ignored him, and then over to Wharton.

"Please, Doctor."

Sydenham walked over to her and they huddled together.

"I cannot see the point in dressing up in pyjamas. Look at it! There's more blood on the table and on the carpet than on the floor of an abattoir! That, plus the fact that this museum is open to all and sundry, must surely mean that any fibres your boy wonder finds about the place will be about as much use as a condom in a convent."

She sighed. He was just being difficult but what he said had some sense. What with Castle behaving like a tourist at the Natural History Museum, she felt the situation could easily degenerate into farce, and she could not let that happen. The prime rule was to get the maximum amount of information as soon as possible.

"Okay," she agreed.

He did at least don some disposable plastic overshoes and rubber gloves, although everyone there knew that these concessions to modern forensics were only allowed because he didn't want to dirty his hands and his shoes, not because he feared contaminating evidence with his own sheddings, organic and inorganic.

More plain-clothes police had arrived. Castle moved quietly around the museum, spending his attention on the exhibits, apparently without awareness of why he was there. It was Wharton who did the orchestration.

Sydenham had been rummaging in his bag. At last, apparently ready for the fray, he looked up at the body, still hanging over the blood-splashed table.

"You don't honestly think I'm going to conduct my investigation while she's suspended like a light bulb, do you?"

He addressed this to a tall constable who had been assigned to assist him. The response to this was a look of uncertainty accompanied by a mouth slightly open. He did nothing more.

Sydenham grew rapidly exasperated. "Cut it down, man. Cut the bloody body down."

Wharton, who had heard Sydenham, looked up from examining a scrap of paper in a plastic evidence bag and nodded at her subordinate.

There then followed a ten-minute sitcom, a play within a play, as comical as the overall production was tragic. No one could stand on the table, not only for fear of treading on evidence, but also for fear of treading on the girl's intestines: in any case, forensics demanded that the rope be cut as far from the body as possible. Thus two policemen were despatched to the metal balcony to reach out with their batons and grab the rope, pulling the body towards them and away from the table. The intestine was pulled smoothly along the oak surface, friction negated by the blood. It flopped to the floor with a slopping noise and hung from her, like a huge green umbilical cord.

Then a plastic sheet was stretched out beneath her, held by two more officers, as if she were a suicide threatening to jump. When at last the rope was cut, she fell into the sheet and almost fell right out again as her two rescuers took the strain, staggered and one corner was lost from their grip.

Upstairs in the office, Russell let out a snort of derision.

"Watching this, you can see why it's so easy to get away with murder," he remarked and Eisenmenger glanced sharply across at him. Russell didn't seem to realize what he had said. He returned to the scene below him. The female detective seemed to have taken charge. He remembered Beverley Wharton well from the Pendred case and had the circumstances been different, he would have quite enjoyed the experience.

But circumstances were different.

The body now restrained in all three dimensions, Sydenham was ready to begin, but as he advanced on his prey his foot kicked something that had been hidden by the copious blood on the floor. He bent down and inspected it. Then he picked it up, holding it between fingertips so that it dangled like a small dead animal.

"The uterus," he pronounced loudly. Wharton came over and Sydenham swung it gently to and fro. "Nearly missed it," he said.

"The uterus was cut out?" she asked.

"Apparently." Sydenham gestured for a plastic bag to be brought to him. He dropped it inside.

"Is that significant?"

Sydenham sighed. "Isn't that for you to discover? Next you'll want me to tell you the murderer's telephone number just by chopping up the deceased's pancreas."

He turned back to the body. Quite reasonably, he commenced with a reading of the core temperature, but not for Sydenham was it to be with an electronic thermometer. He produced a small glass one, one end coloured blue, from a pocket in his briefcase. He peered at it, shook it, peered at it again and then put it where no thermometer ought to go.

The Scenes of Crime man made a face.

"Do you have to?"

Sydenham, whose sensitivities had been bludgeoned to a bloody death some decades before, looked surprised at this complaint, but deigned no reply.

"Was it cold last night?" he asked of the room in general. Johnson said at once, "There was a bit of frost."

Sydenham looked around him as if his eyes encompassed the infrared end of the spectrum.

"It's not too hot now, is it?" he asked rhetorically. Then he bent to retrieve the thermometer, noted its reading and put it back at once in its protective tube.

"Don't you clean it?" asked Scenes of Crime.

Sydenham replied with complete seriousness, "What the bloody hell for? Even if she's got AIDS, I'm sure the next one isn't going to care about it."

Then he turned to the neck. With a large scalpel he cut the rope at a point about ten centimetres from the knot, briefly inspected it and then surrendered it to a plastic bag held out by Forensics.

Wharton returned her attention to Johnson while Sydenham stood in front of the corpse, making notes and directing the Scenes of Crime photographer using unnecessarily loud and clipped commands.

"We'd better speak to the lad who found the body."

Johnson found himself wondering why he took pleasure in pointing out obstacles to her progress.

"You might speak to him, but I doubt he'll have much to say to you."

Wharton's features were fine, her eyes a dark brown, her mouth just a perfect size larger than it needed to be. How, Johnson wondered, could those features move so swiftly and so smoothly into an ugly expression of ire and suspicion?

"What do you mean?"

"He hasn't said more than three words since I arrived. Dr Eisenmenger says that he's in shock."

She considered.

"Eisenmenger? He was the one who phoned us, wasn't he?"

"That's right."

"Eisenmenger." She considered. She had come across the name before. The Pendred case, if she remembered correctly. She asked, "isn't he one of your lot?"

This last she addressed not to Johnson but to Sydenham, who looked up from his notes, squinting his large, hairy eyebrows over his glasses.

"Johnny Eisenmenger? That's right. He wasn't bad either. Not the best, of course, but not bad."

He returned to his measurement and his mutterings.

Wharton turned to Wilson. "Get him down here."

It took Wilson a few minutes to return with his quarry, most of which had been occupied with trying to stop Professor Russell from accompanying Eisenmenger. First the Dean's name then the Chief Constable's name had been taken in vain, Russell uttering these as if they were the names of ancient and powerful gods, while Eisenmenger remained silent, enjoying the other's anger. Wilson's temper was quick but even he knew better than to unleash it under these circumstances.

"I'm sorry, *sir*," he said, the emphasis and a certain sibilance hoisted like warning flags, "I have orders only to take Dr Eisenmenger. You'll have to wait."

He wheeled around and they walked out together, Eisenmenger in front. Wilson raised his eyebrows to Bellini as they passed. Russell, his face a lively shade of puce, stared after them.

Once he had been produced for her delectation, Wharton ignored Eisenmenger for a long time. It was clearly designed to demonstrate to him their respective positions in the temporary hierarchy that had formed around this slaying, but Eisenmenger didn't care. He suddenly felt very tired.

At last, although not to him, she said, "Sir?"

Castle had wandered away and was watching Sydenham silently. He looked up and nodded, but it was a twitch of uninterest, no more.

Wharton said to Eisenmenger then, "I assume you don't mind talking to me here?"

Of course he wouldn't. He was a pathologist; the horror and the desecration wouldn't bother him. He had no feelings. He shook his head, disappointed that she didn't seem to remember him.

She carried on at once. It wouldn't have mattered what his response had been.

"Could you tell me what happened this morning? From your point of view, I mean."

He recounted how it had unfolded, how he had found Stephan Libman, how he had avoided touching anything.

Sydenham gave a somewhat exaggerated cry of triumph. He was crouched over the body, his gloved hand grasping the left thigh.

"What is it, Doctor?" asked Wharton calmly. She had no time for Sydenham's deliberate eccentricities.

"A tattoo, my dear Inspector. A small tattoo on the inner left thigh. Quite high, too. It was, I suggest, a prize, a secret that only the lucky few would ever uncover."

Wharton was mildly interested, since at least it would provide corroborative evidence of identification.

"What is it?"

"A red scorpion. Perhaps she liked to warn those who ventured in that direction that she was not entirely without defence."

Wharton ignored the elaborations but noted the fact of its presence. Sydenham returned to his examination of the corpse, Wharton to her examination of Eisenmenger.

"Do you know who she is?"

Eisenmenger had been trying to chase the vague recognition that had stirred behind the horror but he had failed. He shook his head.

"I've seen her before, but I couldn't say where or who she is."

"No idea at all? You couldn't say if she was a medical student or a nurse?"

Again he shook his head. Wharton tried to minimize her dissatisfaction.

"But it seems likely that she is somehow connected with the museum or the hospital. We can proceed on that basis?"

"Presumably." *I really don't care.*

She couldn't fail to notice his indifference, but she let it pass.

"You obviously have a key to the museum."

He produced it at once, wasn't surprised when she took it from him.

"And when you came into the museum from your meeting, only Libman was here?"

He nodded.

"And he is one of two curators. The other being Tim Bowman."

"Assistant curators."

"So there's a curator as well?"

Eisenmenger nodded and said, "Arthur Goodpasture."

She considered.

"So where's Goodpasture? And where is the other assistant curator?"

Since he didn't know and since it seemed superfluous to say, "Not here," he only shrugged.

"Is that unusual? For them not to be here?"

He didn't like this, didn't want to snitch on anyone, but he also knew that only the truth was going to save him from being compacted on to the tarmac by the steamroller of police process.

"Bowman's often late. Goodpasture hardly ever."

"Have you got their addresses?"

When he shook his head she asked, "Where can we get them?"

He genuinely didn't know. It was not a problem he'd ever faced before, and in his hesitation she saw resistance. She looked hard at him before impatiently turning to Wilson who was taking notes beside her. "You should be able to get their addresses from Personnel. Get round to their houses and find out where they are. Then I want statements from each of them. Take a WPC with you."

Back to Eisenmenger then, but before she could continue Castle wandered up.

"Dr Eisenmenger? My name's Castle. Chief Inspector Castle."

He had a smile on his face, the contrast with Wharton's mix of distrust of Eisenmenger and disgust at the interruption quite vivid. She couldn't believe it. He had done nothing since entering the museum, and he chose now to interfere with her interrogation.

"Could you tell me what this place is exactly?"

Eisenmenger grasped the question and clung on to it. Here was a line of enquiry he found more amenable.

"This is the Museum of Anatomy and Pathology at St Benjamin's Medical School." He knew that he was sounding like a guide, but that didn't matter. "It houses over ten thousand exhibits including pathological specimens, anatomical dissections, models and some unique artefacts, such as the full coronal and sagittal dissections of the male and female." He indicated the halved bodies, upright in defiance of their asymmetry, that faced the corners of the museum. "These, together with the fact that we have over twenty-five thousand books on anatomy, pathology and related subjects, means that this is the most – "

Wharton, it seemed, felt that she did not need this information.

"Interesting as this is, Doctor, I am more interested in the newest exhibit, the one that appeared here last night."

For the first time Castle showed more than passive acceptance of Wharton's claim of leadership. "Background, Inspector. We need background on this one."

The admonishment was gentle but from Castle it was brutal. Wharton took it badly but could do nothing other than take it and appear to take it gracefully. Her pleasant features pinched slightly as she acquiesced with a soft but terse, "Of course, sir."

Castle said then, "How many people would you say visit the museum? On a daily basis?"

No census had been taken and no records were kept. Eisenmenger could only guess.

"Probably on average a hundred per day."

"But there is no record of admission?"

A shake of the head to which Castle murmured, "Pity," but there was no real admonition in his voice.

"Are any of them outsiders?" he continued. "From outside the medical school, I mean."

"Only students and staff of the medical school and hospital are allowed in here. We're very strict on that. They have to display a name badge."

Eisenmenger felt more at ease with Castle, his answers seemingly easier to find.

"And what, precisely, is your role here, Doctor? I mean, you have a curator and two assistant curators. What do you do?"

Being honest with himself he had always had trouble defining his role.

"Overall charge," he replied, using the phrases he always used in answer to that question. "I'm the one who takes the blame when it goes wrong."

He could not help but remember his interview with the Dean.

Castle smiled understandingly. "But never the credit when it goes well, eh? I know what you mean."

Wharton had been following this with increasing incredulity. Didn't the stupid old bastard realize that Eisenmenger was a suspect?

Apparently, however, he did, for his next question was of a distinctly different timbre.

"Where were you last night?"

Eisenmenger had been led along the path quite willingly. To find himself with his foot suddenly stuck in a gin-trap was therefore all the more unpleasant.

"At home," he said at once. How could two syllables sound so guilt-ridden?

"With whom?"

For some stupid reason, the use of the grammatically correct interrogative pronoun transfixed him. The murmuration of the 'm' sounded in his ears and distracted him. He didn't expect policemen, even inspectors, to recognize such syntactical niceties.

"With . . . with my partner," he said at last, almost as if it were an admission to a crime greater than this one.

Castle nodded and smiled, his eyebrows raised, waiting.

"Marie Jacobsen. She's a sister in the hospital."

Castle turned to Wharton to make sure that she had made a note of this. Then, quite abruptly, he appeared to lose interest in things. The smile faded, as did something in his eyes.

He looked briefly at Wharton, nodded, then said to Eisenmenger, "Thank you, Doctor."

And with that he was off. Wharton watched him go, unsure of whether to be impressed or depressed. She reflected that if he behaved like that all the time, he would still be a good officer: presumably once he had. He returned to his previous position, looking intensely at a glass cabinet. It seemed to hold for him an overwhelming, totally absorbing fascination.

Turning to Eisenmenger, she said, "What time did you arrive home last night?"

"About seven, I guess."

"And neither you nor Ms Jacobsen left the house?"

"No."

"And what time did you leave for work this morning?"

"My usual time. Just before seven thirty."

"Ms Jacobsen will corroborate your alibi, of course." She looked directly at him as she said this.

Of course.

Apparently the subject was exhausted for she asked then, "There's just the four of you involved in running the museum, then?"

"Well, there's also Professor Hamilton-Bailey. He's Professor of Anatomy and as such has a say in the administration of the anatomical side, although I have overall responsibility."

The name was noted.

She indicated the great glass window above them, Russell's stony stare retaining all its impotent rage even from this distance.

"And what about him? Professor Russell. What does he have to do with the museum?"

"Normally nothing. Technically he's in charge of the Histo-pathology Department, a sub-division of Pathology, therefore he is my manager, but the museum is outside his direct responsibility."

"But he has a key, I understand."

"That's right."

"Apart from him and the others we've mentioned, does anyone else have a key?"

Eisenmenger could think of no one, save for the Security Department of the medical school.

She pointed at the rope, at its origin so far up at the apex of the glass dome.

"Do you have any idea how that rope might be attached? Is there a hook or something?"

"There used to be a huge central chandelier. I think that it was hung from a hook."

"And how might someone get up there?"

But Eisenmenger didn't know and this at once, he felt, cast him into suspicion. The deeper his ignorance, the worse he felt that it looked for him.

"Who would know?"

"Goodpasture, I suppose."

Sydenham's imperiousness broke in.

"Inspector? Your attention, if you please."

He was standing up, incongruously dapper beside the bloodied, exploded corpse, only the plastic disposable gloves and overshoes spoiling the image of a man of cultured leisure. Wharton looked up questioningly.

Sydenham beckoned with a finger that was streaked with red and dotted with gobbets of something yellow. Wharton frowned but walked over to him. Eisenmenger, feeling forgotten, followed her.

"It's sodding difficult, what with all the blood," Sydenham began and at once Wharton said sweetly, "Fancy."

He glared at her but rode over the interruption with obstinate gravitas.

"There are marks around the vulva."

He ought to have sounded at least saddened and possibly embarrassed, but managed only to appear exultant.

"She was raped?"

He nodded. "It's mostly blood but I think that there's semen in her vagina."

And Wharton? This news of further desecration produced from her only excitement. The fact of the disembowelment was macabre and odd and therefore difficult: rape she could comprehend.

"Raped, then murdered. That's good," she murmured.

Eisenmenger said nothing but he looked down at the girl's body, then up at the glass dome. He knew that rape then murder was a familiar pattern – knew it nauseously well – but they didn't rape and then do this to the victim. He looked across at Wharton, saw that she was happy with the model in her head.

"Inspector?"

One of the forensics team came up holding in gloved hands a wastepaper bin. There was clothing inside it. An expensive-looking bra was on top.

"Where was this?"

He gestured over to the far corner. "Under one of the study tables over there."

She prodded the clothes around. They weren't obviously bloodstained.

"Bag them and label them," she ordered. Then, somewhat unnecessarily, she added, "Don't cock it up." Suddenly she was radiating contentment.

Eisenmenger had found all this interesting but he felt somewhat lost in oblivion. He asked, "Do you need me any more, Inspector?"

And, happy as she was, she let him go, telling him that he could return to work. A formal statement would be taken later.

"What about the Dean? He'll have to be told."

That was easy. That was Castle's job, and one that would keep him out of her way.

"Leave it to us. We'll take care of it. I suggest that you say nothing until you are told otherwise."

Eisenmenger was making his way to the doorway that led directly into the Department of Histopathology when Castle called him over.

"Could you tell me something about this, Doctor?"

The exhibit that held such interest for him was a uterus bisected coronally. The cavity was filled with a mass of grey, haemorrhagic tissue that seeped through the cervix and hung bulbously from the base of the uterus.

"That's an example of something called a Malignant Mixed Müllerian Tumour or MMMT. It's a highly aggressive tumour of older women, most commonly arising in the uterus, but sometimes in the ovary." He was in didactic mode, the words automatically delivered whether to student nurse, student doctor or policeman. "It's usually spread by the time of diagnosis, most commonly . . . "

But it was to be one of those rare occasions when his audience actually knew something.

" . . . to the lungs," murmured Castle.

Eisenmenger, astonished, said, "That's right."

Suddenly Castle shivered. At once he stopped, then he smiled but it was not the best of examples.

"Thank you, Doctor. That's what I thought it was."

Thus dismissed, Eisenmenger continued on his way. Such was his surprise that he failed to spot Basil Russell's glare of powerless fury from the Curator's office as he unlocked the door to the Histopathology Department and left the museum.

When Jamie tried to get to talk to the police, to someone in authority, it was late morning. He hadn't bothered with the rest of the morning's lectures, the time spent first in ringing Nikki's home number then, when no one answered, in driving round to her flat. She lived in a pleasant first-floor flat in a wide avenue about two miles from the medical school. Whereas most first- and second-year students lived in Halls – were glad to live in cheap accommodation that was convenient for lectures and nightlife – Nikki had moved out some six months into the first year. The small, boxlike rooms and shared cooking and washing facilities were not to her taste.

There was no answer, of course. He had known that there wouldn't be. He spent a few seconds wondering what to do, his forehead resting against the red front door, his breathing suddenly loud, but there had really been no choice. His stomach contained glass and acid and he was sweating, although the day was cold. He might be about to make a complete prat of himself, but he had known then that he was going to have to go to the museum and talk to the police.

Lockwood was pissed off. He had rapidly learned that murder investigations were no fun for the uniformed branch since they involved not only being ordered around by the CID but also large amounts of standing around while members of the idiot public tried to interfere, or gawp or even occasionally throw things at him. He had been on his feet for several hours now and he had not consumed any nourishment since seven that morning. These things, allied to the facts that his bladder was full and he was suffering from a severely itchy arsehole due to a combination of poor hygiene and impressively florid anal warts, meant that he was not a happy copper.

Jamie Fournier's approach was therefore destined to be received with less than affectionate warmth. In fact it was received with the suggestion that he should "Fuck off, sonny."

Jamie tried again, persistence born of nauseous fear.

Lockwood, despite all evidence to the contrary, considered himself a patient man, but he wasn't about to put up with some snotty arsewipe of a cocky medical student refusing to obey his orders. He couldn't do anything about Wharton and her lot, but he could do something about some little tit who didn't know when to back off.

He stepped forward, readying himself to enjoy the moment, loading his frustrations and irritations into the breach. He took a deep breath, his immature, rather coarse features settling themselves into a look of anger.

What would have happened then shall never be known, for Johnson came out at that point and Lockwood's ire found itself unexpressed. Jamie turned at once to the older man.

"I'm worried about my girlfriend. She's not been in lectures and she's not at her flat . . . "

Johnson didn't have the faintest idea whether this was significant or not, but he did know that what had happened to the girl would be as nothing compared with what would be done to him if he ignored an important lead. At once he ushered the boy inside and closed the museum door with a meaningful look at Lockwood.

Lockwood, left alone again, said three words, all beginning with a fricative.

The body could not be seen directly, nor the blood, nor the rope nor the actual atrocity, but there was still ample evidence that here was a crime scene, with numerous people peering and pouncing, crawling over the carpet, the desks, the exhibits and the books.

There still remained the looks on the faces of those around him.

Johnson kept him in the front lobby but through the half-glazed, highly polished doors that led into the museum proper Jamie could see enough. He felt as if he was going to vomit.

"Are you all right, son? Do you want to sit down?"

Jamie shook his head, which was just as well since only the floor provided such a facility in the bare lobby area.

"Your girlfriend's missing, you say?"

"Yes. At least . . . I think she is."

"What's her name?"

"Exner. Nikki Exner."

"Address?"

"Flat 2, 39 Olave Avenue."

"And when did you last see her?"

Jamie could have answered that one easily enough, but he suddenly saw where this might be leading. He hesitated, trying to think, trying to decide.

"Son?"

"About ten, maybe ten thirty."

It wasn't long in coming, the question he had foreseen, the question he didn't want to answer.

"Where was that?"

Deep breath, then, "The pub."

"Which one?"

"The Harvey."

It was a pub a few streets away. Johnson nodded, noting the name. He also noted that it sounded like a lie.

"Can you describe her?"

Like all witnesses, Jamie's initial description was vague and all but useless.

"Average height. Short brown hair. Dark eyes."

Johnson recorded this near waste of breath as if it were directions to a treasure chest.

"When you say short brown hair, how short and what shade of brown?"

Jamie indicated a level half-way up his neck. "She'd put henna on it."

"And her eyes were dark?"

"Yeah. Brown."

Johnson began to feel the closest he ever came to excitement.

Keeping his voice neutral, almost uninterested, he asked, "Any distinguishing features?"

Jamie shook his head.

"Nothing? No tattoos, nothing like that?"

Suddenly Jamie remembered, and Johnson saw that he remembered. Feeling oddly embarrassed, Jamie had to be gently led to describe the small red scorpion on the inside of Nikki's left thigh.

Eisenmenger had plenty to do and was busy doing none of it. Not that his professional life was busy to the point of distraction. True there was an unfilled consultant post in the department – unfilled because of Russell's reputation – but the presence of two specialist registrars basically made life quite tolerable. Occasionally Eisenmenger had qualms about the probity of using trainees as workhorses – something that the Royal Colleges piously demanded should never happen – but they were qualms that he could live with. The registrars did the cut-ups and they saw all the cases before bringing them to Eisenmenger or Russell; all the consultants had to do was make sure that the diagnosis was right and that they hadn't missed metastases in the lymph nodes, and other such subtleties.

So there had been a murder in the museum. So she had been disembowelled and stretched from the ceiling. So the police were suddenly all over the museum like scabies mites. So he was one of the suspects.

So, so, so, so.

So Tamsin kept whispering in his head.

"Was it very gory?"

The voice, straight from *Horse and Hounds*, was breathlessly excited as it punctured his thoughts.

Sophie Sternberg-Reed had a profile to slice gold with, and Eisenmenger couldn't believe that she was stupid (although she rarely proffered evidence to the contrary), but she wasn't a pathologist. She sounded now like a fourteen-year-old girl.

"A bit."

"Somebody must have broken in, right?"

Eisenmenger didn't know and didn't want to know, but he also knew the safest answer to give.

"Presumably."

She was tall and leggy. Her long blonde hair was allied to an open almost naive expression that must surely have led her into a thousand misunderstandings with hormonal suitors; misunderstandings that she had probably slid out of without even being fully aware that they had happened.

He indicated that they should return to the case before them and she applied her long eyelashes to the double-headed microscope.

"It is inflamed, isn't it?" she asked and there was some faint desperation about her question.

"Why don't we get some special stains?"

She had bright blue eyes. Why could he not believe that there was something bright behind them?

"Sure . . . "

He knew what was coming.

" . . . Such as?"

"Such as a cytokeratin and a CD45. Just to make sure that it's not an oat cell carcinoma."

Her face collapsed.

"Oh," she said. She wasn't going to cry, was she? "Is that what you think it is?"

He nodded slowly and slightly, afraid of how she would react. It wouldn't be the first time she had crumpled into tearful desolation. Thankfully this time she took the blow with some fortitude.

"I'm not very good, am I?"

"You're inexperienced."

She looked less than convinced.

"It's my 'Rita' next month."

Regional Training Assessment. Specialist registrars had them every year of their training: fail and the Regional Postgraduate Dean got depressed; depressed Deans were, as a rule, bad news for trainee and trainer. Eisenmenger tried not to show that he thought that this might be a problem for her.

"I'm sure that Professor Russell will give you a good mark."

Something changed then. Something that strongly resembled fear and agitation took hold of her. She went very quiet, almost as if he had said something profane.

"Sophie? What's wrong?"

She shook her head firmly.

"Nothing." She stood up, picking up the slides that she had brought to him for checking. "I'll organize those stains."

She was gone before he could argue and then the telephone rang into his bewilderment and Goodpasture's voice drove his feeling of perplexity away completely.

"Doctor?"

"Goodpasture! Where are you? There's been all hell at the museum . . . "

"I'm dreadfully sorry, Doctor. I had some trouble. My wife's had a stroke."

Eisenmenger was at once lost for words while breathlessly Goodpasture continued, "She collapsed. They say she's had a small bleed in the head. I'm in the intensive care place."

He could hear complete lostness in the old man's words. Before he could convey his condolences, Goodpasture was on to more important matters.

"I'm so sorry that I wasn't there to open the museum. I know that I should have been . . . "

"Don't be stupid, man. Of course you couldn't do that."

" . . . only Janey looked dreadful. I couldn't bear to leave her, not even for half an hour."

"Of course not."

"I thought that I'd better phone. Just to let you know what's going on."

He stopped then and Eisenmenger had the feeling that he was being given the chance to say something.

"Is your wife all right now?"

"She's stable. Looks awful, but they said I was to be positive."

Eisenmenger knew that such statements were kindly meant but the gurus of Evidence-Based Medicine would frown sternly at them.

Another gap.

"I know that it's difficult, Goodpasture, but we need you over here as soon as it's practicable. Something's happened."

"Happened?"

"There's been a murder. In the museum."

It is difficult to judge another's reactions on the end of a phone line.

"Murder?"

"That's right. The police are there now. They need to speak to you as soon as possible."

"Oh . . . " He suddenly sounded flustered.

"Goodpasture?"

"I'll be there right away."

"Make sure that your wife's okay first."

He'd stopped listening.

"Goodpasture?"

"I'll be over there at once."

There seemed little point in arguing. Eisenmenger rang off, wondering why he feel oddly unsure of Goodpasture's reaction.

Johnson had noticed before how Wharton could change from one mood to another with such smooth precision and with breathtaking utility. Wharton didn't experience emotions; it was more that they experienced her. She caught them, assumed them like cosmetics, then removed them just as deftly as she probably stripped off for her more welcoming superiors. He wondered if she was capable of generating any of her own, and whether they actually affected her as they affected others.

She was in full, angry flow when Johnson brought her his news. An anonymous young constable had trodden on a bloodstain, and now she was not so much roasting him, as applying a flamethrower to his external genitalia. She had taken the interruption equally badly but when Johnson had conveyed to her his belief that they might have positive identification, the ire had at once melted, gone without a residual. By the time that he had taken her through to where Jamie Fournier was standing in obvious agitated anxiety, there was a smile on her face and her voice was soft.

"Let's go outside," she suggested.

"I'll get the Chief Inspector, shall I?" asked Johnson. He enjoyed her impotent irritation as she consented, the façade of concern stripped away for him and him alone.

By the time Johnson had collected Castle and steered him outside, Wharton had taken Jamie to one of the park benches that were scattered about the periphery of the square. The grass was overhung at the edges by sycamore and beech, and overlooked beyond them by the grimed frontage of the medical school. Castle sat so that Jamie was in the middle: Johnson stood in front of them, the attentive subordinate.

"This is Jamie Fournier, sir. He believes that his girlfriend has gone missing. She's a second-year medical student but she hasn't attended lectures this morning and she isn't at her flat."

"When did you last see her?"

There was hesitation then, and both Johnson and Wharton picked it up, but neither could tell whether Castle saw it.

"Last night."

"Where?"

Another pause that seemed to italicize the previous one.

"The William Harvey."

"And then . . . ?"

He made an effort for this one, not allowing a hesitation, but the strain was obvious and he cleared his throat before saying, "She had to get home."

Wharton had been the primary questioner but it was Castle who asked, "And you?"

"I went back to my room."

Not obviously a lie.

"What time was that?"

He raised his shoulders, making a face, making believe that he was having a problem with exactitude.

"About ten thirty, I suppose."

Castle asked, "When did you meet her in the pub?"

He was being forced to turn his head with every question now.

"I didn't meet her in the pub."

Truth.

"Where did you meet her?" He hadn't even finished turning his head before he started his response.

"In the museum."

Truth.

Castle again. "At what time?"

He turned back, but this time there was a noticeable pause. "Six."

Lie.

Then Wharton asked, "Did Nikki spend a lot of time in the museum?"

He nodded. "She was up for the Anatomy prize." Then, because there was a gap in which no one said anything, he was compelled into adding, "She was doing a lot of revision for it."

Why lie at the end?

In a voice that suggested he was merely being a bit slow and stupid so he would have to be forgiven, Castle asked, "Why did you split up after the pub? Wouldn't it have been more usual to spend the night together?"

"I told you. She was working for this prize. She wanted to carry on and she wouldn't have wanted to be distracted."

The construction sounded odd and he realized it at once.

" . . . If I'd gone home with her, I mean."

Wharton asked, "How long have you known Nikki?"

"We both started here together, just over a year ago."

"And going out with her?" Castle this time.

"About two months."

Wharton asked, her face and tone perfectly level, "When did you last have sex with her?"

He opened his mouth as if intending to answer, but something got in the way.

"You what?" he asked incredulously.

Wharton asked again, same words, same tone, same expression.

"What the fuck has that got to do with anything?"

Softly Wharton advised him, "It might help us if you tell us."

He still didn't seem to know what to say. Suddenly he asked, "What's going on? What's happened?"

He turned from Wharton to Castle and back to Wharton. Johnson noted sourly that she didn't seem to have a suitable emotional coat for this occasion. In the end it was Castle who felt able to relinquish information and take responsibility for the anguish that it would unleash.

"There's been a death in the museum. A young girl."

Obviously he had known that much, but hearing it from such a mouth was a thousandfold worse. His face hardened into fearful apprehension. Castle rushed to head off the question.

"We think it was probably foul play."

The incongruity between the words of the cliché and the reality of their implication was absurd but nobody cracked up, least of all Jamie.

Fearfully. "Is it Nikki?"

"It's a girl who fits the description you've given us," replied Castle. Then he said, "Right down to the tattoo."

Again there was a hiatus while the words and their meaning burrowed into him with their merciless pain. His face became uncoloured and stiff.

"Oh my God," he said softly. "How . . . ?"

"She was hanged?" Castle was almost shame-faced, but whether it was at the lie he told or the truth he gave, it was not possible to say.

He took this in but it went only as deep as the skin. There was suddenly a sound of a car horn blowing loudly. Some starlings squabbled amongst themselves on the grass.

Suddenly a look of consternation amidst the fear.

"Hanged? You mean suicide?"

Wharton was already shaking her head.

"There's no doubt that it was murder."

Into the quiet the wind blew and Wharton said softly, "We have to know when you last made love."

He didn't understand but there were no words left to him. It was in response to his look of consternation that she explained.

"We think that she might have been raped."

There was no sound from him, and the collapse of his face took agonizing seconds, but when the realization came, it subsumed him completely. His tears drowned his eyes and his head dropped down into his hands. His back began to shake, his whole body to rock slightly. At long last there were sounds of sobbing.

Johnson, who had been making notes, looked down at him awkwardly. Wharton seemed to withdraw into herself as if such behaviour was socially dubious. It was left to Castle to put his hand on the young man's back and murmur, "I'm sorry, son."

Minutes passed with Castle leaving his hand on the rough cloth of the rugby shirt.

At last Wharton asked, "Jamie? Can you tell us? We have to know."

She waited patiently and at last he looked up slowly from his hands. His eyes were bloodshot, the skin of his cheeks wet and raw, and his nose was running.

He took a deep breath.

"I lied."

Wharton frowned. "What do you mean?"

Another breath.

"We didn't go to the pub. We went to my room in the Halls of Residence."

"And had sex?"

He nodded. Quickly as if to get it over.

"Let's get this clear. You left the medical school when?"

"Six."

"And you went where?"

"To my room. We stayed there until midnight, together. Then she went home."

A six-hour sex session. Johnson wasn't sure whether to be impressed, disgusted or envious. Even Wharton seemed to think it worth raising her eyebrows for.

It was Wharton who asked, "Why did she leave then?"

"I told you. She had revision to do for the prize."

It was Castle who asked, "Why lie, son? I don't get it."

Jamie took his time, cleaning his face, drying his eyes.

"She shouldn't have been there. It's residents only after ten at night."

Castle glanced briefly across at Wharton who shrugged almost imperceptibly. *It could be the truth, it might be a lie.*

"And you spent the rest of the night alone?"

He was too shocked to be offended by the implication, merely nodding slowly.

"There's no one who can corroborate that?"

Another shake of the head.

"How did she get home?"

"In her car."

For the first time Johnson spoke. "What make and colour? Can you remember the number?"

It took him a long time. "A black BMW. A convertible. I can't remember the number."

"How old?"

He tried to recall. "Uh . . . It was fairly new. Perhaps three years old."

"Where did she park it?"

"I – I'm not sure. In the main hospital car park, I guess."

Wharton could feel that there might be truth in what he said, but she could feel that lies were also lurking in his words. She glanced across at Castle to see if he too sensed it, but he was staring at the backs of his hands. She wasn't sure if he was concentrating on the words of the boy or on his melancholic thoughts.

Jamie asked, "Can I see her?"

Wharton said, "I'm afraid not. Not yet anyway." She didn't have to justify the refusal but she said anyway, "The body has to have a post-mortem examination."

Addressing Castle she said, "Are there any other questions, sir?"

He looked up suddenly, as if jerked back to reality.

"Not now." He stood up and put his hand on Jamie's shoulder. "I really am sorry, son."

Wharton too stood up. "We'll have to take a formal statement. Let the Constable know where we can find you."

He was dismissed with a turn of her back, the two senior officers walking away, leaving him to his devastation, alone but for Johnson.

Having taken the exact addresses of his room at the residency and his parents' house, Johnson said, "Will you be all right?"

Jamie nodded. "I might go home."

"Let us know if you do," advised Johnson, shutting his notebook. He was wondering why the young man was still telling lies, and where they started and the truth ended. He didn't doubt that he would be questioned again. He walked away, trying not to feel like a callous bastard.

"Sir?"

Castle was standing over Sydenham, watching him work, but it was a scrutiny that suggested detachment, that he was vaguely interested only until the bus came or his prescription was ready. He looked up at Wharton.

"What is it?" His voice was tired.

"Can we talk?"

He took a deep breath as if stirring himself. They moved over to the end of one of the halls, close to the spot where Libman had curled himself into a mewling ball.

"We've established that the museum shuts at six. There are no signs of a forced entry and the only keyholders are Security, the curator – Goodpasture, the two assistant curators – Libman and Bowman, Dr Eisenmenger and the two Professors, Russell and Hamilton-Bailey.

Castle seemed to be trying to concentrate.

"Could someone have come into the museum during the day and hidden themselves? Perhaps in one of the store rooms."

Wharton was slightly surprised by Castle's perspicacity. Slightly surprised and slightly irritated. She had a dislike for questions that threatened to bring complexity to basically simple situations.

"That's a possibility we'll have to investigate," she admitted. Why couldn't the old fool either stay out of it completely or take charge?

Castle nodded, returning to reverie.

"There's still the question of the wider implications, sir." There were in reality still a huge number of questions, but Wharton was interested only in steering Castle out of her lane.

He didn't hear or, if he did, he didn't deem it worth reacting.

"Sir?"

Even then it took him a moment. He was examining the titles of the books behind her.

"I'm sorry?"

"Are you all right, sir? You seem a bit distracted."

"Do I?"

Was he taking the piss? For a moment she thought that he was but then he seemed to come to. As she watched he brought her into focus and from a weak, anaemic smile said, "I'm sorry, Beverley. I'm feeling a bit out of sorts today."

"Aren't you well? Should you not go home?" She tried not to sound too keen on the prospect.

"I'll be all right." He paused, then, "You were talking about the wider implications, I think."

He didn't convince her but at least she had his attention.

"This is a prestigious institution. We need to be aware of what that means. The press will be banging on the doors soon. We need to liaise with the medical school authorities."

He frowned. Was he thinking this through or was he wandering again? *Out of sorts* could mean anything, she mused. Anything from a cold or a mouth ulcer to impending death.

"You're right, of course," he agreed. "The Dean, I suppose, would be the man."

There was another break.

"Will you go, sir? I think it should be the most senior person."

He smiled at that, but it was a fleeting, secretive smile, as if he guessed her motive.

"Of course."

He ran his fingers along the spines of the books at her side. She noticed that his hands were covered in tiny cuts and that they were shaking.

"There's so much knowledge here," he said softly. "So much sadness."

She didn't know what to say, but he saved her from inanity by continuing more loudly, "Why here?"

"I'm sorry?"

He sighed as if the effort of explanation was beyond him.

"Why the museum?"

She didn't know and couldn't see that it mattered.

"It's quiet. It's locked at night."

He shook his head after a few moments in which maybe he was considering these aspects, but maybe his mind had gone elsewhere.

"They're linked," he pronounced firmly. "The place and the crime."

"Possibly," she agreed cautiously. She knew he could be a good detective but found she no longer knew when it was whimsy and when it was insight.

He nodded, apparently satisfied that she would take his pronouncements into consideration.

"While I'm gone, check out how she was suspended from up there. What the access is, that kind of thing."

He walked off and she looked at his back until he had gone through the doors that led to the main lobby.

Johnson called to her.

"Neither Bowman nor Goodpasture is at home. According to the neighbours, Goodpasture's wife was taken into hospital last night. He went with her, so presumably he's still with her."

"Which hospital?"

"This one."

"And Bowman?"

Johnson shrugged.

"Nothing. The neighbours don't hear or see anything, and they're certainly not going to tell us about it."

So where was Bowman? It could probably wait for the time being.

"Find out which ward Goodpasture's wife is on, then get him over here if he's with her."

Johnson didn't bother with a nod, just turned away to organize things. It could have been a sign of a perfect relationship. Two people who understood each other perfectly.

But it wasn't.

She didn't have the luxury of time to consider Johnson's attitude.

"Inspector Wharton?" Scenes of Crime, taking a breather from prancing around Sydenham, had retreated to a study cubicle in a far corner. It was from here that he was now calling her.

"What is it?"

"I think you should look at this."

Frowning she walked over. He was looking down at the surface of the desk, but it wasn't the graffiti that he was admiring. There was a thin covering of white dust in the corners.

"Could be cocaine," he suggested.

Wharton licked a finger and dabbed it at one edge of the powder. She put it to the tip of her tongue. A small smile came over her face.

"Could be," she agreed.

She called over Forensics but a stentorian shout of "Inspector!" forced her to delegate supervision to the Scenes of Crime Officer while she walked over to Sydenham, who was calling imperiously for her attention.

"How kind of you to find the time to join me."

He had grown, she thought. His chest was rounder and the shirt around the girth that forever threatened his buttons was pleading for mercy. No comb but he was a cockerel.

She walked over to him.

"I've finished here. Let's get the body over to the mortuary."

"Is there anything else you can tell us at present?"

"She died between 10 p.m. and 2 a.m. I'll be more specific once I've been able to do a proper post-mortem."

She nodded. Nothing he had said was a surprise.

"How did she die?"

If there was a pause, a delve into the well of confidence, it was quickly and smoothly done.

"She was disembowelled."

"And then hanged?"

"That's right."

"Alive?"

"I would say so."

Wharton looked down at the body, suddenly feeling slightly sick. She wondered how anyone could do such a thing, how anyone could state the facts so baldly. "You're saying that somebody ripped her open, pulled out her bowels, then hanged her by the neck until she was dead?"

"More or less."

"What does 'More or less' mean?"

He paused but it was for effect. "I would say that she was more or less dead by the time she was suspended."

Wharton hoped fervently that it was 'more' rather than 'less'.

"What was the blade?"

"Sharp and long."

She made a face.

"Is that all you can say?"

Sydenham's patience had always been a precious commodity, much sought after. Clearly the little he carried around with him had now been used.

"What do want? The murderer's name and inside leg measurement?"

"Anything at all," she said as sweetly as she could.

He raised his eyebrows. His voice was level and slow.

"Let me try it this way. Which do you want? The wrong answer quickly? Or the right answer when it's ready?"

"I need as much information as you can give me, as quickly as you can give it to me."

Oh, the smile on his rather plethoric features! His reply, when it came, was slow and so laden with irony it barely achieved take-off velocity. "Well, the blade was sharp and . . . " The pause nearly outstayed its welcome before, " . . . it was long. Further than that, will have to wait."

There was no point in doing anything other than ignoring the challenge implicit in his refusal to elaborate.

"Can't you even give an estimate as to how long it was?"

There was a sound that could have been a sneeze suppressed. Then in a voice that was positively begging for an argument, "It was long enough for the job."

They stared at each other for a few moments. Then, unexpectedly, Sydenham lowered his eyes.

"There's one other thing," he admitted. His voice was low, as if ashamed.

"What?"

He looked up and for the first time in all the years that she had known him, he looked genuinely sorrowful.

"I can't be sure when she was raped."

She didn't grasp what he meant for a long time. When she did, it went at once to her stomach.

"Christ."

"I would guess that it was the first act, but it is possible that it occurred quite late in . . . " He looked back down at the body. " . . . in what happened to her."

She had never seen him like this before.

"But surely she was raped first," she protested.

All he said in reply was, "I hope so, Inspector. I bloody well hope so." He smiled but it was a tight contraction of the cheek muscles, nothing more. "God help the human race if she was raped after she was slit open."

Castle had to wait to see the Dean. Others in his position might have insisted on immediate attention but he was not of that kind and he was not in that frame of mind. He wanted time to sit and think. He took out a photograph and looked at it as he sat in one of three armchairs opposite the Dean's secretary. The picture was of Jo, his only child. At twenty-four she was close enough to her prime for him to be able to appreciate that here was a beautiful woman and far enough away from the traumas of the teen years for the shadow of her tantrums and insolence to have faded. Qualified as a solicitor, she had repaid her parents' faith a thousandfold.

Would that she had not been an only child.

He recalled the day she had been awarded her degree, the day that it had rained and the car had broken down on their way back home, but nothing had gone wrong; nothing that mattered anyway.

Well, it had gone wrong now.

He felt something growing inside him and he was relieved when the Dean's secretary called out to him, "Would you like some coffee, Inspector?"

Somehow, whatever the words, the implied sense was, *You don't want any coffee, do you?*

He shook his head, putting the photograph back in an inside pocket. The door to the Dean's office opened and the Dean put his head out. He smiled the most charming of smiles to Castle and said, "Come in, come in."

As he shut the door behind Castle, he added, "I'm sorry to have kept you waiting." The room held one other individual, introduced to Castle as Martin Berry, the Bursar.

"I'm sure you know why I'm here," began Castle.

"This appalling business in the museum," interrupted the Dean. "Yes, yes."

"The press have been on to us already," said Berry, using a tone that suggested this was one task too many in a life full of inconvenience. Berry was of average height, average build and average ugliness. He even managed to be an average Bursar.

And then he added, his voice suggesting irritation, "And on to the hospital."

Castle missed the significance that was clearly implied, although Schlemm replied at once, "I hope that you told them, politely, that we were quite capable of dealing with the situation."

Berry proffered the requisite assurances and the Dean turned his searchlight smile upon Castle.

"Contrary to public perception, the hospital and the medical school are entirely separate institutions with different funding sources, different ways of doing things and different views on what is important."

He might have been speaking about a separate branch of the family, the one from the wrong side of the bedsheets.

"Do I take it you don't get on?"

The Dean tried a smile in the face of this blunt and, he considered, somewhat tactless question.

"We chafe occasionally," he conceded and, leaving the visions conjured by this slightly biological metaphor, he proceeded with, "We know of course that a body has been found in the museum. Am I to assume that you consider it suspicious?"

Castle failed to smile at the Dean's underestimate. With a straight face and official demeanour he informed the two men of what appeared to have happened.

The Bursar's slightly adipose and pale face seemed suddenly oversensitive to gravity, for blood drained from it and the features threatened to follow. Even the Dean, an aristocratic stoic in the face of everything except poverty and lack of etiquette, managed a look of discomfort.

"I see."

"But, good God!" said the Bursar. "Do we know who she was? Who did it?"

"We believe that the girl may been Nicola Exner, a second-year medical student. Do you know her?"

The question was born not of suspicion but of hope, although both men rushed to assure him of their innocence, even of this, minor charge.

"I wondered. Apparently she was up for a prize – the Anatomy prize – so it occurred to me that you might have come across her name."

The Dean said at once, "There are over nine hundred medical students here, Inspector. You will excuse my ignorance, I'm sure."

Castle duly did so. "As for the person or persons who did it, we are keeping an open mind."

"An intruder, I'm sure," opined the Dean, apparently possessing deductive skills that bordered on the supernatural. The Bursar rushed to agree.

Castle murmured, "Perhaps."

"Is there anything we can do?" enquired the Dean, the plural pronoun actually referring to the Bursar, and the Bursar alone.

"Don't talk to the press. Refer all enquiries to us. We'll be setting up an incident room at the station – we'll let you have the telephone number.

"It seems likely that we may have to circulate photographs of the dead girl about the medical school and the hospital. We will need your co-operation with that."

The Dean couldn't quite hide completely his distaste for that notion but he said nothing. He allowed the Bursar to nod.

"Obviously over the next day or so we will have to interview various people – perhaps a lot of people – in the medical school and hospital. I trust that there will be no problem with that?"

The Dean could not bring himself to react while the Bursar, apparently under the impression that he should not only co-operate but do so enthusiastically, nodded vigorously.

Schlemm allowed only the smallest of pauses before saying, "Well, if there's nothing else, Inspector . . . ?"

The rising inflection, the fine, crescendoing eyebrows and the thin smile all signalled the end of the visit. Castle stood and thanked them for their time. It was, he was assured, nothing.

He left and the Bursar soon followed him with orders to co-operate as much as possible.

The Dean sat and thought for a long time, staring at the telephone on his desk. Eventually he picked it up.

"Miss Hunner? Could you get me Professor Hamilton-Bailey?"

Wharton looked around the workshop. It was square and benching ran around the walls, while most of the centre was occupied by a large table made of stained, scored wood. Above the benching were shelves on which were chemical bottles, retorts, paints, pestles, funnels, beakers and measuring cylinders. Under the benching were large paper sacks, drums of liquid, buckets and a great number of glass and Perspex jars in a range of shapes including cylindrical, cubical, spherical and even icosahedral. Any available wall space was occupied by anatomical charts.

Wharton wrinkled her nose. The room was pervaded by a curious smell, not unpleasant but certainly not fragrant.

Goodpasture's appearance was sorry indeed. His skin was always rather pasty and greasy – almost corpselike in the monochrome fluorescence of the lighting in the workshop – but a night spent awake and worrying had dehydrated it to parchment. His eyes were sunken and red, his whole demeanour crumpled. He was shaking as he watched her through fearful eyes.

They sat at the benching on tall wooden stools. He had appeared about fifteen minutes before, looking scared and lost and small. He had at once been descended upon by Lockwood who, sensing Brownie points, had restrained his initial impulse to grab him by the scrotum and escort him from the premises, and actually established his true identity. Within minutes he had been passed to Johnson, thence to Wharton.

Wharton's skirt was tight around her legs so that a generous expanse of her left thigh was exposed, but if she had meant to excite this curious little man, she had misunderstood her quarry. He was too exhausted and anxious to notice such enticements.

"What do you do in this room?"

He looked surprised, as if he couldn't comprehend why this should be asked.

"It's where we make the models for the museum. We repair them here, too."

"So you're the clever man who makes those fantastic models! You must be very talented."

He looked genuinely nonplussed. Perhaps it was the fact that he was unused to flattery: perhaps it was bewilderment that they should be discussing such things at all. For a short while he said nothing, then, "Dr Eisenmenger said that there's been a *death* in the museum."

"That's right."

"Who?"

"We think it was a medical student. Nikki Exner. Do you know her?"

He shook his head at once.

"Are you sure? You answered very quickly."

Again the shake of the head. "I don't know any of the students. Not personally."

"How long have you worked here?"

At once he said, "Thirty-seven years." The pride dominated his voice.

"Man and boy, eh?"

He nodded, pleased.

"I'm told that you hardly ever miss work."

"No. I haven't had more than five days off since I started. Except for leave, of course."

She smiled.

"A bit of a coincidence, then," she suggested mildly.

He frowned. "What do you mean?"

"That you shouldn't be here the day that a girl gets herself murdered in the museum."

For a moment the room held itself in check. Goodpasture looked as if she had squeezed his testicles while Wharton just looked quizzical.

Suddenly it burst out of him, alarm and indignation vying for supremacy. "But you know why!"

She smiled and said at once, "Oh, I know! I was merely commenting on how extraordinary coincidence can appear. That your wife should be taken ill on the same night that this dreadful thing happens."

He peered at her suspiciously while she maintained the bright smile.

Then she asked, "When was she taken ill?"

"About ten o'clock. She suddenly collapsed in the kitchen. She went down without a sound. It was terrible."

"And you called the ambulance right away?"

He nodded.

"How long did it take to arrive?"

"About fifteen minutes."

"Did you go with her in the ambulance?"

He nodded.

"I expect they took ages in Casualty."

He hastened to disagree. "Oh no. They saw us quite quickly. They said it was a stroke."

"And she was admitted to Intensive Care?"

Another nod.

"Did you stay with her? All night?"

"Yes. She hasn't come round yet."

Wharton wanted this point to be quite explicit. "You didn't leave her side at all?"

He hesitated a mere fraction of a second, then, "No. Not at all."

Wharton sensed the lie. "Are you sure about that, Mr Goodpasture?"

Another pause, then he dropped his head. "I went out once. For about fifteen minutes." He stopped again, then in a voice full of shame he said, "I had a cigarette." Looking up as if asking for absolution: "I haven't smoked for twenty-five years, but I just had to."

Could he have done all that had been done to Nikki Exner in just fifteen minutes? Wharton doubted it, but it would have to be checked.

"You went for a cigarette?"

His nod was as guilty as if he had confessed to the murder.

"And that was the only time you left her side?"

"Of course."

Of course.

"Can I see your key? Your key to the museum?"

He didn't have to look for it. His fingers found it at once, as if it jumped towards their questing presence in his pocket. Yet when she held out her hand for it, he was suddenly reluctant. It was as though she had asked him for a body part.

"You'll get it back in due course," she assured him.

"But how will I open up?"

She said simply, "You won't. Not until we let you."

He dropped the key reluctantly into the smoothness of her thin palm, almost pained by the loss.

Then she asked, "Is there a way to gain access up to the glass dome? What about cleaning and maintenance? Is that all done from the roof?"

He seemed at a loss, as if relinquishing the key had diminished him. "Access?" he began, then stopped. Then, "There's a passageway over there."

He barely lifted his head, and his chin hardly moved in a direction directly behind her. She looked over her shoulder and saw for the first time that two charts showing the venous system and the arterial system in fact hid a door.

"That leads up to an attic. It's used as a store room. You can gain access to the glass dome at its centre."

Wharton slipped down from the stool and went to the door.

"Caplan? Fetch Johnson."

Johnson appeared a minute later.

To Caplan she said, "Stay here and keep Mr Goodpasture company." To Johnson she said, "Come with me."

She turned her authority upon Goodpasture.

"Is it locked?"

He shook his head.

She went to the door. There was a round handle by the left hand of a curious individual who was composed solely of veins. She turned it and pulled the door open. Stairs led up to the left and on the wall was a light switch. She could see no blood on the bare wooden floorboards.

Johnson followed her up. At the top was another door, this one leading into darkness. Another light switch was to their right, a thing of Bakelite that flicked down with a heavy thud. The light was yellowed with age and the shadows nearly swamped it, but they could see a huge attic space that must have been thirty metres across. It was full of exhibits, some clearly very old, all exceedingly dusty and cobwebbed. The larger were covered by dustsheets and they loomed in the shadows, phantoms from the half-darkness. They were all apparently identified, white postal labels hanging from each, black ink scrawled on the thick paper. Some of the shapes looked threatening, as if monsters from the deep lurked beneath. There must have been many hundreds of items.

A path led through this collection to the centre of the room, in which there was a round structure perhaps two and a half metres across. A single small door faced them.

The floor was bare wood. Still no bloodstains.

Wharton advanced warily as if she feared that the murderer might lurk somewhere under the dust. The doorway in the round structure was half-height and secured by two heavy bolts that were clearly very old. Wharton fished for a small torch in her jacket pocket and inspected them.

"They've recently been opened."

She searched again in her pocket, this time producing disposable gloves which she put on before pulling back the bolts. They were stiff and she had to pull back on them repeatedly. The door opened and daylight pushed its way in. Wharton poked her head through the gap.

She found herself looking down to the museum floor, a vertiginous thirty metres below. She pulled her head back with a jerk, her hand tightening on the frame.

"You all right?" Johnson sounded genuinely concerned.

She nodded. "A bit unexpected, that's all."

She put her head back out.

The table was directly beneath, the blood's pattern on its polished surface and the surrounding carpet even more impressive when viewed from this all-encompassing perspective. Lockwood, squashed by the distance and the angle into a head of hair and a few surrounding bulges, was scratching his backside. Past her head the pink rope hung down, now ending prematurely having been shorn of its burden.

She looked up.

The glass of the dome began just above her and her view of the grey cloud cover was spotted with raindrops on the panes. Spanning the diameter of the dome there was a metal bar from the centre of the underside of which a hook protruded. Hanging from this, easily within reach, there was a pulley. The pink rope passed through this, and was then tied around the bar.

"Have a look," she offered to Johnson as she ducked back inside. He put on disposable gloves and leaned out. He spent a few minutes looking around. Wharton looked at his back and thought that he would be so easy to push . . .

"It seems fairly straightforward," remarked Johnson as he turned back to her. "There was no need to drag the body up here. Just thread the rope through the pulley, lower it, make a noose, put it round her throat and haul her up. Tie it off and leave."

"A few trips up and down, though."

Johnson shrugged. "So what? He had plenty of time."

"Or she. Using a pulley means that it didn't need too much strength."

He acknowledged her point with a nod. Then she said, "You get the rope and the pulley. I'll get Forensics up here."

She left him leaning out again.

Goodpasture was sitting where she had left him, fidgeting and looking miserable. Caplan looked on, his face suggesting that the little man was subhuman.

"There's a pulley hanging from the dome. Has it always been there?"

Goodpasture had looked upon her reappearance as a dog does the return of its master. He nodded eagerly.

"It was used when the conference table was installed, some ten years ago. The table was brought in on a low trailer. It allowed us to lift the table off the trailer."

"Who would know it's there?"

Goodpasture said at once, "Everyone. You only had to look up."

Maybe. But you'd have to have bloody good eyesight.

Johnson appeared, the rope looped in his hands, the pulley at its centre.

Goodpasture asked, "Have you finished? Only my wife . . . "

They let him go with the usual provisos. He scuttled from the room, Wharton staring at the odd figure that he presented.

It was during Wharton's interview with Russell that Bowman arrived at the museum.

This particular segment of the investigation had not been going well. In fact it had been going exceedingly badly. Wharton had never encountered anyone like Russell before. True, she was quite capable of handling his towering arrogance, born of an ego that would have dwarfed Caligula's, but it was allied to an intellect that was sharp and a temperament that was describable only as bastardly. Russell had been inconvenienced and that meant he was in turn going to inconvenience everybody and anybody who came his way, especially if they were members of the constabulary.

Libman had been taken to Casualty so severe was his trauma, leaving Russell alone, save for Bellini, in the curator's office. By now Bellini was sick of standing in the room, even a room as oddly ornamented as this, and he felt mutinous. His face, always on the edge of sourness, had become terminally sullen.

Thus it was that, when Wharton entered, it was into a locus of disgruntlement emanating from both her junior colleague and her witness. Within a second she received a verbal assault the mere fallout of which threatened to wither the foliage of a particularly impressive yucca plant in the corner behind her. It was some minutes before Russell stopped and in that time he had used such a range of expletives that Wharton, her own well of obscenities hardly shallow, felt as though she were an acolyte come to the Master.

"I'm sorry if you've been inconvenienced, sir . . . " she began as soon as she was allowed, but it was to be a beginning without end, for Russell started again. Bellini's only problem now was to stop smiling.

"Professor," she said in an attempt to halt the tirade. Then, "Professor!"

The shout worked. Russell paused and in this lacuna she continued quickly, "I appreciate that you have much important work to do and I can only apologize for the delay, but we will be through much more quickly if you let me ask the questions that I must ask as part of this enquiry."

Russell scowled but said nothing.

"You're the head of the Pathology Department?"

He said, "I am," as if this were the equivalent of running a small European state.

"But Dr Eisenmenger runs the museum . . . ?"

It was half a question, half a provocation.

Russell sneered.

"The museum is an anomaly. It is a distinct entity outside both the Pathology and Anatomy Departments. It has its own budget."

"So you have nothing to do with the museum?"

"Nothing at all."

He made it sound as if he was denying an association with sodomy.

"But you have a key."

"Of course." And when she waited for more, he said merely in a tone that spoke as from a great height, "I *am* the Professor of Pathology, Inspector."

"What time did you leave here last night?"

He considered.

"Well, it was probably about half-past seven."

She raised her eyebrows.

"Are you always so late in leaving?"

Russell smiled and Wharton found herself preferring his scowl.

"Oh, frequently. The problem is," he went on in a voice that was not just patronizing, it was patronage through and through, "I have so much expert opinion work sent to me that what with the usual surgicals from the hospital theatres, and the teaching commitments, there just isn't time in the day for the really interesting stuff. For instance, I'm trying to edit a new text, and then there's the research – "

Wharton had the distinct premonition that on subjects such as these, Russell could profess with the best in the land.

"And what time did you arrive home?" she interrupted.

Russell paused in mid-sentence and there was about his eyes a look that suggested to be interrupted was a new and not entirely pleasant experience.

"About eight, I suppose."

"You live nearby then?"

Russell shrugged.

"It's expensive, of course, but the convenience more than makes up for that."

"Could I have the address?"

He gave it to her reluctantly. It was a flat some mile and a half away. She knew it to be very expensive and very, very exclusive.

"I trust you won't be coming round and bothering my neighbours," he said. "They wouldn't be used to the police."

Like they wouldn't be used to Afro-Caribbeans or Asians, he seemed to imply.

Wharton's smile was so faint and cold it must surely have been dead before it hit her lips. "If we do have to call, I'll warn the men not to piss on the flowers."

There then followed one of those silences that signifies, silences in which it feels as if God were suddenly listening very intently. Russell stared at Wharton and she returned the compliment.

"Quite," murmured Russell after a few seconds but there was a hint of stormy weather somewhere abouts.

"Did you leave the flat at any time during the night?"

"No."

"Can anyone corroborate that?"

He hesitated. "No."

She waited before, "You're sure?"

He overreacted at once. "Of course I fucking am! Do you think I don't know when I'm alone?"

She smiled broadly. "You do of course realize that you are running the risk of prosecution if you refuse to divulge information that might be of importance to this investigation?"

He snorted. "I was alone."

We'll see.

She decided to leave it at that for now. There was time enough to squash Russell later.

"Did you go into the museum for any reason yesterday?"

He considered this for perhaps three seconds, then, "No."

"Do you know the victim, Professor?"

At once, "No."

"You're sure? You were very quick in answering. It couldn't be someone that you've taught? A medical student, perhaps?"

"I was quick in answering, Inspector, because I am positive that I have never seen her before."

Even Wharton, who had an armoured hide and the temperament of a polecat with piles, could see that there would be little gained from trying to break down such arrogant self-confidence.

"Inspector?" It was Caplan at the door.

She looked up, partly in irritation, partly in curiosity, then stood and walked over to him. There was a hurried discussion. Returning to Russell she said, "That'll do for now, Professor. You may go."

Yet strangely, now that it was finished, Russell appeared to want to prolong the interview. He raised his eyes from her legs.

"So soon?" he asked. "Is there nothing else I can help you with, Inspector?"

"Not at present, sir. A formal statement will have to be taken, of course."

His smile this time was subtly different.

"Will you be taking it?"

The shock that he was suddenly flirting with her, as if the termination of the interview had pitched them into a different, unrelated context, as if the formal work was over so it was time to play, found her wanting for words.

Eventually she said, "No, Professor," but what she meant was, *You have got to be joking, Professor.*

His smile didn't change in the slightest, but there was something about his eyes that hardened.

"Shame," he said.

Behind her Bellini just had time to straighten his face before she turned abruptly and walked out of the room. Russell followed at once, buttoning his double-breasted jacket and pulling his linked cuffs clear of the sleeves.

"Where did you put him?"

"He's in the office first on the right. He's in a right fucking state."

Caplan spoke as one who didn't much care for people 'in a right fucking state'.

"So I gathered."

"He came in looking like he'd just been dug up from the graveyard, but as soon as he saw the uniforms he nearly fainted. Tried to get back out and when we stopped him he began to shout a bit. Got quite violent. Took a bit of an effort to quieten him down."

"You didn't hurt him, I hope."

"Of course not."

They exchanged looks.

Johnson was waiting outside the assistant curators' office. Wharton walked in without looking to right or left: Johnson followed her in, waving the uniformed constable away.

Tim Bowman sat with his back to his desk, his body hunched, his hands clenched and his elbows on his knees. His chin was on his chest. Wharton's first impression was of exceeding thinness, almost emaciation. That and agitation. He was almost quivering and his breathing was shallow and loud, as if he had just run for his life. Perhaps he had, she mused.

He was dressed, if dressed was a word appropriate to the bundled, dirt-streaked clothes hung about his bones, in a loose and grey sweatshirt, ripped jeans and trainers. His wrists were exposed by his body's position and Wharton was interested to note that they were scabbed.

"Tim Bowman?"

He looked up, as if kicked, straight into her eyes. His head went down at once but it was too late.

"Well, well," she murmured.

Grinning, she turned to Johnson and for once she didn't mind his perpetual air of disapproval.

"You two probably haven't been introduced. This might be Tim Bowman now, but when I first met him he enjoyed the name of Tim Bilroth." She turned back to Bowman. "We got to know each other quite well, didn't we, Tim?"

The object of her affection said nothing, keeping his head very low.

Suddenly Wharton looked hungry, looked as if she had found something that she could taunt, exhaust and then eat.

"How have things been, Tim?"

Solicitous, mocking; Bilroth could take his pick.

"Not too bad."

She smiled. "Remind me, Tim. What happened last time we met?"

"I got off." He tried this with bravado that lasted just as long as Wharton commented, "On the kidnapping charge."

He ducked his head again at that.

"What about the rape, Tim? What about the ABH? Got you on those, didn't we?"

Nothing from Bilroth.

Wharton kept looking at Bilroth, although her words were meant for Johnson.

"Tim's got a bit of form. Graduated from indecent assault to rape about five years ago."

Johnson raised his eyebrows. "Started young."

Wharton said, "Oh, very young." Then she leaned forward so that she was speaking directly to Bilroth's bowed head. "Do you know what he did, Bob? Do you know how he used to get his nasty little end away?"

"Tell me."

"Tim's into drugs. Did a bit of dealing, too, in the good old days. Tim found the girls were a lot easier to handle when they were a bit the worse for wear, so he took to mixing in a little downer. Just enough to make them slightly more compliant."

"Not nice."

"That's right, isn't it, Tim?"

Bilroth was still not inclined to comment.

Johnson asked, "When did you get out, Tim?"

Suddenly Bilroth raised his head, defiance emerging from somewhere. "A year ago. I changed my name and I changed my ways."

Wharton smiled. "I'm sure you have, Tim."

"I have! I got this job, didn't I?"

Wharton snorted. "Only by lying. Only by using an assumed name and forgetting to tell anyone that you'd done four years for rape."

Bilroth screwed up his face in disgust. "How else am I supposed to get a job? What else could I do?"

Wharton sighed and leaned back. "So now you're a good boy, are you? Given up the old ways, back on the straight and narrow."

He dropped his head again. "That's right," he confirmed to a stain on the carpet.

"No dealing, no drugs?"

A shake of the head.

"No rape?"

He looked up at that. Johnson saw something pass across his face before defiance masked it again. "No."

She stood up, walking behind Johnson. It was a cue for a change of attack.

"Why were you late today?" asked Johnson.

Bilroth shrugged. He looked shifty but Johnson could imagine that he had probably looked that way from the moment his head squirted from between his mother's thighs.

"Where were you last night?"

He bowed his head, seemed to find nothing there of succour and looked up. "At home."

"All night?"

"Yeah."

"I don't suppose that there's anyone who could corroborate that, is there?"

Bilroth shrugged.

"What time did you leave here last night?"

At once he said, "Half five."

"And you got home at . . . ?"

"Half six."

"And you didn't go out again?"

He shook his head. His greasy hair resisted the challenge and stayed glutinously firm.

"Why are you late?"

He opened his mouth, hesitated, then just shrugged.

"Come on, Tim, it's eleven o'clock. Where have you been all morning?"

He said in a voice that was little more than a whisper, "I didn't feel good. I was sick in the night."

She poured disdain on him like it was concrete. "Oh, yes? But you suddenly felt better so, being a conscientious lad, you thought you'd better come in. Is that it?"

He nodded but kept his head down. There was a long wait while no one moved, then she walked up to him and commanded, "Stand up and turn out your pockets."

He was at once alarmed and this made her smile. "But . . . " he stuttered. His face was turned up to look at her, his eyes jerking to and fro between her face and Johnson's.

"We can do it here or we can do it at the station," she reminded him wearily.

There was of course no option for him. It was slow and it was almost painful but eventually he did as she ordered and, amidst the Polo packet, the scraps of paper, the cigarette papers, the tobacco and the smallest of small change, there were five packets of heroin.

Wharton didn't say a word. She looked directly into his eyes and said, "Why this job, Tim?"

He was now extremely wary, as if Wharton was wielding a knife at him. "What do you mean?"

"Why a job in a Museum of Anatomy and Pathology?"

He made a face. "Why not?"

She considered for a second. "It is an interesting place, I can see. Lots of fascinating models. A great deal of learning."

He just looked at her.

"Lots of blades, too," she continued. "Lots of needles."

Bilroth scowled. "I told you. I don't do drugs any more."

Johnson suddenly grabbed his wrist. Bilroth pulled back but couldn't break free. Johnson pushed the sleeve of the sweatshirt up to expose several healing puncture marks at the elbow.

Wharton smiled. "Oh no?"

Johnson released him and he pushed the sleeve back down, saying nothing.

Wharton continued, "So we've established you're lying about that. What about other things?"

Still nothing.

She sat down in front of him, then leaned forward so that she was facing him directly. "And what about murder? Tried your hand at that, have you?"

Panic swamped his face. "What do you mean?"

"Murder, Tim. Easy enough concept, even for a rapist."

Johnson counted the seconds. Three of them before Bilroth finished looking from face to face.

"I haven't murdered anybody!" His voice was at once raised. "What's going on here?"

Johnson was thinking, *He's telling the truth*, but if Wharton was thinking that also, she kept it well hidden.

"Oh, come on, Tim. You mean you don't know?"

Again he was looking from Wharton to Johnson, his eyes flicking as if jerked by cotton threads. "What's happened?" he demanded.

As if playing a game, Wharton said, "A medical student has been murdered, Tim. Murdered in the museum. But before she was murdered . . . guess what, Tim?"

He looked fearful, certainly enough, and he was running on reflexes, not thinking deeply. But it was obvious to Johnson that he could think just deeply enough to guess what had happened. Just deeply enough to open his mouth but ask only, "What?" in a voice that betrayed its fears.

Through a smile that a killer might wear, Wharton whispered, "She was raped, Tim."

"He did it, Johnson."

Johnson said nothing. He could see why she might think that Bilroth was the culprit – there was an abundance of circumstantial evidence against him – but Johnson didn't take well to leaps of conclusion.

"Well?" she demanded, as if his agreement was crucial to her.

"It looks as if he might," he admitted.

"You bet it does!" Whom, he wondered, was she trying to convince? "Where's the Chief Inspector?"

"He's still with the Dean, I think."

That she had sent him there was no excuse for his absence when she required his presence, it seemed. She made a face of irritation and disgust.

"I'll just have to take the initiative myself."

As if, Johnson wryly thought, that was a problem. "What are you going to do?"

She smiled. "Mr Bilroth's going to take me home so that we can have a look around his flat."

"Has he said he's happy to do that?"

"Not yet."

She didn't even smirk. He tried not to show his disapproval of her methods, but perhaps he failed for she said then in a rather abrupt manner, "I want you to interview Hamilton-Bailey, the Anatomy Professor. Then I want you to find the girl's car and make a few checks on Jamie. Find out a bit about him.

He nodded, keeping his face neutral.

"And then," she went on after a pause, possibly for breath, possibly for bile, "I want you to go to the medical school office and find out everything they've got on her. Then check out the girl's flat. Ask around."

He was thinking, *And after lunch?* while nodding, his face neutral.

"What about the post-mortem?" he asked.

She looked at her watch.

"That won't be until five. Plenty of time to find all those little pieces of evidence that will nail Bilroth."

Find them? Or place them?

"Do you want me to attend?" he enquired.

She shrugged. "If you've got everything else done."

Before the lunchtime meeting of the Academic Heads, it was customary to spend fifteen minutes eating the buffet and socializing. It was during this that Dean Schlemm took Russell to one side with a look of stately concern to the foremost, the frown on his brow managing a regularity of peaks and troughs that hinted at the Olympian.

"What is happening at the museum?"

Russell sensed from the Dean's voice that he was safe in displaying arrogant ignorance.

"God only knows, Dean."

One of the tricks was to infuse nearly every sentence with the word 'Dean'.

A nod of sympathy.

"Not too disruptive of your work, I trust?"

Russell snorted.

"I was held captive there for almost the entire morning! All my routine work will have to be done this afternoon. What right do these people have to take away my liberty? It isn't as though I had anything to do with the beastly business."

"Oh, quite."

"And, as I am sure you realize, Dean, events such as these tend to distract the staff. I've had the most terrible trouble trying to keep their minds on departmental matters."

"Ah, yes." The sympathy in his voice was the emotion of one superior being to another when confronted with the regrettable antics of an inferior breed.

Hamilton-Bailey wandered past. He had not eaten, did not look as if he would ever eat again. Even amidst an assembly of learned professors that could rarely, if ever, be described as animated, he appeared significantly distracted, so that when Schlemm called out, "Alexander?" he was not graced with a reply.

"Alexander?" He did not so much raise his voice as raise the level of asperity within it.

His quarry looked up, his head almost employing a flicking motion. His eyes widened and he attempted a smile.

"Dean?"

"We were just talking about this unfortunate business in the museum. Basil tells me that it is proving something of a distraction in his department."

Hamilton-Bailey opened his mouth. Words must have been inside, but they were reluctant to emerge and, when at last they did peep shyly from their hiding place, they had a strange, affected tone. "Business?"

"Surely you've heard?"

But it appeared that he had not. The Dean expressed polite surprise. "Well, perhaps you are that little bit removed from the incident."

There was no one present who felt it right to remark upon the use of the word 'incident'.

Hamilton-Bailey formed his delicate features into an expression of puzzlement. "What's happened?" Again the tone did not sound quite right.

Suddenly the Dean found someone trying to attract his attention and with a brief apology he moved away, grace and decorum falling from him like fairy dust. Strangely when Russell looked in the same direction he saw no candidate for Schlemm's attractor. "Perhaps Basil could explain," he suggested and was gone.

Left together the two Professors looked at each other in embarrassment. Stiltingly Russell explained that someone had been murdered in the museum, and Hamilton-Bailey offered shock and horror. "How terrible!" he opined, a truism that was as effective as nerve gas in decimating any meaningful discussion.

"Bloody awful mess," reflected Russell.

At once Hamilton-Bailey said, "Mess?"

"Yes. Strung up from the ceiling like a side of beef, then disembowelled. Blood and intestines everywhere. It was like . . . "

But he had lost his audience. Hamilton-Bailey's face had crumpled into complete horror and nausea. "Oh, my God!" he breathed through this mask of shock. He seemed about to lose consciousness.

Russell looked at his colleague through surprised eyes. "Are you perfectly well, Alexander?"

Hamilton-Bailey, draining to an even greyer colour by the second, took some time before assuring Russell that he was, indeed, fine.

"I expect that you'll receive a visit from the police soon," pointed out Russell.

Hamilton-Bailey's eyes told of extreme apprehension. "Me? Why?"

"You're a keyholder. They seem to consider that grounds for suspicion."

The Professor of Surgery apparently found this an unpalatable morsel for he seemed then close to a fainting attack.

The Dean chose that moment to call the assembled academics into the committee room to begin their meeting and they were parted. Russell continued to stare at Hamilton-Bailey, his head full of questions.

On the whole, Wharton was pleased with the way things were going. Sydenham might not have been her first choice of pathologist, but he had given her some useful preliminary information. It appeared that Exner had died after midnight and possibly as late as three o'clock in the morning. The mode of death was probably exsanguination, which suggested that she had been alive when she had been eviscerated. It was his opinion that she had been suspended only at the point of death, or possibly just after death.

There were no signs of a break-in, which was highly pleasing, since it reduced the number of potential subjects. True, it was possible that one of the hundred or so people who had visited the museum on the previous day might have hidden in one of the store rooms, but that was better than having to sift through a few million city-dwellers.

And now it just might not matter.

Now she had Bowman, or Bilroth, or whatever he chose to call himself.

A convicted rapist working in the place where a rape had been committed.

She could have hugged herself for joy.

Georgina Budd, Hamilton-Bailey's secretary, busied herself with work that was brought in to her by the four senior lecturers who worked in the Department of Anatomy: from the Professor himself she received no work, and had not done so for several days. His much-trumpeted new edition of Gray's Anatomy, a project that had occupied most of her working hours for the past few months, appeared to have been forgotten. She thought that she knew enough of her boss's private life to prepare a shrewd guess as to the cause of his inactivity.

Irene Hamilton-Bailey.

And, to judge from his distracted, miserable demeanour that morning, things had reached a crisis.

On the telephone in front of her, a light went on.

A woman of great curiosity, Georgina had quickly learned in the course of her employment that the offices were not completely soundproof. If the laser printer were switched off, and the door to the corridor and all the windows closed, there was a sufficiency of quiet in the room for her to hear, standing close to the wall and apparently contemplating the disused cemetery that the office over-looked, what was said in the adjoining room. This position she now adopted, holding a mug in both hands as she stared outwards, as if lost in coffee and thought.

"Irene?"

She knew at once that this was a call of interest. Hamilton-Bailey never called his wife.

"I need to talk with you."

Why can't it wait until tonight?

As if Georgina were privy to the thoughts of Mrs Hamilton-Bailey, this was apparently the question that was now posed by the Professor's wife.

"Because it's urgent. Very urgent."

Really?

"It's about last night."

A small child could be heard wailing somewhere outside.

"Please, Irene. There's no need to react like that . . . "

There was quite a long pause after that, until in a firm voice, a voice that Hamilton-Bailey usually only used on medical students who had failed to meet his expectations in their knowledge of some artery's course or some organ's relationship with its neighbours, he said, "I don't know who you were with . . . "

Georgina almost gasped. Clearly this was devastating stuff, and from Hamilton-Bailey's rising tone it had been effective in provoking a response from his spouse.

" . . . and I don't care," he continued, as if battling through the storm of his wife's protestations. "Something's happened. Something terrible . . . "

In her three years with Hamilton-Bailey Georgina had heard some choice gossip, usually of an academic, back-stabbing variety, but this promised to be of a different order altogether. Altogether indeed.

"It may be that the police will . . . "

The door to Georgina's office opened and two of the senior lecturers came in. They were arguing because they were always arguing, and they were doing so loudly. She turned around, putting the mug down behind the computer monitor so that they would not see that it was empty.

"I'm sorry, Georgina," said one. "We didn't realize that you were having a break."

She smiled over her frustration. "That's all right. What can I do for you?"

They then proceeded to bicker again, this time over whose work she should do first. By the time they had compromised, each had explained what they required of her, and they had left her to solitude and stillness, there was no further conversation from the office next door.

It took Johnson some time to discover anyone who knew anything about Nikki Exner. It was Berry, the Bursar, who finally relieved him of the growing paranoid suspicion that there was in the medical school a conspiratorial silence concerning the dead girl.

"In an academic institution of this type and size, it is almost impossible to know a student well. There are nearly two hundred students in each year, each year being taught by perhaps fifteen different departments, in each of which there may be four or five lecturers. Students don't get to know lecturers and lecturers never get to know students."

This utopian ideal unfortunately failed to help Johnson.

"So who would be able to help me? Who would know about Nikki Exner?"

They were in Berry's office. Ornate and undoubtedly impressive, it was considerably less splendorous than the Dean's.

"Her personal tutor might," he offered, but the hesitancy suggested that Johnson should not risk his life savings on a wager.

"Might?"

Berry sighed. "Each medical student is assigned a personal tutor when they start here. Some of the tutors are very good and take an active role in the pastoral care of their students, others adopt a more passive method."

"And who was Nikki Exner's tutor?"

It took Berry little time to locate the information, the file being on his desk. "Professor Hamilton-Bailey. He's the Professor of Anatomy."

But Johnson, of course, knew exactly who Professor Hamilton-Bailey was, despite appearing to write the information down with great assiduity.

"Thank you, sir," he said, standing up. "Where might I find the Department of Anatomy?"

Johnson's arrival in Georgina's office presented some problems, and these were only circumnavigated with liberal use of his warrant card, gravitas and implacable inexorableness. His appearance before Hamilton-Bailey, Georgina Budd gesturing impotence behind him, caused further disturbance that was ended only when it became plain that Johnson was not going to leave without his desired interview. The Professor grudgingly acquiesced and Johnson was offered a chair with an exasperated sigh and a peremptory wave of the hand.

The only other incumbents of the room were a skeleton and a bird-eating spider, the former hanging open-mouthed from its stand by the desk, the latter stuffed and presenting a menacing attitude because of it. The spider was perched on a shelf above Hamilton-Bailey's head, the skeleton stood at the side of the desk, appearing to listen with open-mouthed attention.

Hamilton-Bailey's frame suggested to Johnson that he too had been stuffed, but the fact that he was trembling and exuding almost palpable agitation suggested that the process of packing had been attempted quite recently.

Despite Hamilton-Bailey's puffery, Johnson did not fail to notice that he looked oddly unkempt. His bright red bow tie was slightly loose at the collar and his shirt looked creased as if it had seen more than one sunset unwashed. He was sweating a trifle too freely as well, given the ambient temperature.

"I am exceedingly busy, Constable. Can this not wait?" Hamilton-Bailey might have been small but was quite capable of issuing arrogant disdain in great abundance. Unfortunately, this particular attempt at brusque dismissal did not come off.

Johnson was well practised in implacability. Ignoring his demotion, he observed that the desk in front of the good Professor was neat, tidy and practically empty.

"No, sir, I'm afraid that it can't."

Hamilton-Bailey's sigh sounded as if there was something stuck midway between his epiglottis and uvula and it was in danger of heading for his trachea.

"Very well. What is it?"

"I understand that you're involved in the running of the Museum of Anatomy and Pathology."

"Not really. Eisenmenger is the man you want."

"Oh. I'm sorry but I was told that you administered the anatomical side."

Impatiently, Hamilton-Bailey put some flesh on his skeletal answer.

"Technically speaking, the anatomical exhibits and models are the property of the Department of Anatomy. As such, I have entitlement to determine which of them are exhibited and how they are exhibited, and to ensure that they are kept in good repair."

The Professor's circumlocution gave Johnson some trouble but eventually he had the gist of it recorded.

"Could I ask where you were last night?"

Hamilton-Bailey opened his mouth as if to make reply, but then his face folded itself into indignation.

"May I ask what that has to do with you?"

Johnson had seen so much indignation in the course of his employment, it had long since ceased to have an effect.

"This morning the body of a young woman was found in the museum. We believe that she had been murdered."

Clearly Hamilton-Bailey was tired – a fact that might or might not be of interest – and so Johnson found it difficult to judge his reaction. He opened his mouth, as if about to castigate the policeman for his impertinence, stopped, took a short, sharp breath and then said, "Good God."

Johnson said nothing more. The reaction wasn't quite right, but then it wasn't patently false either. He found the silence that grew between them quite pleasant but Hamilton-Bailey had more difficulty with it.

"I still don't see what this has to do with me," he said.

"You have a key to the museum, I believe."

"Oh, I see." Hamilton-Bailey, having seen the point, allowed Johnson the benefit of his co-operation. "Yes, that is correct."

"May I see it?"

Hamilton-Bailey paused as if he didn't understand the question, then felt in his pockets. He found it in the second one he tried and held it up for the Sergeant to see. Johnson politely took it from him while Hamilton-Bailey uttered a faint "Oh."

There then followed another brief interlude until Johnson said, "And yesterday evening?"

The Professor started as if at that instant the bird-eating spider had found sufficient resentment at its predicament to jump down the back of his neck. A pause ensued. Johnson said nothing and assumed a questioning expression as Hamilton-Bailey appeared to wrestle with some internal dilemma.

At last he said, "I was at home."

Johnson didn't exactly fall off his chair, but he did manage to lift one eyebrow and murmur, "Oh?"

"With my wife," continued Hamilton-Bailey. And then, for good measure, "All evening."

Johnson reflected that it was a close-run thing which was the more suspicious, too much information or too little.

"Your wife will confirm all this?"

Hamilton-Bailey's exasperation raised his voice several octaves. "Of course she will!"

He continued, "Now, if you've finished . . . " But if the Professor thought that the interview was at a conclusion, he was met again with disappointment.

"We believe that the dead girl's name was Exner. Nikki Exner. Did you know her, sir?"

Hamilton-Bailey's reply came at once. "Nikki Exner? Good Lord! I was her personal tutor."

"So you knew her?"

The Professor was busy expressing shock at the news so he didn't respond at once. When he did it was to place as much distance as possible between himself and such unsavoury occurrences.

"I had obviously talked to her on a few occasions. Made sure that she was happy, that there were no personal problems, that kind of thing."

"When was the last of these talks?"

Hamilton-Bailey couldn't remember. He had to call in Georgina who, having been listening to every word, was not at all surprised when she was summoned and asked to consult his diary. At last the information was obtained.

"At the start of the year. October the tenth."

"And she seemed happy? Nothing worrying her?"

The Professor had to disappoint Johnson, however, and said with a sympathetic smile, "As far as I can recall, that was the case. However, it is not policy to make records of such discussions, unless the student wishes something to be done formally."

Georgina returned to her listening post and Johnson at last felt that he had gone as far as he could on this occasion. He stood.

Relieved, Hamilton-Bailey burst into a smile and also took to his feet.

"If there's anything I can do, please let me know," he offered, generosity suddenly overflowing.

"Someone will come and see you to take a formal statement."

"Of course, of course."

Hamilton-Bailey was ushering Johnson to the door.

"A terrible business, a truly terrible business." Then he asked, "How, precisely did she die?"

Johnson had reached the door. He said only, "She was hanged."

Perhaps it was then that the bird-eating spider took a nip of Hamilton-Bailey, for Johnson saw him react with some surprise.

"Hanged?" he asked. "But I thought . . . "

Johnson looked on with interest as he slowed to a halt. "You thought what, sir?" he enquired.

Hamilton-Bailey suddenly seemed very confused. It took him a few seconds to say, "I . . . I was told that there was some form of atrocity."

"And who told you that, sir?" Johnson was interested, no more. It was as if he was asking for directions.

Hamilton-Bailey stared at him for a second, then, "Basil Russell." With a rush he added reassurance of Russell's innocence. "He saw it this morning."

Johnson nodded and noted it down. Then waited a while, as if expecting more: from his relaxed posture he might have been there for eternity.

Eventually Hamilton-Bailey had collected enough composure to ask, "Is there anything else, Constable?"

Johnson stared at him for a few moments longer before shaking his head slowly and murmuring, "Not at the present, sir."

He left the Professor in his office, his mind trying to sort out what had just happened, aware that Hamilton-Bailey's reaction had been slightly off-key, slightly strange.

The coffee lounge was dull, dilapidated and dirty, but Johnson was so tired he would have sat down in a scabitic doss house. The coffee was scalding, the plastic cup thin enough to allow light through and the currant bun so dry that it was only the thick layer of margarine that held it together. When the drink had finally cooled enough to allow him to place some in his mouth, it was clear that few if any coffee beans had been sacrificed in its manufacture.

But, he reflected, it was liquid and he was no longer on his feet. He leaned back and closed his eyes, trying to ignore the nagging suspicion that the designer of the sofas had either been deformed, an alien or a sadist.

Peace.

He began to relax.

The sofas were arranged in threes around tables forming open squares. There were few people in the lounge when he first arrived but by the time he had seen off the currant bun and most of the brown coffee-like liquid in the cup, quite a few more people had arrived and the background noise had risen considerably. Inevitably he, a stranger, was left to solitude, but the sofa adjacent to his became crowded with students.

Talkative students.

At first the discussion was about the fact of the murder, then it moved on to details – most of them beyond fantasy – while Johnson sat with his head resting against the dark green emulsion of the wall and a smile that stretched his face.

"Mind you, she had it coming."

Johnson didn't lose the smile, didn't even change the pattern of his breathing, but he was suddenly very interested.

The speaker was a girl, short, dark-haired and not particularly attractive. Johnson wondered if the remark was born of envy, but he was soon corrected in that supposition. Despite the fact that all but one of her five companions were male, all appeared to hold similar opinions.

"She was a snooty cow," admitted a spotty boy with fair curly hair and the kind of face that was just asking to be smacked.

The first girl snorted. "She was a tart."

Her slight Welsh accent sounded hysterically judgemental. The spotty one declined to comment further about that, but another young man – more athletic and better looking than the first – said, "I didn't really know her."

"She only looked at second years and above." This from the other girl, a long-haired blonde.

"Sometimes a long way above." The Welsh accent was beginning to grate with Johnson, but he wondered what she meant.

And then they stopped talking and the atmosphere changed. He had not looked directly at the students, and did not do so now, but he did at that point flick his eyes across the room. Approaching the students from the coffee bar was a young man in a white coat. He was holding a can of Coke and was clearly a year or two older than the group next to Johnson.

He was also clearly upset.

He walked past without acknowledging anyone and sat down, alone, in a far corner of the room.

Johnson heard the Welsh voice say, "I don't know why he looks so miserable. She dumped him months ago."

The remainder of the coffee was cold and Johnson couldn't imagine what it would taste like now. He got up as unobtrusively as possible and walked over to the subject of her commentary.

"May I?" he asked. His reply was a silent grimace that barely made it to the facial muscles before it scurried back inside. The young man was hunched over his Coke can as if protecting it from the light.

Johnson saw no reason to prevaricate. He fished in his breast pocket and produced his identification.

"Detective Sergeant Johnson. I wonder if you'd mind having a chat."

The young man closed his eyes and leaned back with a quiet "Shit."

"I'm sorry but I don't know your name."

Something was whispered, Johnson knew this because his ears told him so, but the lips didn't move and the face – aimed at the ceiling – didn't alter.

Johnson was prepared to be reasonable for a little while longer.

"I'm terribly sorry, but my hearing's not too good today. Could you speak up?"

"Matthew Sacks."

"What year are you in, Matthew?"

"The fourth."

He was good-looking and athletic, that much even Johnson could appreciate. He was semi-smartly attired under his slightly grubby white coat. The breast pocket was filled by pens and two penlights: the side pockets bulged with small paperback books and notepads. A stethoscope – the badge of his office – was hung ostentatiously around his neck.

"I was wondering if you could tell me anything about Nikki Exner?"

He jerked his head down and for the first time looked at Johnson.

"It's true then? She's been murdered?"

"She's missing. We need to find her."

"But there's been a murder? In the museum?"

"A body has been found there, yes."

He wouldn't let it go. Clearly it was important to him.

"But if Nikki's missing – "

And rather than carry on this dance around the young man's suspicions, Johnson interrupted him with, "Do you know Nikki?"

Sacks stared at him for a minute. Just stared as if they were in the midst of a child's game then, clearly the loser, he dropped his gaze.

"Yeah."

"Well?"

"We . . . went out for a while."

"For how long?"

"Couple of months."

"How long ago?"

He thought about it. "Summer last year, I guess. June, July."

"So what happened?"

He had a bloody good idea what had happened, but much of his job required him to ask questions to which he already knew the answers. Whatever words he expected, he was surprised by the reaction, for Matthew Sacks began to cry.

At first there was just silence, but from this fertile ground of reflection there grew slowly tears. His face tried to fight it and became masked and stiff, until quite suddenly he ducked his head into his hands and sobbed. Johnson waited, just as he had had to wait ten thousand times before.

At last, a deep breath taken as if air, not time, were the antidote, he looked up. "She broke it up. We had two great months, and then she just said to me one day that it was over."

He spoke in a tone of wonder and hurt. He had thought that love and affection were enough but they weren't, not for some people anyway.

Johnson said nothing. Any of his words of comfort would have been worse than harmless. In any case, he didn't need to, for Matthew now wanted to talk.

"I still can't figure out why. It was a good thing we had. We didn't have a row or anything. Not one, not in all the time we were together. She went home for the summer break, but I had to stay on here. When she came back, suddenly it was over. After that she wouldn't even speak to me."

He paused and Johnson waited.

"She started dating Fournier a couple of months after that. The gap was odd. It certainly wasn't like Nikki to be without somebody for weeks on end."

"Perhaps," suggested Johnson, "she was doing work for the Anatomy prize."

Sacks frowned.

"You know she was astonished when she was short-listed for the prize. A change came over her; I'd never seen her like it before. She hadn't expected to do so well, and it really caught hold of her."

"There we are then."

"Maybe," he admitted, but he didn't seem convinced.

Johnson said, "She didn't live in the Halls of Residence." He used the past tense and cursed himself, but Sacks didn't notice.

"It cramped her style. She had the money, she moved out."

"Her family are well off, are they?"

Sacks' reply was odd. "She said they were."

"Didn't you believe her?"

He was taking a drink of Coke. The coffee lounge was quite crowded now, but nobody had tried to join them.

"I saw her father's car once. It was a beaten-up Ford. Nothing special."

"Are you sure it was her father?"

"She said it wasn't, but I knew she was lying. He was just leaving as I arrived. They kissed and hugged, but I could tell it was a family thing, nothing more."

Johnson wasn't sure that this young man, perhaps twenty-one or twenty-two, knew enough about anything to make that judgement.

"Does she do drugs?"

He had been deliberately abrupt. Sacks was upset but he wasn't going to be caught by that one. He was, however, a poor liar.

"No, not at all."

He was back at the Coke and Johnson wondered if there was something Freudian in this. The policeman sighed and asked again, "Does she do drugs, Matthew? She's gone missing. If she did the occasional jazz Woodbine or snorted the odd line, it is just possible that it might be connected."

He waited, confident that Sacks would think better of continuing the deception. He was not disappointed.

"Yes, she did," he muttered.

"What did she do?"

He was clenching his hands between his knees.

"Mainly coke and cannabis."

"Mainly?"

He shook his head and muttered something.

"What?"

"We tried heroin."

There had been a subtle change in their relationship. Matthew Sacks was no longer just a casual witness, now he was confessing to crime.

"What does 'tried' mean?"

"I only did it once."

All interrogations were like this. He often felt like a mosquito trying to suck enough blood to fill a blood bank.

"And what about Nikki?"

And the silence told him a volume more than the eventual answer.

"She seemed to be used to it."

Nikki Exner was gradually becoming an interesting person. The corpse was nothing, the previous person gone and no amount of inspection would fill the lacuna, but the person, once found, was a different thing.

"Where were you last night?" he asked.

Sacks looked up at that one.

"I was on call. I'm on a medical firm and it was their take night."

"What does that mean?"

"The firm was the one that accepted all emergency medical admissions."

"So you were busy all night? Someone was with you?"

He did look tired.

"I got to bed at four. Until then I was with the houseman for the whole time."

Something occurred to Johnson. "Did you admit someone called Mrs Goodpasture? A stroke, I think."

The other nodded. "She was in a bad way."

"What time was that?"

But he didn't really know. "About eleven?" he suggested vaguely.

"Was her husband with her?"

Sacks nodded. "He was really screwed up. Really jumpy."

"The whole time?"

"Couldn't get rid of him. He was always in the way."

Johnson had almost finished. The questions were largely asked. His next enquiry was unlikely to yield anything useful.

"Where did she get the drugs?"

Sacks didn't really want to say but he wasn't a natural or an easy liar. Eventually, after Johnson had stared at him for a while and then said, "Matthew," he replied.

"A guy called Bowman. He's one of the curators in the museum."

"You're quiet."

The truth of this statement was undeniable. As was the tone of expectant triumph in Wharton's voice. Bilroth kept his face stony, his eyes on the increasingly depressed streets that they were passing through. He was sweating and he was noticeably shaking. Wharton, who sat in the front, had to glance back over her right shoulder to look at him. She wrinkled her pretty, powdered nose, not sure if she could really smell the odour that seemed to come from Bilroth.

Perhaps he's withdrawing, she speculated, but it was a disinterested, clinical thought, soon gone.

She could sense he was guilty. She could touch his lust and his delight as he had raped the girl, then killed her and in an insensate psychosis dismembered her.

And when she had proved it, when she had presented the world with the demon who had raped and sliced open and then hanged a beautiful girl, she would be unstoppable. Castle would be a mere speck on the backwards horizon and (it was this that gave her most cause to despise him) probably unconcerned.

She felt now that all that had gone before in her career was about to be justified. All the whispers and the discreet conversations, the nights on her back, and the smiles and laughs at other people's weak jokes; all might be granted a legitimacy that before now her secret rationalizations had failed to conjure. Christ, perhaps even the unpleasant few minutes she had spent with Superintendent Bloom, her back against the wall of the New Caledonia Hotel, his hot breath in her ear and his prick rasping her cunt, would now seem less sordid and dirty.

She crossed her legs.

Perhaps not.

The car stopped but for a moment she couldn't shake off the feeling of prostitution.

"Inspector?"

The driver knew her, was aware of her moods.

She lied briefly with "I know," then opened the door. Standing by the car she waited for Bilroth to be dragged from his seat, passing the time by looking around. He had chosen to live on a different planet, she decided. This wasn't Earth, this was some realm of punishment, a cosmic penal colony where only the lost were sent.

Wherever she looked there was a sign of hopelessness, an expression of total acquiescence to despair. Paint peeled, cars rusted, rubbish collected in heaps and graffiti was scrawled. Everywhere. No matter which direction she twisted her head and allowed her eyes to settle there was the same shit, the same loss of humanity and all that humanized.

Bilroth's chosen residence was the upstairs flat in a terraced house. Outside there was a car; the car was in the metre-long front garden. The car had at some point been torched and, judging by the state of the front of the house, it could easily have been done where it now rested. The front door had once been solid wood but a combination of rot, boots and dog urine had conspired to consume and warp it into nothing more than a vague ill-fitting shape in the way of the frame.

"Christ." The driver was wrinkling his nose as if he could detect something nasty in the woodshed.

They were having trouble getting Bilroth out of the car. When he finally emerged, handcuffed, his eyes were on the dog turds that lay scattered like seed upon the pavement. Wilson had a hand on the neck of his sweatshirt, screwing it up so that it dug into the flesh of his throat.

"Got a key, Tim?"

All sweetness and blight, she turned to Bilroth. They stood and looked at him, but he had found a particularly interesting crack in the pavement.

"We could break it down easily enough," suggested the driver.

Wharton turned to Bilroth. "Well, Tim?"

Still there was nothing. She nodded at the driver and he went at once to the boot of the car where, quite astonishingly, he managed to locate a sledgehammer.

"Last chance, Tim."

And he was so engrossed in a particularly soft pile of dogshit that some unfortunate passer-by had previously skidded on, he didn't apparently hear the question.

The door took only one blow, a pathetic response that inevitably led to a feeling of police overkill.

They proceeded up the stairs, silencing with a warrant card the old man who came out of his ground-floor flat to see who had come to call. Bilroth had to be literally dragged up the bare wooden steps.

There was a single door at the top of the stairs. The landing was minute but someone had found room to place a pile of vomit. Still, it masked the stench of urine.

"Tim?"

This time Bilroth heard. He produced a key.

It was just after she had taken the key. Obviously Wilson loosened his grip and obviously eyes were on the key in Wharton's hand as it moved towards the lock. Obviously too Bilroth had an itch to be elsewhere.

He shoved Wilson, making sure that his elbow went deep and fast into the policeman's abdominal cavity. The grip went, Wilson tottered into the vomit with a despairing and inaccurate "Shit," and Bilroth spun round. He put one foot out for the stairs, missed and ended his escape attempt by sliding his leading foot down the steps, widening his involuntary splits and crying out despairingly. He made a few grabs at the banisters and succeeded eventually in halting his painful descent, but by then the driver had hold of his sweatshirt in both hands.

He pulled Bilroth back up with little regard for personal dignity or for the seams of his attire.

Wharton was smiling as Bilroth was more or less deposited in front of her.

"Did you forget something, Tim?" she asked. She stood and looked at the top of his head for a long while, making sure that everyone was calm. Wilson spent this time wiping the contents of someone's stomach from the seat of his trousers and uttering profanity in abundance. It was only when he had completed as best he could this operation that Wharton turned again to the door, key in hand.

The key went into the lock and turned easily.

The door opened and Wharton walked through.

She looked around, then back at Bilroth. Her face was triumphant.

"Oh, Tim," she breathed. "Oh, Tim!"

There was a photo of Nikki Exner pinned to the wall.

It was nominally a bedsit but in reality it was a shithole. Barely furnished, untidy and damp, it bathed them all in squalor. Wharton had her nose permanently wrinkled because of the smells of drains, old cooking, sweat and ammonia. Wilson moved around the place kicking things and continuously blaspheming, the clinging fragrance of puke his constant companion. The driver stayed by the door to make sure that no one escaped.

Bilroth had been made to sit in the only chair present, surrounded by empty beer cans.

"Now, Tim, are you going to tell us where we should look, or shall we just rip this stinking hole to pieces?"

There was no answer, so Wharton merely sighed and indicated with a look that Wilson should proceed.

It didn't take long. Wilson found energy for the first time in the course of the investigation and worked his way rapidly through the various drawers, tins, crannies and nooks. Then . . .

"Sir?"

He had found a biscuit tin at the back of the wardrobe and the contents he showed to Wharton. She examined them eagerly then turned in delight to her suspect. "Got you," she said simply.

Just as rapidly as it had filled, as bit-part players had entered, uttered lines with almost insulting familiarity and taken their cues with ill-disguised boredom, so now the museum emptied. The body had gone long since, accompanied by Sydenham and funeral directors, unaccompanied by any form of oration or oratorio. Forensics had wrapped up shortly after that, closely followed by Scenes of Crime, garlic and all, moaning about how he would now have to go to attend the autopsy. There were only a collection of uniformed officers and Johnson when Castle came back into the museum. Johnson wondered where he had been for the past hour or so, but didn't ask directly.

"Where's Inspector Wharton?"

"She's gone with Tim Bilroth, the assistant curator, back to his flat."

Castle's curiosity had lasted no longer than the question and he asked for no further information. Johnson felt compelled to elaborate.

"Apparently he's got form for rape and drugs."

Castle was greyer than ever, as if not only had something disagreed with him, it was positively out to get him.

"Interesting," was all he said and that in an uninterested murmur. They stood together in the museum, close to the table and its irregular red cover. By Castle's side was a hand and forearm with all the muscles and their bony attachments exposed and labelled.

"What's wrong, Jack?"

They had known each other a long time, and never before had Johnson used his first name, but surprise or any other form of reaction seemed far beyond Castle. He looked at Johnson, appeared to be about to say something, thought again. With a smile he said, "Not doing very well, am I?"

"Not very. No."

For a second Johnson thought that was it, that Castle would refuse to open up any further, but he said, "A bit of bad news, that's all."

"Is it Eve?" Johnson knew that Castle was devoted to his wife.

Castle was looking at the forearm. The fingers were splayed and slightly clawed, as though it had burst through from below, grasping for freedom.

"So the theory is that this chap Bilroth drugged her, raped her and then strung her up. Is that it?"

Johnson shrugged. "I guess."

"Do you think he did it?" Castle asked.

"I don't know. He's got the right form."

Castle looked up at the glass dome. "Why doesn't it fit? Why doesn't it smell right, then?"

While Johnson was struggling for an answer, Castle had returned to the forearm. He said quietly, "Eve's dying."

Johnson hardly caught it. He stared at the Chief Inspector. "Dying?" he said stupidly.

Castle had moved around the forearm. With his eyes still on it he said, "A few weeks, they reckon. Got the Macmillan nurse coming round tonight."

"Oh, shit. I'm sorry . . . "

Castle looked up. "Why should you be sorry? You didn't give her cancer, did you?"

"No, but . . . "

"Shut up then." Castle looked him in the eye. "Don't tell anyone. No one at all. This stays between you and me. Got that?"

"But what about Inspector Wharton?"

Castle's expression didn't changed. Still staring at Johnson he repeated, "No one at all."

Eventually Johnson nodded and dropped his gaze.

Caplan came up to them. "I've sealed off the scene. That's the only way in and out now." He indicated the double doors to the medical school. "Is there anything else you want me to do?"

Castle ignored him and it was Johnson who dismissed him. He collected Lockwood and they left the museum to Castle and Johnson.

A deep breath and Castle straightened his back. "What's to be done?"

A fucking lot actually.

103

Johnson said as smooth as shining brightness, "Not much. Why don't you get over to the nick? I expect Inspector Wharton will be getting back there soon."

Castle looked at him for a long time, as if the lie were written across his eyes. Then he said quite slowly, "Okay," and turned to go.

As if afraid of letting a rare moment go, Johnson said to his back, "She's out to get you, you know. She'll stab you in the back and tread on your carcass to get where she wants to go."

Castle stopped but he didn't turn round. Nor did he ask whom Johnson was talking about. All he said was, "My wife's about to die. Do you think I care about that?"

He carried on walking. Only when he had reached the glass doors that lead out to the medical school courtyard did he turn to face Johnson. "If I were you, I'd watch out as well. You're not out of her sights."

He walked out and left the door swinging.

Russell spent the afternoon in a foul mood. That this was worthy of comment, that it was even noticeable as straying from the norm, was testament enough to the magnitude of the event. His reporting session, in which the day's specimens were examined under the microscope, diagnoses reached and reports written, was always a tense affair, but that afternoon's two-hour ordeal achieved new heights of agony for the two registrars and a visiting Chinese doctor. This last gentleman spoke little English but had gleaned enough to realize that Basil Russell enjoyed humiliating juniors and foreigners who didn't speak much English.

When Sophie Sternberg-Reed and Belinda Miller emerged, both sported tight lips and slightly watery eyes. Even the Chinese visitor, a tall and patently correct young man, threatened to burst asunder the oriental reputation for inscrutability. Sophie rushed off to the Ladies without a word, brushing past Eisenmenger as if he were a thing of smoke and tears as he entered the secretaries' office. Gloria was talking on the telephone and sticking a pencil in her ear. Her way of coping was to ignore everything that she didn't want to know about.

Eisenmenger raised his eyes at Belinda, who was made of a sterner fabric, and said, "Good session?"

She forced a smile but didn't answer directly.

"I've got a hysterectomy to show you."

They went into Eisenmenger's office, leaving Sophie in the loo and the Chinese visitor brewing tea with a shaking hand.

"Something up with Basil?" he asked when the door was shut.

Belinda was small and stocky, dark-haired and dark-eyed, and hard to dislike. She snorted at Eisenmenger's question. "He obviously didn't get his end away last night."

Russell had a reputation for womanizing or at least attempting to womanize. Eisenmenger had never been able to fathom Russell's complete lack of insight in this area.

"He was bad, was he?"

She was lost for words to describe Professor Russell's behaviour. "Compared to that man, the devil looks worth a squeeze," she said at last. "No one could do right this afternoon."

Eisenmenger had had many such conversations. Russell's moods oscillated only between arrogant and corrosive.

"Mind you," she continued, "this morning he was all sweetness."

Russell was not only one of the most devious, back-stabbing bastards who had ever passed water, he was also capable of turning on charm of such dazzling brilliance that the unwary were inevitably consumed by the light.

"If I were you," he advised, "I'd be grateful for any respite that came my way."

She looked less than convinced. "I don't think anything that pleases the Professor can possibly benefit me."

She was probably right, and the same went for Eisenmenger, but there was no point in dwelling on such matters.

"What have you got to show me?" he asked.

Belinda had brought in a tray of slides that she now put on the bench by the microscope. There were sixteen glass slides, each with a pink and blue section on them.

"It's part of the hyperplasia study."

The gynaecologists had set up an ongoing study on abnormalities of the womb lining. Hysterectomy specimens were received fresh in the department so that tissue samples could be cut out and frozen, then sent to the Department of Anatomy. This involved a convoluted protocol to follow involving taking small blocks of tissue from numerous sites in the specimen. Eisenmenger was the named pathologist and, although it was the registrars who did the bulk of the dissection, it was he who had to fill in the long and tedious paperwork.

"These bloody things are coming thick and fast. We must have done eight in the past month."

"There should have been another one last thing yesterday."

Belinda was doing the cut up for Eisenmenger that week and, as such, he was slightly surprised by her uncertainty. "Should have been?"

"It's gone missing."

"Not another one." Specimens going AWOL were a continual problem. Theatres blamed Histology, Histology blamed the porters, the porters didn't give a toss.

"Theatres swear blind that they sent it down, but it's not there now."

"Have you told Russell? He'll need to log it as a Serious Clinical Incident."

She nodded. "That was when he turned from nice to nasty." Belinda had a prominent mole at the corner of her mouth that Eisenmenger could not help staring at when he talked to her. He watched it now as it rode her grimace. "Poor old Sophie got the brunt of it."

Eisenmenger had begun to look down the microscope. He sighed. "Is there something going on here? I'm getting worried about her."

Belinda was sensible: he could trust her and, he hoped, she could trust him. "I'm not sure," she said.

The telephone rang. Gloria's superb tones boomed out, informing him that there was a policeman to see him. With apologies to Belinda, he told her to show the visitor to his office.

Johnson looked tired, pissed off and ready to hit something. He refused Eisenmenger's offer of tea or coffee and slumped in a chair. "You'll have to look for another assistant curator."

Eisenmenger raised his eyebrows. He wasn't sure if Johnson was referring to Bowman or Libman. Libman was sedated on a psychiatric ward, in deep shock.

"Bowman's been arrested for rape and murder."

The news had come through as Johnson was driving out to Nikki Exner's flat to ask a few questions.

Bilroth's flat had been a stinking mess, but it was a stinking mess that contained a watch bearing the inscription, *To Nikki, with love on your eighteenth birthday, Mum and Dad*. There had also been a not inconsiderable quantity of heroin, cocaine and cannabis.

Johnson heard all this with mounting shock, not least because the message from Wharton that accompanied the news was triumphal in tone.

"You can forget about interviewing anyone else for the time being. I've got him."

I've, he noted.

Johnson had known what that meant.

"What do you think?" he asked Eisenmenger.

And Eisenmenger had no answer. "I think anyone can murder," he said unhelpfully. "Anyone at all."

"Yeah, I know. But did Bilroth do this one?"

Eisenmenger didn't know. "It sounds as if he might have done," he said cautiously.

Which was what Johnson hadn't wanted to hear; but he had known it was almost certainly what he was going to get.

It was dark when Johnson finally found time to return to the museum. He was tired, tired to exhaustion, but he wasn't ready to stop yet. Not while it felt so *wrong*, while he felt disturbed about the way things were going.

It was dark and all the entrances were taped off but he went in anyway, using one of the keys they had taken from the assembled players in this drama. The silence was broad and deep and once again, as Johnson stood staring into the dense blackness before him, he was struck by the strength of the resonance with a holy place.

It took him a while to locate a light switch, but fumbling eventually produced a satisfactory result. Suddenly light chased out the darkness forming a perfect cone near the centre of the room, the blood-cover conference table half-outside its circumference. For a moment he was surprised by the brilliance of the light and feeling stupid because of it.

He walked forward, enjoying the coolness and the space. The rope had gone and the body had long since been removed but it was really all still there. The whole enormity of the thing that had happened here still remained despite the removal of much of the physical evidence. In effect only the bloodstain remained, so huge as to be almost cartoonish, splattered like a drop of blood from a towering Titan, but that was enough. The memory of the girl's desecration lingered, as solid and horrifying as the reality.

Yet it wasn't just the act of murder that bothered him. As awful as it was, he knew that the feelings deep within him were not born of disgust or shock at the blood and the suffering.

He crouched down, looking up into the heart of the glass dome.

No, what bothered him was symbolism. It was no mere murder, done for gain, or for revenge, or in fear, or for sex, this was a statement. This murderer wanted to tell a story, make a statement, catch the attention . . .

But why?

And what precisely was the statement?

He dropped his gaze to the far end of the hall where ten hours before Stephan Libman had curled up into a quivering ball.

An odd reaction, despite what Eisenmenger had said.

The table was spread out in front of him, still crimson and glutinous, a huge wooden pizza. Almost as if willed by an outside force he reached out to touch it.

He wondered why he felt an undercurrent of such sorrow.

Mark.

His brother had died not six months before, a sudden heart attack taking him just as it had taken their father. And it was in the quiet of the huge crematorium, a small group huddled together in cold grief despite the warm sunshine outside, that he had rekindled his distant memories of church and solitude and mortality.

He felt that same emotion now . . .

"I know why I'm here, Johnson, but what about you?"

For a moment his heart stopped and he thought that he would join his brother. His sympathetic nervous system, usually hard to awake, was electrified and his heartbeat thundered back into his chest so loudly and so forcefully that he could feel blood sucking and rushing out of his veins and into his atria.

He whirled around and Wharton walked out of the shadows.

"Bloody hell!"

This was as blasphemous as Johnson ever got.

Wharton was smiling but it was not the fulsome expression of an old friend or lover.

"I thought for a moment you were praying."

He tried to smile, didn't want her to see that he had been so startled by her sudden appearance.

"I didn't realize you were here."

She shrugged.

"I wanted to work things out. Where better than where it happened?"

He couldn't resist putting a faint jeer into his voice as he commented, "I thought it was all wrapped up."

"I think that. Don't you?"

Now there was a question.

He ought to have said, *There are a few points I don't understand.*

"No."

She smiled, but this time it was the real thing. In fact it turned eventually into a laugh. "Please, Johnson. Don't be shy."

He shrugged. "You asked."

Suddenly the laugh stopped and the smile followed it. "You don't like me, do you?"

He considered. "Does that matter?"

"If you mean does it matter to me personally, then no. If you mean does it matter to the investigation, then yes."

"But the investigation's over," he pointed out.

"Yes. This one is."

He made a face and looked to the carpet.

She walked forward so that she was beside him, facing the bloodied table. "Tell me, then. Tell me where I've slipped up."

And she was pleased to see that he had to hesitate.

"I just don't think that he did it," he said at last somewhat lamely. Then, "It's all completely circumstantial. You can't place him at the scene of the crime."

"What about the cocaine?"

"There are nine hundred students here. That could have been left by anyone, at any time."

She tried not to sound too impatient, but didn't overtax herself. She was sure now that this was merely pique. "You didn't see his room. The drugs paraphernalia, Nikki Exner's watch, the photograph of her on the wall. The guy's a known drug abuser and has a conviction for rape as well as one for ABH that involved a knife. He can't give a satisfactory explanation of where he was last night and you, yourself, have uncovered a witness who claims that he supplied the dead girl with drugs. What more do you need?"

But Johnson wouldn't relinquish his doubt. He looked up at the glass dome again. "It took a hell of a lot of effort to suspend her like that."

"So?"

"So I can't see a young man who's out of his head on narcotics managing to organize it."

She too looked up but saw it with different eyes. "I don't see why not. He had an obsession with the girl. Out of his head, that obsession was all that mattered. He raped her because he wanted her. Used her in any way that he fancied, then he had to kill her."

"Like that?" he asked incredulously.

"Why not? With the cocktail of narcotics he had inside him, he probably thought it was entirely normally to do that to someone."

He let it go.

"And then there's the overall feel of it all."

"What of it?"

Again he lapsed into speechless rumination for a while.

"There's a grand design about it. A sense of theatre, of symbolism, perhaps."

"The church thing again," she said mockingly.

"It doesn't square with Bilroth."

"There was a grand design, but it was in his head. Bilroth raped her, slit her open, then strung her up."

Still he wouldn't admit defeat. "It wasn't him," he insisted.

"You're wrong, Johnson. Or rather you're desperate for me to be wrong."

He wasn't surprised that she should think so and he had to admit that there was an element of truth in her accusation. But whatever pleasure he might derive from showing her to have erred, it was subordinate to making sure that the right person was caught.

He honestly believed that.

"Why should I want that?"

He was raising the temperature, quite deliberately enticing her to commit.

"Because you've got a problem. Because you could never cope with my promotion."

They had never talked like this before, a game of dare.

"I've seen plenty of coppers get promoted. I've never considered it a problem."

"Until now."

What was she saying? What did she want him to say?

He shook his head. "You're seeing things that aren't there."

"Am I? Why me, Johnson? Why should it give you such indigestion because I was made Inspector? Especially when you admit yourself it didn't bother you when other people got promoted."

"I haven't got a problem with your promotion," he insisted but he heard the lie as plainly as she did and he suddenly thought, *Why don't you tell her?*

They were standing within a metre of each other. Smiling, she moved towards him so that her breast was nearly touching him.

"It's not because I'm a woman, is it?" she asked softly.

If she intended to provoke him, she succeeded. He felt a surge of disgust and, turning half away, he said, "No. No, it's not because you're a woman."

She moved her hand up to his face, stroking his cheek with the back of her hand. He stiffened, emotions suddenly mixed and therefore muddied. Her breast was now brushing against him and he had to concede that she was attractive, with full lips and eyes large in the poor light.

"I'm glad you're not sexist, Bob," she said softly. "You and I could be a good team. We could go far together. A very, very long way."

Then she smiled as she added, "In more ways than one."

At once he was flooded with near nausea, so full that he couldn't speak.

"What do you say, Bob?" she asked quietly and her finely plucked eyebrows were arched gently, faint creases forming on her forehead.

He looked directly into her eyes and through stiff lips he said, "Harlot," in a voice almost as quiet as hers.

The word was ludicrous, and he wondered why he had used it. Cowardice, he supposed. A sudden fear that some of the other words he might have employed – tart, prostitute, station bicycle were all terms that some had used about her – were too strong perhaps.

Yet if Wharton thought it ludicrous she didn't laugh, far from it. For a moment she was silent, shocked, but it was only while her expression caught up with her emotions. Her eyes narrowed and her skin turned white, her lips barely surviving as they were stretched and thinned to sharp edges around her mouth.

"You bastard!" she hissed.

And now he was on this path, he found that he didn't want to stop and he certainly didn't want to retreat. It was with huge exultation that he said, "I know about the Eaton-Lambert case, don't forget. I know what happened."

For a second she looked surprised, then afraid, then this emotion was vanished, replaced by mockery.

"Oh, you know, do you? What do you know, Sergeant?"

"I know that you planted evidence, that you pressurized him into admitting to it."

She smiled and Johnson was forced to admit that it was bloody confident construction. It wasn't the uncertain glance of someone who was afraid of him: more like the full-on stare of a tiger shark facing a whelk.

"I don't have the faintest idea what you're talking about," she said. Before he could answer she continued, "But if you have evidence that there was something amiss in the investigation of the Eaton-Lambert case, I suggest you take the matter to a superior officer."

She knew that she had him and that made him angry.

Too angry, as it turned out. With nothing much to say he said anything. "I would if I could find one you haven't slept with."

The first thing she did was actually to flinch, as if the blow had been concrete. Then her eyes narrowed and he waited.

111

She slapped him so unexpectedly that it was gone before he could react. Almost as part of the same balletic movement, she wheeled around and walked quickly from the island of light in the centre of the room. The door slammed in the darkness beyond.

The slap hadn't really hurt but Johnson found himself rubbing his cheek. He stayed in that position for a long time.

Hamilton-Bailey's return home that evening was, at least initially, little different to the usual. Irene and he had long since ceased to function as a unit but, both recognizing that credit outweighed debit if they continued on a purely mechanical level, their domestic arrangements had evolved into a state of complementation. Thus they occupied either the same space in the house, or the same time, but rarely both at once. Irene would cook early, retiring to the sitting room or to her own room for the remainder of the evening. This allowed Alexander the run of the spacious kitchen when he arrived home, after which he invariably retired to the study, thence to his bedroom. Mornings and weekends were similarly contrived in their choreographed routine, and the wonder of it was that it was accomplished by both dancers without constant clock-watching.

Entertaining – something that Alexander considered they did with distressing frequency – was accomplished with the help of a catering company and the erection of a structurally flimsy but cosmetically impressive façade. That no one was fooled did not matter: the play was the thing.

Hamilton-Bailey was somewhat surprised that Irene chose not to engineer a meeting at the earliest possible opportunity. He concocted a fair imitation of a chilli con carne with the groceries he had picked up on the way home from his local shop (he hated shopping in supermarkets, feeling conspicuous and pathetic as he trudged around the aisles), then scurried for his study. At once he switched on the radio and then poured himself a large cognac as Mahler filled the half-light of a single desktop lamp. In weeks past he would have begun work on Gray's, but he had not done this for several days now. He sat down in an armchair and stared straight ahead, the bowl of the brandy glass resting in his palm. He had much to ponder. Much indeed.

The knock at the door came some twenty minutes later.

"Come in, Irene."

Irene Hamilton-Bailey was in her late forties, but time had passed her by so that, in contradiction of the generally accepted pattern, it was her husband who looked frayed and unappealing while she retained her youthful attractiveness. Tall, statuesque and with eyes that were deep blue, large and long-lashed, she had made many men fall in love with this construction of femininity, grace and wealth.

How had it started? How had the marriage vows stretched and twisted, and then bound his hands while she had used his love and devotion to escape the normal moral confines of wedlock? He had asked the question so many times before, asked it but never answered it, that he no longer posed it seriously. It had happened, and he had allowed it to happen: these were the only matters of importance now.

Irene had bathed and changed for bed. She entered now, fragrant and clean, the very paradigm of femininity, all the more alluring because for so long it had been unobtainable.

She seated herself in the armchair opposite her husband's.

"What's going on, Alexander?" Irene had never developed the habit of prevarication.

Hamilton-Bailey said nothing.

"I mean the phone call."

Still he was silent.

"They said on the radio that there was a murder last night, at the medical school. They said that a girl had been killed."

Irene didn't watch the television. Her world was of an entirely different substance.

He avoided looking into her eyes. He was afraid of what he would concede if she were to see his face, of what he would have to confront if he were to see hers.

"And now you want me to lie, to say that I was with you all night, that . . . "

But even Irene could not voice the truth of her latest infidelity. Instead she asked, "Why, Alexander? I don't understand."

He reflected that they had never got to the abbreviation stage. She had remained 'Irene', he 'Alexander'. It was a symbol of their failure in marriage.

"Did you do it, Alexander?" Her voice was fearful but he could not but help wondering bitterly if the fear was for him or for herself.

"Of course not!" he protested. "Do you know what was done to her? It was horrible, horrible . . . " But he could not expose her to the awfulness of it all. She was still his wife, after all.

She looked both reassured and uncertain. "Then why?"

He sighed, but could still not find the words. A sip of brandy, however, helped.

"You're my wife, Irene," he said simply.

She looked uncomfortable. Irene had never liked overmuch attention paid to facts such as that. She asked him for some brandy and as he poured it from the decanter on the low table near the door, he said, "Think how it will look, Irene. No matter what you and I might know or desire, the police consider me to be a suspect. They will want to know what I was doing last night and . . . " He turned around and brought the glass of brandy to Irene. " . . . who I was with."

She sat and thought about it.

"I would much rather," he continued, "that they were not privy to our domestic affairs. I am sure that upon consideration you will be of a like mind."

For the first time he dared to look into her eyes, trying to ignore the inevitable feeling of melancholic lostness that her beautiful eyes always brought to him.

Irene said nothing while Alexander, ashamed at having to admit to his wife's adultery, even to her and especially to himself, drank brandy. At long last she drained her glass in one and stood up. He raised tired eyes to her.

She proffered the glass and tried to smile.

All she said was, "I understand."

She left the room.

Eisenmenger arrived home early that night. It was his turn to cook but he didn't feel like it and so had resolved to get a takeaway. Marie wouldn't like this – she would see it as a de facto breach of their understanding that there was a strict alternation of domestic chores – but he couldn't help that. He was tired and he was strangely disturbed by the events of the day and he didn't know why. He wanted time to think, time to place this latest incident into context. Marie wouldn't be home until after nine thirty and he needed the silence of the empty flat.

He showered and changed, poured some wine and sat on the blue leather sofa. The suite had been Marie's choice and he would not deny that she had good taste. It showed in the venetian blinds, the glass coffee table, the uplighters and the potted palms. It showed, too, in the rugs dotted about the polished floorboards, the border and the stencilled walls. He found himself looking around the room and wondering where his choice had gone. For a moment he felt like a guest in the flat and try as he might he couldn't deny this proposition. After all, he was effectively a guest in her life, so why not in her flat?

Ignore the fact that he paid the mortgage and the bills, that he paid the price for all that filled her life, somehow and somewhere he had been turned into another of Marie's possessions: a bloody useful one in that it could wave credit and debit cards, it could write cheques and it did half the cooking, ironing and cleaning.

It even occasionally got to shaft her. Not lately though. Not for a long time, in fact.

He sipped some wine.

Not that he could really complain. When he had first got to know Marie, she had been what he had been looking for. Someone to bring regulation to his life. His wife, Deborah, had been the same, he supposed, albeit less insistent on a fanatical fifty-fifty split of labour. She, too, had been ordered, but she had been happy for him to be disordered. If he didn't fold his clothes at night, she did it for him: if he didn't get around to cutting the lawn, she always seemed to find the time. If only she hadn't had such a problem with what he did, they might still be married now. The fact that she was almost physically sick at just the thought of his day job was bad enough, but there was also the ever-present possibility that he would be called out to some other murder, some other body found in a wood or a flat.

It was happening at too many dinner parties, on too many quiet sunny days at home, and it was spoiling too many meals that she had prepared for him.

Always there was another stabbing, shooting, beating . . .

Tamsin.

Abruptly he got up and walked out of the sitting room, through the narrow dark hallway and into the main bedroom. The bed was a four-drawer divan and he rummaged in one of the drawers. At the bottom was a large brown envelope. He pulled it out and returned with it to his wine.

Tamsin had been beautiful. It shouldn't have mattered but it did. Everything about Tamsin's death seemed to bring greater guilt to him, even the fact that she was pretty. Wide blue eyes, slightly snub nose and an expression of grinning impertinence that could have been irritating but was exactly otherwise.

He stared for a long time, not breathing and not even aware of it.

Before he knew it, he could smell burnt flesh, feel the oily, char-flecked grease, hear her small voice.

Where's my mummy?

The photograph had been blown up from one the police had found in her mother's flat. Marie had found it once, during her periodic and unbelievably thorough cleansing offensives, and had innocently asked who it was. She hadn't understood his reaction, his uncontrolled, sudden and apparently irrational anger, the way he had snatched it from her as if she could not be trusted not to mark it or tear it or lose it. They had rowed after that, the acrimony made worse because he could not tell her what it meant to him.

That, he had long ago decided, was another aspect of the problem. He could not tell her about this thing, this event that had exploded into his life – that had exploded his life – and that had altered him irrevocably. Oh, she knew of it – just as she knew of famine in Africa and the relief of Mafeking – after all, she had been a nurse on the psychiatric ward where he had sought relief, but she didn't know the truth of it. That he had hidden it, and hidden it deep.

He knew that he should have been capable of confiding in her, indeed he knew that not to have shared this with her was as great a deceit as adultery would have been, but he also knew that it was beyond him. Perhaps, he had often told himself, it was the test that would determine his perfect partner, the one to whom he could talk about poor little Tamsin.

The glass was empty, the bottle in the fridge and the trip to the kitchen at least chipped away at his melancholia.

Why Tamsin? Why now?

Obviously because of the murder in the museum but, then again, not obviously.

This one was patently different. This one was like all the others had been – a puzzle, nothing more. Certainly his shock at the discovery had been merely an exaggerated form of surprise. No one could fail to be startled by the naked body of an eviscerated young woman hanging from the ceiling, but it had ended at that. Libman's reaction might have been far more extreme, but then he was unused to seeing corpses, or at least whole corpses. When Eisenmenger had seen the body, he had felt no great emotional involvement.

So what then?

He lay back, so that his head was overlying the back of the sofa and he was staring at the ceiling. Marie had decided that there should be coving and that the ceiling should be painted a delicate shade of rose pink. It was all in exquisite taste. In fact it was so fucking exquisite he occasionally felt the urge to scream.

Nurses and doctors formed relationships all the time. Admittedly pathologists, who saw only the dead and freshly excised pieces of

116

the living during professional hours, were not usually prone to the same temptations that clinicians endured, but his had been a special case. He and Marie had met under slightly different circumstances but the result had been the same. He wouldn't be so ungallant as to say that Marie saw him as a means to financial and social betterment – although this was a virulent disease epidemic amongst the nursing profession – but it was clear that she considered herself to have bagged a prize specimen. Certainly her parents had been obnoxiously delighted when he had been produced, like a particularly magnificent salmon, at one overwhelmingly embarrassing Sunday dinner.

Their attitude had bothered him and it had made him suspicious of Marie's. Did she really feel for him, or for what he could do for her?

And then of course, there had been the circumstances of their meeting. He had been vulnerable, and he could not help but wonder if she had taken advantage of that. True her phone call had been made after a few weeks, when he had left the hospital and was resting at home, but it had been *her* call, not his. She had been the active one, the hunter.

It had come at a time when he had been feeling lonely – his own fault for he had refused outpatient follow-up – the only other person to call being Johnson, and he wasn't about to enter into a relationship, deep or shallow, with that good gentleman.

And now here was Johnson again.

Was that the problem?

He drank more wine, then closed his eyes.

No, it wasn't just Johnson. It was the whole lot of them. Johnson, if anything, was the best of them, the least tainted by inhumanity. The morning's events had taken him back to a time when he hadn't cared about the person, only the body. The crime had been a whodunit or a howdunit, but rarely a whydunit and never a realization of what it meant. Meant to the victim as he or she died, or the murderer as they fired the gun, pushed in the blade, smashed open the skull or, God help him, eviscerated the hanging girl. Meant to the parents, the children, the siblings of the deceased. Meant even to the parents, the children, the siblings of the perpetrator when they realized that little Johnny had become that worst of all social outcasts, a murderer.

Wharton, Castle, the others, none of them was capable of feeling anything but cardboard sorrow for the players in the tragedy; he saw in them his own past self.

117

Tamsin had changed all that, and he had escaped, he thought, to academe, where the post-mortems were few and the deaths were attended by no desecration of God's law.

He heard the front door open and it was with a shock that he realized it was already nine forty-five.

"John?"

The voice from the hall was fifty per cent anxiety and fifty per cent irritation.

"In here."

Marie came in, her short tight skirt showing her legs to good advantage.

"What's the matter?"

He smiled. He could tell they were about to have a row, it was like listening to a countdown in his head.

"Nothing. Want some wine?"

"Aren't you cooking?"

He got up and fetched a glass anyway.

"I'm sorry, I didn't feel like it. I'll get a takeaway. What do you want?"

He hadn't expected this to work. Marie was methodical to the point of asinine obstinacy. One thing at a time. Perhaps he would put this on her tombstone. She ignored the proffered glass.

"But you're supposed to be cooking tonight."

Eisenmenger didn't want a row, or at least that was what he told himself as he said, "I've had an extremely bad day, Marie – "

Even he could hear the irritation in his words.

"And I haven't?" she interrupted.

He sighed. Of late she had been become more erratic, more labile, her emotions swinging from calm to frenzy in seconds. This was a near-daily occurrence now.

"I don't know," he admitted and found himself wondering why this should be considered a shortcoming.

"It's not fair, you know, John. You promised that you'd do the cooking tonight. I can't be expected to come in at this hour and starting getting a meal, can I?"

"I didn't expect you to – "

"You have no idea how awful my day has been. One of the bulimics died today. She managed to get hold of a blade. She shut herself in the bathroom and it was twenty-five minutes before anyone realized. There was blood everywhere."

Clearly this had upset Marie greatly. She was capable of a level of commitment and involvement that Eisenmenger not only could not emulate but could barely understand.

Nor was it surprising that she hadn't heard what had happened in the medical school. The Unit of Academic Psychiatry was an entirely separate building some two kilometres from the main hospital-medical school complex.

"I'd said I'd get a takeaway, for Christ's sake! What's the matter with that?"

She began to cry, but there was enough anger within her to make that little more than a distraction.

"You don't bloody understand, do you? You're so bloody self-centred and lazy."

That was so funny he actually laughed. And as he laughed, he knew that only spitting in her eye would have been more inflammatory. He desperately wanted to tell her what had happened to him that day. He wanted to describe in pixelated detail just what had been done to the girl in the museum, each fractal shape that the blood had made, every colour of every viscus.

But he couldn't. Not because it would have been cheap, but because he found that he was not capable of opening up the experience to her. And finding himself thus silenced, he felt yet more guilt and sadness and even, oddly, pleasure, while Marie's anger exploded before him.

That evening Goodpasture's wife had still not regained consciousness. He was virtually forced from the intensive care unit by concerned nursing and medical staff who feared that he would collapse from nervous exhaustion if he didn't get some sleep. Only the kind but unrelenting insistence of the sister and consultant eventually persuaded him that there was nothing to be done, that he might just as well leave, that they would call him as soon as there was any change.

And so he departed, giving the impression of a desolate figure, bowed down by sheer pathos. No one was sure whether to mock him or to cry for him.

He lived a twenty-minute bus journey from the hospital, his home a neat and decidedly spruce terraced house in a long street of the same. There were times, when the weather was hot and the air shimmering, that the street gave the impression of going on for ever, poking through these three dimensions into a mirror universe, a universe where life was better and God always smiled.

Not today, though.

Today God frowned, angry and vengeful. Today there was a cold wind and drizzle licked him with its lascivious tongue. Today, for the first time in forty-three years, he was alone.

He found his house without thinking, an automaton whose feet knew the pavement and the garden walls, the lampposts and the cars better than ever his thinking brain had done. He put the key in the lock and pushed open the door, wiping his feet carefully, avoiding the two letters that lay on the mat. These he picked up, didn't look at and placed on the kitchen table, so that they were propped against the fruit bowl. It was what he always did with letters.

Taking off his coat, he hung it up in the cupboard under the stairs, then swapped his shoes for slippers. The photographs on the fire surround caught his eye and with a guilty start he realized he had completely forgotten about Jem. Jem would have to be told.

He went out into the hall and picked up the telephone receiver. He knew the number off by heart. He waited but an answerphone cut in. With a dreadful feeling of loneliness he left a message, telling of what had happened. Having put the receiver back down he waited a long time just staring at it, hoping that it would ring, that the world would remember him, but he was to be disappointed.

Then he sat down in the kitchen and listened to the silence.

The only thing that broke the silence that night was the sound of his weeping.

Basil Russell returned to his exclusive flat and for the first time ever found its exclusivity depressing. His neighbours in the mansion block were on one side a colonel, recently retired from the Royal and Sutherland Highlanders, and his wife, and on the other a woman novelist. He knew none of them and had preferred it that way until now. Now he wanted to be able to talk to someone.

Should he ring Linda? After all he had cancelled her last night, the first time for many years. He knew that she would happily come, but he knew also that he would not call. Linda came on Wednesdays, never Thursdays: that was a wall too high to climb. This acknowledgement only deepened his feeling of doom.

It was not within him to feel sorry for himself. Like licking his own genitalia and juggling, this was a skill that God had neglected to bless him with. He had always thought that this lack was in fact a strength. That, along with his invincible belief in his own intellectual superiority and his unconquerable certainty that everyone, but everyone, was out to betray him and to laugh at him, was what kept him going.

Until now.

Now he had glimmerings of something that he had not before known, that might have been alien but was recognizable.

He was afraid.

Castle's house was in darkness when he returned that night and he was glad. It was much later than he had planned, such that he had missed the Macmillan nurse, and, even if Eve would not be angry, he was nevertheless cross with himself.

He opened the door as quietly as he could, then closed it by twisting the knob of the Yale lock and gently releasing it again. He stood for a long time in the hallway darkness, the street lights casting diffuse, distorted beams through the stained and frosted glass. Just standing, listening to nothing, seeing little of consequence was what he needed.

He wondered how he had managed to get through the day. How he had endured the long hours at the medical school. Hours in which Eve had died just a little bit more. Hours in which he had not once lost the knowledge that soon she would be dead, soon she would be and think and love no more. Soon she would be gone from him.

At least, he thought without any emotion – contentment, envy, bitterness, satisfaction – Wharton had solved the case.

Then, almost as if unbidden the thought had pushed into his awareness from outwith his head, he wondered, *But is Bilroth guilty?*

Now there was a question, but Castle had been a policeman long enough to know that it was most probably irrelevant. Innocence and guilt, as abstract, philosophical concepts, did not exist for those in law enforcement. If evidence could be found sufficient to persuade a jury to convict, that was enough.

On that criterion, Bilroth's future seemed fairly certain and if further investigation showed that the picture thus far concocted was not quite a perfect reflection of reality, then so be it.

"Dad?"

The call was whispered but it still gave him cause to jump.

"Jo?"

His daughter came out of the darkness from the living room.

"I heard the door," she said quietly. "Thought it was you, but when nothing else happened, I got worried."

She gave him a kiss on his cheek.

"I'm sorry. I was just standing and thinking. I didn't realize you were home."

She tried a smile but it wasn't a good fit. "Of course I am."

121

They went into the living room where Jo had been sitting and reading by the light of a single lamp.

"How's your mum?" he asked, full of dread.

"She's not too bad. She got tired so she went to bed."

"What about the Macmillan nurse? Did she call?"

He was suddenly aware that he spent all his life asking questions and he decided he didn't want to any more.

"She phoned and said she'd have to postpone it until tomorrow."

He nodded. "Good. Maybe I can be there."

She tried the smile again, but this time it was tears that got in the way.

"Are you going to stay?" he asked, hoping that she would say yes.

"I've got to get back. I've got papers to go through. In fact," she looked at her watch, "I ought to go now."

"Of course," he murmured and they both stood at once as if engaged in courtly ritual. They hugged and she whispered to him, "Be strong, Dad."

She let herself out, the door barely making a sound.

He stayed a long time in the living room, wondering at the tears as they fell.

That night, Marie lay curled up on her side of the bed while Eisenmenger lay on his back and looked at the patterns of phosphorescence against the darkness of his eyelids. They hadn't eaten at all in the end, retiring to bed at the tailing end of their row, neither completely satisfied, the dispute still flickering with life.

He kept thinking about Tamsin, about her cracked, black flesh, about her inability to comprehend what had happened to her, and it was because he didn't want to think about such things that he said, "I'm sorry."

She said nothing, didn't even move.

"Marie? I said that I'm sorry."

For a long while he thought she was going to refuse his offer of peace, but eventually she sighed and turned over to face him.

"So am I."

She smiled and he saw within it a few of the reasons why he had chosen to become her lover. Hers was a round face, the features small and finely crafted. Bleached hair, blue-grey eyes and a small mouth with lips that were too thin and always needed lipstick.

He had always known that he would have to tell her and now was as good a time as any. It still felt like pushing on the lid of a buried coffin.

"Someone was murdered in the museum last night. A girl."

Her smile turned to horror. It was genuine, too; not simulated anguish but the real thing, like butter compared with butter spread. Trouble was Eisenmenger found himself preferring spread.

He told her what had happened, reserving the gorier details.

"But who could have done it?"

Anyone. Anyone at all, he thought, although he said, "I should imagine it was someone who broke in."

He didn't mention that there had been no signs of a break-in.

"Do they know who it was?"

"A medical student. A second-year."

She was quiet for a moment before whispering, "How awful," and again he could hear that she really meant it.

"The police will probably be in contact. They'll ask you to corroborate my alibi."

"Oh, yes. Of course."

Of course she would, but he noticed that she didn't say that now she understood why he had been the way he was, that it was reasonable that he hadn't wanted to cook.

They lapsed into silence, but six-year-old girls are persistent.

And because words hadn't been enough to keep the pictures of Tamsin away from him, he leaned over and kissed her. She seemed to respond and so he gently took her chin and kissed her again. His hand moved down to her breast, feeling the nipple harden beneath the cotton of her T-shirt. Then he moved down to the hem of the shirt, feeling the smooth top of her leg and the thin band of her knickers stretched across it. He kissed her again, harder this time, full on the open mouth, while his hand worked up her belly to her breast.

She pulled away.

"Not tonight, John."

That was it. No explanation, no apology.

And he of course said that it was okay, and they kissed – politely – and she turned away to sleep on her side.

Tamsin returned to cry into the night in his head.

There were hourly checks on the prisoners and the Custody Sergeant was a fastidious man. He checked on Bilroth regularly after the interrogation had finished. Thus at one, two and three o'clock, he looked through into the cell and found Bilroth to be lying in the cot, clearly rather agitated. The Sergeant had seen thousands of prisoners lying on the harsh metal benches and Bilroth looked no different

123

to any of them. In fact the Custody Sergeant would have been considerably more worried if there had been no movement from the prisoner. Usually they went to sleep eventually.

When he looked at four o'clock, however, he could see that Bilroth had managed to find peace not in the arms of Morpheus, but in the rather more rigid arms of Death. He was hanging from the bars of the high window by a noose that he had ingeniously constructed from his trousers.

Sadly his last act was his most creative by far.

Part Two

Johnson would never be able to forget those moments, the sudden transition from an ordered, peaceful Sunday morning – the day off, a trip to the garden centre planned – to complete chaos, shouting, yelling, shoving, banging. The conflict of emotions – embarrassment, fear, bewilderment and growing anger – that grew more potent as disbelief transmuted to indignation.

He and Sally had been lying in bed, not really awake. It was early when it began, although he could not have said precisely what time. First there came a thunderous crash, as if the front door had been struck by a sledgehammer. Both he and Sally jerked awake and sat up almost as one. Before they could do or say anything of consequence, it came again. Then the voice.

"Come on! Open up!"

Once more the crash.

"Ten seconds or we'll break it down."

Johnson snatched one glance at his wife's frightened puzzlement, got out of bed and grabbed his dressing gown. He nearly fell down the stairs, the cord of his gown tangling around his legs.

And all the while, although he didn't comprehend any of this, he was very afraid that he recognized the situation. He ought to have done, he had been in it any number of times, only on the other side of the door.

He got to the front door and could see complex shadows through the frosted glass. Before he could get the chain off and the door unbolted and unlocked, there came another command to "Open up!" followed by another crash that shook the door. When at last he did so – perhaps all of fifteen seconds after the first assault – the door was at once pushed open, forcing him to step back, and a foot came in to stop him closing it.

It was as he had feared, for immediately a warrant card was thrust forward into his face. It was held too close to read and, had he not been himself a policeman, completely unrecognizable as official identification of a policeman: it could have proclaimed the bearer to be a member of Secret Squirrel's gang. The next thing he took in was the face behind it, a hard, vicious look about the eyes: eyes that not only didn't care, they didn't comprehend. Then he was shoved aside with a solid shoulder that pushed him into the door and caused his head to bang into the glass. Six of them came in, and at once split into two groups of three, one going upstairs, the other around the ground floor.

He called up to Sally, "Put some clothes on, Sally. Come down here." Then he went in search of the man with vicious eyes, finding him in the sitting room.

"What's going on?" he asked, although even then he knew. "Has there been a complaint?"

The other turned. "What do you think?" Then he was back searching the room with his eyes while one of the others pulled out drawers from the bureau and emptied them into a sack, then examined their backs and their undersides.

"Who are you?"

He didn't even turn this time. "Commander Liddle."

Sally came in. She was terrified, holding her dressing gown around herself tightly, tears only kept away by fear.

"Did they touch you?" demanded Johnson more harshly than he intended. He knew what sometimes happened, but she shook her head.

"What's going on, Bob? Who are these men?"

He looked at Liddle who was picking through the stuff in the bag. Their letters, their mementoes, their whole lives. A photograph of a holiday in Polperro, Sally's birth certificate, his old, expired passport, even his dead mother's wedding ring: all passed through this stranger's hands and were discarded as useless, valueless, not worth even a second's contemplation. How could he do this? What right did he assume? How could even God claim the authority to expose Sally to this? But the anger that this induced was too weak to spark anything in him.

To Sally he said, "They're police. Complaints Investigation, I guess."

Liddle didn't react. Sally's eyes widened.

"Complaints? I don't understand."

But Johnson was beginning to.

"Let me guess," he said to Liddle. "An anonymous call? What was it about? Drugs? Arms? Stolen goods?"

And when Liddle didn't even turn to face him, when all he did was crouch before the ever-filling sack of Johnson's life and rifle through it with bored indifference, Johnson suddenly broke through the barrier of ingrained obedience and grabbed at the other's arm, commanding, "Answer me!"

But Liddle only looked at the hand on his right arm, saying nothing, and Johnson let it drop, the pathetic show of resistance shown up for what it was. Liddle returned to his reading.

Johnson turned back to Sally for comfort, but when he looked at her he saw more than fear and bewilderment on her face, he saw that her eyes held questions that he couldn't answer and, irrationally, he felt offended that she should be asking them.

And then he understood. He knew that they would find what they had come for, though he didn't know what it would be. Knew too that they were acting on anonymous information.

Knew too the source of that information.

He took a deep breath, the knowledge bringing dread and certainty that his life was about to change irrevocably.

The cry from the kitchen came as no great surprise. Johnson tried to smile at Sally but, although she returned the gesture, it was a far from reassuring thing. They followed Liddle and discovered him kneeling down in front of the sink. The cupboard under it was open and from this the lower half of a body could be seen protruding, as if unconscious: to give the lie to this occasionally a hand would appear and give something to Liddle who put it into a large plastic bag. This went on for several minutes while they looked on and again Sally gave him that questioning look.

Liddle got up and there was a look of satisfaction on his face. He didn't show them the bag and he said nothing but Johnson had seen the plastic-wrapped packages, strapped with parcel tape, that now nestled within it. The size said it all. Money.

He ran through it in his mind as he watched the playlet follow its script before him. The serial numbers would be checked and, he was certain, they would be interesting. Perhaps they would be numbers that the police had been given by the banks, banks that had been robbed. Or perhaps they would be the numbers of banknotes involved in money laundering.

He found himself admiring the subtlety of it all; how these bundles of money would suggest his culpability in *something* but not definitely in anything. They would taint him and make him less than clean.

And still it went on. It went on for three long hours and twice more Liddle was called and went unhurriedly in response, the second time to the garage, the last to the cupboard under the stairs. Each time there were a few more such parcels and each time the chaos in the house grew around them. Nothing was untouched; every drawer pulled out and emptied, every item of clothing in every cupboard removed and searched, every item of food in the kitchen taken from its place and examined.

They left them eventually, but only after Johnson had been cautioned and told to report to the police station at eight the next morning. He would be reporting not as a police officer but as a suspect.

"Dr Eisenmenger?"

Gloria had put the call through and, as was ever her way, she had decided at once the characteristics and intentions of the caller. Thus she confidently informed him that the owner of the voice was a woman (with high probability), attractive (with medium to low probability) and interested in Eisenmenger as a man as opposed to a histopathologist (with near-zero probability).

"Speaking."

"My name's Helena Flemming. I work for Wolff, Parkinson, White – "

"Solicitors?" he interrupted.

"Yes. "

Solicitors meant forensic work.

"I'm afraid that I no longer do forensic work."

"Oh, I know," she hastened to reassure him. "I was only telephoning you to arrange a meeting. I was just wondering if you could provide an opinion on a forensic pathology report."

He hesitated and, as with the great moments of history, perhaps it was this small pause that decided between two courses of events, for into his hesitation she said, "Your name was recommended to me very highly. I would so like to meet you."

She had a nice voice, he decided. Husky and low, but also somehow innocent.

"Just an opinion?" he asked.

"That's right."

Still he wasn't sure and, he appreciated later, she was prudent enough to say nothing more.

"Well, I don't see why not. When would you like to meet?"

"Oh, thank you," and she sounded genuinely pleased so that he found himself irrationally delighted with himself. "How about this afternoon?"

It was then that the pleasure dipped and he wondered for the first time if he had been lured, hooked and landed. Why the rush?

"This afternoon? I'm afraid that's impossible – "

"I meant after work, of course. If you came to my office at about five thirty. It's only on Golgi Street. Only a short walk from the hospital."

He was sure that he was missing something.

"Forgive me, Mrs Flemming . . . "

"Miss Flemming but, please, call me Helena."

" . . . Miss Flemming, Helena. I can't help feeling that I'm being rushed."

She laughed and Eisenmenger found himself thinking that it was a pleasant sound.

"Not at all!" she protested. "To be perfectly honest, I've only just been given the brief. It struck me as sensible to get an independent expert opinion on the pathology as a first move."

It sounded reasonable, but then Vlad the Impaler had probably had his less histrionic days. Nevertheless, Eisenmenger couldn't see the harm in gaining a few pounds sterling merely by writing a report. He looked at his diary and found nothing that would prevent him attending the meeting.

"Okay."

"Oh, good!" She sounded so pleased he felt as if he had granted her redemption. "Five thirty, then."

She was about to ring off when he asked, "What case is it? Have I heard of it?"

The pause was small but it betrayed her. That and the faintest hint of knowingness in her voice.

"It's the Exner case."

Before he had a chance to take in the breath to protest, she had rung off.

It had been only three weeks since Nikki Exner had died in the museum but those twenty-one days had seen interesting effects. Nikki's death had caused the usual imperturbability of the medical school to be rocked, the oscillations travelling far beyond the museum, through the Departments of Pathology and Anatomy, out into the wider political pool of medical academia as a whole.

The Dean's usual regal disregard for the minutiae, the tactical picture as opposed to the strategic overview, was tested close to collapse and was forced to withstand titanic forces. Questions were asked of him in council, questions that demanded much of his imperturbability. How had this dreadful event been allowed to occur? How had the personnel procedures been so lax as to allow the employment of a convicted rapist? How large was the drug problem amongst the student body? If the Dean did not know, why did he not know?

And, as is the way of such things, the Dean's experience was subsequently taken by him, inverted and played out again to those beneath him. The Human Resource Directorate was asked to institute immediate enquiries about how Bowman – or Bilroth, as they now had to think of him – had fooled them so easily and to alter procedures so that it might not recur. The Bursar was commanded to discover the size of the drug problem and to convene a task force to eradicate it.

And then there was Eisenmenger. The Dean was sorry but he felt that Eisenmenger's part in this tragedy was large, as was his culpability. That Eisenmenger had sat on the small interview panel that appointed Bilroth was bad, that he should have allowed the museum to become the centre of drug dealing was beyond redemption. He was summoned again to the Dean's palatial office, there to find Dean Schlemm flanked by Professors Hamilton-Bailey and Russell.

King Charles the First must have experienced similar emotions upon his final encounter with Oliver Cromwell; *Oh shit,* or some such seventeenth-century equivalent.

He was to be removed from his position of responsibility over the museum: Professor Russell was gracious enough to agree to take this over. Professor Hamilton-Bailey fully concurred with this change. All three of them felt that Eisenmenger had let the medical school down.

Eisenmenger didn't argue. He had about him a kind of tired acceptance that this was as it would be, no matter what he said or did. At least, he consoled himself, it should lighten Russell's mood which had been never less than thunderous ever since the murder. With this darkness of mood had come the usual acolytes – back-stabbing, non-cooperation, slanderous whisperings and sheer, bloody rudeness – that Eisenmenger knew well but had never really been able to accept calmly. On three occasions Sophie had feigned illness in order to escape the worst of Russell's evil.

In any event, for the present it was a meaningless change, for the museum had not reopened. Goodpasture had been given long-term compassionate leave in order to nurse his wife who had regained consciousness after three days but who had been left with a complete left-sided paralysis. Stephan Libman had been given long-term sick leave for, although he had recovered from the acute effects of his shock, his general practitioner felt that he was unfit for work and would be so for some time. It was doubtful if he would return to his job as assistant curator at the museum.

But not as doubtful as Tim Bilroth's chances of taking up his old employment.

The ramifications of his death had been almost as consequential as those of Nikki Exner's had been. For the police there had been a huge amount of adverse publicity as another death in custody had embarrassed them, although for Inspector Wharton it had been wholly advantageous. Bilroth's suicide had convicted him for the rape and murder of Nikki Exner far more incontrovertibly than any jury could have done. Even while the press were demanding an enquiry into how Bilroth could have been allowed to kill himself whilst under supervision, they were calling him a rapist and a murderer, a fiend and a demon who had sliced apart Nikki Exner.

Thus the subsequent enquiries concerning Nikki Exner's murder were cursory, not helped by the absence of Castle. His wife had died shortly after Bilroth's suicide, the post-mortem examination showing that she had died from massive, bilateral pulmonary emboli, although the malignant mixed Müllerian tumour had frozen the organs in her pelvis and spread to the lungs. Yet it was the fact, not the cause, of her death that mattered to Castle and his daughter as they stood side by side at her open grave.

Jamie Fournier had been left to mourn alone. His relationship with Nikki had been too brief for her bereaved parents to accept him as part of the family and, when they had travelled up to identify their daughter, their meeting with him had been awkward and laden with embarrassment. Certainly they were not capable of sharing their devastation with a stranger, no matter that he claimed to have loved their daughter.

Yet gradually normality had reasserted itself, albeit a normality that was altered irrevocably and substantially. Matters were settled, not always to the satisfaction of those affected, but at least they were settled.

Eisenmenger knew that he shouldn't have kept the appointment with Helena Flemming and couldn't find within himself the reason why he did. Yet at just after five thirty he was outside her office, having thought many times that afternoon about ringing her to cancel the meeting, and having thought an exactly equal number of times that perhaps he shouldn't.

Shouldn't cancel it for two reasons, one prurient and to the fore, the other in the background but ill defined. Quite simply he knew that he wanted to see Sydenham's report because he suspected that it would be poorly structured and ill conceived, but there was also a vague uneasiness about Bilroth's condemnation by the world and he wanted to see if Sydenham's autopsy proved or disproved the case.

After all, he reasoned, it was purely an academic exercise.

And so, the judgement made, he was there at the appointed time, in the darkness and a damp, cold drizzle. The door to the office was locked but there was a speakerphone and a buzzer. Helena Flemming's voice answered and he was let into the subdued lighting of the reception office, place of pastel shades, metallic blinds, deeply upholstered and deeply uncomfortable chairs, and potted palms.

A door opened at the back and a short-haired redhead came through. Her smile was wide, the intense greenness of her eyes was visible from across the length of the room. She was dressed in a trim suit of dark green, the skirt cut short and the shoulders padded.

"Dr Eisenmenger?"

She advanced, her hand outstretched, the walk slow but confident. When they shook hands her grip was surprisingly firm. There were no rings.

"It was kind of you to come."

"No problem," he replied. Then, indicating the deserted office, "You work late."

She broadened her smile. "It's often the best time to get things done – either now or early in the morning. Anyway, it's also often the only time that people can find the time to talk."

She led him through to the office at the back. It was more of the same, only smaller. He sat in a straight-backed chair of tubular steel and canvas, one of two in front of the desk. Around the austere, steel blue carpet's edge there were drunken, tottering piles of files.

"Tea? Coffee?"

He declined and she picked up a pencil, holding it at both ends, her elbows on the desk. With this totem in place she said, "I should perhaps begin by giving you a little background."

"Well, I have to admit to being slightly intrigued by the interest of a solicitor."

"Because the case is closed?"

"Isn't it?" He wondered why they were playing this game.

"Tim Bilroth's dead, but that doesn't necessarily mean that he was Nikki Exner's killer," she pointed out.

"The last I heard, the police thought otherwise. They're not looking for anyone else, are they?"

She seemed abruptly to tire of the game and her voice was lost in something that sounded like exhaustion. "I have been retained by Tim Bilroth's family – specifically his parents – to look into the strength of the case against Tim Bilroth for the murder of Nikki Exner. A subsidiary point is to investigate the possibility of bringing an action against the police for negligence."

A death in police custody. Inevitably the police were to blame.

"Were they? Negligent, I mean."

As if she detected scepticism underpinning the question, her tone was wary, the look on her face suggesting she was ready for an argument.

"Some would say almost by definition. He didn't die a natural death, after all."

"But he went to great lengths, didn't he? I would have thought it would have been impossible for the police to have foreseen quite how determined he was going to be."

"Luckily," and she was smiling as she said this, "we don't have to worry about what you think on the matter."

He thought about replying in a similar vein but hesitated, unsure of how far this was a game and how far she was serious. Into this she said, "Tim Bilroth was a known abuser of heroin. He had been arrested and questioned for rape and a murder of horrible brutality. That he should be depressed should not have come as a great surprise to the police, nor should the possibility that he might have been suffering from narcotic withdrawal. It is the family's contention that the police could also reasonably have expected that the two states might act together to induce suicidal thoughts.

"They should at least have had him seen by a police surgeon. No such examination took place."

Maybe, but Eisenmenger had been on the receiving end of too many complaints to cast stones based on a solicitor's testimony. Lawyers, he knew from sour experience, spent their lives looking in retrospect, usually at genuine mistakes committed as much through misfortune as through culpability. That didn't stop them from making you pay, though. Payment in stress, loss of confidence and depression, as well as in money.

"You want me to look at the Exner autopsy report," he said.

Her desk was a mess. Extrapolation suggested that there were three piles of papers that had elided into a general hump, but extrapolation is notoriously inaccurate. Eventually she found what she was looking for – a buff cardboard file. This she opened and from it she produced a thin document.

"I'll copy it for you."

She walked out past him and he inhaled perfume. He tried not to look at her legs, but not as hard as he might; they were nice legs doing a good job supporting a nice torso. From behind him, through the opened door he heard the sound of a photocopier warming up. The perfume was nice, he decided. Maybe he could forgive her for her earlier put-down.

The copier quietened down suddenly, leaving loud silence through the door. He noticed that she had a photograph of two small boys on her desk. They were sitting in the forked bough of a tree and were perhaps six years old. The photocopier started its rhythmic churn but abruptly stopped almost at once.

"Oh, damn!"

He looked around. "Problem?" Although he knew what had happened.

"The copier's jammed again. If it does it once a day, it does it ten times."

She kicked it and there came from it a dull clang. He noticed that the casing around its nether regions was scuffed and dented with abuse.

He got out of the chair and went to her side. The machine was old and clearly had received so much verbal and physical punishment during its photocopierhood that it no longer cared. Helena Flemming was down on one knee trying to wrench the door open but either it was jammed or it was fighting back. He joined her in apparent supplication before the machine.

"May I?" he enquired. She relinquished her hold with an expression that was unreadable. The casing was so battered it was slightly bent out of true. Instead of just pulling outwards on the door, he tried pulling out and up at the same time. On the third tug the door came open, the intimacies of the copier's secrets suddenly bared. The offending paper sheet was crunched between two rollers.

"He-man," she commented in a tone of mockery. He had his hands in the machine's body cavity, trying to work the paper loose without causing it to rip.

"Not really," he replied as the paper came out. "In the final reckoning, it's common sense that matters."

She took the paper – indeed, nearly snatched it – shut the copier and stood up, moving away to throw the paper in the bin. To his sorrow, the legs chose to go with her. He sighed and stood up.

Her second attempt at photocopying was more successful and he was at last allowed a copy of the precious report. She returned to her desk and he followed.

Barely had he sat down when she said, "We would like your comments in writing as soon as possible. When can you manage?"

Somewhat taken by surprise he replied, "Well, it's hardly a large report. How about the day after tomorrow?"

She nodded. "Friday would be fine."

She was writing something now. She had hardly looked at him since his remark about common sense. Was she offended?

"What about a fee?" he demanded.

She looked up in surprise. "A fee?"

He could have laughed. Here was a lawyer who didn't know what a fee was. He would have been more likely to meet a poor orthopaedic surgeon.

"Yes. For my opinion."

She nodded slowly. "Of course. If you feel that it is appropriate, then feel free to submit an invoice. I am afraid, though, that there has been a misunderstanding. The Bilroth family is not in receipt of legal aid and is certainly in no position to pay excessive fees to expert witnesses. I understood that you would be claiming only reasonable expenses."

He couldn't tell whether it was the shock of being told that there was no money, or the unpleasantness of being made to feel selfish and acquisitive (and by a solicitor, for God's sake!), but he was acutely embarrassed. In this state he replied intemperately, "And what about you? Or is it only your fee that they can afford?"

She looked at him severely. In a cold voice she said, "I am acting *pro bono.* I shall claim no fee."

Eisenmenger's mood as he arrived home was dark. It was just after seven and Marie was in their small, crowded but perfectly ornamented kitchen. Even the aroma of the food that faintly permeated the flat did little to alleviate his irritation.

How could that have happened? In all the thousands of encounters he had had with exponents of the law, never once had he felt less than them. Never once had he failed to feel that he and his profession had higher ideals, a greater sense of what was right in the universe, than did practitioners of the legal profession.

Until now.

Not once had it occurred to him that Helena Flemming might be acting *pro bono* – 'for the good,' or 'for free' – that her motives might be more than mercenary. Why should it? Lawyers acted *pro bono* only when there were other gains to be made, for instance publicity or increased standing in the eyes of their peers. What could Helena Flemming possibly gain by taking on the apparently hopeless case of Tim Bilroth, drug abuser, drug peddler and rapist of this parish?

Not that it mattered. Whatever her motives, he now appeared in her eyes to be money-grubbing.

And they were beautiful eyes, that had to be admitted.

"Is that you, John?"

He went into the kitchen and Marie turned to him with a smile, her fingers covered in chopped onion. Things hadn't been too bad since the day of Nikki Exner's death or, at least, there had been no major rows. Was that 'being not too bad'? He guessed that it was.

"Hi," he said.

They kissed, Marie's hands held away and down so that for a second the word 'penguin' popped unbidden and quite impertinently into his head.

Her nose wrinkled. "Is that perfume?"

"Can't be. I forgot to put it on this morning."

She audibly sniffed this time.

"That's definitely perfume," she decided.

He shrugged, made a face. *So what?*

Frowning she turned back to her cooking. Facing the pasta jar but presumably not addressing it she said, "I tried to phone you."

He had turned away to get changed in the bedroom. He stopped and raised his eyes to the top of the architrave. The words were light, the tone was dark. *Incoming on radar.*

"Did you? What time?"

"Just after five. They'd said you'd already left."

He turned around but all he saw was the back of her head as she played havoc with a yellow pepper. Even from that disadvantage point he could see she was upset.

"So I had," he said steadily. He left it at that, half out of curiosity as to where this was leading. Trouble was, a secret part of him admitted that it was half out of sheer bloody belligerence.

For a long time that was probably only five ticks of the kitchen wall clock (an old railway clock that he had been assured was cheap at three hundred and fifty) there was silence. Then he sighed and turned away again. Once more he didn't make it through the doorway.

"Where were you?" she enquired of the pasta. How could a voice be so brittle?

He sighed. He shouldn't have done, at least not so loudly, but once done it could not be undone. The wind that blew on the road to hell was made up of such sighs.

"I had a meeting to go to. With a solicitor. She wanted me to – "

"She?"

He paused, incredulous. "Yes. What of it?"

She turned around. There were tears in her eyes and he found himself thinking, *For God's sake!* She said, "Is it her perfume I can smell on you?"

He could see where they were going as clearly as if it was the route along a floodlit runway. Straight there, and no stopping or turning.

"Possibly." He could have tried protestation but he knew from past encounters that it would do little good: indeed, it had before served to heighten her suspicion of him, as had the 'don't be silly' approach.

As did the 'possibly' approach.

"What does that mean?"

He decided quite abruptly and, he had to whisper to himself, quite objectively that he had taken a sufficient quantity of baseless suspicion, self-pity and emotional aggression.

"For Christ's sake, Marie! I had a meeting with a solicitor who happened to be a female. She also happened to be wearing some pungent perfume. That does not mean that I took her from behind, across the desk or over the photocopier. It means she asked me to give an opinion on an autopsy report, and nothing more."

Marie said nothing. Her eyes were already overfull and the muscles around her eyes were doing some odd twitching movements that didn't bode well. He knew that they were about to explode into a row. He also knew, however, that she would run away, that he would not want to talk about their real problems, and that she would spare him the pain by saying nothing with her mouth and bloody great sentences with her feet. This was her latest tactic, laden with far more potential than staying put and indulging in verbal histrionics that would inevitably expose the basic illogicality of her arguments. Using this ploy she could indulge in lonely and undisturbed recrimination, inventing a world where she was the wronged woman and he the cause of all her woe.

She had been getting worse, of that he was in no doubt. Always possessive, she had now taken this trait and worked it into a thing of monstrousness: now it was a question not only of possession but also of complete control over him. At the start, when he had still been convalescing, he had looked for that, he supposed – someone who would take the decisions, make the course changes. Now, though, Marie not only wanted to navigate; she wanted to drive and to put him in the boot, bound and gagged. Yet even as he recognized this change in her, he knew that he was not without blame. His refusal to total commitment had always bothered her, his inability to give everything to her had first raised these suspicions. He had provided the substrate for her jealousy, ironically without ever giving her real cause for invoking the green-eyed phantom.

And now he waited, almost begging the strike to come.

"How could you?" she demanded, or shrieked, for either verb applied.

"How could I what?" The question was posited with exasperated tiredness. "What have I done?"

"You've been with another woman! I can smell it on you."

"You can smell a trace of her perfume on my clothes. No bodily fluids were exchanged, Marie, I assure you."

"I don't believe you!"

He shrugged. "I can't say I care, Marie."

But that was mistakenly, or perhaps deliberately, provocative.

"That's the trouble, isn't it?" She was crying. He felt detached, watching with fascination but no engagement as the long-threatened weeping commenced. *Not long now*, he thought tiredly.

"I don't know what you mean," he said, as much to supply a line in a playlet as to elicit any utilizable information.

"You don't care! You don't care about me!"

"Oh, that's crap, Marie, and you know it."

"Is it? Is it?" she demanded but then she ad-libbed. She should have been reduced to inarticulate generalities, to ceaseless and meaningless automatic denial of everything he posited. Yet suddenly she asked, "Do you love me, John? I mean as much as you used to?"

It was a clear question, asked straightforwardly. The answer, too, did not require an extensive and technical knowledge of some obscure branch of learning.

Thus it was a shame that he muffed it. First he paused then, when he had found the required syllable – "Yes" – he dropped his eyes at once.

He had plenty of time to rehearse how it should have sounded as she walked quickly from the kitchen, slamming the door behind her.

Better go back to stage school.

Beverley Wharton returned from the bar slightly drunk but alone. Her companion for the evening had wanted otherwise but she had been forced to disappoint him, claiming biological rather than psychological reasons for her refusal: he hadn't liked it, but what could he do?

She let herself into her top-floor flat, switching on the light and leaning against the whitewashed walls for a moment or two. She was tired and her head was beginning to ache, just behind the eyes.

The flat was in a converted warehouse that overlooked the river. It was tremendously fashionable and no less tremendously expensive, but for all the advantages it was undoubtedly encumbered with several disadvantages. The noise proofing for example. Converting a single, extremely large volume into forty considerably smaller volumes had been achieved with a few square kilometres of partition walling and suspended ceilings; the ambience was wonderful, the practicality less certain. And the decision to use polished wooden flooring in all of the flats might have won critical plaudits from the design and fashion authorities but it also meant that she could hear when her neighbours hadn't bothered to remove their stilettos or their steel-tipped Doc Martens.

She could also hear when they reached noisy, homosexual climax together.

At first this had bothered her, but now she was used to it – even enjoyed it. Some of her guests enjoyed it too, she noted wryly.

She slipped off her shoes and crossed the sea of polished wood that lay between the front door and the window. She should have put up curtains, she knew, for even on the fourth floor she was perfectly visible from the ground or adjoining building, but that would have diminished the view and she knew that she could never do that.

The view was magnificent, for the warehouse had been built on a hill that rose away from the river. No one who came here failed to remark upon it. When she stood here in daylight the broad sweep of the river lazed fatly away from her, the disused dockyards and warehouses on its banks giving a bleak, industrial romance to the foreground, while the background trudged away in rows of houses and minuscule parks. At night, lit by a thousand lights and a million reflections, it became almost ethereal, divorced from humanity's grubby touch, almost kissed by angels.

She would spend long periods looking at that view, often with the lights off, a glass of red wine in her hand. It fascinated her, though why she should be held by such captivation she could not say. Yet at the same time her desire for this thing saddened her, for she was sometimes afraid that it was the only thing that she could truthfully say that she loved.

She stood there now; the only sounds she could hear were distant and therefore disconnected, the noises of people in different flats and essentially in different universes. She was alone with the night-enfolded river, its billion lights flaring before her. In the most secret of secret places.

Why was she so depressed?

This was the question that would not leave her, that gnawed at her, that ached deep within her bones.

She had achieved exactly what she had wanted. She had nailed Bilroth, quite rightly taking the credit. Castle had not bothered to block her – the old fool had stupidly let her phrase the reports so that his part had been shown to be minimal instead of ensuring, as most of his colleagues would have done, that he and he alone was seen as the great detective. That Bilroth had subsequently chosen to string himself up by his trousers was inconvenient for the uniformed branch but quite fortuitous for her. It had functioned to embed his guilt deep within him as far as the public was concerned, and it had meant that she had been required to perform only the most perfunctory of follow-up enquiries.

Castle's family tragedy had also proved fortuitous for, in the light of her stunning performance in the Exner case, she was now acting up as Detective Chief Inspector.

And then there was Johnson.

Johnson had got what he deserved. A shame, but there it was. She could have worked with him. True he was old, but that was not necessarily a bad thing, and he was undoubtedly a good copper. He would have been no threat to her and she would have taken him with her as she ascended the ranks. It really could have been a very productive relationship.

Such a pity he had chosen to reject her offer. Didn't he realize that this was how you did things these days? Couldn't he see that she knew how to get results and that results were all that mattered to anyone and everyone?

She shook her head at her companion, the river, and her faint reflection sympathized.

Maybe he would try to fight it out, maybe he wouldn't. If he didn't, if he resigned, end of story. If he did, there was the simple matter of strengthening the case around him, of firming up the vague suspicions that she had created. So it was all sorted.

So why was she pissed off?

From nowhere a gust of rain splattered the glass in front of her and she suddenly shivered. Abruptly she felt alone and for a second she regretted her decision to come back without a companion, but it was only for that second. It wasn't some prick with a sweaty man attached that she wanted now. No, certainly not that.

The problem was that she didn't know what she did want.

Russell slammed into the secretaries' office and demanded of Gloria, "Where's Eisenmenger?"

She looked up from her typing. Her smile was broad and indistinguishable from the genuine article, and therefore incongruous in the face of such discourteous vicissitude.

"Is he not in his office?" she asked, as if a small child's tantrum was being enacted before her.

"Of course he isn't. I wouldn't be asking you if he was anywhere to be found."

Belinda came in with a tray of slides and several request cards. "Do you want to go through these now?"

Russell stared at her as if she had asked him to rod the drains. "Of course I fucking don't," he enunciated quite clearly, his tone one of patronizing contempt. "Take them away. I'll let you know when it's convenient." Then, to Gloria, "Tell Eisenmenger I want to see him at once."

He turned and walked back into his office, the door slamming behind him. Belinda looked at Gloria who raised her eyebrows in response. "Clearly a bad day. Perhaps he's lost his rattle."

Gloria's booming laugh made pious men fear for the Second Coming. Russell must have heard it and must have had a fairly good idea of what it meant, but he didn't respond.

It was then that Eisenmenger entered. He had been lecturing to a group of final year medical students who, despite having their Pathology exams in less than four weeks, showed no knowledge and no hope of knowledge about the subject.

"The Professor wants you," Gloria informed him. Her voice was sly.

"Oh dear," he sighed. "Is it one of those days?"

"And a half," said Belinda.

Because it annoyed Russell he always knocked on his door just once and just lightly. Then he would go in without waiting for Russell to invite him.

Russell was reading correspondence at his desk, an ornate affair of mahogany and brass that was large enough to have served as the desk of a head of state. The only reason that it didn't look out of place in Russell's room was that Russell had a room the size of a small aircraft hangar. It was easily the biggest office in the medical school (excepting possibly the Dean's). Even Russell's bulk was reduced to more aesthetic proportions within it.

He looked up murderously.

"You wanted me, Basil?" *Keep the tone light.* This approach seemed to have the delightful result of giving Russell severe oesophageal reflux.

"Yes. The damned museum."

Bereft of verbs Eisenmenger was forced to wait for sense.

"You didn't tell me that there was this bloody investigation into the specimens, did you?" His tone suggested he had been duped. "I've just received a letter from the Dean 'reminding' me of the deadline."

Of course. The panic about organ and tissue retention. Eisenmenger had quite forgotten it but was delighted to be reminded and delighted to find that the good Professor now had full and sole responsibility.

"Didn't I?" he said. "I am most terribly sorry, Basil. To be honest I assumed that the Dean would have told you when he suggested you should take over. It must have slipped his mind."

"How the hell am I supposed to get anything done while Good-pasture's away?"

Eisenmenger shrugged, his face covered with an exceedingly thin veneer of concern.

"Well, he'll be back soon, I expect. And while the museum's closed, it'll give you an excellent opportunity to make a start. Clear out all those dusty store rooms."

Russell turned puce, always a satisfactory result, and would perhaps have exploded, perhaps have hit something, except that the telephone rang. Eisenmenger, some five metres away, could clearly hear Gloria's voice as she informed Russell that there was a phone call for Dr Eisenmenger. Russell scowled and Eisenmenger left him with a sweet and loving smile, a small measure of happiness the better.

Gloria held the phone out for him. He raised his eyebrows and she shrugged.

"Dr Eisenmenger."

Helena Flemming's voice was teasing. "Your secretary's a happy woman, Dr Eisenmenger. It must be fun in the Department of Pathology."

That was a laugh.

"Ms Flemming – "

"Helena, please."

"Only if you call me John."

She acquiesced with "Very well," uttered in a teasingly low tone. This achieved, he asked, "Helena. What can I do for you?"

"I was just wondering if we could meet tonight. Discuss your impression of the report."

He looked at the clock on the wall. Half eleven.

"I haven't even looked at it yet."

"But it shouldn't take you long. It's quite a short report."

Bloody hell, she was persistent.

"I really don't see – "

"Please?"

She had adopted a tone that was almost a small girl's. Supplication, shot through with something else. Surely it couldn't be implied sexual promise?

He hesitated, and into this she said, "I really would be most grateful. Perhaps we could discuss the report over a drink somewhere . . . ?"

There was no doubt now. He should have rejected the overture, but his ego was preening itself in the mirror while chatting up his autonomic nervous system. He didn't have much chance.

"Where?" he asked, and wondered whence this came.

Mrs Goodpasture sat in her chair in the middle of the ward and looked straight ahead, although it seemed unlikely that it was the gentleman opposite (who was coughing up luminescent green sputum flecked with blood) who held her rapt attention. She shook gently but persistently and a small trickle of saliva seeped from the right-hand corner of her mouth. She was dressed in a thick nightdress and covered with a woollen shawl. Her eyes were yellowed and veined, like overgrown desert stones, her hair greasy.

Her husband sat beside her and talked. He talked half to his wife and half to no one, or possibly to himself – there seemed little distinction. His voice was low and whenever people passed they heard snatches of talk about neighbours, about the weather, about television, about events in the newspapers and about what he had done that morning. She did not respond.

In the three weeks that had passed since her stroke she had made little progress beyond regaining consciousness and responding slowly and seemingly unwillingly to verbal commands. She had no speech; her eyes were lifeless. She had soon given up trying to talk for all that had been left to her was to moan. She was at least continent, and would demand help with this by drawn-out moans and flicked movements of her left arm. Goodpasture found that feeding

143

her was the most distressing time, when no amount of rose tinting and rationalization would conceal the fact that he was spooning food into an unresponsive carcass, that she had quite simply been devastated by what had happened.

But still he hoped.

She had survived the first few hours and that was good. The consultant had said that if she made progress now there was a chance that she would win back some control over her body, perhaps even learn to speak again. Not that she had ever been much of a conversationalist, but anything would have been an improvement on this.

And so Goodpasture persevered. Coming in every day at just after nine and staying by her side for nearly eleven hours, during which he would sit and talk. He became a familiarity for the staff and the other patients.

Too sad and lost to be laughed at, but too pathetic to evoke much sympathy: embarrassment, if anything, was the feeling most of the nurses tried to suppress. During all this time she had only one other visitor, he an infrequent one. Jem, her son, his stepson, called but had appeared to find it all too much. His tears had been bitter. Goodpasture, it seemed had been left to continue the vigil alone.

And always he talked. The wonder was that he did not run out of words to use or sentences to construct, all of the highest standards of inanity, as only lovers can do. 'Talk to her,' he had been told, 'let her hear your voice,' and so he set to with initial enthusiasm. Yet as the days passed and as his wife stayed all but motionless and seemingly uncaring, it was only natural that he should gradually falter, that he should become as morose and low in affect as his wife. The nurses and the doctors saw it and they felt for him.

But they did not know his secrets.

So now, after twenty-one days, still he talked, but it was not a thinning of the seam that led him to stray gradually from the domestic and the mundane to matters more spiritual.

Or one matter at least.

"Why did I do it, Janey?"

He asked this quite suddenly and seemingly without reference to his previous topic which had been on the subject of next door's incessantly barking Jack Russell. Perhaps it was coincidence that he made this enquiry when there was no chance of being overheard. Whether Mrs Goodpasture, with matters of her own to contemplate, knew what he meant cannot be assessed, but if she knew the answer she held nothing forward by way of reply.

There followed a long pause before, "I should have said no." He dropped his head. He would have been seen to be agitated, had eyes been cast upon him. "Why didn't I say no?"

A nurse came by. She smiled briefly at him, then passed on.

More silence, more restlessness as if, now embarked and sailing, he could not return to the safety of land. "Oh, God, what have I done?"

And the good Mrs Goodpasture?

Whether she heard or not, and whether having heard she understood, and whether having understood she cared, there is no one to judge. In any case she began to moan softly and to rock, her left hand jerking up and down. Her stiff neck allowed little movement but her eyes watered.

She wanted to use the commode.

"Is it convenient?"

Belinda wasn't carrying slide trays and she looked worried, two negatives that rang faint alarm bells. She wasn't the first registrar to come and tell him how much of a pig Russell was.

"Of course," he smiled.

She sat down and emanated embarrassment with silent clarity.

"Would I be right in guessing that this is to do with Basil?" he asked.

She laughed once and said, "Who else?"

He sighed. "What's he done?" Several things were running through his mind: commanded her to review three hundred cases of Osgood-Schlatter's disease by next Wednesday, refused to allow her study leave, or merely bollocked her for no very good reason. The variety of ways that Basil Russell could make the life of a specialist registrar miserable was impressive.

"He's propositioned Sophie."

She was genuinely upset, as if it had happened before.

Jerked out of complacent anticipation of the usual Russell behaviours, he was astonished. "He what?"

She nodded. "Three weeks ago. You remember you wondered why she was so odd? Eventually she told me."

"What happened?" he asked but inside he was asking if he really wanted to know the details. Was this just prurience?

"Well, apparently it happened the day before the murder. He'd been on at her all day – her reports were crap, she was useless, she was lazy, nothing out of the ordinary – and she'd had to stay late, first because there was a late frozen section, secondly because he'd made her rewrite practically every report she'd written."

Thus far they were on well-trodden territory. Frozen sections – when the surgeons demanded an instant opinion while the patient was still anaesthetized – were an occupational hazard and occasionally they came late. Only Russell, however, would expect the registrar to stay late to do them.

"What time did she finish?"

"About eight. At which time she went in to Russell because he had told her that she wasn't to leave until she had shown the rewritten reports to him.

"Apparently he leafed quickly through the reports then . . . " Suddenly she lost the words. " . . . it happened."

Portentous, but nebulous.

"And what does 'it' stand for?"

She seemed to find the desktop very interesting. "She's a bit vague."

The charges against Russell seemed to be evaporating somewhat.

"But he did something . . . inappropriate?"

She was quite definite. "Oh, yes . . . " She paused, then said, "I think he implied that she was likely to fail her 'Rita', but that they ought to talk about it."

It was hardly going to simulate Semtex at the disciplinary meeting. Eisenmenger waited for something with a slightly greater whiff of scandal.

"He put his hand on her leg and then suggested that they should discuss it over dinner."

It was better, but would it suffice? Much as he wanted to see Russell pay some sort of forfeit for his attitudes and behaviours, he couldn't see that such testimony, unsupported and coming from a failing registrar, was going to topple him. His next questions were asked from hope and without expectation.

"Were they alone?"

Of course they were.

"Do you think that she'd be willing to put this in writing?"

Belinda didn't think so.

"Could I persuade her?"

Sophie didn't even know that Belinda was telling him.

He breathed out a long sigh. "Then there's nothing much to be done," he decided. "I'm sorry."

She stood up. "I didn't think that there would be, but I thought you ought to know anyway."

"Thanks," he said, but it was singularly lacking in gratitude.

She left and it was long minutes before he picked up the Exner autopsy report.

As soon as Eisenmenger walked into the cafe-bar, he felt a primary immune response beginning to peek out from behind his lymph nodes.

It was chic and expensive and vacuous. Style was all, with no room left for feeling. He knew that the waiting staff would be arsy, slow and poorly trained, but he knew just as well that they would look superb. The food would be decorative like a dried flower arrangement and about as appetizing, while the drinks would be expensive and come in glassware that was angular, heavy and crying out to be dropped.

Helena Flemming was not yet there – he was ten minutes early but not, he informed himself, because he anticipated anything to come of this appointment – and he seated himself at a table near the back, trying not to look too dislocated.

The waitress found him eventually, handed him an absurdly large menu and asked him what he wanted in a voice that suggested that he was already too far gone in matters of style and taste ever to be redeemed by his choice of drink or food. He ordered a bottled beer with an East European name, but only because all the beers were in bottles and all had East European names. He declined food, a refusal she took badly for she raised one eyebrow and grunted. She left him, snatching the menu away as if they'd lost a lot of menus to people like him.

There was background music of course. Sibelius followed by Delius, and the effect was to make him revise slightly his opinion of the management. His beer arrived, replete with small doily but no glass. He cursed himself for his pusillanimous refusal to ask for one.

Delius changed to Debussy just as the clock swept past six fifteen and on to the half-hour. The bar began to fill with the kind of people that he found depressing on a good day and odorous on every other. People who had good lives and smiling, joking faces because they didn't give a fuck about anyone else. People who were the winners in life because in some indefinable but very important sense they were detached from it. People who didn't have to face death or disease for long stretches of their lives.

Debussy bowed out and on came Mozart, and Eisenmenger began to feel that he had been stood up. His beer was reaching its end and his buttocks had discovered that the triumph of style extended to the furniture.

He caught sight of Helena Flemming through the front window and momentarily he was excited, at once telling himself it was merely because now he would have a chance to stand up. Yet if that was the case, it was odd that the sight of Johnson walking purposefully along beside her should cause him a sudden gust of sadness.

Johnson? What was he doing here? Serving policemen had no business in the company, no matter how delectable, of defence solicitors.

In the doorway, she paused and looked around, spotting him only when he stood up. She said something to Johnson and they came over. She was smiling at him as she said, "I've brought a friend of yours to join us." Eisenmenger really couldn't tell quite what the smile meant.

"Johnson? This is a surprise."

Johnson hesitated briefly before saying smoothly, "Just having a drink with a friend. Nothing more."

His tone was slightly strained as if this were a party line, no more.

They sat down and somehow a miracle occurred and the waitress was there and Helena was talking to her as if she had returned to her ecological niche. The waitress, too, sensed that here was one who belonged. She listened attentively and with an air of deference that had been totally lacking in her encounter with Eisenmenger. Helena ordered wine and, to Eisenmenger's surprise, Johnson was happy with this: Eisenmenger felt it proper also to concur.

"Sorry I'm late. Bob and I have been having a chat."

Eisenmenger was looking for landmarks and not finding them.

"Isn't it a bit unusual for a member of the police to be having meetings with a defence solicitor on a murder enquiry?"

Helena looked across at Johnson.

"The circumstances are unusual," he said. "Technically speaking, I'm not a serving police officer, since I've been suspended."

Eisenmenger at first thought he was joking. Superficially his tone had been light, almost facetious, but his face clearly told otherwise. Berlioz took over from Mozart as Eisenmenger looked from Johnson to Helena Flemming, then back to Johnson.

"What happened?"

"Apparently there is a suspicion about my honesty. Apparently they're worried about various sums of money found around my house and garden. The serial numbers on the notes are interesting."

Johnson the criminal. Close cousin to Johnson the ballet dancer and Johnson the nuclear physicist.

"And they believe this?"

He smiled but it was sad as if his lost love had just walked by in the street. All he said was, "Apparently."

"But surely they'll show that it's rubbish?"

Now Johnson spoke as if telling him that the tooth fairy was a myth. "It's being investigated, if that's what you mean. The reality is that I've been questioned and questioned and questioned until I am ready to confess just to get them to stop. They've poked and they've pried. They've talked to my friends, they've talked to my colleagues and, I'm afraid, they've talked to my enemies. They've dug and they've dug and they've sifted and, eventually, they'll almost certainly find something. It'll probably be petty – an arrest that wasn't properly processed, a conviction that was subsequently found to be unsafe, a piece of slime who's willing to whisper that I've not always been a good boy – but that won't matter. It'll be something.

"And if, by some miracle, they don't, as far as my future is concerned, it doesn't matter. I wasn't destined for much, but from now on everyone is going to wonder. Everyone is going to have that minute germ of doubt."

He took a deep, deep breath. "I don't think I'm ready for that," he finished.

Berlioz put down the baton only for Butterworth to pick it up, just as Eisenmenger picked up on an odd inflexion in his voice. "Enemies? Have you got any?"

It was Helena who answered.

"Only one."

There was something going on, but then the waitress returned with the wine. She seemed to know Helena and certainly she assumed that she was in charge. Eisenmenger felt as if he were the only one in the room who didn't know much about what was going on.

"Who would that be?" he asked of Johnson when they were again alone.

But Johnson didn't reply directly.

"I ought to fight it of course, but with only three years to go, I'm not sure it wouldn't be better just to resign straight away."

"No!"

The vehemence of Helena Flemming's reaction was striking.

"Would one of you two care to tell me what's going on?" asked Eisenmenger. The wine was crap.

They hesitated, looking at each other before Johnson said, "I'm fairly sure it was Beverley Wharton."

"Wharton? Why would she do that?"

Johnson was about to reply but he was interrupted.

"She's a bitch, that's why."

There was a lot of anger in her words. Eisenmenger remarked, "I take it you're not in the fan club either."

"Hardly." Suddenly she wasn't just angry, she was furious. She drank the wine as if it were drinkable.

Johnson said, "Have you heard of the Eaton-Lambert case? About three years ago?"

It was vaguely familiar but the details eluded Eisenmenger.

"Jeremy Eaton-Lambert's mother and father, Helena's step-father, were found in their Richmond townhouse, both with their throats cut. The father was in the sitting room, the mother in bed. There was evidence of an attempted break-in and over a thousand pounds, worth of jewellery was missing.

"The police arrested Jeremy Eaton-Lambert after just one day. The prosecution case was that he had faked the robbery and that, with this cover, he had murdered them both. They produced in evidence some of his clothing that was bloodstained, and a pair of his father's cufflinks that they found in his flat."

Vaguely Eisenmenger recalled it. "The will was in his favour, right?"

It was Helena Flemming who said, "He stood to inherit four hundred thousand pounds."

Johnson continued, "Jeremy never admitted anything. He was questioned for two days, then charged. He was held on bail and during that time further enquiries uncovered a knife in the garden of the house: it had Jeremy's fingerprints.

"He was tried five months later and, inevitably, he was found guilty. Sentenced to life, he was sent to Wormwood Scrubs."

"He died, didn't he?" There had been quite a fuss, Eisenmenger remembered.

"He committed suicide." Helena's voice was curious, almost lost in another place. "After three months of bullying, abuse and sheer, vicious nastiness, he cut his wrists on a jagged edge of his bed. He was in solitary confinement and managed to die with his back to the cell door so that no one could see he was bleeding."

That there was a parallel with Tim Bilroth was clear, but the rest of it was opaque. He sipped some wine and suppressed a minor shudder. He looked at Helena and asked, "And what has this to do with Nikki Exner?"

It was Johnson who said, "The officer who discovered the knife, who found the bloodstained clothing and who suggested that I should look in just the place that I found it was Beverley Wharton."

There were so many implications of his words it was a wonder they didn't dent the floor as they fell. If Eisenmenger had been worried that he didn't know what was going on, he found himself suddenly very much afraid now he knew. He looked at Helena Flemming. She was staring at him intently.

"Am I on line here?" he asked her. "Is this more about destroying Beverley Wharton than about proving Tim Bilroth's innocence?"

She replied, "Not at all. This is entirely about proving the innocence of a wronged man." Then she smiled. "Of course, if it can be shown that Inspector Wharton has acted improperly . . . "

Eisenmenger's glance flitted between the two of them: Johnson looked calm, Helena Flemming looked determined.

"But you've got it in for her, haven't you? Your whole attitude suggests that if she burst into flames you wouldn't even spit on her."

"My attitude to Inspector Wharton is not at issue in the first instance."

Lay off.

He turned to Johnson. "Why haven't you told anyone before about these allegations?" he demanded.

"I kept quiet until now because no one was going to listen and because I had no proof that I could take to a superior officer. As to why I'm speaking out now, there are two reasons. The first is easy – I've got nothing left to lose. The second is harder to define but I guess that it comes down to a faint uneasiness about the Bilroth case. I don't know if she 'helped' things along this time, like she did with the Eaton-Lambert case, but one thing I do know is that Bilroth didn't do it."

"Are you so sure? People have been convicted on less convincing evidence than there is in this case."

"People have been convicted wrongly, too." Helena Flemming whispered this. Eisenmenger heard something like melancholy.

Johnson said, "I'll concede that there are aspects of the case which seem to implicate Bilroth – the apparent rape, the toxicology – but the way that it was done? To hang her, draw her and quarter her? That's not Bilroth."

"But he had an obsession about her, didn't he? He had a photograph of her on his wall, didn't he?"

Johnson said, "So he had a crush on her. Hardly a signed confession."

"And weren't there books in his flat?"

"There was quite a library," admitted Johnson. "Stuff about all aspects of death. Murders, executions, death rituals, myths. He had some really quite expensive encyclopedias, as well as hundreds of magazine articles. All of it was carefully compiled and catalogued."

"And how did he explain that?"

"He said that it stemmed from his work. That he had always been interested in things like that."

Eisenmenger didn't comment on the likelihood that his job had stemmed from his obsession rather than the obverse.

"Still, you can see why people might raise their eyebrows," he said drily.

But Johnson was dogged. "He didn't do it. I know it, and I feel it." Then he added very deliberately, "A bit like the feeling that you've got."

Eisenmenger stared back at him for a long time, trying to work out just what his feelings were. Then he shrugged, "Maybe."

As if tired of the preliminaries, Helena Flemming said, "What about the autopsy report? Have you read it? What did you think?"

Eisenmenger fished in his briefcase, landing the report. He held it up.

"My opinion? It's thin."

He let it fall to the table surface where it lay half across the tubes of white and brown sugar that protruded from a small pot in the middle.

"Is that it? Thin?"

It was as if she had paid him thrice the going rate and been given an answer that was no answer at all.

Johnson picked it up and looked briefly through it while she demanded, "What does that mean?"

"It means," explained Eisenmenger, "that most forensic pathology reports these days are thick. Not only are they thick, they are dry, they are turgid, they are pedantic and, most important of all, they are full of caveats.

"This," he gestured at the paper that Johnson held, "is none of those things."

"Isn't that good? Shouldn't the report be clear and concise?"

Eisenmenger hesitated. "It depends whether the case is clear and concise."

Johnson said, "That's the whole point, isn't it? If you believe the accepted version it is, but if you don't, there are a few questions to answer."

He held it out for Eisenmenger to take.

Helena asked, "Are there any specific places where you think that there might have been procedural errors or where his conclusions are not directly supported by the evidence?"

"A few."

She took out a notebook and a pen. "Such as?"

There was something about her attitude that didn't quite chime but Eisenmenger couldn't identify it. He put the report flat on the table and indicated the first page.

"Well, let's start with a few general points about the autopsy examination. His external description is skimpy, to put it kindly. Half a page is hardly comprehensive. True, he notes the ligature mark around the neck; specifically how it corresponds in thickness and depth with the rope, how it is deepest anteriorly and fades beneath the mandibular angle on the left, again corresponding with the knot.

"What he doesn't mention, though, are any other marks that were on the body, with the exception of the vulva."

Helena frowned. "Perhaps there weren't any."

Eisenmenger chose not to show his condescension. "Yes, there were. There always are. Everyone's got them, even you. The faint, fading bruise where you knocked your elbow last week, the hangnail that you pulled yesterday so that it bled, the spot you squeezed this morning."

"Perhaps he didn't consider them important."

Eisenmenger shook his head. Beethoven was given a go at entertaining the subconscious. "It's not his job to consider them unimportant. It's his job to *examine* the corpse. It's his job to collect data and from those data to construct a hypothesis."

"While we're on the subject, he doesn't mention her nails either."

Johnson's intervention surprised Eisenmenger. How the hell had he picked up on that?

"The nails? What about them?"

Should she be asking questions like that? It was Johnson who explained about rape and about resistance to rape. She made notes. As she wrote, her forehead puckered and her mouth was just the slightest bit open. Her lips were glossed and Eisenmenger found himself wondering if she had ever had them injected: surely not, not at the age of . . . thirty-two, thirty-three?

His hypothalamus, which had been whispering to him for quite some time, coughed abruptly and pulled on a few strings inside his head.

"You mentioned the vulva." She had finished with Johnson and turned now to Eisenmenger. Even as his lascivious id was enjoying hearing a beautiful woman utter the word 'vulva', he was thinking, *Like a tyro.*

"Almost inevitably, in a case of rape, there is trauma to the vulva. The degree varies, depending on how much resistance is offered, but it is almost inevitable that there will be some, unless the victim is first drugged."

It was Johnson who pointed out, "But the toxicology reports suggest that she *was* drugged."

"Exactly. Midazolam – the date rape drug."

Once again Helena Flemming seemed to be slightly behind her two companions.

"So what does Midazolam do?"

Eisenmenger explained. "It's related to common tranquillizers like Valium and has similar properties, only more so. In particular it causes the taker to relax, to have a reduced level of consciousness and, most importantly, to have almost complete amnesia. If you're going to rape someone, it's tailor-made."

She asked, "But isn't that what Tim Bilroth used before – when he was convicted? How does that help our case?"

Once again Johnson surprised Eisenmenger.

"I think what Dr Eisenmenger is getting at is that if Bilroth gave her Midazolam, then why are there marks on her vulva? She wouldn't have resisted."

She considered this and the frown was delightful. Somewhere deep in his head a spring of warm pleasure came to life. The waitress came by and seemed upset that no one was drinking the house nectar.

"Then the fact that there were no marks on the body or that the nails are normal doesn't matter."

"That's not the point," said Eisenmenger. "The point is that they weren't mentioned at all."

"He didn't do a thorough autopsy." At last she was getting it.

The spring was growing stronger, the pleasure warmer. He tried to carry on talking through this peculiarly pleasant diversion.

"Sydenham's old school. He's used to writing short reports."

"So?"

"So . . . " and Eisenmenger hesitated because he didn't want to be too judgemental. "So pathologists like Sydenham are of a time when the pathologist told God what the disease was. He was born into medicine when doctors told the patient what to do and the patient doffed his cap and wept: when what the pathologist told the clinician was the Truth as delivered to Moses on Mount Sinai."

"How times have changed." Helena Flemming's voice and expression were impossible to read.

"Yes, they have," admitted Eisenmenger.

"He's got into trouble in court because of that attitude," pointed out Johnson.

"On more than one occasion," agreed Eisenmenger.

"So he's crap? Is that what you're saying?"

"I don't know," he said after a pause and had the pleasure of seeing the frown again. She leaned back, crossed her legs and for the first time there was a smile on her face that seemed genuinely amused. Her legs were enveloped by some very lucky stockings. He was starting to feel smothered by the gushing enjoyment in his head, almost dizzy with its exuberance.

"What do you know?" she asked. Johnson kept quiet and drank his wine, and Eisenmenger had the feeling he was on his own.

"I know," he said carefully, "that even the best of us make mistakes, and I think that Sydenham is far from the best."

"But you can't prove it."

"Not from the report, no."

She hadn't lost the smile. Her eyes were Irish green. When she spoke, the teasing tone was back. By now Eisenmenger's neocortex was receiving a battering from all sides: where once, and not long ago, he had looked upon Helena Flemming as a pretty girl but no more, now and very quickly, he was being told that she was something special.

"That's a shame," she said quietly.

As if afraid of what might happen in the silence, Eisenmenger said quickly, "There are a few other things."

She raised her eyebrows as if amazed.

"For instance the forensic reports."

"In what way? I was going to ask you about those."

"The vaginal samples were heavily contaminated with blood, but the samples from the clothing were very interesting."

"Three different types of semen." Helena seemed excited by this.

Johnson said laconically, "A nice, middle-class girl."

"One of which was presumably Fournier's, but one of which was definitely from Bilroth," pointed out Eisenmenger. "Not a piece of evidence that helps the cause."

"But if there was a third person, then there's a possibility that it was he who drugged and raped her."

"Yes. That is possible," agreed Eisenmenger.

"Well, that's good, isn't it?" She noted this down. Then, "Anything else?"

"The description of the internal organs is perfunctory, but that is not perhaps entirely surprising – after all, if death was not due directly to injury to one of them, all that is necessary is to ensure that natural disease did not play a part.

"What worries me, though, is the uterus."

"That was one of the organs that was cut out, wasn't it?"

"Strictly speaking, it was the *only* organ that was cut out. No other was actually separated from the body."

Johnson said, "But she wasn't pregnant, was she? Sydenham told us specifically that she wasn't."

"There was no evidence of that."

Helena asked, "So why does it worry you?"

"Well, without going into too much gore, it's not the first organ you might expect to be removed if all you do is slice open the abdomen and make a few slashes. In fact it's buried deep in the pelvis and sandwiched between the bladder and the rectum. It's generally a bloody fiddle to get it out."

"It was removed deliberately?"

Eisenmenger didn't know and said so.

"But that is the inference."

He nodded but it was reluctant. Helena sat and thought. Johnson finished his wine and Tchaikovsky took over in the background. Eisenmenger waited and tried not to let his hormonal and autonomic nervous systems run his life.

She sighed and at once Eisenmenger found himself thinking that it was almost a theatrical gesture, and yet not minding in the least. "Do I get the impression that there are things about the report that you're not happy with, but you're basically hampered by just having a written report to read?"

It seemed reasonable but, he appreciated afterwards, he was being distracted.

"That's right. The report alone isn't enough. After all, it's only one person's viewpoint . . . "

Suddenly he realized what was happening: she wanted him to perform a second post-mortem. She had that look on her face. He looked to Johnson to see that he, too, was strangely amused. Eisenmenger suddenly appreciated that he was being expertly but deliciously manipulated.

"I can't," he said to Helena. "It's just impossible."

She frowned and he had actively to stop himself from smiling like a smitten schoolboy. "Why not?" she asked and it was as if he had refused to accept that women should have the vote. How could he be so unreasonable?

"A lot of reasons . . . "

He was about to carry on – he was sure that he was – when she enquired softly, "Such as?"

It unsettled him: that and the glance at Johnson, whose expression was plainly saying, *She does this to people.*

"Well," he began but the feelings in his head were at it again and there was a pause while he tried to get his head above the surface of how much he was attracted by her. "I was a suspect, for God's sake. If I'm trying to prove that Bilroth didn't do it, I am in effect putting myself back as a theoretical suspect."

"I can't see why that should worry you. You're not suggesting that you did it, are you?"

Christ, she could tease for England.

"No. But I can see that my evidence at any trial proceedings would be attacked for being tainted."

"But the case is closed, as far as the police are concerned. Your evidence would be viewed against that background."

Would it? He didn't know.

"In fact," and as she said this, she leaned back in her chair and crossed her legs. She did this in perhaps two seconds, but in Eisenmenger's head they were seconds in which continents collided, mountains rose and coastlines changed. She knew what she was doing, and he knew what she was doing, and (Eisenmenger could see out of his eye's corner) Johnson knew what she was doing.

It mattered no jots at all.

After a couple of aeons she continued.

"You would surely be in a uniquely advantageous position. Few defence pathologists have the advantage of having seen the body at the crime scene . . . "

There followed a pause. Helena Flemming did nothing but drink the undrinkable. Johnson examined a fly that was doing particularly interesting things on the ceiling.

"If you're thinking of getting a second post-mortem, you're going to need the permission of the Exner family."

She didn't even allow a second to pass before she said, "As soon as the Bilroth family had instructed me, I contacted Nikki Exner's parents. I pointed out that the evidence against Tim Bilroth had been circumstantial at best, and that had he not died the defence would have been entitled to a second post-mortem in any case."

Eisenmenger was astonished.

"They've agreed already?"

She smiled sweetly. "Not yet. But when I explain to them your opinion of the quality of the first report . . . "

He looked to Johnson but if there had once been help there it had long since run for shade and, with that hope of rescue apparently gone, he could say only, "Shit."

Helena Flemming looked satisfied, but Eisenmenger was suddenly facing things he didn't want to face. Eisenmenger was suddenly facing the past. It had been easy to walk away; it would be proportionately harder to turn back.

"I don't do forensic work any more . . . "

Helena now said nothing. Her eyes somehow managed to grow larger and more appealing but, as much as his hormones were begging him to please her, he knew that it was a step beyond what he could manage.

He shook his head.

"No."

Perhaps it would have ended there, and thereby perhaps it would have been for the better.

But Johnson didn't keep quiet.

"I think you've got to do it," he said quietly. "Not for us, not for the Bilroth family, not for the Exner family, but for yourself."

Eisenmenger opened his mouth to rebut that but Johnson was inexorable.

"I know what you went through with the Bright case and I know how terrible you felt. It was only human – I was pretty sick as well – but it's time to stop hiding behind the sofa, John.

"You were pretty good and when you departed, we were left with the likes of Sydenham, and crap like that." He indicated the report. "If you do this now, you'll not only be helping to clear Bilroth's name, you'll be healing yourself."

Helena Flemming clearly didn't follow all the references but she had enough nous to keep quiet. She waited while Eisenmenger tried to find the words to tell Johnson to sod off.

But they weren't there.

All he could hear was Tamsin asking for her mummy.

At last he nodded. "Okay."

And Ravel's Pavane began to play in the background.

He was late, of course. Very late. He expected a row and the quiet and the darkness of the flat when he opened the front door only served to heighten his sense of apprehension.

He had stayed in the bar and talked, but it had been conversation with a sense of forlorn longing, for it had been with Johnson rather than with Helena Flemming, who had left shortly after his agreement to undertake the second autopsy on Nikki Exner.

Her departure awoke again his sense of having been manipulated: yet, he reflected, there were some manipulations that could bring the deepest of pleasures.

"You realize, of course, that if you continue to be associated with this, your career in the police force is finished."

The briefest of angry looks and then Johnson had said, "The way I look at it, my career – such as it was – is over already, one way or another. I can take early retirement in a year or two, but I don't think I'll be getting that far anyway. Beverley Wharton will see to that."

He spoke matter-of-factly, his words trying to build a façade of stoicism, but underneath there was much, much more. Johnson said then, "So tomorrow I resign."

Eisenmenger couldn't believe it. "Resigning? Just like that?"

"It has been pointed out to me that this way I can avoid any risk of being prosecuted." Johnson had a tense grin on his face but it was only a rictus.

"But if you didn't do anything . . . "

"You don't understand the Force. This kind of thing isn't decided by who's right and who's wrong, it's more a question of taking the broader picture. What's right for the greatest number. If I fight it from inside, it gets messy. If it gets messy, the usual method of dealing with things is to bury the troublemaker under a hundredweight of manure."

"You really think Wharton's behind it?"

Again the rictus. "Oh, yes. She's behind it. Like a virus with a mean temper. She wants me out of the way and what Beverley wants, Beverley gets."

"But you should fight it. You can't just give in."

They had reverted to the bottled beers. Johnson shook his head. "Even if I did contest the allegations, I have a shrewd idea that something else would turn up. Something just a little bit more incriminating."

"So she gets away with it? As easy as that?"

"She's done it before, John. Anyway, I am fighting her, only this way I can do it unhindered. Helena wants me to start digging around quietly. Fill in the background on Nikki Exner and what happened on the day she was killed."

"And when this is over?"

He shrugged and drank beer. "Maybe do private work for a living. Just to supplement the pension. I'll have to see."

They lapsed into a few minutes, silence while Eisenmenger wondered how he would handle being framed and then forced to resign.

"She's quite a girl, isn't she?"

Johnson's remark momentarily lost Eisenmenger in its wake.

"Helena," he explained and Eisenmenger made a sort of noise. Then Eisenmenger asked, "How did you find her?"

"I didn't. She found me. She talked me into this. Suggested that, given my situation, I could do the most good by helping her. I'd known her vaguely from before, but it was basically she who pointed out that our aims were identical. To show that the police have got it wrong on this one."

Eisenmenger considered. The tape loop was by now repeating itself, giving them another opportunity to appreciate the wonder of Debussy. The place was considerably busier than it had been earlier, the waiting staff even less inclined to wait.

"She's certainly got it in for Wharton not suprisingly."

But at least Helena's altruism was explained. Eisenmenger asked, "So that was where you first met her? During the investigation?"

Johnson nodded.

"And you told her what you knew about Wharton, that she had manufactured the evidence against her stepbrother?"

There was another pause. It was almost with shame then that Johnson said, "I should have told her a long time ago, but things were different then . . .

"When she came to see me last week, it was to discuss the Bilroth case. She'd kept track of Wharton and the similarities between this case and her stepbrother's were obvious. We got to talking and I got to thinking that maybe it was time to make amends." He looked down. "Should have done so a long time ago."

They had talked on after that, talked about this case and about other cases that they had both been involved in until it was closing time and even the great composers had been silenced. Yet while they had talked, Eisenmenger had been wondering about Helena Flemming and about her obsession. Was it wise to become involved in someone else's crusade? Hadn't she duped him into this? What was he going to gain by involvement in the affair?

Then he had thought of her legs and her mouth, of the coyness and the teasing.

"Marie?"

He whispered the name into the darkness of the bedroom but she didn't answer. Surely it couldn't be that easy? He had expected another row, more accusations of infidelity, more fantasies spun out of imagined evidence.

He undressed and slipped into the bed. She didn't move a single muscle, and even her breathing refused to break rhythm. He knew then that she was awake.

For a while he wondered whether he should talk to her, explain where he had been and why he was late, but then the memory of the last argument persuaded him otherwise. Best, he decided, not to protest too much. If she thought him unfaithful, no amount of rhetoric on his part was going to alter that. At least this way they would avoid the row for the time being, that much was a plus.

Once he would have gently woken her perhaps. Once they might have made love. Once, but not now.

He kept silent and just lay there, wondering what he was becoming embroiled in. His final thoughts before sleep were of Helena Flemming.

For Wilson the following day was not good. None of his days were ever brilliant but this was a rancid stinker. He had spent the morning interviewing three women, all of them witnesses to a gentleman who had taken to indecently exposing himself on their doorsteps. The interviews had not been easy, to the extent that even he (not a good judge of such things) had a vague inkling that Wharton would not be overjoyed to read his conclusions.

"For God's sake, Wilson, this is sheer, fucking crap! You haven't gleaned one useful piece of information from any of these witnesses. We don't know how old he is, how tall he is, whether he's bald, whether he's bearded. We don't even know if he's got one, two or three eyes."

Wilson felt unjustly treated. He had asked questions of the three women who had been exposed, as it were, to the offender's exposure but, perhaps quite understandably, they had been distracted during the encounter. Their descriptions had been sketchy and contradictory.

"They weren't looking at his face," he pointed out.

They were in Beverley Wharton's office, or rather in Castle's office where she was temporarily stationed. It was not a nice office – bare and utilitarian – but it had one major attribute: it was a Chief Inspector's office. Already she had been led to understand that she had the eye of her superiors, that her talents were not unappreciated.

Beverley Wharton's prospects were good, even if the office's prospects were of a doss house and a sandwich bar.

161

She shook her head slowly in exasperation.

"Who ties your fucking shoelaces up in the morning, Wilson? Is it your mother or your minder?"

He didn't answer, although it wasn't immediately clear whether this was because he had the wisdom to keep quiet or the stupidity to have forgotten.

"You haven't even found out if he was white or black," she pointed out. "Presumably he wasn't piebald. Presumably his dick was the same colour as the rest of him?"

When still he didn't reply, although this time the look on his face made it plain he hadn't actually asked the question, she threw the report across the desk and said, "Get back to the witnesses and this time don't return without something useful."

When he had gone, she smiled. There was something quite pleasant about shouting at stupid people, about exasperated anger. It helped to get her through the day.

That and news like the snippet of information she had been given earlier that morning.

Johnson had resigned. Just like that. Just like a lamb.

No fuss, no silliness. Just accepting the inevitable.

It had all been really rather easy.

She got up and went to look out of the window. Someone had been sick on the front steps of the doss house and the caretaker was hosing it down and into the gutter. He didn't seem to mind that the splashes were hitting the windows and passing through the open doorway of the sandwich bar. Who would know the difference?

Johnson had been the last big problem, and now he was gone. The pressure she had applied in various quarters to prevent him contesting the allegations had been successful: he would take early retirement without a hint of impropriety, while she was free of his irritating attention to righteousness.

The phone on the desk started to ring.

"Beverley?"

She recognized Superintendent Bloom's voice. It was only vaguely Lancastrian, although she had had occasion to note that in times of extreme emotion the accent became far broader.

"Yes, sir?"

"I thought you ought to know. We've just been notified by the Coroner's Office that there's to be a second autopsy on Exner."

She felt suddenly worried and she didn't know quite why.

"What on earth for? The case is closed."

162

"Presumably the Exner family aren't quite so sure. Anyway, it's fixed for Friday evening. Seven o'clock. I want you there."

She agreed, or rather she acquiesced to the command, and put the receiver down.

Something was going on. She could feel it. Vague undercurrents, shifts in the sand, ill-defined patterns. Something was stirring beneath her feet and she felt uneasy.

Bilroth had done it, of that she was certain. All the circumstantial evidence supported the conclusion, not least his track record, and if she helped things along in the interests of speedy justice, she could see no great crime in that.

And the toxicology supported her, as did the forensic report on the semen samples.

Bilroth had done it.

What was the problem?

"Shit," she whispered.

On their anniversary, Johnson always took his wife out to dinner. Normally they went to a small Italian trattoria but this was their twenty-fifth and Johnson was enough of a romantic to attempt something grander, of more significance. Accordingly he booked a table at an expensive and rather intimidating eatery in the West End, followed by a night in a riverside hotel.

The evening did not start well. The traffic was atrocious so they were late. The drinks were served by a foreign gentleman who clearly considered politeness – not to mention God's gift of language – too precious to dispense to the likes of the Johnsons.

And then there was Sally's attitude.

Oh, she made conversation, she smiled and laughed, and she radiated gratitude that he had splashed out in such a manner, but he could tell that there was something else beneath the veneer. His work had endowed him with insight into the moods and motivations that lay beneath the words: often on social occasions it was something of a nuisance, a distraction from the small talk that was demanded of him, but at least it made him receptive to Sally's underlying moods.

At last, as the desserts were being cleared and they were wondering about liqueurs with their coffee, he asked, "What's wrong?"

He asked gently, almost as if it was an item on the menu. Sally's blue-grey eyes, wide and underlined by mascara, stared up at him from above the oversized card in front of her. "What do you mean?"

"Something's bothering you."

She knew better than to deny it. The menu went down and she sighed. "You're out of a job."

He frowned, as if this was a complete surprise to him. *So?* His expression implied *What of it?* He said calmly, "Yes."

Irritation flitted across her face. "That's why I'm bothered!" she said. "Because all you can say is, 'Yes.'"

"What more is there to say?"

Her head was leaning towards him, close to the table as if she was aiming some sort of weapon. "Bob, all that money was found in our house! Money connected with crime! You were nearly thrown out in disgrace!"

"That money was planted."

"But that's even worse! You didn't fight; you didn't even make a fuss. You just walked out – "

"We went through this," he interrupted. "There was no point in doing anything else. It would have been counterproductive."

"But look at you now. You've done nothing about getting another job."

"I told you what I'm doing. I'm trying to sort out the Exner case."

"For which you're not being paid."

"No," he admitted, "but it's my way of making a fuss. If I can show that Bilroth was innocent, it'll make life uncomfortable for Beverley Wharton."

"But what use is that to us? I can't live on Beverley Wharton's discomfort."

Sally had found it hard to settle to the life of a policeman's wife – the closed world, the barriers that separated the police and the rest of the world. He knew that she had done so only out of love and he was humbled by such devotion.

"There's my pension."

She snorted. "Why are you in such a hurry to be a pensioner?"

The waiter came by but he waved him away. "I told you what I wanted to do. If I can make a go of this, then I'll set up a detective agency."

But she was shaking her head. "That's wishful thinking."

As he well knew, but he wasn't about to smash his dreams just yet, certainly not in public. She said, "How much does it cost to set up something like that? Have you worked it out? What about premises? What about equipment?"

He didn't answer and she took his silence, quite correctly, as proof of his ignorance. "It won't be cheap and you'd probably have to use our savings, wouldn't you?"

He looked at her and said slowly, "I don't know. I can't say . . . " But it was a lie and they both knew it. She snorted. They resumed their perusal of the liqueur menu, but it wasn't long before Johnson said, "Just let me help with this Exner business. Then we'll see."

She looked directly into his eyes for a long time, then nodded quickly and almost infinitesimally. The movement was spastic and suddenly cruel memories flared into Johnson's mind.

"You're all right, aren't you, Sally?"

As though she were having to find the courage to overcome pain she took a breath before smiling and reassuring him. "Of course I am."

She repeated the smile, this time more convincingly, and Johnson at last returned it. She asked, "Well, what are you going to have?"

The rest of the evening passed, but Johnson kept wondering.

Russell let out a shuddering sigh so deep and so long his paunch oscillated very faintly with its carrier wave.

"Fuck," he breathed. "Oh, fuck."

He leaned against the flock wallpaper, its harsh surface catching the abundance of grey-black hairs across the broad, freckled expanse of his back and causing a rasping sound as he moved. His mouth was open and from its corner a thin lick of spittle clung to his jowl.

"Oh, yes," he breathed slowly. "Oh, yes."

Below him – below his belly – Linda knelt and worked her magic. She moved her tongue and lips around the professorial member with the dexterity of a concert hall oboist while above her the sexual clichés were whispered into the sitting-room air.

Why, she wondered, *was it always the sitting room?* And not just always the same room, but always the same corner of the room, opposite the window and below the ghastly portrait that she assumed was of his mother. Poor bastard, with a mother like that.

Russell was crooning delightedly now. It was following the familiar pattern. She glanced surreptitiously at her watch without disturbing the rhythm of her mouth. Ten minutes gone and ten to go; then on to act two, when he would require her to squirm on the floor, the fingers of his left hand supposedly taking her to the heights of passion, while he wanked himself silly with the right. She had another appointment at seven but there would be plenty of time to get to it. At least Russell was well and truly back into his routine now.

With consummate skill she decided that it was time to take him a little bit higher. Accordingly she took one of her hands from the shaft and began to squeeze his testicles. The sighs became louder. *Whatever turns you on, dear.* She had been doing the job for too long to ask questions, although she was too intelligent not to pose them in her head. Why did he always want her to strip naked if all she was going to do was to give him head? Why did he want his balls squashed? Why did he insist on giving her a glass of Madeira wine afterwards?

But he was a regular source of income, and she valued that. Same time, same place, same day. Week after week: even Christmas day (although then there had been some concession to the festive season – a Santa hat for her and a little ring of tinsel for him).

He put his large, podgy hands on her head, an indication that he was nearing climax. She went back to work with renewed concentration for a moment.

Regular, except for that time a few weeks ago when he had called unexpectedly and cancelled her visit. First time for years that he hadn't wanted his little blow. He had sounded odd, as if near to collapse, but she hadn't asked for a reason: that would have been unprofessional.

Anyway, it had been only one week, although he hadn't seemed to her to be entirely normal on the next few occasions. At least he seemed not too bad now. Not quite normal, perhaps still a bit strained, but certainly good enough for her.

His grip on her head became tighter, threatening to dislodge the pins from her blonde hair. He began to move his hips back and forth and she in turn stopped her lingual gymnastics and puckered her lips into a soft, moist tube. His movements became more energetic, more uninhibited, rapidly increasing in violence until her head had to ride every thrust. Then, quite suddenly, he stopped deep inside her mouth, almost making her gag, and she knew that there would be a short wait, a short groan and another hundred pounds.

As she swallowed, she idly wondered what that made the total volume now.

At eight the next morning Johnson was standing outside the offices of Wolff, Parkinson, White wondering why it had to be so early. It was cold and what little sunlight there was cast only gloom. He knocked on the glass of the door, peering into the dark empty office, feeling like a fool. Was she there?

It took a little while but eventually Helena Flemming appeared and let him in.

166

"Thanks for coming."

She led him into her office and offered coffee. While the kettle was boiling he asked, "Why eight o'clock?"

She poured the water into the mugs and then splashed some milk into his.

"I work better early," she said and he missed the lie.

He sipped the coffee, as much to gain some warmth for his hands from the mug.

"Are you sure about John Eisenmenger?" she asked after a moment. "He doesn't seem too keen."

"He was good. You won't get better, not for free. Besides, I think it's just what he needs."

"*Was* good. I hope he still is."

"He is," he reassured her.

She let it rest.

"Which brings us to me," he said, "since we're talking of working for free."

Helena looked at him quickly, a worried look on her face. "You're not backing out? You said you didn't mind not having a fee."

He put the coffee mug down. "I told you, it's probably for the best. If we do prove anything against Beverley Wharton, I want to look squeaky clean."

"Of course."

"I think I should warn you, though, I doubt we'll be able to show that she planted evidence."

Helena Flemming had been looking through her desk drawer. She looked up at Johnson. "No? But we must."

"You'll be lucky. Beverley's clever. There'll have been no witnesses, no one in her confidence. She's beholden to no one: that way there's no one to use anything against her. She learned her lesson with me."

"A mistake she's now put right."

"Exactly." He tried the coffee again, this time finding it cool enough to drink. "No, the most we'll show is that Tim Bilroth didn't do it, and maybe that there's proof of who did."

Looking disappointed, Helena said, "But is that enough? She's hardly likely to get punished for it, is she?"

Johnson had heard the tone in her words before. She wanted something more than mere justice for Tim Bilroth; more even than vindication for Jeremy. She wanted vengeance.

"Maybe not. But it won't look good for her. There'll be questions asked, some annoyance. Just as they'd rather I left than fight an alle-

167

gation of corruption, so they'll start to think that Beverley's a liability. They hate that more than anything."

"Incompetence and corruption are acceptable, just don't get found out?"

He finished his coffee and put his mug down on a file that was labelled *Miller vs. Miller.*

"Isn't that always the way?"

She wasn't happy, that much was clear from the way she stared at her clenched hands on the desk.

"I want her to pay for what she's done. I want everyone to know who and what she is."

"Fine. It's just that I'm too old to expect happy endings all round. I'll settle for a tiny bit of satisfaction – it's better than none at all."

Her coffee was growing cold and she wasn't drinking it. Johnson asked, "What do you want me to do?"

She looked slightly lost by the question. "You're the detective. You tell me."

Another of the files on her desk was marked *Martius vs. Martius.* To Johnson it looked oddly like a divorce case. He said, "The first thing I want to do is to talk to Libman. I still think that his reaction was wrong. Then I'll find out some more about Nikki Exner. Almost always the answer comes from knowing enough about the victim, especially in a case like this."

"Like this?"

"You don't hang, draw and quarter somebody unless you know them and you hate them." He paused. "Unless . . . "

Helena looked at him. "Yes?"

"Unless you have something to hide."

"What on earth can you hide by doing that to someone?"

Johnson smiled. "Some murderers are like magicians. Misdirection is the name of the game. The important thing is not to forget about other possibilities. As long as you don't forget that you've always got to go back to basics. Find out as much as you can about the victim, from there you find possible suspects, and from there you find out all about them. Sooner or later you discover your killer."

"As easy as that?"

He nodded but then added, "As easy as that, but then the hard part comes – getting the evidence to prove it. That," he said standing, "is hard enough for the police. For people like us, it's going to be bloody impossible."

He walked to the door.

"Thanks for the coffee. Daily reports okay? Or would you prefer to hear from me only when I've got something to say?"

She looked uncertain, he thought. He suggested, "When's the autopsy going to be? Friday? How about after that?"

She frowned in an attempt to look confident. "Fine."

"You were late last night."

What did that mean?

"I said I would be."

Marie frowned. "I didn't think you meant that late."

In truth neither had Eisenmenger, but that, he reckoned, was life.

"We got talking. I didn't realize the time."

They were eating supper. Eisenmenger had made it even though it wasn't his turn, an attempt to appease Marie. They hadn't actually communicated with each other since the night before because she had been on an early shift. He had lain in bed and pretended to be asleep as she had showered and dressed and even with his eyes shut and with no words spoken he had known she was angry.

There was a break in the conversation, but it was a conversation that had consisted largely of such pauses interspersed with unconnected sentences uttered in strained tones. She wasn't really eating anything, just stabbing and chopping it with a fork. Eisenmenger wondered what she was seeing as she mercilessly despatched a piece of broccoli. The slightly sullen look around her mouth did not bode well. What with that and the way she had barely bothered to acknowledge his kindness in cooking the meal, he knew that there was a lot of resentment building inside her.

"Was she there?"

She? Already it had become a case of 'she'? As if Marie now saw it as a menage a trois, with him cast as the rampant philanderer and Marie the wronged wife. A costume drama with the pair of them dressed in the fool's motley.

Inevitably as he opened his mouth to reply he was wondering whether it was worth it. Not, he had to admit, the best basis for reconciliatory words.

"She? Whom do you mean?"

Just a question but he knew instinctively that his grammatical pedantry would, as it had several times before, infuriate her.

"Her," she said at once as if now that the battle had commenced, the smell of blood was exciting her. "The lawyer."

He frowned but was at once thinking that he was playing a part, no more. Why couldn't he behave as he really wanted to?

"Yes," he said slowly and deliberately, "she was." He waited, knowing that those three words were boring into her like slivers of metal under the nails. *Why not?* he asked himself. *Why shouldn't I do this? I'm innocent and this is purely of her own imagining.*

But still he felt guilt.

"And so was Johnson," he added then. "It was Johnson who stayed late and talked with me."

Marie snorted, unbelief contorting her face into a mix of hurt, self-pity and anger. "What were you talking about? You and this lawyer."

"Flemming. Helena Flemming," he said and knew at once that it was a mistake, as if the giving of her name gave Marie power.

"Well, then. What were you talking about, you and *Helena?*"

His part was now to be rational and calm, to explain the truth. Yet he knew that it would not be enough, that his relationship with Marie, which had been ending for weeks now, was finally starting to decay. And with this realization there came the insight that not only did he want the relationship to end, but he wanted it to die at the hands of Marie. He wanted her to club it to brainlessness with her jealousy, while he held up his hands and said, *"Non mea culpa."* In fact what he wanted was a normal 'let's be nice and have sex occasionally' type of relationship, one he no longer seemed to posses.

And so he explained. He told her about Nikki Exner and Tim Bilroth, about Beverley Wharton and about Helena Flemming. And all the while Marie sat, the food now left to untasted oblivion, the look on her face not changing, except perhaps for the worse.

When he had finished, he looked at Marie, tried to make eye contact, but she just sat there and stared at the cruet.

"There's nothing 'going on' between me and Helena Flemming, Marie," he said quietly and, he imagined, earnestly. "It's a professional relationship, nothing more."

Still she stared. Idly Eisenmenger wondered if she were having some sort of telepathic conversation with the pepper mill – asking for advice perhaps. He began to eat again but it was cold and the little flavour it had once possessed had gone, wasted on the sweet suburban air.

Marie did nothing for a short while, content, it seemed, to stare at her food. Eisenmenger might have assumed her asleep had she not suddenly sobbed. When he looked up, it was to see water-drenched doe eyes above large, rolling tears. He felt a curious mix of exasperation and regret. Before he could speak, she said, 'I'm sorry, John. I'm so sorry.'

She reached out her hand it was not without reluctance that he took it. She continued, "I love you so much, John. I couldn't bear to lose you."

And he allowed himself to believe that here was genuine emotion. "And I love you," he said gently. She nodded, smiled and resumed her meal.

Silence followed, before, "Is she attractive?"

Afterwards he wondered if, had he not lost his temper then, things might have been different.

Of course he told himself that no, they would not.

"Oh, for fuck's sake!" He flung down his fork and bits of congealed rice were flipped across the table in a miniature mockery of confetti. "Listen to yourself! What's wrong with you? Why can't you just accept that I'm not trying to get into her knickers?"

But she didn't hear him, it seemed.

"She is, isn't she?"

Now there was eye contact and he suddenly wished that there wasn't. Even through watery salt-laden tears she seemed to be seeing things within him that were not for her knowledge.

"It doesn't fucking matter what she looks like. She's only interested in the Bilroth case, not whether I'm going to perform cunnilingus on her!"

Marie looked shocked, as if the word was beyond the limit, as if their positions were those of mother and son.

"How dare you?" she screamed abruptly. "How dare you be so disgusting?"

She got up, knocking her glass of wine over and sending the barely eaten meal skittering across the table. "You bastard, you bastard, you bastard!"

She was backing away from him, crying but bending forward as if better to spew out the invective.

"Marie . . . " he said, half worried but half relieved.

"Shut up!" she shouted, and this made her sob, hysteria driving her on beyond reasoning. "Shut up! You don't love me! You probably never have!"

He tried not to think about the truth that maybe lay curled up and asleep in that.

"Please, Marie, you're just being silly . . . "

Was silly such a terrible word to use? Was it worse than 'cunnilingus'?

171

Maybe it was to Marie. Maybe the trivialization of her behaviour was to her a worse insult even than the thought that her suspicions were true.

Whatever the reason, there was a short sharp pause during which her face passed through a curious sequence of stuttering emotions, then . . .

"S-S-SILLY?" she thundered, the word coming out asthmatically, so that she seemed to asphyxiate as she aspirated.

Then in the shock that her bellow had produced in Eisenmenger, she lunged forward to the table, picked up her plate and flung it at him. It was a pathetic throw, missing him by a wide gap, although flecks of onion caused collateral damage to his cheek. The plate hit the modern, steel standard lamp in the corner, the one that had cost Eisenmenger an eye-watering five hundred pounds but Marie had insisted was perfect for the room. Luckily, he noticed, it appeared undamaged.

Marie took deep, shuddering breaths, then pronounced, "We're finished."

She turned at once, rushed from the room and made for the bedroom, banging the door shut behind her. Eisenmenger heard the key click loudly.

He sighed in a heartfelt manner.

"Well, thank fucking Christ for that."

The Chief Constable called the Dean, a golfing partner and member of the same lodge. It was purely a courtesy call, nothing that could be construed as unethical or of dubious morality, certainly not by those of right and proper sensibilities.

"Daniel? It's Marvin here. Sorry to bother you when you're probably up to your neck in work."

Dean Schlemm surveyed the rolling vistas of his impressively empty oak desk and murmured, "Not at all. What can I do for you?"

"You recall, of course, the Exner case."

The Dean closed his eyes briefly. Even this mundane action was achieved with a degree of aplomb that most people would never achieve. "What of it?"

"I'm afraid it looks as if it hasn't gone to bed as we hoped. At least not quite yet."

The Dean leaned back in his leather chair, his eyes looking over the ornate decorations of the ceiling. "In what way?"

"Apparently the Exner family have given permission for a second post-mortem to be carried out."

"That, I believe, is their privilege."

"Of course, of course . . . "

"Is it a problem, Marvin? Are you not comfortable with this scrutiny? Surely you have confidence in the work of your officers."

The Chief Constable had looked through the papers relating to the case and discovered what he had known would be there. The circumstantial evidence against Bilroth had been strong, but not completely without weakness. His convenient death had resulted in perfunctory follow-up that had not tidied everything up. This was understandable and quite normal. Why waste valuable time and money on pursuing a dead man?

"Of course, of course."

"Well, then. What is the problem?"

The Chief Constable had always felt slightly intimidated by the Dean, a feeling that was not uncommon. It was rare that he had the means with which to nettle this paragon of intellectual imperturbability.

"I thought that I ought to warn you. The pathologist who is performing the second autopsy works in your medical school. Eisenmenger."

The Dean came close to a start; but only close. Still, it was an uncharacteristically rapid movement that found him sitting upright and frowning. "Eisenmenger," he repeated.

"That's right," confirmed the Chief Constable with something approaching a smile about his chapped lips. "It occurred to me that if he were to find something . . . awkward, it would open up the whole business again. Bad publicity, all that sort of thing." A brief pause for contemplation, then, "And what with it being one of your own chaps doing the digging . . . Shitting in his own nest, as it were."

The Dean could have done without the vividness of the metaphor but appreciated the point. He rang off, leaving the Chief Constable satisfied with a task well completed, and leaned back in contemplation.

Eventually he picked up the telephone again.

Johnson rapidly came to regret his decision to start with Stephan Libman. It was easy enough to establish that the assistant curator was to be found at home, or rather, his mother's home, but there the facility ended. She it was who answered the doorbell, presenting her rounded, worried face with its ruddy cheeks, double chin and frightened, blue-grey eyes to Johnson from behind the stained glass and heavy wood of the front door.

"Yes?" Not querulous but definitely suspicion-filled. The world was a dangerous place, and the answer was to keep it out. Her face, with its broken veins and over-applied mascara, was at a height of five feet. It emerged from the darkness behind her, so that Johnson had the impression of a funeral parlour.

"Mrs Libman?"

"Yes?" This time there was imminent hostility in the affirmation-cum-query.

"My name's Johnson. I'm investigating the death of Nikki Exner . . . "

"Are you police?"

Johnson had debated how he should answer this question. Tempting as it would have been, he had decided that he had to be honest, if only for his own protection. There was no point in supplying the bullets for Beverley Wharton to shoot him with; she would have liked nothing better than to hang him for impersonating a police officer.

"No, I'm – "

"Are you press?"

"Oh, no . . . " Too late he realized that he had made a mistake, for she began to shut the door at once. Someone who liked talking to the press? So they really did exist.

"I'm working for Nikki Exner's family," he said quickly, putting his hand out to stop the door from closing. "They were worried about the trauma that Stephan has suffered . . . "

The lie – well, only a small one – worked. The door was allowed to open slightly again.

"Worried?"

"They heard about him. What he had been through. Even in their grief, they realized that it must have been a terrible experience for him."

Johnson was discovering talents in acting and fabrication that had lain unseen for decades. He heard the words and wondered whence they came.

The door was opening wider with every syllable. Clearly the key to Libman mater was through her son.

"He's suffered terribly."

Now he could see her left bosom. Suppressing the thought that it was, under other circumstances, something he would rather not have seen, he turned the key further.

"They asked me to visit him, to check that he was all right."

Suddenly he was treated to the whole of Mrs Libman but luckily Johnson was made of strong fibre. His face remained impassive as he surveyed her bulges, talcum powder, neurosis and bright, floral patterns. It was like looking into pure motherliness.

"He's ill," she announced. "He's terribly ill."

"May I see him?"

The most transitory of frowns crossed her chubby face, but Johnson added at once, "To thank him personally for everything that he did."

What Stephan Libman had actually done was not obvious to Johnson, but clearly Mrs Libman was privy to information that Johnson was denied. She stood aside to allow him in and said, "Of course, of course."

He entered the house and felt at once at home and repelled. The house was a homage to maternalism, to domesticity, but in a very dated, oppressive way. It was as if he was back at home, back when he was ready to leave, when he didn't understand anything about his parents and they understood nothing about him, when he metamorphosed into an alien in front of their alarmed expressions and he suddenly saw them as human and therefore flawed.

Thus the decor was brown and unmistakably faded with scattered rips in the wallpaper, worn patches in the overwhelmingly patterned carpet and every horizontal surface covered in ugly or cheap, or ugly and cheap, ornaments. There was even linoleum below, but then there were pelmets above.

The house was small and all the rooms that he saw or passed through – the front, the back, the hall, even the kitchen – were the same in style, or rather in the same complete lack of style. Taste had been killed and then embalmed with a lipless grin.

As she led him through this tunnel of hideous memory he noticed that in the hall, opposite a large and ornate gilded mirror, there hung a child's painting. Johnson summoned all his strength to stop a shudder running through every muscle of his body.

The kitchen had never been fitted in any way, shape or form. The Belling gas cooker stood as it had stood for fifty years, the Fridgidaire obtruded in the corner, curves and sheer bulk straight from an era of Teddy Boys and bobby sox, the butler sink square and brutish next to it. The kitchen table was set for lunch, the pale blue Formica chipped away at the edges.

There was a small conservatory at the back of the house, looking out on to a long, thin garden that was carefully tended. Johnson didn't need to search for the garden gnome that he knew would be there.

Stephan Libman sat in the conservatory on old wicker furniture reading a book. He looked better than he had the last time that Johnson had seen him, but then Johnson had seen roadkill that looked better than Libman had that day.

"Stephan?" Mrs Libman spoke as if afraid of terrible retribution. Stephan, however, appeared to have little intention of inflicting terrible retribution on anyone. His pallid face turned to his mother and if he had the power of instant annihilation at his command he hid it well. A frown passed by as he caught sight of Johnson.

"This is Mr . . . "

But she had forgotten and looked to him for help.

"Johnson," he supplied. "I've come to find out how you are."

"Mr Johnson comes from the . . . Exner family."

The slight pause said it all.

Stephan nodded slowly, then returned to his book.

Mrs Libman asked of Johnson, "Would you like some tea?"

To Johnson other people's tea was usually to be avoided but it occurred to him that it was only this or a nuclear strike that could have been used to separate mother and son.

"Lovely," he lied.

She left them – bustled away would have been the apposite term – having determined that her son – clearly her only son – was not thirsty. Was there a Mr Libman? Had there ever been?

"How are you, Stephan?"

Stephan looked up. His eyes were large and pale, as if they couldn't muster the energy to be anything brightly coloured. Was he weak or had he just been assured that he was weak?

"Okay," he said. He continued to stare at Johnson. Did he recognize him?

"It must have been a terrible shock for you."

At once he returned to the book and Johnson knew better than to press the matter. Yet even as he did so, he suddenly realized that now he had a problem. He had been a policeman and all his previous interviews (a euphemism for interrogations) had been undertaken with that premise. The basis of the exchange had been that he had possessed the right to extract information from the interviewee. Full stop. There had been no need for subtlety, no need to sidle up to the other and gently squeeze out what he needed with guile and deceit. No need to pick the mind's pockets.

Suddenly he saw that he had a new skill to learn.

"What are you reading?" Not exactly likely to extract news of a smoking gun, but then at least it was neutral.

Stephan showed him the book. *Bleak House.*

"Ah, Dickens," said Johnson knowledgeably. "Good, is it?"

Apparently it was, for Stephan nodded briefly and returned to its embrace.

Time was running out. The return of Mrs Libman would, he was sure, terminate the opportunity for useful discussion. But how close could he go? How near to the fences and alarm systems? Panicking slightly, Johnson tried a risky tactic.

"You heard about Tim, of course?"

Stephan looked up suddenly. It was the most energetic movement he had yet made and Johnson was at once afraid that he had made a mistake. For a long moment Stephan just stared at him, a curiously impassive look on his face that contrasted with the implied hostility of his fixed gaze.

Then, "I liked Tim. He was a laugh."

He dropped back to the book and Johnson relaxed into a routine.

"Did you get on well?"

Stephan considered. "Pretty much."

"He kept odd hours, didn't he?"

With a smile Stephan said, "He didn't keep the ones he was supposed to."

"Late mornings, eh?"

"Something like that."

"And the evenings? Did he disappear early?"

"Sometimes. When he could."

"Bet that irritated your boss, Goodpasture."

The smile broadened. "Goody hated him. Used to go red in the face. We thought that one day he'd burst a blood vessel."

"Row a lot, did they?"

"Oh, yeah. Practically every day there was . . . "

And then he stopped as if too much had been said. Johnson at once spoke with a knowing grin. "Sounds like my office. There's always someone who can't loosen up."

A long pause before, "Yeah." He returned to his book.

Johnson had established contact, but he was afraid that he would spoil it with hesitation. The boy had actually looked up at him. Progress indeed.

"And I understand that sometimes Tim stayed late, right?"

Now there was a long wait. The boy's eyes were back on his book but Johnson could see that he wasn't reading, that he was actually making a decision.

Then, "Sometimes."

"Why?"

He had hoped that the sudden arrival of a direct enquiry would surprise Stephan into admitting more than otherwise he would. Yet there was another pause and Stephan's answer when it came was presented in a surprisingly prosaic manner.

"He dealt in drugs."

Johnson's surprise must have shown for he continued, "It wasn't a secret. Anyway, he's dead, isn't he?"

"What drugs?"

Stephan looked up at the small window in the whitewashed wall of the house. Through it his mother busied herself doing motherly things, just as she probably had for all of Stephan's life. Where and who was Mr Libman? Dissolved into soup by the acidic, maternal love that oozed from his wife?

"Anything. Cannabis, coke, heroin, MDMA . . . Whatever gear you wanted."

Johnson looked up sharply. Stephan's sudden knowledge of the intricacies of drug nomenclature was illuminating. In fact it made Stephan suddenly far more interesting. More, perhaps, than he at first appeared.

They didn't have long. Mrs Libman was rattling crockery.

"And what about Nikki Exner? Did she buy?"

Stephan smiled but it was a poisoned thing that rode across his face.

"She was one of his best customers. 'Special', he called her."

"Special?"

The smile broadened and somehow became a leer.

"Yeah."

Johnson had been a policeman for twenty-six years and in that time had had occasion to observe how the drug culture worked.

"How did she pay, Stephan?"

He shrugged, but the look on his face refused to budge.

"How?" Johnson insisted.

He waited a minute, perhaps thinking how to phrase it. "Sometimes she paid with money."

He couldn't have made it plainer without actually using words like 'let', 'shag', 'she', 'him' and 'her'.

"And what about that night? What about the night she died?" Johnson sounded eager, sounded, he knew, as if her terrible death were merely an oddity.

Stephan opened his mouth. Suddenly they were both aware that it had gone quiet in the kitchen. Mrs Libman was approaching.

"What do you mean?" asked Stephan.

How could he be so dim?

"Did he stay late? Did he meet Nikki to deal drugs?"

Please be quick. Please speed up your thought processes.

But Stephan was not one to be hurried. Could he be just a tease? Could he actually want to string Johnson along?

He considered. At last he said, "Oh, yes. He stayed late all right."

But it was wrong. Johnson heard it at once. A lie had been told, or maybe a truth not told, but before he could pursue it Mrs Libman, replete with tray, appeared.

It was as bad as Johnson had feared. Not only was the tea stewed to a dark brown bitter sludge that no amount of milk would lighten, but she had taken the opportunity to bring out a plate of jam sandwich biscuits that were clearly a treat for the focus of her life that was her son. Johnson sat and drank his tea, refusing the dubious pleasure to be had from the sweet, sickly biscuits, suppressing shudders and trying to remain polite, interested and unnauseated.

And through it all, it seemed to Johnson that Stephan was no longer the slightly feeble mummy's boy. Under all his acquiescence to his mother's suffocating ministrations Johnson detected a seam of something darker. What before had seemed to be meek foppishness, a complete and total acceptance that his role in life was to be the eternal youngster, the object of his mother's affection, was now to Johnson tinged with a knowing slyness. He was using her, enjoying the deception.

Which meant that he wasn't such a *naif*.

Which meant that perhaps he knew a lot more than he had thus far admitted.

After twenty long minutes Johnson managed to escape. Mrs Libman showed him out, leading him away from her son. As she left the conservatory first, Johnson looked back at Stephan.

He was reading his book, the dutiful, obedient son.

Sophie Sternberg-Reed caught him as he returned from a particularly excruciating urology meeting. An hour and a half of bladder carcinomas, one after the other, all identical and all shown to an audience of surgeons who were completely uninterested always drained him, but on this occasion it was worse than usual. It could have been connected with the fact that this had been an especially heavy meeting – forty-seven cases – and it could also have been in part due to a migraine, but he suspected that it was mostly because he had slept badly, although not because he had spent the night in the spare bedroom alone.

Rather because he had not once been alone all the long night.

Tamsin had been with him.

That morning when he had left the flat the main bedroom door had been closed and he hadn't bothered knocking or calling out to see if Marie was in there. He had simply washed, dressed and gone out.

"What is it, Sophie?"

"Can I have a word?"

She looked more scared than usual, more of the depressed, hunted air about her. Apparently Russell had commented that morning in public that he thought her to be "More rabbit than human, although perhaps not quite as bright as the average bunny."

He didn't want to talk to her, felt that he had barely enough time or compassion for his own problems, let alone those of the delightful but hopeless Sophie Sternberg-Reed with her double-barrelled name and single-barrelled intellect.

"Of course. Come into the office."

She followed him in and sat nervously while he dumped the slides in the out-tray. Then he too sat down.

"If it's about what Russell said . . . "

She shook her head. "It's not. At least not directly . . . "

He thought he could guess then. "Look, Sophie. I think I know what you're getting at . . . " She looked slightly lost by what he was saying, but then she always did. "About what happened . . . If you wish to make a complaint, I would support you all the way . . . "

It took a while but eventually she arrived. Her eyes opened wide and her mouth followed shortly after.

"Oh, my God! I didn't realize you knew! But how did you find out?"

Her embarrassment spread to Eisenmenger. Flustered he explained quickly, "Belinda came to me. She wanted advice about it. About what to do." When Sophie continued to look horrified, he added, "I'm sure she thought that she was acting for the best."

Suddenly the expression on her face crumpled. She went from aghast amazement to depressed acceptance in under a second. "Oh, well, it doesn't matter now." She tried a smile. "I've resigned."

It was Eisenmenger's turn to be startled. "Resigned? But why? Surely not because of Russell? You can't let him win!"

Her shoulders moved up and down in a sort of shrug. "Its the easiest way. I don't think I'm cut out to be a histopathologist, do you?"

Eisenmenger tried to lie, but her eyes were on him and he hadn't the cruelty to continue the deception. He dropped his gaze to the desk and said, "Maybe not."

She took in a long breath as if his answer had finally killed her hopes. "I've written to Personnel and I've just put a copy on his desk. I thought I ought to tell you straight away."

He was just about to thank her for her courtesy when Russell arrived. His appearance in Eisenmenger's room was abrupt, to say the least, but then it always was. He never knocked, just came in. On this occasion he seemed to burst forth into the room, the door swinging away from him as if in fear.

He was scowling but that was no clue to his temper since it was a fixture that was so deeply etched it was probably went down to bone. His body language, however, was spectacularly clear on the subject of his mood. It was obvious that he had not anticipated Eisenmenger to be in company, but he didn't allow that to delay him.

"You," he said, meaning Sophie, "please leave. I have business with Eisenmenger." Even for Russell this was unusual, this ulceration of the veneer of politeness. As she passed him, her attitude one of near-supplication, he added, "I have seen your letter. For the first time since you arrived in this department you have shown good judgement."

When the door had closed behind her, he turned his attentions to Eisenmenger.

"Now," he began but Eisenmenger had had enough. What he had been thinking for once he expressed.

"How come you get such enjoyment from being a complete and utter fucking bastard, Russell?"

If he was shocked by such candid sentiments, Russell failed to show it.

"I'll ignore that," he decided. "I wish to talk to you about your extra-contractual activities."

"My what?"

"When you took this job, you failed to inform either me or the medical school that you would be continuing to function as a forensic pathologist."

"I haven't been."

Russell raised both eyebrows. He was such an obese man it must have expended a considerable amount of energy.

"Really? Then I have been misinformed. I was led to believe that you were about to perform a second post-mortem on the girl who was murdered by Bilroth."

Eisenmenger stared at him, wondering how he had found out, wondering what the hell it had to do with Russell. "I am," he admitted cautiously.

Russell smiled. "But you are not employed here as a forensic pathologist."

"What the hell does that matter? I'm doing it in my own time."

Russell snorted derisively. "That is not the point."

"What is, then?"

Russell frowned and walked from his station at the door. It was a sign of confidence, Eisenmenger felt. "The point is, Dr Eisenmenger, that as a senior lecturer in this medical school, you should consider very carefully the wisdom and merit of reawakening interest in this particular case."

At last he comprehended, even if he didn't understand.

"You're warning me off?"

Russell at once dismissed this with a wave of podgy fingers. "I am saying that you should be careful of a conflict of interest."

"Why should any question concerning the death of Nikki Exner result in a conflict of interest for me?"

Russell appeared to find this an obtuse attitude. "The publicity concerning the murder was harmful to the medical school. Any further investigation would not only prove fruitless, since the guilty man was found and is now dead, but would attract further attention; prurient attention that could only harm the reputation of one of the world's great schools of medicine."

"You're certain Bilroth was guilty?"

"Of course. As are the police, I believe."

"I'm not." Eisenmenger knew that he sounded obstinate, unreasonable, but quite enjoyed the anger that this produced in the fat man.

"Well, let me tell you," and here Russell came close to Eisenmenger and stuck a flesh-rolled forefinger in the general direction of his face, "that if you persist in this, it may affect your career in the medical school. Bear in mind that you have already lost your position with regard to the museum. That may not be the end of the matter."

Eisenmenger wondered how Russell was coping with his new role as curator, sort of hoped that the question of the provenance of many of the specimens was giving him much trouble. He couldn't raise the energy to be sorry that it was no longer his problem, but he was intrigued by this move from Russell. Was it prompted by the Dean? Was there possibly more to this than mere fear of public scrutiny?

Eisenmenger smiled because he knew it would infuriate Russell. "Thanks for the concern, Basil. I'll certainly keep that in mind when I do the autopsy."

Russell's face showed a spasm of intense anger but nothing came of it. He grunted, scowled a bit more then withdrew from Eisenmenger's immediate vicinity. At the door he said, "If you put any specimens from this autopsy through this department, they had better be properly labelled as such so that the department can charge you appropriately."

When Eisenmenger didn't say anything, he added, "And you'd better make damned sure you do this in your own time."

He opened the door and stumped out, slamming the door behind him. Eisenmenger sighed and leaned back in his chair. Of course, he reasoned, it might just be that people were worried that if Bilroth didn't do it, then suddenly everyone else was a suspect again. And that included a few distinguished people.

Johnson found Jamie Fournier in the students' bar and, perhaps not surprisingly, he was drinking. The bar was impressively long and indeed was, the girl behind it told him, the longest student bar in the country. Johnson admired it for a while, taking in its highly polished beech surface, the three sets of pumps and the four stations of optics. Behind him, the whole room must have been forty by thirty metres, large enough to hold a spacious dance floor and numerous seating areas. It was mostly empty.

"Are you a member of staff? I'm afraid I can't serve you if you're not; not unless someone signs you in."

Johnson hastened to assure her that he wasn't thirsty. He was looking for Jamie Fournier. Her face changed, almost sinking to a scowl. "Oh, him. He's over there."

She indicated the far corner of the room, to Johnson's left.

Walking over in the direction indicated, Johnson saw at once the reason for her expression. Despite the fact that it was only five o'clock, Fournier was drunk. He looked dishevelled and was crouched forward over a pint of lager that was a quarter full. Johnson sat beside him and said nothing, Fournier glancing up and staring at this breach of privacy.

"Do I know you?" he asked.

"Johnson. We met during the investigation of Nikki Exner's death."

A long pause, then, "Oh. Yeah. Police."

There was no inflection of disgust that Fournier could put on the word that Johnson had not heard a few thousand times before. "I

183

wanted to talk to you," explained Johnson, not exactly denying the accusation. "About the death of Nikki."

Fournier was clearly very drunk but he had enough awareness to say, "What for? It's over, isn't it?"

Johnson said nothing.

"That cunt, Bowman – Bilroth, whatever – killed her." He suddenly grabbed at the beer glass and poured the rest of the lager down his throat, spilling much of it. Then without another word he got up and walked unsteadily back to the bar. Johnson watched him and wondered if he would be served. Wondered, too, if he would return to his seat.

Judging by the body language, he had trouble persuading the barmaid but eventually he succeeded. He turned and made his storm-tossed way back to Johnson. By the time he reached harbour he had lost a not inconsiderable quantity of cargo. He flopped back down in his seat.

There was a pause, then, "So what do you want?"

He was leaning back in his chair, his eyes closed, his voice slurred and bored. The front legs of his chair were off the floor. Johnson watched him. He was pissed, he decided, but he wasn't that pissed. There was acting there.

"How well did you know Tim Bilroth?"

The answer came at once. "He was a creep. I never liked him."

Everyone has a retrospectoscope, and everyone uses it.

"You knew him, then? Knew him well?"

This one was handled more cautiously, with a shrug. "A bit."

There was much psychology in Johnson's art: knowing when to leave, when to pull: when to shout, when to whisper. Now he felt it time to pull.

"But he sold you drugs." Not a question, a statement.

Fournier didn't move. "Did he?" he drawled.

Johnson leaned forward and kicked the back legs of Fournier's chair. It had a satisfying effect as Fournier was brought to the worn, stained carpet with a thump.

Johnson leaned into his opened eyes. "Yes. He did."

Fournier looked for the glass. "Not me," he muttered after a few swallows.

"No? Are you saying it was just Nikki?"

Fournier looked at his beer mat. Nothing that Johnson could see there was going to provide much in the way of a mnemonic.

"Well?"

Fournier shrugged. "I guess."

Suddenly Johnson demanded, "What the bloody hell does that mean? Did she or didn't she buy drugs off Bilroth?"

Maybe Fournier decided that it no longer mattered. Whatever the reason he said with a soft sigh, "She bought them."

"What were they?"

"Usually coke or cannabis. Sometimes heroin."

"And you?"

That was different, it seemed, for at once Fournier was more reticent. "I tried it occasionally."

That was a laugh, but Johnson didn't pursue it. Fournier had more to drink. His skin was sallow and sheened with grease. He looked ill, and maybe it wasn't all the drink. Why was he in such a state? Was he pining for his lost love?

"But she used them regularly?"

He nodded.

"Did she deal?"

Fournier tried to look surprised at the notion at the same time as he tried to look convincing with his denial. It didn't work.

Johnson shook his head. "Wrong answer, son."

Fournier tried to answer but something about Johnson's expression changed his mind. "A bit," he admitted.

Which meant a lot.

"What happened that night?"

Fournier rubbed his hands together, crushing the palms as if obliterating something between them. When he didn't answer, Johnson said, "Well?"

Fournier made a face. "I told you."

Johnson leaned forward so that he was only half a metre from Fournier's face. "You told us a pile of shit," he said. "Now tell me the truth."

Or else, he was implying, although this could only be a bluff.

Fournier looked up and searched his face, looked into his eyes. Then he dropped his gaze. "What do you want to know?"

"How about starting with what happened from about five o'clock. Where were you and where was Nikki?"

It couldn't have been classed as a great feat of memory but Fournier seemed to be having difficulty. Moments passed in which Johnson looked round. The bar was noticeably busier now; both students and older people crowding around the bar and starting to spill out into the room, an after-work diaspora.

"I was in lectures at five. I don't know where Nikki was."

"Wasn't she in the library? Working for the Anatomy prize?"

185

There was another pause. Then, as if he had made a definite decision, he sat back in the chair with a sigh and said, "Hardly. Nikki didn't give a shit about the poxy thing. Sure, she told everybody she was hard at work for it, but I never saw her do any."

"She didn't care about it?"

He laughed. "She said to me, 'There's no need to bother. I don't see the point.'"

So just how bright was Nikki Exner that she didn't need to work? Johnson's question brought about a matter-of-fact reply. "We're all bright here." There was no need to boast about it, Fournier was saying.

"But she wasn't outstanding, I gather."

Fournier shrugged. "She had her moments."

Johnson considered, then, "So what about after lectures?"

"I came up here. We normally met here, in the evening. Nikki showed up at about six. We had a couple of drinks, then she suggested we should go down to the library."

"Why?"

A simple question. Maybe it was the answer that was complex. Whatever the reason there was a long period of hesitation before Fournier said, "Nikki liked it in there. We used to go there a lot. She said she liked the quiet and the peace."

"But," pointed out Johnson, "the library closes at six."

"Bowman used to let her in."

"Ahh," said Johnson as if he hadn't already guessed most of this. "Peace and quiet in which to trade, then?"

Fournier didn't reply at once. He glanced quickly and sheepishly up at Johnson before nodding his head. Johnson frowned.

"Peace and quiet for something else as well?" he asked slowly, catching an undercurrent. Fournier was embarrassed and Johnson suddenly knew why. "You used to make love in there."

A nervous little laugh. "Yeah."

Johnson waited and watched Fournier. Then, "She got quite a thrill from it. We used to do it on the big table. Stripped naked. She loved lying on her back and staring up at the glass dome while I fucked her."

Bloody uncomfortable was Johnson's reaction.

"And Bowman? What about him? Where was he while you were doing this?"

"He'd make the deal and leave."

"Leaving you two alone? But what about getting out again?"

"The door to the Histopathology Department has a Yale lock. We used to go out that way, then out through the fire door."

Was he telling the truth? Johnson wasn't absolutely certain but he couldn't say definitely that these were lies.

"And that night? You went to the library, then what?"

He shrugged. "It was like usual. Bowman and Nikki haggled over some coke, but eventually agreed a price. Then he left."

"And you two . . . ?"

Fournier looked at him as if he were stupid, or naive.

"We did some coke. Then we shagged."

To Johnson, who still remembered shag tobacco and shag pile carpets, this particular slang term still struck off-key notes.

"When did you leave the library?"

"About ten, I guess."

"Just you? Or Nikki as well?"

"Together."

"Where was her car?"

"She'd parked it in the car park nearest the library. It was normally pretty empty at around that time."

"And you left in it?"

"That's right."

"And then what did you do?"

His face showed something. Disappointment, perhaps, or maybe guilt at a lie. "I went to the pub. Nikki went home to her flat."

"You didn't spend the night together? Was that usual?"

Within the space of two questions Fournier had clamped down. "Sometimes we did, sometimes we didn't." His voice was low as he tried to stop himself entering places he didn't want to revisit.

"But that night? You had expected to, I think."

Johnson could sense something and now he felt sufficient confidence to take a tentative step further. The young man had been answering Johnson's questions for long enough to allow some pressure to be applied. Some, but not too much: it was a thin and delicate line he used.

Fournier shrugged. "I guess."

"What did she say, Jamie? Why didn't she want to spend the night with you?"

Fournier was back there; almost as if Johnson no longer sat beside him and asked him questions. "She said she was tired."

"A lie?"

Fournier smiled a small smile. "Yeah. I knew her well enough by then to spot the lies."

So there was more than one. A whole storyboard of them, maybe.

"But you've no idea where she went or what she did?"

He shook his head.

"And you went to the pub with your mates?"

"Yeah."

Johnson got out a notebook. "Give me some names, Jamie," he suggested.

Returning in the evening Eisenmenger expected to find Marie in her usual post-domestic state – sullen, self-pitying and manipulative – but she had not been there. Was she on a late?

He looked in the main bedroom and discovered the chest of drawers and the wardrobe doors opened. It looked as if they had been burgled but he knew that wasn't the case. It was with relief that he checked and found all of Marie's clothes gone. Even when he had noticed half of his own clothes gone – subsequently finding them ripped to shreds in the spare bedroom – he didn't mind. It struck him as typically clichéd of her to have done such a thing.

Yet there was no note, no long diatribe of vindictive slander and self-justification, and for that he was grateful. In this one thing he felt that for the first time since he had known her, she had done something adult and ended it quickly.

He opened a can of beer and sat down to think through the rest of his life.

Irene Hamilton-Bailey stood in her husband's study for a long time, wondering. He had left the house some two hours before, the front door slamming in the wind so that she had looked up from her window to see him trudging slowly away from her through the cold, damp air. He had been heading for the Common, a place where he spent increasing amounts of time, huge doses of green solitude and melancholy, swimming in deep introspection.

Even two lives as tangential as theirs intersected sufficiently for Irene Hamilton-Bailey to appreciate that he was troubled, that his very soul seemed to be diseased. She had looked on over the past few weeks and seen her husband fade through fretting, a silent wasting that their mutual past prevented her from succouring.

Now, as she looked around her, she saw more symptoms of his malaise. The editorial papers for his beloved *Gray's Anatomy* lay uncared for, clearly shocked by their sudden fall from loving attention: some of them even appeared to be marked with coffee rings. His houseplants were dying from dehydration and he had left a half-eaten chicken sandwich on the mantelshelf, as if it had been placed there after an interruption and subsequently forgotten.

Only once before had she known him like this and then the cause had been easy to understand. Her brief but intense dalliance with Daniel Schlemm had caused poor Alexander such grief, she recalled. It had been the first of her affairs that he had known about, and it was therefore before their mutual understanding of the best way forward. The pain of realization that she demanded more than his inconstant attentions, and that she could and would take what she needed when she needed it, had been severe for him. Severe, too, had been the consequent recognition of his inferior status: he had no franchise because he had no money. His only currency had been social status for her, a quantity that was externally valueless but was at least desirable enough to keep her with him.

The problem now, however, was not so obvious.

She walked into his bedroom. The bed was unmade, the wardrobe open. Dirty clothes were piled on a chair. As she looked around she felt rising nausea at such slovenliness. She walked away from it, back into the study as if gone from sight would be gone from the world. And still she wondered why, unable even to guess

Unless . . .

She could date the change exactly, but she didn't want to. Not at all a woman to bury unpleasant facts, this one nasty suspicion she found herself hiding from. Surely not. Surely not Alexander . . .

"Irene? What are you doing in here?"

He made her start. If only he had made her start a few times earlier in their marriage.

"Oh! Alexander. You gave me a shock."

"What are you doing in here?" he repeated.

Trespass. She couldn't blame him for being aggressive. She had made the rules: breaking them was therefore a more serious crime for her. She tried a smile.

"I was worried about you."

"Were you?" The change was abrupt and startling. From irritation to uninterest in a single sentence. It was as if he had lost the strength to support his anger.

She found herself embarrassed; not a feeling she knew well. Looking around the room she saw the papers on the desk.

"How's the book going?"

His gaze followed hers, then slipped away. "Fine," he lied quietly. He didn't point out that she had never before shown interest in his academic workload. He came into the room and stood in front of the desk as if to hide the truth. He looked awful, she thought. Never the most rugged or handsome of men, now the air of dissolution and neglect only added to his intrinsic, diminutive shabbiness. When had he last shaved? She knew that he hadn't been into work for some while now.

"Alexander," she began spontaneously. "What's wrong? Why are you like this?"

She didn't know what would be worse – that he might be like this because of her latest liaison (in the banking world, kept a flat in Mayfair, kept a wife in ignorance), or because of something far, far darker. And surely it couldn't be her little affair? Surely he was used to it all by now.

"There's nothing wrong."

"Yes, there is. Look at yourself. You're in a terrible state. You haven't been to work for days, you've stopped taking proper care of yourself. You're behaving like a condemned man."

He looked again around the room as if this was all news to him.

"Something's terribly wrong, Alexander. Please tell me."

She took a small step towards him and this brought his eyes around in slight alarm. It was as if she were threatening him rather than trying to offer him support.

"Is it . . . that dreadful murder?"

There. She had said it now. The demon was named and therefore possibly incarnated. Now she could only wait and hope that it would not do dreadful damage.

He opened his mouth, his eyes not leaving her face. She could sense a struggle within him but she dared not do or say anything more. At last his mouth closed again, then his eyes. He stood there for a moment, as if dreaming of his childhood. The words when they came hardly moved his lips and there was an impression of a medium's fakery as, his eyes still closed, he said, "Something awful happened, Irene. Something horrible."

Johnson had spent so many years working on enquiries such as this that he had no longer to analyse why he did what he did. He did not therefore need to consider why he spent a whole day in the students' coffee room, this time deliberately not keeping himself aloof but speaking to as many students as he could. He did not at conscious level have to formulate specific questions – *How well did you know Nikki Exner? Did you ever hear anything bad about her? How well did she do in her exams?* – because these sprang from the same autonomic source as his basic strategy. Get to know Nikki Exner and since, by definition, he could not meet her bodily, he had to meet her virtual self that existed within the minds of those who had known her.

He wanted to construct a model of Nikki Exner because he knew that it was only through this that they would have a chance of finding her killer. She had been murdered in a curious, ritualistic way; a way that had meaning certainly for her killer, almost certainly for her. Find Nikki, find the reason for her death and the reason for her mode of death, find the killer.

He began with the medical school and the Bursar's office but when he explained his mission (he thought it unwise to attempt a deception) their attitude changed. It was subtle but it was real. Polite smiles from Berry but no, he would not be allowed to see her academic records. Nor would he be welcome to conduct further interviews with the academic staff in connection with the late Miss Exner. The case was closed and there was no point in any such enquiry.

He sought to vault the Bursar and tried to contact the Dean but, strangely perhaps, the Dean was unavailable and the Dean's secretary told him coldly that the Bursar was entirely correct in refusing Johnson permission to see confidential records or to interview members of staff. When he left the office he felt chilled to the bone and slightly bruised as if he had hit a solid metal door.

He contemplated ignoring the command and going to talk to the relevant staff anyway, but decided against this: Helena, he felt sure, would not condone such a course. This left him with the student body, where at least he might peer beneath the official picture and see a different side to Nikki Exner. He had thus returned to the coffee room.

It was exhausting and he was forced to consume innumerable plastic beakers of their brown, opaque beverage (he first tried the tea, then decided that it was worse even than the coffee), and it was slow. God, it was slow.

And largely fruitless.

Most of them knew the name (of course) and a lot of them had known her in life, but only vaguely, only as a pixel in the background (or so they told him). Very few of them had anything to add that was of consequence. There had been occasional rumours of drugs, but none had attached specifically to a name, certainly not to Nikki Exner.

And then there were the ex-lovers. A not insubstantial cohort of athletic, good-looking young men who recalled the late Miss Exner with varying degrees of fondness, although all of them either implied or directly expressed a feeling of calculation and coldness about her. Over half of them had been dumped without ceremony, without apparent feeling.

Moreover not one of them knew anything of drug abuse. An observation that made Johnson smile the smallest of smiles.

It was near the end of this labour, this endless rifle through denial, ignorance feigned and real, and fading interest, that a name was mentioned that made his instincts twitch out of their wearied slumber. It was mentioned by an attractive blonde who had been in the same year as the dead girl and who had perhaps been a rival to her: whatever the reason she had little of pleasantness to say about Miss Exner.

"She was a cold-hearted cow. Took up with someone, used them, squeezed them dry and then moved on. The poor bastards still queued up, though. Still kept flocking around her pussy like flies around dogshit."

This was too vitriolic for Johnson. He mentally downgraded the value of the information, seeing it as tainted and thereby unreliable.

Did she use drugs?

"It wouldn't have surprised me. Certainly she looked fairly wasted most of the time. Not that she attended lectures much, so I didn't see her about a lot, except in the evenings in the bar or the pub."

Johnson took that as a 'Don't know.' He asked a few more questions, not expecting much and not receiving much. Then, as he was about to leave she said, "If you want to know how much of a bitch she really was, ask James Paneth."

Who, he enquired, was James Paneth?

"Used to be a medical student. Got chucked out or decided to leave; nobody ever discovered which. Whatever it was, Nikki Exner was involved in it. That much I do know."

Where might he find this gentleman?

She shrugged. She didn't know and she didn't give a proverbial.

The pharmacy was subterranean and cramped and it smelt. Johnson couldn't quite place the smell; there seemed to be traces of disinfectant, damp and something that seemed to him to be sweet and sickly. It had been extremely hard to find, not helped by signs that were presumably placed to help the patients find their way but that were actually confusing and contradictory in their directions.

In the end it had been the head porter of the medical school who had been able to tell him where James Paneth had gone. This man sat at a desk and commanded the portering staff, thereby commanding great power. Clearly he knew this, for his attitude was laced with regal disdain. He viewed Johnson with some suspicion until Johnson passed two ten-pound notes across the dented wooden surface of the desk.

"I got him a job at the women's hospital down the road. Pharmacy porter. They owed me a favour."

Johnson thanked him humbly and departed, wondering but not asking what the original favour had been.

In front of a crowd of those who were obviously patients admixed with those who were less obviously cursed by illness he had asked to see James Paneth. The middle-aged woman of whom he had asked this had peered out at him from behind a counter, emanating suspicion, discontent, menstrual problems and sheer, constitutional grumpiness. It struck him as curiously fitting, given that this was a women's hospital.

"Who are you?"

"I'm investigating an incident at St Benjamin's. We believe that Mr Paneth may have some information of value to us."

She had raised her eyebrows but thankfully had not asked to see identification.

He had been ushered through to the pharmacy itself, a place which the patients were not privileged ever to view, and he had become at once disorientated, confused by the numerous bays – each identical, each lined by white shelves, all of which were covered with boxes, bottles and small tubs – the nooks, the doors, and the very brightness of the place.

His quarry was unpacking cardboard crates, checking their contents against a stock note. He was a tall, thin young man in his early twenties perhaps, not unhandsome but spoiled by a sour expression. The ghost of acne lurked around his cheeks. Johnson's guide grunted and left them.

"James Paneth?"

He had looked up but his eyes didn't find Johnson's face for more than a second before dropping again. It gave him a shifty look.

"Who are you?"

"I'm looking into the death of Nikki Exner."

A frown. "I thought you'd got someone for that."

He returned to his work. Johnson sighed. "I'm just filling in a bit of background. Trying to iron out a few inconsistencies. I want to talk to those people who knew her best."

Abruptly Paneth laughed. "So you've come to me!"

"Is there something funny?"

With symmetrical abruptness he stopped laughing. He looked again into Johnson's eyes, this time for longer, and Johnson noticed a squint.

"No. It's not funny at all."

Johnson looked around, found a box that contained tubes of haemorrhoid cream and sat down.

"You were a medical student, weren't you?"

"A long time ago."

"You knew Nikki Exner?"

Paneth shrugged.

"How well?"

"Too well."

Johnson wanted to go to the toilet. He was hungry and he had a slight headache.

"Look, Mr Paneth. You may find Raymond Chandler a model worth following in everyday life, but I've got a job to do and a limited amount of patience. Do you think you could drop the world-weary cynicism and oblique references and just tell me what I need to know?"

Paneth was back at his unpacking. For a second there was silence then he stopped, stood up straight and turned to Johnson. "Six months ago I was looking at a career in medicine with everything going my way: now I'm looking at a shitty job as a fucking pharmacist. Added to that, I've got an incurable disease and I've got big family troubles. I think I've got some justification for world-weary cynicism, don't you?"

They stared at each other for a moment. Johnson wanted to ask him about his 'incurable disease' but before he could speak, Paneth sighed and said, "I was a first-year medical student, so was she. I hardly knew her, except that everyone but everyone knew Nikki Exner because she was fucking fantastic to look at and, it was said, she was great in the sack."

Johnson considered this. "People I've talked to say that something happened between you and her, that she got you thrown out."

Paneth snorted and gestured at the shelves and their boxes. "I don't do this for the pay, you know."

"So tell me."

But it was plain that it wasn't that easy. Paneth was still reluctant.

"This is a murder enquiry, remember." Johnson hated himself for that but it worked.

Paneth considered, then relented. He said slowly, "It began with a microbiology practical. They were usually a bit of a dead loss and

194

a lot of people didn't bother turning up. I was certainly surprised to see Nikki Exner there – she hardly bothered with lectures, let alone the poxy practicals – but there she was. We were put into pairs and I found myself with her. I couldn't believe my luck . . . "

He paused, then with a wry smile he said, "Still can't, I guess."

"So what happened?"

"The practical was to do with serology. We were supposed to test each other for Hepatitis B and HIV using an ELISA kit."

Johnson let the jargon wing its way past him without comment.

"I did her, she did me. Took blood then tested it. Easy as piss. Except . . . mine was positive."

Johnson, who was writing this down, looked up and asked, "You had hepatitis?"

"HIV. AIDS." *Blunt. No other way to be.*

Johnson continued to stare, his face trying to convey sympathy. Only when Paneth looked directly at him did he say, "I'm sorry," and continued writing.

"Why should you be? It's not your fault: trouble is, it's not mine either. I'm haemophiliac. A few years ago it was an occupational risk."

There was an awkward silence into which the young man whispered, "I hadn't even thought, you see. The Factor 8's supposed to be clean now. Not like in the early days when you didn't know if the next injection was going to be the one that started the clock ticking."

Johnson waited a second before trying to steer him back. "What did you do?"

"Repeated it, of course. Then, when it wouldn't stop being positive, begged Nikki to say nothing. To let me think about what to do."

"You didn't tell anyone?"

Paneth looked at him as if he were being stupid. Perhaps, he conceded, he was.

"And end my medical career after five months? Nobody likes doctors with AIDS, you know."

Johnson wondered about the ethics but it wasn't the time to enter intellectual debate.

"And?"

"And . . . I made a stupid decision. I decided not to tell anyone. I made a few enquiries and reckoned that as long as I stayed out of the surgical specialities, it was nobody's business but my own. I told Nikki as much. Made her promise not to tell anyone. She agreed."

Apparently, then, no problem. Except that Johnson knew that there had been: he just didn't know what it had been. Several people had told him that *something* had happened, that it had involved James Paneth and Nikki Exner, and that it hadn't been good, but nobody knew quite what it was. Or, at least, they weren't going to tell him.

"Then, about four or five weeks later, she suggested that we should go out together." He paused and remembered and, even though he seemed to hate her, he smiled slightly at what he saw in his mind. Johnson again wondered just how beautiful and captivating Nikki Exner must have been.

"I thought it was fantastic. I thought that she had been misjudged because here she was befriending me despite the fact that she knew I was HIV positive."

"It wasn't quite like that, I take it."

He looked across at Johnson, his eyes large, his mouth sour. "I'd misjudged her all right. Completely underestimated how much of a piece of human excrement she was."

Johnson said nothing.

"We just went out for a pizza. She was charming and I thought life at last was getting better. I'd been fairly depressed. The sudden realization that I had HIV had completely blown me apart, and I wasn't having much luck trying to come to terms with it. She was great and I felt special." He paused, brooding. "We didn't go to bed of course, but it was still one of the best nights of my life. Then, about a week later, we went out again. Only this time, after we'd had a few drinks and I was starting to think that my life wasn't at an end, she sprang it on me."

"What did she spring on you?"

"She suggested that since my family is well off and since we got on so well, I might care to give her some money."

"Just that? Just a suggestion?"

"Not for long. I was surprised by the idea and I thought it was an odd thing to say. I felt as if suddenly things had changed. She was still smiling but now there was something underneath the expression. Her eyes were no longer quite so inviting either.

"Anyway, I asked her what she meant and she basically said that she wanted money to keep quiet about my HIV status. She pointed out that since I had said nothing about it to the medical school authorities, it would look bad for me."

Johnson could hear a tremor in his voice. "What did you do?" he asked.

"I said I'd have to think about it. The evening was at an end in more ways than one and we said our goodbyes. I spent that night and most of the next day wondering what I should do."

"What did you decide?"

James Paneth suddenly started to weep. His face remained set but there were small tears rolling down his face. It was a moment before he could speak. "I'm here, aren't I?" His face distorted into a sneer. "*Pharmacy technician*. With a bit of luck I'll get a place to read pharmacy at university somewhere. Won't get another place to read medicine, can't do dentistry if you're HIV positive. Too dumb to be a vet. Not a lot else, really. In the meantime I managed to get this job to fill in the time."

"Did you tell anyone what Nikki Exner had tried to do?"

The laugh was short and bitter. "Where was my proof? It would have been ten times worse if I'd tried to implicate Nikki Exner in a blackmail plot. She'd have denied it for sure."

Johnson felt as if he was in a condemned cell. Paneth seemed to embody despair and loneliness, and he could offer no succour at all. Indeed, the only thing that he could offer was suspicion.

"Where were you on the night of the murder?" he asked. Paneth's face showed a journey through emotions – incredulity, anger, contempt, then acceptance. He said at last with a sigh, "I was working. Overtime on the night shift as a general porter. You can check it easily enough."

It was with awkwardness and a sense of embarrassment that Johnson stood and said his thank-yous. Paneth got out a handkerchief and cleared his nose. Then he looked up and said, "And I've still got HIV."

Johnson departed, feeling as if he was leaving a morgue. Before he left the hospital he checked with the head porter. James Paneth had indeed been on duty for the whole of the night in question.

Eisenmenger had never been there before and he could not understand why. Was it fear, but if so, of what? Fear of ghosts or fear of himself? Who was the more terrifying?

Yet he knew where it was. He had made a point of knowing, had taken that information around with him for years now. A form of tenuous contact with the past.

With the dead who still lived in his head.

A small cemetery in the west of the city, bordered by terraced houses on three sides, a hospital on the fourth. There was a tiny chapel in its centre, stone and brick, alive with cobwebs like decayed spirits.

Most of the graves were well tended, some with flowers – fresh or browned with age – most without. He had had to search for three-quarters of an hour before finding the one he wanted.

An old man, apparently dementing, had been there, sitting on a bench by the wide gravel path with its whitewashed kerb. Food crusted on his lapels and in his beard, while his shirt cuffs had been frayed white as if bleached. He had shaken and dribbled, but what struck Eisenmenger as he had passed was that he had been happy. Happy to mumble to himself, happy to shake, happy to live in the world, even if it wasn't the world that Eisenmenger inhabited, for he continually laughed gently to himself. A gentle, happy sound of satisfaction.

So struck by this had he been that Eisenmenger had stopped just past him, as the dusk drew in and the greyness of the sky came ever lower, and looked back at him. And as he had looked, he had found himself growing increasingly depressed, closer and closer to tears.

Abruptly he had turned and continued his search, leaving the old man, who had never once acknowledged him, to his thoughts and his soft laughter. Only when, in a dark, overgrown corner, he had found the grave he was looking for, did he think again of the old man.

His depression had not been for the dement, but for himself, left behind in this world, left behind without the gentle laughter.

There had been no one to tend Tamsin's grave, no one to remember as they walked past. It was a small grave and he had thought then that no grave should be small. The grass had been cut but only roughly, and the small marker stone was chipped and knocked out of true as if kicked. No flowers were there, nor probably ever had been. It was as if the world colluded with her terrible death.

Eisenmenger had stood in the darkness for a long time, aware that it was cold, aware that it was late, aware too of the faint sound of the old man's mumbled laughter in the distance. He had stood at the foot of her resting-place and cried dried tears while listening for the sound of her voice, wondering if he was doing the right thing.

When at last he had walked away, past the old man who still sat and mumbled happily while he shook, he had still not been sure.

Sally looked at the spike where bills for payment were kept. It wasn't any fuller than usual but she kept thinking every time it caught her attention that it soon would be. They hadn't spoken of Bob's future since the night of their wedding anniversary and in that time and in that silence, her fears had grown. Her father had been a clerk in the deep, dark bowels of a multinational, a small parasitic protozoon symbiotically eking out its existence within the relatively safe confines of a higher organism. He had been perpetually poor, forever teetering on the edge of fiscal cataclysm, and this had embedded deeply within her a need to remain financially secure.

It had taken a long time to accumulate an even half-way decent store of savings. Not only had Bob contributed, but she, too, had worked, quite willingly, long and hard hours as a nurse.

Long enough and hard enough to threaten her health.

And Bob was threatening to waste it on some pipedream, some wish-fulfilment.

She felt an itch in her palm and idly she began to scratch it.

"Where the hell is he?"

As if Johnson knew the answer, but apparently he was to blame for recommending Eisenmenger. Clearly Helena foresaw disaster and perhaps she thought it time to search out the culpable.

"He'll be here," he assured her with certainty that came from hope alone.

"He's already half an hour late."

They were in the cramped mortuary office, a box of varnished wood and untidiness, the frosted windows deep blue with the night, giving the impression that out there was the limit of known space.

"He'll be here."

She looked doubtful but didn't comment. Johnson again noticed in her a driven quality, this time manifesting as touchiness and a constant fidget. He himself tried to remain still, although in truth he was starting himself to wonder where on earth Eisenmenger was.

Outside the office there was a long, dark corridor, narrow and high, and lit only by underpowered light bulbs housed in suspended spherical shades that were milky white. This led to changing rooms on the left, the dissection room on the right. In the dissection room there had gathered a crowd of disparate individuals, occupying their waiting by some desultory conversation that was invariably whispered and exchanged without eye contact.

Sydenham was there, already attired in shirtsleeves, white wellington boots and an inadequate green plastic apron. He had his arms folded and occasionally he sighed loudly and looked pointedly at the wall clock opposite to indicate his irritation. So, too, was the mortuary technician, Clive, who leaned against the wall and watched from the corner of his eye the trim figure of Beverley

Wharton. Turned away and apparently deep in discussion with Wilson, she may have been able to see this openly lascivious attention or she may not, but she knew Clive well, knew his mind, perhaps even liked to guess what he might be doing in his imagination. The only concession she had made to health and safety was to don a pair of blue disposable overshoes, making Wilson do likewise. The last person was a short, rotund individual who had entered in a blazer, white shirt, striped tie and pale grey slacks: this rather suave and quite astonishingly smart attire had given the impression of someone promenading on the poop deck, an illusion that was strengthened yet further by the camera around his neck. Difficult though it had been to envisage, he now looked even more ridiculous because he had put on a voluminous green overgown and overshoes.

"Who's the friggin' dandy?"

Wilson was incapable of subtlety and his whisper found no hiding place amongst the harsh surfaces and sharp angles of the dissection room. Wharton winced, flashed a look of intense irritation and said in a tone barely above breathing, "He's a photographer, stupid. Hired by their lawyer."

She pronounced the last word with some venom. Her meeting with the defence team had been something of a shock. It was bad enough that it should be led by an attractive woman (something that Beverley Wharton always took as an insult), worse still that she should turn out to be the stepsister of Jeremy Eaton-Lambert and clearly possessed of little love for Beverley Wharton, but for Johnson to be there as well was beyond credulity. Clearly he had enjoyed her consternation and her discomfiture, had taken particular pleasure in deepening the wound by enquiring, "Lost any more suspects, Beverley?" His use of her first name signalled that he now considered himself her equal.

But that wasn't the only signal she was being sent and nor was it the most significant. Their presence alone told her that this was no formality, that the body of Nikki Exner and the questioning of Bilroth's guilt were the pretexts only. The real issue was Beverley Wharton.

"I really can't hang around much longer, you know." Sydenham's voice was full of tired irritation, drawled into a dying fall. Since no one knew what time Eisenmenger was going to arrive, and since no one could do anything to alter it, no one replied and they did so with thundering indifference.

Sydenham returned to his repetitive behaviour pattern with a snort of contempt. The photographer glanced nervously about him and silently wondered if this was worth fifty pounds, while the mortuary technician sharpened a brain knife.

The buzzer sounded and there was a palpable leavening of the atmosphere. Sydenham looked up and said loudly, "About time," while Wharton straightened herself, checked the time and sighed. The photographer began to fiddle nervously with his lens, much as a conjuror might check his props before entering stage right.

Clive went out of the dissection room, past the office and opened the small side door. Eisenmenger came in with barely any acknowledgement of Clive's greeting. His entry to the office was greeted by Helena with the words "At last," uttered in an amalgam of relief and irritation. Johnson said nothing.

"We'd better get started." Eisenmenger's voice was tired and he sounded as if he really didn't want to be there.

Helena was aghast. "Is that it?" she demanded. "Don't we get an explanation?"

"What do you mean?" Eisenmenger didn't seem to grasp what she was talking about.

"You're nearly forty minutes late! Where have you been?"

This appeared to come as news. His abrupt look at the clock (an ornate affair that had been appropriated from an hotel) was the first sign of real animation he had shown, yet his reply when it came was in a manner that Marie would have found only too familiar.

"I had someone to visit."

"What does that mean?" demanded Helena but Johnson recognized the signs. He said, "Perhaps we should get started," and got up.

They trooped along the corridor in single file, a curiously motley line. Their arrival in the dissection room provoked a similar mix of reactions with Wharton turning a mask of indifference towards them, Sydenham making curious huffing noises and the photographer breaking into a wide smile much as General Gordon must once have done at Mafeking. While Eisenmenger got changed, the two opposing groups separated like hostile tribes meeting on common holy ground, and Clive wheeled a trolley, on which was a white body bag, into the dissection room. Everyone watched as he single-handedly pulled it across on to one of the six stainless steel dissection tables.

Eisenmenger emerged in theatre-style blues and white clogs. He had been in the mortuary many times before and knew its layout well: he knew Clive well also. He went straight to the large plastic box where the gowns were kept and wrapped one around himself. Then he took a thick heavy apron off a hook and put on first one pair of plastic gloves then, over these, a second pair.

Once he had finished, he seemed to change, to relax. For a minute he just waited in the corner alcove where the gloves were kept, looking around the mortuary out of sight of the others, as if reliving memories. Then he caught Clive's eye and beckoned him over.

"I'm sorry, Clive. Stagefright, I guess."

"No problem. Guessed as much." Clive was a man of small vocabulary, a lexicon in which he dispensed with words that others considered useful but he, it seemed, despised.

"Fifty okay?"

"Fine."

It was essential to keep Clive onside: an autopsy conducted with an unhelpful technician was worse than doing one alone since he might give him blunt knives and scissors that wouldn't cut, and he might happen not to be around when he was needed to weigh viscera or hold skinflaps and the like.

"Did you help at the first post-mortem?"

Clive smiled. "Stingy bastard only gave twenty."

A small victory but an important one.

"What kind of PM did he do, Clive? How long did it last?"

Clive's face took on the expression of a connoisseur. "Ninety minutes," he said. "Ninety minutes and crap."

Eisenmenger had suspected as much but it was good to get confirmation. The background now sketched, he felt it was time to start on the main subject. He advanced into the dissection room and nodded a greeting to Sydenham who said, "Evening, John. This isn't going to take long, is it?"

His tone was ambiguous, falling between a plea and a command and consequently possessing the force of neither.

Eisenmenger shrugged. "Only as long as it needs, Charles. Only as long as it needs."

He turned to Johnson. "Bob, would you mind taking notes?" Then to the photographer, who was following him with his head and eyes much as a spaniel might, "Thanks for coming, Anthony. Two copies of everything, and include measuring strips where appropriate."

He barely looked at Wharton.

He nodded to Clive who undid the body bag, pausing only once when the zip snagged. Inside was Nikki Exner.

An autopsy is the examination of the body after death, conducted to discover usually the medical cause of death, occasionally, if that is known and the relatives consent, to investigate the effect of treatment on incurable disease or some other aspect of the patient's medical condition that might prove of benefit to future sufferers. The second autopsy, however, is an entirely different affair. In this case, the death was suspicious and the first autopsy would have been performed by a forensic pathologist approved by the Home Office. A person or persons will have been charged with in some way causing the death and the second autopsy is performed at the behest of defence council: it is, in effect, a chance for a second and independent examination in order to ensure that nothing has been missed and that the interpretation of the findings is correct. It is as much an examination of the first post-mortem as of the body.

Nikki Exner had been frozen following her first autopsy and, now that she was thawed there was the usual curious discoloration of the flesh, like livid streaks, but, like the violent manner of her death, it had done little to diminish the lustre of her beauty. Even now, pale and waxen, marked by huge cuts that had been sutured with beige strings, it was easy to see that her figure had been wonderfully proportioned, while her features had been appealing – coquettish, almost – with lips that were full and red and undoubtedly inviting.

Eisenmenger checked the two name tags, one on her little finger, the other on her big toe, to ensure the correct identity and told Johnson to note that he had done so. Clive told him her height and weight, which Johnson noted, and Eisenmenger settled down to start a detailed examination of her external appearance, Sydenham at his side making a constant critique. At Eisenmenger's direction, Anthony began taking full body shots from every angle. Then Eisenmenger took samples of hair and scrapings from under the fingernails, two of each: one was put into formalin, the other into a sterile container. Both were labelled meticulously by Clive under Eisenmenger's direction.

The most striking abnormalities were the rough, cruciform incisions that ran from pubis to throat and left to right under the ribs. Clive had sutured them neatly enough but this had only served to accentuate their slightly jagged, serpentine course. Clearly Sydenham had felt no need to make further cuts and Eisenmenger remarked on this.

"I thought she'd been desecrated enough, old boy. Didn't see the need to reproduce the Tube map by making more."

Eisenmenger didn't say what he thought of this, but instead told Anthony to photograph them, then asked Clive to roll the body over completely so that the back lay brightly lit.

"Nothing there," concluded Sydenham, as if saying it would make it so. Eisenmenger maybe didn't catch his words, for he began to peer at her back closely, bringing the movable spotlight down close. He spotted three faint bruises that were duly photographed with measuring strips alongside.

"So which of those do you think was the fatal blow?" enquired Sydenham, overcome with wit. He was ignored as Eisenmenger moved down to the anus. He pulled the buttocks apart and paused, then looked up.

"What do you make of these, Charles?"

Sydenham moved forward and Wharton too was suddenly interested. There had been nothing in the original report about the anus.

"Where?"

"There, at three o'clock. I think it's a tear, and there appears to be some bruising and some abrasion." He looked up at Johnson. "Make a note of that."

Sydenham scoffed. "I saw those marks. They're nothing. Everyone's allowed the odd anal tear, my dear chap. It doesn't necessarily mean that they've been buggered, you know. Anyway, it explains why she was constipated."

Eisenmenger looked up. "Really?" Wharton noticed this and was at once attentive.

"Oh, yes." Sydenham frowned at him. "Even the young are allowed to get constipated, you know," he pointed out, "especially if she got searing pains in the backside every time she did number twos."

Or perhaps she was constipated because of opiate abuse.

Eisenmenger smiled at Sydenham, and nodded, and murmured, "Absolutely, Charles." Nevertheless he asked for the anus to be photographed and he cut out two ellipses of skin from the area of the tear telling Clive, "Just label them 'Anus'."

There were no other marks on her back: when she was turned over there was some ill-defined bruising on her shins and there were two puncture marks in her left forearm, none of which Sydenham had felt worth commenting on, all of which Eisenmenger described, had photographed, and cut samples from.

Yet it was Nikki Exner's nose that interested Eisenmenger the most.

"The septum's ulcerated," he decided after peering at it for long minutes.

Sydenham, who had again been exhibiting signs of over-exaggerated exasperation, took this announcement with a sigh of patronizing disbelief. Even when he had spent thirty, maybe even forty, seconds examining her nose, he could manage only, "It's a bit red, but I wouldn't go farther than that. Anyway, she must be the first person ever to die of a snotty nose if you think that it's important."

Yet Eisenmenger quite clearly heard Wharton mutter the word, "Shit," as he told Johnson to note what he had found and told Anthony, as best as he could, to photograph it. Again he took samples.

Having completed his external examination, he then asked Clive to open the body, using the longitudinal incision. It was at this point that he began to lose his audience.

Clive was a good technician, taking pride in what was necessarily a difficult, under-regarded job. The mortuary fabric was aged and decaying – it desperately needed several hundred thousand spent on it – but he kept everything clean and tidy, the knives were always exquisitely sharp and the paperwork was always up to date. Likewise with his stitching. When Clive reconstructed a head after a shotgun had exploded it or an articulated lorry had squashed it, the result was usually viewable by the relatives. Similarly, when he stitched a body after post-mortem, it was done so as to ensure that no body fluid could possibly leak from it. Yet this meant that its reversal entailed much snipping and tugging, pulling the coarse twine through the flesh with small gobbets of red meat, like minced pork, hanging off it. The body often twitched and jerked, occasionally even writhed, as he did this, so that it performed an intermittent dance: not one that was in any way lifelike, but it was all the more disturbing for that.

And this was not the worst, for when the stitching had finally been unpicked, there was exhibited the enormous abomination that is an eviscerated corpse.

When opened, the pristine body shows the economy and preci-sion of God's plan in the intricate way that the organs are packed together, the varying shapes and hues contrasting to create some-thing that may not (except by Goodpasture) be described as beauti-ful, but that can at least be admired and appreciated. It may have lost its function but it has yet to lose its form.

That is the pristine body, however; the body that has yet to feel the hand of man. The body that is to undergo its second post-mortem examination has lost both function and form. The plan has been despoiled, each organ not only removed but also hacked so that no secret should escape. And then, when finished, there is no attempt to recreate that which has been defiled, for such would be a wasted, vain excursion. Instead, the organs that God and a multi-million-year trawl of evolution have made are piled together and slopped first into stainless steel bowls, thence into a yellow plastic sack, then into the body cavity.

It was this bag that Clive now pulled from Nikki Exner, knotted but the contents clearly visible as it passed in front of the spotlight so that red liquid and irregular shapes were silhouetted.

Wilson was the first to protest, a near-silent affair that merely involved a grunt as of despondency, a swift look at Wharton with soulful eyes from a pallid face and a quasi-dignified walk-cum-dash for the door. Eisenmenger looked up at the noise, found Helena's eyes that were large and bright, and smiled. She smiled back but it was the kind of expression a mouse might thrust forward when it entered a cattery. On the other side of the room, Wharton leaned against the wall and tried to look bored but she was watching everything he did and there was a hint of worry about her mouth.

Clive put the heavy bag into a steel bowl and, at Eisenmenger's request, sponged the surplus blood out of the cavity so that it could be inspected. Then, while Eisenmenger was directing Anthony to photograph the cavity and was giving Johnson some brief notes on its description, he carried the bowl over to the dissection bench. Eisenmenger also unpicked slightly the transverse cut, the one forming the horizontal part of the cross. From the edge of both incisions he took samples. Then he turned away from the body.

From now on his back was to both Helena and Wharton, but neither of them made a move to come closer. Sydenham, now that the external examination was over, had also lost interest, a phenomenon that Eisenmenger noted with some amusement. It was typical of a forensic pathologist that the internal organs – to the average pathologist these formed ninety-five per cent of the examination – should be of so little importance.

Nor could it be said that his ennui was because he knew the corpse of Nikki Exner too well, for the first autopsy examination appeared to have been cursory in the extreme. The brain, extracted by Clive with no little effort and dexterity, and having first been constructed by God with unsurpassing skill, incomprehensible knowledge and wondrous love of humankind, had not been dissected, it had been hacked; quartered like a grey, set yoghurt, and then discarded. The liver, not nearly as intricate but still weighing fifteen hundred grams, measuring perhaps thirty-five centimetres across and simultaneously capable of scores of metabolic and homeostatic functions, had been slashed. Once. The kidneys had been partially incised, no more; the lungs similarly treated. The heart, a double pump comprising four chambers, four valves, an intricate circulatory supply and a microscopic electrical conduction system, had been, it seemed at first sight, given to a large Rottweiler to chew.

Eisenmenger spent fully thirty minutes carefully reconstructing and then, once their parts had been more or less put properly together in their correct relation, dissecting these organs, not letting his contempt for Sydenham's slapdash technique show too much. In particular, he did not betray any surprise when he quartered the uterus (Sydenham had only halved it) and discovered two fibroids previously hidden: one of these was nearly two centimetres across, the other only a centimetre.

From all the organs he took samples, one fresh, one in formalin.

At last he had finished and Sydenham, who had spent the time making odd expiratory noises and once even humming in what was clearly meant to be a pointed and bored manner, moved over at once.

"All done?" he asked brightly. "I didn't expect you to find much, but still . . . " he lowered his voice at this point and adopted a tone of conspiratorial camaraderie, "second autopsies so rarely do. Complete waste of time if you ask me. Still, I don't suppose you'll complain about the fee."

Eisenmenger felt suddenly tired, but not of work. He said, "I haven't quite finished yet, Charles."

To Clive he said, "Put the block under her back. I want to take a good look at her neck and face."

Sydenham's reaction was an incredulous "Well, really!" He looked across at Wharton and shrugged as if to express his powerlessness in the face of such obstinate stupidity.

There had been a shaped rubber block supporting the head and neck. Clive now put his gloved hand behind the neck and, with muscles that Eisenmenger for one did not think he himself possessed, pushed the body up so that it bent forward at the hips and the whole of the back was off the table. The block he now placed about half-way along the thoracic spine so that, when he gently lowered the body back down, the head was back and the neck was exposed and extended.

Eisenmenger took the scalpel and made an incision from side to side across the clavicles. He ignored Sydenham as he heard him mutter, "Metropolitan or Victoria?"

He didn't announce what he was about to do, but he did glance up at Helena who was frowning slightly and, he thought, looked pale. She was also breathing rather rapidly.

Then he began.

Working slowly and carefully with scalpel and forceps, he began to peel away the skin from first the neck, then the chin, then the face.

To the experienced eye it is a remarkable demonstration, exhibiting the complex musculature of the neck and face, the superficial vasculature that supplies it, and the way that it shapes the mouth, nose and lips. It is anatomy made incarnate.

To the initiate, however, it is scientific flaying, nothing less. It is barbarized investigation, seemingly inexplicable in terms of its purpose and therefore unnecessary and therefore unforgivable. Sydenham's attitude – constant muttering about the requirement for such a procedure, with continual appeals to the gallery – hardly helped. The reaction of those present was varied but on the whole negative. Only Clive – who had seen this done a hundred times before and did not consider it his job to question what the pathologist did – and Johnson were seemingly unaffected. Johnson took notes, though, with even greater concentration than he had heretofore shown. Anthony, perspiring freely and wearing a look of bewilderment, was kept busy taking numerous photographs as Eisenmenger worked, but it was clear that the remuneration now seemed somewhat inadequate. Wharton had turned away slightly and was looking at her black patent leather shoes, her arms folded tightly across her midriff. Helena, however, made the mistake of watching quite closely what Eisenmenger was doing and her expression as he carefully peeled back the skin from the neck, then from under the jaw and then, the grotesqueness climbing ever higher, from the lower jaw, grew ever more filled with an amalgam of nausea, horror and shock.

It was just as he asked Clive to help him by holding the dissected skin as it lay folded up over the eyes, the lipless grin of muscles and teeth exposed, that he happened to look up and saw Helena. She was grey and was swaying slightly but perceptibly. Within the space of perhaps a second he saw her face lose comprehension and the swaying grew in amplitude.

"Bob," he said, nodding at Helena. Johnson put down the notebook and hurried over to her just as she began to lose it completely. He took her shoulders, turned her round and steered her from the room. Eisenmenger was looking at them, but then his eyes caught Wharton's look of amusement. He turned back to the corpse.

When the face had been totally removed, he examined the tissues beneath minutely but it was the neck that arrested his attention. He spent perhaps fifteen minutes on his examination of the ligature mark, having it photographed from every side, taking samples from several points both along it and, to Johnson's surprise, both above and below it. Several times he laid the skin back over it, then lifted it.

At long last he straightened his back, stood back and nodded at Clive.

"Thanks."

He peeled off his gloves and turned to Sydenham who suddenly looked like a dog whose master had unexpectedly returned.

"All done then?"

"I think so."

Sydenham looked at his watch. "Three and a half hours. Certainly earned your money there."

Eisenmenger smiled. "I think that perhaps I did, Charles. I think, perhaps I did."

He rather enjoyed the look of concern not only on Sydenham's face, but also on Wharton's.

After the post-mortem, Eisenmenger showered and changed. By the time he emerged Wharton and Wilson had gone (according to Clive neither had looked particularly happy, although probably for different reasons) and Sydenham was just going. It was obviously only supreme self-confidence that kept his voice loud and his optimism to the fore.

"Bye, Johnny. Good to see you again. Perhaps you should think about taking the job up again."

The door thumped shut behind him. Eisenmenger fished his wallet from his pocket and found five ten-pound notes. "What do you think, Clive? Should I?" he asked as he gave him the money.

Clive's expression was indistinguishable from innocence. "I suppose it'd be good to work with a half-way decent pathologist again."

Johnson and Helena were in the office. Johnson looked tired and was fidgeting: Helena excited, charged almost. "What did you find?" Her eagerness contrasted strikingly with her normal detachment but Eisenmenger was tired and it was not his way to build hypotheses from fresh assumptions and newly found data, not without considerable thought.

"I'd rather not say. Not yet."

Clear disappointment and irritation formed her features. "What do you mean?" she demanded.

"I want to think about what I found. Try to work out how it all fits together, and how it affects what we had previously known or surmised."

Frustrated, Helena asked eagerly, "But you've found something? Something significant?"

He sighed, too exhausted to defend himself too vigorously. He said merely, "I'm sorry. I hadn't realized just how crap an autopsy Sydenham had done." He wanted very much for her to shut up, but it was obvious that she wanted something positive from him. "I think there are one or two things that are interesting. I think there may be some evidence to question the original hypothesis about what happened."

She opened her mouth to ask more but Johnson interrupted. "Perhaps we should let Dr Eisenmenger cogitate a bit before asking him any more questions."

At first she looked unhappy but then she relaxed and said, "Of course. I'm just anxious to get on, that's all."

"Anyway, I've got to go," said Johnson. "I'm late already. Are you coming?"

Eisenmenger had not realized that Johnson had given her a lift. Helena hesitated. "What about discussing progress? You said you'd give me an update."

Johnson looked at his watch. "It's just that I said I'd be home by ten thirty at the latest. I hadn't realized that it would take quite so long."

"What about meeting tomorrow? Say ten o'clock at my office?" asked Helena of Johnson. She turned to Eisenmenger. "Would you be able to make that?"

Saturday morning. The weekend had seemed an emptiness anyway. He nodded, as did Johnson. Apparently mollified, she stood and it was then that Eisenmenger said, "I'll give you a lift, if Bob's got to rush."

She hesitated and for a second he saw that she was going to refuse, almost as if the offer were too dangerous to contemplate. Then, "Thanks. Is that all right, Bob?"

Johnson couldn't deny that it was. It would have been out of his way anyway. His eyes rested on Eisenmenger for a moment then he said, "I'll be off, then. Ten o'clock tomorrow."

In the car, Helena was quiet but Eisenmenger assumed this was the result of tiredness: in any case, ever since he had first met her she had struck him as somewhat taciturn and uncommunicative. He felt that he didn't know her at all well, that she was entirely happy with things that way.

"You don't drive?" he asked.

She was looking ahead, through the first of a splatter of raindrops on the windscreen. There was a slow strobing effect as they passed streetlights. Her perfume was strong; Eisenmenger found it almost inebriating.

"No, I don't." She asked, "Does that make me a freak? I only ask because I seem to be in a small minority these days."

"Not at all. Is it a deliberate decision or an inability to pass the test?"

She turned her head to look at him, her eyes large in the neon-blushed darkness. "Actually, Dr Eisenmenger, I've never bothered to learn." Then, "Are you always so unmannerly to young ladies?"

It sounded as if Jane Austen had cadged a lift. A glance sideways told him that there was a smirk below her eyes. Abruptly she said, "Take the next right." Then, she said, "There's nothing wrong with being unusual. In fact, it's a state to be cherished."

It was an odd remark and it left Eisenmenger off balance. After he had negotiated the turn he said, "I didn't say there was anything wrong with it. It was an observation."

She didn't reply, as if bored with the conversation, so he commented, "I take it eccentricity is all right with you."

For a long time she didn't respond, then she said, "Second on the right, then first left. Pull up on the left opposite the large block of flats. I live there but there's no point in trying to park in the court-yard. It's bound to be full."

Fair enough.

It was only after he'd parked as she had directed, opposite the ornate, neo-Georgian apartment house, that she said, "My stepfather always told me that to be different was to be liberated."

Still she wouldn't look at him. He said gently, "Your stepfather's dead, I think."

She wasn't going to show any emotion. "Bob told you, I guess." At last she looked across at him. Her face was set but it didn't do any harm to her looks. "I seem to be rather careless. First I lose a father, then a stepfather."

She was looking directly into his eyes and for some reason he thought her perfume was strong and wonderful.

"Don't blame Bob," he said.

She shrugged. "I don't."

Abruptly she opened the door and got out. Taken by surprise, Eisenmenger was a few seconds behind her. He was out and after her as quickly as he could.

"Helena?" he called.

She stopped in the middle of the road and turned questioningly. "What?"

He didn't know what to say now that he had her attention. They faced each other over the roof of the car. "When this is over, I'd like to take you to dinner."

He could have stuck his tongue in a light socket. *What the hell was that?*

Despite his embarrassment, she seemed to think about it. A car's engine could be heard coming down the road. It was loud and echoed slightly against the background noise of traffic. "Really?"

Her face was impossible to read. The car was coming closer, accelerating. Helena glanced at it and began walking back to his car. She had just reached it when a streak of red metal shot past. Eisenmenger just glimpsed the side of a woman's face, then it was gone, down the road then turning sharply right.

"Look," he said, "I realize that while we're working together, things have to be professional, but there's no reason why afterwards we can't develop things on a personal level."

She was smiling now, enjoying herself. The smile was not a small thing. "A personal level," she repeated as if she had heard it but she didn't quite believe it. For a few seconds she looked gravely at him and for the first time she seemed to warm just a little to him. She moved to the back of the car and he did likewise so that they were facing each other across the gap, she in the road, he on the pavement.

"What, precisely, does that mean, Dr Eisenmenger?"

"Well . . . " he began, but it was without hope of finishing. A pause, then, "It's just that . . . "

But whatever the words were, they were camouflaged in a mass of cringing discomfiture. He heard another car turn into the street, this time from the other direction.

When he didn't say anything more, Helena helped him out. "Are you asking to take me out, Dr Eisenmenger. Are you, perhaps, asking to have a drink now?"

Her voice was slightly odd and her face was trying hard to keep intact.

The car was accelerating. Eisenmenger glanced up and saw that it was red.

"Well, if you're offering . . . " he said but his mind wasn't in it.

Was that the car that came by just now?

"You think that was an offer?"

He tried to smile because suddenly they were flirting but then again suddenly he was thinking of something else.

Was that Marie?

"I kind of hoped it was."

The street was long but the car was fairly racing along it now. It was moving so quickly that it appeared to flash on and off as it passed the street lamps.

"Hope and reality. Such a wide gulf." The car wasn't slowing. Why did the sound of its engine seem so menacing? "I hardly know you, indeed I know absolutely nothing about you. You could be – "

Suddenly he lunged forward and grabbed her forearm. Before she could react or even speak he had pulled her toward him, between the parked cars and out of the road. At the same time the red car, now only ten metres distant, braked sharply, skidded and steered, perhaps accidentally perhaps deliberately, into the side of Eisenmenger's car. It scraped along it, pushing the side panel in and making a scream of torn metal that was shockingly loud in the night.

Helena, still held by Eisenmenger, looked back over her shoulder with a look of stunned incomprehension. The car had passed over the spot where she had just been standing.

The red car's engine was still running and they heard the gears crunched into obedience, then saw it reversed two metres, the wheels spinning on the tarmac, the brakes applied like a land anchor. Marie's face looked out of the open window. Her eyes had been crying but there was a vicious, hateful spite over the rest of her face.

"I knew it!" she hissed. "I knew it!"

They both stood watching her, Helena completely lost, Eisenmenger completely incredulous. Suddenly Marie started shouting. "BASTARD! Fucking BASTARD!"

"Marie," he said, but it was really only because he felt that he ought to try to say something. "Marie – "

"SHUT UP! SHUT UP, YOU BASTARD!" She began to cry again, but it was a curiously self-centred, self-considering thing. "I knew you were cheating on me. I knew all along. How could you? How could you?"

A few lights had gone on in the apartment blocks around them. A few silhouettes were looking out. Street theatre: not as good as rubbernecking at fatal road traffic accidents, but pretty entertaining.

"Marie, I don't know what you're thinking," he said which, he had to admit to himself, was a bit of a porky, "but I think you've got hold of the wrong end of the stick."

213

What was he saying? Why didn't he just tell her to bugger off, since she had left him and shredded half his wardrobe? What was this to do with her?

Her voice became wheedling, pathetic. "I love you, John! Why don't you love me any more?"

He took a deep breath. "Do you, Marie? Do you really love me? Are you sure it isn't possession you want? Someone to matter, someone to parade for friends and neighbours?"

But she wasn't listening. Now she was mumbling. A few silhouettes disappeared as there was no more shouting and as no blood had escaped its vascular confines. Helena was recovering and glanced at Eisenmenger. Abruptly, Marie uttered a curious noise – half scream, half sound of revulsion – and turned again to Eisenmenger.

"I'll make you sorry, John. Sorrier than you've ever been before."

And with that she assaulted the gear box once again, laid more rubber on the road and accelerated away, her offside front wing looking almost as sorry as Eisenmenger's front passenger door.

For a minute there was silence, then Helena asked, "Friend of yours?"

She took pity on him and invited him up to her flat. It was on the fourth floor and spacious, but its furnishing and decoration were unusual and suggested someone who liked to be different, who wasn't going to conform. They sat and drank coffee in a large sitting room that had a distinct Continental air, with large plain floor tiles dotted with rugs, wooden-framed three-piece suite and curious, modernistic lights. They sat on opposite sides of a glass-topped coffee table as he explained about Marie. When he had finished she leaned back in her chair, her head on its back, exposing her neck. It displayed for the first time her figure, displayed too a remarkably attractive figure.

Yet he could tell that she was alone and he wondered why.

"Well," she said after a while, "even if she left the flat, she doesn't seem to have left you."

Her voice was almost a drawl and there was still that hint of amusement.

"You do believe me, don't you?"

But he wasn't about to be allowed the comfort of reassurance.

"Does it matter whether I do or not? After all, what possible significance has your private life for me?"

"None, I suppose." He tried a smile but the implications of her question made him wonder. She had meant to imply that she wasn't involved in his private life – was teasing him with that fact – but Marie clearly now believed otherwise.

He said, "Marie can't seem to accept that it's over. The ironic thing is that she ended it."

"Perhaps she thought you would beg her to come back."

He hadn't thought of that but it would fit with what he knew of Marie. "I think you're probably right. Marie's is a hysterical personality, and that would fit."

Helena asked, "Hysterical?"

"It's a personality type," he explained. "They tend to be manipulative and somewhat shallow. They make a fuss but they don't ever quite get around to doing something about anything."

"She certainly made a fuss of your car."

The comment unsettled him. She certainly had gone beyond what he might have expected. How much further would she go? "Yes," he agreed softly, suddenly wondering.

The conversation lapsed. There was an ornate, apparently antique carriage clock on a small table beside the open fireplace. It ticked lazily away into the room around them. The time stretched and so comfortable was it that Eisenmenger could quite easily have stayed there for the rest of his life. Indeed he found himself falling asleep. He pulled himself up and reached for his coffee mug to drain it. She was looking at him, almost as if trying to assess him.

"Bob's told you about what happened to my family, of course," she said.

The option was to feign incomprehension but he found that he couldn't lie to her. "Yes." It sounded like a shameful confession.

She nodded and said nothing for a while. Then, "The clock belonged to my parents. It was the only thing I kept."

He didn't know what to say, for no words of his would sound anything other than trite and vacuous in the face of her tragedy, but he didn't need to. Helena seemed to want to talk, if not directly about what had happened, at least about its periphery.

"I didn't appreciate what family was until I lost them. Like safety ropes, they either get in the way or are so unobtrusive you don't even notice they're there, but when I lost mine I went into free-fall. Big time.

"It took me a year to stop grieving, another to start working, but I don't suppose I'll ever stop hurting. Certainly I'm not about to stop hurting over Jeremy. Losing my parents was bad enough, to have my only brother killed by the police was too much too soon."

As gently as he could, Eisenmenger said, "But you're a lawyer. You know that the law isn't perfect."

She looked directly at him and he could see that here was passion. "The law is imperfect in many ways but we're not talking about the law. We're talking about corruption at its worst. We're talking about self-serving, self-promoting abuse of everything that matters. If you think that what happened to my family can be excused or explained by a failure of our legal system, think again. While there are people like Beverley Wharton about, the system will fail and fail again, and the only ones who'll walk away better off are Beverley Wharton and her like."

She put down the coffee mug and sat in the chair, holding herself tight. It made her look small and vulnerable, whatever the look on her face. He wondered what she had meant by 'free-fall'. It suggested a period of chaos and dissolution. Looking at this self-controlled, attractive young woman and at this immaculate, tidy, ordered space around her, it was difficult to imagine any such aberration.

"You're not a specialist criminal lawyer, are you?"

The question appeared to startle her. Certainly she didn't answer at once while she looked at him from striking green eyes that were thoughtful and intense.

"No," she admitted.

He tried a smile to lessen what he thought must be embarrassment.

"I guessed not."

"Does it matter?" Aggression was back, the defences taller and stouter than ever. "I mean, does that make me somehow inferior because all I normally deal with are divorce, wills and civil disputes?"

"Not at all. Inferiority is one thing that I would never associate with you." Perhaps not unexpectedly this ineptitude had no appreciable effect, other than a snort.

"Anyway, a good third of my work is criminal."

He said nothing and she added with a sigh, "But this is my first murder."

"And your first post-mortem, I think."

She squirted a smile from full red lips. "That obvious?"

"Just a bit."

She leaned forward. "That business with the face. Why did you do that?"

And so he explained about abrasion and laceration, about tissue reaction and about the cellular changes that helped him decide how and when they occurred. He didn't suppose that she followed half of it, but she maintained polite interest.

"I still don't know how you can do it."

"Do what? Layered dissection of the face, or autopsy work in general?"

"Any of it. All of it."

Sooner or later everyone asked, "Why?"

And, in truth, it was not an easy question to answer. Why spend your life dissecting human cadavers, trawling through others' misery, others' cruelty, others' uncaringness? Why do a job that involved opening the stomach to look through chyme and vomitus for tablets, cutting down on needlemarks, trawling through excrement and bile and pus?

Why, indeed. He had asked himself that question many, many times and been unable to provide an answer that seemed correct for longer than the time it took to formulate. Sometimes it was because of the intellectual satisfaction in knowing enough about the wonder that is the biology of man to be able to determine how and why it malfunctioned; sometimes it was a feeling of triumph that he could make a blind, deaf corpse describe the killer, whether that killer was a disease or a murderer; sometimes it was merely because it was highly paid and better than male prostitution.

He looked at his watch. It was after midnight. Much as he wanted to stay and talk – just staying would have been enough and more – he stood up.

"Another time, I'm afraid, Helena. I must be going. I've got a report to write and some thinking to do."

Surprised, Helena said, "You'll do that tonight? But it's so late."

He smiled sweetly. "Why shouldn't I? After all, I'm living alone now, aren't I?"

Helena laughed. "Of course. I'd forgotten." For some unaccountable reason he was delighted.

She showed him to the door. As he was about to step outside into the corridor amidst the deep red carpets, subtle wall lighting and framed abstract prints, he turned and said, "Seriously, Helena. Keep your eyes open."

"What for?"

"For Marie."

Her mouth opened, unsure whether to smile. "Oh," she murmured. "Why?"

He found himself unsure how to phrase it. "I don't think she'll do anything but, even if she doesn't know your exact address, she knows you live around here."

Helena considered what he said, then murmured, "I see."

"I'm sorry. It's really nothing to do with you . . . except I'm not sure Marie will see it that way."

She said nothing, just stared at him for a while. Then, as if it were a concession, "I see what you mean."

Then, as they stared at each other, she suddenly leaned towards him and kissed him on the cheek. Then she closed the door on him.

The telephone was ringing when he got back to the flat, which meant that in rushing to open the door he tripped and smacked his knee against the doorframe.

"Hello?"

Nothing. Just an open line that went dead after a couple of seconds. Rubbing his knee he put the receiver down with a small sigh.

Of course it was Marie. He didn't know whether to be amused or sad – Marie seemed to be modelling her life on old films and older novels – but the one thing he couldn't manage was fear.

He knew Marie too well. Knew that she was, when it came to it, ineffectual. She considered that emotions were not passing affect, not moods that passed through her in response to external events and internal ideations, but were things to be expressed and thereby used. Used to make people love you, used to make people sorry for you, used to make people do things, buy things and say things, but always *used*. She used objects, she used situations, she used people and she used her emotions.

And she was so predictable. Her responses were apparently programmed by her cinematic experience. Get pissed off with your lover? Start stalking him and start making silly nuisance phone calls. This whole situation had arisen because she couldn't be content with a stable relationship; she had to imagine that he was an adulterer, for in that delusion lay the opportunity for self-pity and, now that he considered the matter, it was self-pity that motivated most of what Marie did.

Manipulation and self-pity. Suddenly that was all he could see in Marie.

He poured himself a glass of whisky and turned his attention to the death of Nikki Exner, trying to forget Marie. At least that problem could be approached more objectively.

He started by writing out on the computer in the spare room a complete report of what he had found, beginning with a full external description, then moving on to a detailed commentary of each organ system. Then he turned to the notes he had dictated to Johnson and incorporated them, where necessary. Then . . .

Then the phone rang. He looked at the clock: it was just after one in the morning. He picked up the receiver and said, "Hello?"

He heard nothing but the indescribable noises of an open line.

"Marie." Not a question, a statement, and one said in a tired, almost condescending tone.

Still nothing.

He put the phone down and went back to his report. He printed out a copy, then went through it with a pencil, ostensibly moving paragraphs around, changing words, correcting the spelling, but all the time thinking about what he had seen, trying to put it into a pattern.

He poured more whisky, typed the changes into the computer and then printed off another copy. Then he got up from the desk and went to sit on the sofa in the sitting room, the whisky bottle, glass and report on the table in front of him.

He was tired, desperately so, but he had to think about this now, while the sights and the smells were still within, while his mind held a small part of Nikki Exner and she was real, or at least as real as she ever would be.

He read through what he had written, highlighting with a fluorescent marker the things that seemed most significant. The body had a story to tell but it wasn't going to shout it loud. Rather the story was disjointed and told without necessarily attending to temporal order. It was as if it was being whispered by a dysphasic in a delirium, snatches cast softly here and there to be caught only by those who were quick enough and attentive enough.

The phone rang again. He got up and pulled the cord from the wall without even bothering to answer it. He did so with a distracted look on his face, Nikki Exner and her mutilated body still occupying most of his thoughts.

Marie would have to wait. He poured himself another whisky and tried to listen to the whisperings.

Beverley Wharton lay on her back with her eyes closed and her mouth open. In her hands she held the head of Luke, a young inspector from the Fraud Squad: he was sucking on one of her nipples, drawing it out and caressing it with his tongue. With one hand he worked rhythmically around and inside her vulva. She was breathing loudly and crooning encouragement, occasionally shifting her body or arching her back.

Luke was a good lover. Not exactly a donkey but empathetic to her needs and quite gentle. It was about the fifth time they had made love and always before Beverley had enjoyed it greatly – this was lovemaking for pleasure, not for career advancement – but not tonight. Tonight no amount of cunnilingus was going to take her mind from its reiterative worries.

He shifted position, putting his hand under her so that he was holding her buttock. His lips moved up to her mouth, his penis erect against her clitoris. He began to rub up and down as he kissed. For the first time she began to feel genuinely aroused. Perhaps she wouldn't have to fake it after all.

What to do?

It was so difficult not knowing exactly what Eisenmenger had found, although it was clear that he had seen significantly more than Sydenham. Old fool – should have been pensioned off years ago. Why hadn't she insisted on someone else?

She brought her leg over his hip so that she was half straddling him.

Clearly, Eisenmenger was wondering about sodomy . . .

As if by divine comedy the grip on her buttock shifted and his fingers moved to touch her anus. She took a sharp breath in.

Was that important? So what if Bilroth had turned her over while she was drugged and out of it? Rape was rape whether it was vaginal or anal.

And what else had he found? Why dissect the face?

His hand found her breast and this extra stimulation had its effect. She shifted her pelvis so that his prick found her labia and with a small thrust he was inside and she felt suddenly warm. He began to work it slowly and she breathed a soft moan into him, their mouths still clamped. Holding him tight she turned and pulled him on top of her. She bent her legs, then brought them up and crossed them over the small of his back.

He broke away from her mouth and through clenched teeth he murmured, "Christ."

For a moment he just waited above her, his eyes closed. She grinned as he at last opened them, then stretched her arms above her head to grasp the bedhead, displaying her breasts to their best advantage.

"Come on, then, Luke," she invited. "Fuck me."

Afterwards, when he had gone back to his wife and baby son, she lay in her bed and tried to sleep, but loneliness claimed her, a sporadically recurrent affliction that she could not banish. Oddly, it did not often come when she was physically alone, but was more likely when she was in a social gathering, perhaps sitting with her colleagues in a pub or a restaurant. At these times it would come upon her quite rapidly, as if a paradigm shift showed her that she was destined always to be apart. The contrast of being with a crowd and feeling suddenly separate from it – separate in a fundamental and irredeemable sense – heightened the feeling of depression.

Now, the stigmata of recent intercourse still palpable, it subsumed her as the darkness subsumed her and, though she did not cry, it dissolved the lingering pleasure of sex. Why, she found herself wondering, did she use sex as she did? Why did she devaluate it so much?

She had not always been like this. Once she believed that her career in the police force would progress through her abilities in law enforcement, not in bed, but that had proved naive and quickly so. True, her intellect – far above most of her peers and a good few of her superiors – would probably have forced an inevitable rise through the police hierarchy, but the pace would have been excruciating. In any case, it had not been her idea to use her body: that novel concept had been suggested to her on quite a few occasions, whispered in empty corridors or in busy pubs, before she had decided that maybe it was the only sensible route.

But, she was forced to admit, the habit had come easily once started.

And now?

Now she was sleeping higher and higher, like a sort of metaphysical, sexual mountaineer, clambering up the rockface of police promotion, reaching nearer and nearer the top. Would she soon become the Chief Constable's concubine? And what if she should make it to Assistant Chief Constable? Would she have to start sleeping with the higher echelons of the Home Office?

In the blackness she smiled but it was without humour.

The cost had been high. True she still enjoyed sex and, if anything, craved it more than ever. She knew that she was attractive, knew that most men were just pricks on legs if the chance of sex with a beautiful woman was offered, but the distinction between sex for gain and sex for pleasure had somehow become eroded. Luke was for pleasure, but at the back of her mind there was the thought that he could help her: not yet, not with anything specific, but there was the strong possibility that one day he might be of use to her in her career.

Did that make it love or prostitution?

The first time that she had dared admit to herself that she was prostituting herself she had broken down and cried. The shock of this realization had been with her for days but then it had faded. Now, with a prostitute's determination, she lived with the knowledge, telling herself she had only been upset because it had dawned on her that that was how they thought of her. To them – 'her colleagues' – she was nothing more than a tart.

Yet her one defence had always been that she was a bloody good copper and with that she could spit in the faces of those who looked down on her, for all that she did behind closed doors. Those who attempted to sneer her out of existence had always been forced to concede that.

Until now, perhaps. Until Bilroth.

He had done it, of that she was certain. The problem was that the little shit had killed himself before confessing and the case had remained circumstantial. There were questions to be answered that hadn't even been asked. Pressure of work had curtailed the work that should have been done to strengthen the case, but that was no excuse in retrospect. If it should turn out that he didn't murder Nikki Exner, it would be held against her.

She couldn't allow that to happen.

Her options, though, were restricted by lack of certain knowledge. *What had Eisenmenger found?*

He had found something: she became more convinced of this the more she considered the matter. Soon it would seep out. Little gobbets of knowledge and rumour, like stains on a sheet, gradually soiling her reputation and fouling the air.

She had to find out soon.

She turned to lie on her back. The feeling of loneliness was gone and she was very much awake. She switched on the light and sat up. Opposite the bed was a large mirror and she absently admired her breasts in it as she always did. Then she got out of bed and walked naked to the kitchen to make some coffee. She had to think.

Eisenmenger knew and soon he would tell the Flemming girl and Johnson. The Flemming girl was beyond her reach, although it might prove possible to ask a colleague to talk with her. She thought at once of Luke and filed that for future reference: she didn't want to involve anyone else at present. Johnson? She ventured a wry smile. No, she didn't think he would be well disposed towards her.

Which left Eisenmenger. Not unattractive. Was he married? She had heard something about a divorce but that must have been some while before. In any case, that was not much of a problem.

Always have an alternative.

The advice had been her father's, a civil engineer who loved motorcycles. Loved them to death when she was fourteen.

Very well. That was easy. If sex was one strategy the other, inevitably, was politics. A sexual carrot and a political stick.

Sitting, still naked, at the table in the lounge, she spent an hour working out a strategy.

It had about it a taint of unfairness, of callous disregard for justice. It suggested that the universe was not only uncomprehending of human concerns, it was active in trying to bugger them up. Even the nursing staff of the ward – who saw daily just how nasty and vindictive the universe was and thus had, in their human way, lost the ability to appreciate it – were moved to comment that the sudden death of Mrs Goodpasture was hard luck indeed.

She had been convalescing well, considering the size of the cerebrovascular event that had eradicated much of her left parietal lobe with bloodied ease, a sudden explosion of pressurized crimson that had ripped through the delicate grey blancmange of her brain. She hadn't regained the ability to speak, but both she and her husband had been gently warned that that was gone and gone for ever. She had however, been mobilizing well, the Zimmer frame enabling her to shuffle at a steady if unspectacular rate across the ward. And the distressing droop of the right side of her face, like pink-grey wax melted in a fire's glow, no longer proved quite the obstacle to mastication as, miraculously perhaps, she had slowly begun to compensate for the terrible price she had paid.

Terrible price.

Goodpasture looked at her a hundred times a day and with every look the words appeared before him again. She had paid the price that should have been visited on him. God had punished him by punishing her, by blighting her and thereby cursing him to see the results of his actions every minute of every hour of every day. Even when he was alone at night, in the small, neat house that was no longer quite so clean, quite so tidy, he would make himself some hot milk and sit and stare at the television seeing not the soap opera or the nature documentary but the lost, distant look in his wife's rheumy eyes. The look of incomprehension, the look of the innocent unable to understand *why*.

He knew why.

But how to make amends? This question worried at him, like a pain in his bones, never letting him rest. How to atone, both to his wife and his Maker?

The answer was obvious but not easy and perhaps (he told himself in consolation for his inaction) worse than the problem.

But then Mrs Goodpasture died, quite unexpectedly, some ten minutes before nine on a morning when the wind outside was cold and gusty, and when she was due to have shepherd's pie for lunch.

And Mr Goodpasture had already left the house on his way to her side and so could not be contacted. The son, Jem, proved similarly uncontactable.

And so his arrival on the ward found the curtains around her bed drawn and the nurses worried and distressed and not able to look him directly in the face. The sister smiled a smile that the eyes told him was no thing of pleasure and ushered him into her office.

He looked over his shoulder at the curtains and the nurses there saw a terrible look of fear in his watered eyes.

Johnson had already arrived at Helena's office when Eisenmenger got there, fifteen minutes late. It was threatening rain in the tired sort of way that deep winter had.

"Sorry," he said but Helena said nothing. She didn't look at him either. He went through to her office, Helena following.

"Hi, Bob."

"You look tired, Doc. Are you all right?"

Eisenmenger said only, "Busy night."

Helena said, "Coffee?" She was standing beside a filter machine that was almost full. When he nodded, she filled a mug and gave it to him.

"Where do we start?" he asked as she sat down at her desk.

There was a silence for a short while then Eisenmenger said, "Perhaps Bob should tell us what he's discovered." It felt for a moment like a therapy session. Helena was trying to hide a look of uncertainty. "Fine."

Johnson had made notes and these he now produced from an inside pocket. He stirred in his seat and sat up a little straighter. He even cleared his throat and it was clear that he was back in court, presenting evidence. He opened his mouth but before he could speak Eisenmenger said, "There's no need to read the stuff verbatim, Bob. Just give us the basic facts and your conclusions."

Surprised, it took him a moment to alter course. Then he said abruptly to Helena, "You've met her parents. They must have given you some idea of what she was like."

She nodded hesitantly.

"Let me guess. She was bright – she must have been because she was a medical student. She was beautiful – my God, even after dying like that she was still beautiful. She was vivacious, full of good humour and she was considerate." He raised his eyebrows. "Is that more or less what they said?"

"More or less. But then, what else would you expect?"

"Most of the people I spoke to at the medical school were of the same opinion. They saw her as stunningly attractive, bubbly, good company and intelligent. Apparently she was in all respects a popular member of the student body."

He paused. Eisenmenger observed, "'Most'? 'Apparently'?"

"The more people I spoke to the more it occurred to me that the better they knew her, the less positive their attitude."

Helena asked, "Including Jamie Fournier?"

He smiled but it was tainted by cynicism. "Jamie was in love with her."

"Love is blind?"

"Love is . . . tolerant. Up to a point, anyway. Even he seems to have seen that Nikki was a thing of physical rather than spiritual beauty."

"So you're saying what? That she had an unpleasant streak?"

Johnson shook his head firmly. "Oh, no. More than that. She was a scheming, money-grubbing bitch."

Helena was clearly surprised by his candour. Even Eisenmenger could be heard to mutter, "Say what you mean, Bob."

Helena breathed in slowly. "Perhaps you'd better go through what you've discovered."

He briefly recounted what he had been told, what Fournier had admitted to him, what her ex-lover had said and what those who had worked with her had said.

"I don't think that there was much doubt that she was using drugs pretty regularly. I think that her supply – her main supply at least – was Bilroth."

"That doesn't exactly help us in our efforts to clear Bilroth," pointed out Eisenmenger.

"Not obviously." He turned to Helena. "Have you been to the Exners' house?"

"Once."

"Is it large? I mean, are they rich?"

Helena shook her head. "Not at all. It was a semi, but it wasn't grand. I think her father's a civil servant or something."

"And yet Nikki Exner moved out of the student accommodation into a flat of her own, she drove a BMW, she used to miss lectures to go shopping and she could afford as many drugs as she wanted."

"So where did she get the money?" Although Eisenmenger didn't find it hard to guess. After all she had apparently had the semen of three men inside her as she had been slit asunder.

"Sex. I think that she had sex with Bilroth to pay for the drugs, then those she didn't use she sold on for the money."

Eisenmenger was writing all this down. "Do we know she definitely sold drugs? Has anyone admitted that they bought them off her?"

Johnson had to acknowledge that he hadn't found anyone who would confess to it.

"Still," said Helena, "how else could she have got her money?"

Johnson said quietly. "There was one other way – blackmail."

Eisenmenger looked up sharply. "You have proof?"

"Well, I've one student's testimony." He told them about James Paneth.

For a second no one said anything. Then Helena murmured, "A bitch hardly describes it."

"Can we rely on this evidence? Could he be making it up?"

Johnson shook his head firmly at Eisenmenger's question. "He was real."

"And he has an alibi?" Johnson nodded, then added, "So, I think, does Fournier. According to his mates from the pub, he was with them until eleven o'clock by which time he was practically paralytic. They had to help him up the stairs to his room. He wasn't capable of the murder."

"Anyway, it was hardly a crime of passion," remarked Helena.

It was barely a whispered thought as Eisenmenger said, "Oh, I don't know."

His tone was so odd, Helena asked at once, "What does that mean?"

Eisenmenger didn't answer at once, as if thinking deeply. He sounded to the others almost reluctant as he began, "All this is preliminary. It'll need histological assessment and it'll need DNA analysis to confirm it."

"DNA?"

He nodded absently as if still thinking about what he had found. Then, "The secret of science is not to know the answer, nor even to know how to find the answer, but to know the question to ask. Only then can you make progress."

He shifted forward in his chair.

"Why do that to her?" he enquired of neither of them and both of them. "That's the question to ask here."

"Why was she hung, drawn and quartered, you mean? Or why was she raped?"

"Both. Neither." He looked up at Helena. "You're asking a lot of questions there, you know. For a start, I don't know that she was raped, or at least not in a technical sense."

"But there was marking around the vulva," protested Johnson. "And you said that there were marks around the anus."

But Eisenmenger didn't respond, instead pointing out, "Strictly speaking she wasn't hung, drawn and quartered either. That practice involved being hanged by the neck until the victim was almost dead, then taking them down, slicing open the abdomen to draw out the intestines, then hacking the body into quarters for public display."

Helena looked slightly nauseous at this and even Johnson took a couple of deep breaths. "Sorry," murmured Eisenmenger, although it wasn't clear whether he was apologizing for the graphic detail or the didactic pedantry.

"Was it supposed to look like hanging, drawing and quartering, though?" Johnson asked. "Maybe it was symbolic of it."

Eisenmenger regarded Johnson in a silence born of distraction. In his mind he was still thinking through the murder, through his findings. Then he said, "Maybe."

Johnson followed this up. "As soon as I saw her, I was struck by the peculiar sense of splendour about the death, the theatricality of it. That was why I couldn't see Bilroth as the murderer, certainly not in a drugged-up stupor. It was almost religious in its setting, almost Messianic."

Helena stood up and got herself some coffee. She said, "Tim Bilroth wasn't particularly religious."

Eisenmenger shook his head violently. "No. That's not the point. That's the window dressing, the distraction. The whole point of this was to make you ask the wrong question."

Helena looked lost. "Which is . . . ?" she prompted.

"Everyone, and I mean absolutely everyone who came into the museum that morning, as well as those who've seen the photographs and read the reports, everyone has just one question in their heads. It's the first thing that comes into their minds."

Johnson was frowning, perhaps thinking back. "*Why?*" he said quietly. He looked up. "That was the first thing I remember thinking. *Why has this been done to her?*"

Eisenmenger slammed the desk and made Helena start slightly. "Exactly. It was done to shout out in the minds of ordinary God-fearing people, *Why?* Shout it out so bloody loudly that you don't even realize that there are other questions to be asked."

"Such as?"

"Such as, *What?*"

Again Helena needed help. "I don't follow."

"What was done to her and, probably even more importantly, what was not done to her."

She shook her head. "You've lost me." She looked across at Johnson who was frowning but clearly also unsure. "After all, she was possibly raped, possibly sodomized, she was hung, drawn and quartered – or as good as – there's not much left, is there?"

Eisenmenger suddenly began to laugh. It was a quiet laugh and in the context it was bizarre, as if he had suddenly flipped over into insanity. Johnson was staring at him with a look of worried bewilderment and Helena's eyes became very large.

Abruptly he stopped and looked from one to the other, an apologetic smile apparently a peace offering. "I'm sorry. You probably think I'm mad." No one argued. "Actually, there is one thing you left out."

Warily Helena asked what it was.

His smile broadened. "Necrophilia," he said simply.

Helena had gone to get more water for coffee. Johnson asked, "You are joking, aren't you?"

Eisenmenger sighed. "To be frank, I can't be sure as yet, not until I've looked at the tissue samples, but I'd say I'm more than half convinced. And no," he added, "I'm not joking."

Helena returned and filled the machine. Then she turned to Eisenmenger and said, "Perhaps you'd better explain what you found and what you think happened, John."

She wore a worried, almost distressed look, as if feeling unwell. He tried to get her to smile at him but she had looked down at once, only interested in her damned notes. He felt guilty at having to discuss such things with her, but he was only doing a job. The irony was that he was doing it out of goodwill and at her behest.

He had brought with him a box file and this he now opened. He took out three copies of his post-mortem report, each four pages long and each stapled.

"This is preliminary only. The final report is going to need microscopy and, as I have said, DNA analysis, so what I'm saying today is only tentative."

He handed them each a copy.

"Read it at your leisure. For now, I'll just run through the most significant findings."

He waited for their assent, then put his copy of the report on the desk and placed his hands flat upon it.

"When you open up the human body, the most striking thing is the beauty of the packing. In the chest the lungs fill either side, moulding around the heart and assuming a concave lower surface where each rests on the domes of the diaphragm. In the abdomen the same is true, but the greatest amount of space is occupied by the small and large intestines. For the most part the large intestine is at the back and at the periphery, held firm against the posterior abdominal wall by the peritoneal membrane. The central part is the domain of the small intestine and this is allowed more freedom in that it is not held tight against the wall but has a leash – the small intestinal mesentery. The mesentery ties it to the posterior abdominal wall, but not oppressively so."

"Is this necessary?" asked Johnson. He had glanced at Helena and not seen appreciation. Eisenmenger ignored him, as if the question was too unintelligent to require acknowledgement. "In order to do what was done to Nikki Exner – to extract the small intestine and effectively to lay it out like a string of sausages – isn't easy. To do it well requires experience."

"That hardly helps," pointed out Johnson. "All of our suspects must surely qualify."

"Including you." Helena's voice was so desiccated even Eisenmenger seemed to get the message. He smiled. "True. And there is no doubt that this was done supremely well. The stomach, which is basically a thin-walled sack of chyme, overhangs the small intestine and was untouched. The liver would also have been in the way and that, too, was untouched."

"Where is this leading?" It was difficult to tell from Helena's voice whether she was genuinely at a loss or genuinely distressed by his dedication to detail.

"I suppose you could say that it's leading south." Before she could explode he went on, "The uterus always struck me as odd, you see."

Johnson was looking through the report. "That was removed as well, wasn't it?"

"Which was what was odd. The uterus is tucked away in the depths of the pelvis, well away from the small intestine. Not only is it unnecessary to remove it when you're fastidiously dissecting out the small intestine, I would say that it's impossible to do it accidentally, and yet it was the only other organ that was disturbed."

Helena was suddenly animated, her malaise apparently forgotten. "It was taken out deliberately? Is that what you're implying?"

"I think so."

"But why?" she asked and then a look of comprehension came on her face. "She was pregnant?"

Johnson was ahead of her. "But she wasn't. You report says that the cavity was empty."

"My report also states that there were leiomyomata, or fibroids, in the uterine wall."

"Meaning?"

"I suppose it's possible that at the tender age of twenty she had developed significant fibroids, but it would be unusual."

Helena was shaking her head. "I'm lost again."

Eisenmenger looked at Johnson who shrugged his own uncertainty.

"I don't think the uterus found at the scene was Nikki Exner's. I think it was a substitute. This whole business of desecration was performed to cloud the issue of the uterus being removed and another one replacing it."

There was silence while the other two digested this. Eisenmenger stood up and went to the window. Outside it was raining halfheartedly, a drizzle that couldn't be bothered to clean the overgrown scrub in the backyard, that only turned the dust to mud.

A movement in the bushes at the far end of the garden caught his eye. He wondered what it was but couldn't make anything definite out of it. Probably a bird.

"What?"

He had missed what Johnson had said.

"How can you prove that the uterus we found wasn't hers?"

"Analyse a sample tissue from Nikki's body – anything will do – with one from the uterus. Compare polymorphisms. We can have the result in a few days."

"And where is Nikki's uterus? If we could find that . . . " asked Helena.

"Destroyed by now, I should think," interrupted Eisenmenger. "It would have been easy enough to put it in a clinical waste bag. That goes once a week for incineration."

Her face darkened.

"At least we have an explanation of why the body was treated like that," pointed out Johnson.

"We have more than that, I think. We have a motive and we have therefore an indication of who might have done it."

Helena abruptly sat forward. "Explain." Eisenmenger was surprised by the rapid change in her mood: from sulk to intense excitement in the space of two sentences.

"The immediate motive was to remove the uterus and distract attention from it. Ergo, she was pregnant. Ergo, the motive was to hide that fact. Now, working on the assumption that we are dealing only with those who had after-hours access to the museum – that is, Hamilton-Bailey, Russell, Bilroth, Libman and me – we have to ask which of those would care enough about Nikki Exner being pregnant to murder her. After all, I can't imagine Tim Bilroth being bothered about it, can you? He's quite possibly fathered a score of illegitimate babies in his time; why should this one bother him?"

For the first time since he had met her, he saw sheer delight in Helena's face. "Yes! Of course!"

Johnson said, "Libman's mother would have a fit if her darling boy suddenly announced that he was a daddy, but I can't see him topping the girl because of it."

"And there was his extreme shock, don't forget."

Eisenmenger's remark made Johnson pause. In truth he had forgotten about Libman's reaction to the crime.

"Which leaves Russell and Hamilton-Bailey," said Helena, to which Eisenmenger added with a smile, "And me. You really shouldn't leave me out."

"But Russell isn't married. Would he have a strong enough motive to murder her?"

"Oh, yes. The medical school would have quite a lot to say about one of their professors, married or single, impregnating a second-year student. It would certainly lead to disciplinary action and, quite probably, to dismissal. Neither Russell nor Hamilton-Bailey would escape extremely strong censure.

"The same," he continued as if determined to ensure he was considered equally, "would go for a senior lecturer such as me."

Johnson came to life. "Hang on a bit. Can we just get things a bit straighter before we send for the handcuffs? First of all, if you're right and the uterus found at the scene was not Nikki Exner's, can you explain where it came from? Even in a medical school or hospital, they can't be that easy to get hold of."

"They're usually not. Even most of those that are removed at hysterectomy are put straight into formalin fixative in theatre. They would have been entirely unsuitable for the murderer's needs.

"However, it so happens that in the Pathology Department we're participating in a research project that involves receiving the hysterectomy specimens fresh. If they arrive late, they would be put in the fridge until the next day. I think that's where it came from."

"But that would mean that a specimen would have to go missing. The one from the fridge can't have been replaced with Nikki Exner's because we're assuming that she was pregnant."

"That's right. And, believe it or not, one did. The next day."

The three of them looked at each other.

Helena asked, "But surely that implicates Russell pretty conclusively, doesn't it? Only he would know what specimens had come into your department, wouldn't he? Hamilton-Bailey works in a different department."

"It should," said Eisenmenger apologetically, "but unfortunately it doesn't. The project is a joint one between the Departments of Obstetrics and Gynaecology, Histopathology and Anatomy. Whatever Russell knew, Hamilton-Bailey knew as well."

Helena breathed a word that could have been 'Shit.'

"Well," said Johnson, "it certainly looks as if your theory about the reason for the desecration fits the available facts, but I'm still not clear whether we have a motive. After all, if she was pregnant, why not just get it terminated?"

"Perhaps they had a row," suggested Helena. "Perhaps she didn't want to but the murderer did."

Eisenmenger shook his head. "No. I don't think so. There was little evidence to suggest a struggle or a fight. Certainly there was nothing about the body to support the hypothesis that she died in a fight. In fact the available evidence would suggest a degree of premeditation. Don't forget she was drugged before she was killed."

"Very well. They had already had the row about the pregnancy. Somewhere else, on a different day. The murderer decided quite calmly that she would have to die and plans it accordingly. Arranges to meet her in the museum after hours, drugs her, kills her and then cuts her open to take the uterus."

"That interpretation certainly cannot be excluded with the facts we have at present," admitted Eisenmenger, "But it doesn't feel right. For a start, Nikki Exner had a lifestyle to keep up and I can't see that she'd be arguing to keep the child: in fact, I would imagine she'd be horrified at the idea of motherhood, especially if the father was Russell or Hamilton-Bailey."

Johnson had been silent for a while. He said suddenly, "But if she found that she had accidentally become pregnant, she'd use it to her own ends. She'd blackmail the father."

"Exactly," agreed Eisenmenger. "She'd use it."

"But how would the murderer be certain that he was the father?" objected Helena. "He couldn't be certain that it wasn't Fournier's child, could he?"

"He couldn't be certain that it was either. The risk would be too great to call her bluff. She was promiscuous, we know that, and most probably she didn't really know who was the father, but why let that little problem stand in the way? There was money to be made."

Helena had picked up the autopsy report. "Hang on a minute. Aren't you forgetting something? This nice little scenario might be neat and it might not be contradicted by the facts, but it doesn't explain them all, does it? She had sex with three men that night, and there's a suggestion that she was raped and possibly sodomized. Where does all that fit in?"

"And don't forget," added Johnson mildly, as if reminding him to put the milk bottles out, "you mentioned necrophilia."

They had left the office and were now in a small Italian restaurant a few streets away. It was slightly shabby and there was a taste of tiredness in the air of the proprietor who greeted them. He obviously knew Helena well and even managed a smile as she walked in, but it was clearly a great strain for him. They were shown to a table in the corner and the menu cards were given to them with the mix of flourish and boredom that is unique to Italian waiting staff.

"We know that three people had sex with Nikki Exner on the night that she died. We also know that one of them was Jamie Fournier. We have to assume that intercourse on that occasion was not forced and that she entered into it willingly."

Eisenmenger had opted for a clam pasta, whereas Johnson had decided on something safe and was therefore making slow but steady progress through spaghetti bolognese. Helena had before her a green salad and nothing else. Just looking at it made Johnson feel hungry.

"But was she raped or wasn't she? I thought it was fairly certain that she had been, but you seem to be casting doubt on it." Johnson had splashed some bolognese sauce on to his tie and was trying to remove it with his napkin. His efforts only worsened the problem.

"There are marks around the vulva, and there are marks around the anus. They suggest some trauma and they therefore certainly imply some sort of forced intercourse. My problem is their faintness."

"You mean they're old?" asked Helena.

Eisenmenger considered this then shook his head. "No, I don't think so. There was no altered pigmentation suggesting breakdown of extravasated haemoglobin, as one would normally see in old contusions. No, I think that they're faint because the penetration occurred shortly after death."

Helena hadn't looked as if she was particularly enjoying the salad and Eisenmenger's words didn't appear to increase its flavour. Johnson saw a forkful of rocket change course and land by the side of her plate. Eisenmenger, he noted, was oblivious to this.

"Of course it'll depend on the histology, but I'd be surprised if it can be explained in any other way. The other thing to be noted is that there was no great scarring around the anus, so she wasn't in the habit of enjoying anal sex."

He put some clams and pasta in his mouth and chewed meditatively while Helena took a drink of sparkling water, then picked up the fork again.

"I should imagine from a legal point of view, the act of necrophilia cannot be considered rape since consent doesn't really come into – "

The fork was again taken on a detour, this time landing on the plate with a clatter.

"For God's sake, shut up about necrophilia, will you?"

The waiter, who had been heading their way with the obligatory over-sized pepper mill, paused, bobbed his head on one side and then decided that he was too much of a professional to be put off. His offer, however, was waved aside by all three in silence, Eisenmenger's face betraying his surprise.

"I'm terribly sorry, Helena, I didn't realize you weren't happy."

She accepted the apology. "I'm not quite as clinical as you are. Perhaps in time, but for the present I'd rather eat my lunch without considering the grossest aspects of human depravity."

The meal resumed without conversation for a while. Then Johnson said tentatively, "So how do you think she was killed? Was she killed by hanging, then cut down and . . . " He looked across at Helena before venturing forth again with, "desecrated, only to be hanged again afterwards?"

Eisenmenger seemed to him suddenly nervous as he answered. He hesitated for a second and then covertly glanced at Helena before replying in a tone distinctly less enthusiastic than before, "When I dissected the neck and face, it became apparent that, although it wasn't obvious from the skin mark, there were in fact two ligature marks around the neck. The one from her suspension was fainter and I should judge was made after death and therefore presumably after the desecration. The mark that was made first was the one that killed her. She was strangled. The ligature was thin, about five millimetres in diameter."

Helena had finished the salad and perhaps felt more inclined to join in with the discussion. "How can you tell that the two marks were from two different actions? Perhaps she struggled as she was hanging there: perhaps the rope just slipped."

"Because death by ligature strangulation results in a clean, fairly uniform mark that doesn't fade at any point: death by hanging results in a mark that tends to fade where the knot is – usually that would be at the angle of the jaw. In this case there was a sharp ligature mark corresponding with strangulation, but about one and a half centimetres above it there was a second mark that was much fainter but that faded to nothing at the angle of her jaw. That fits with the body being hanged just after death."

The waiter took away their plates. They declined dessert but had coffee instead. It was only after this had been brought that Johnson asked, "How come there are two marks around the neck when there was only one on the skin?"

"Although the killer took great care to align the rope with the ligature mark he'd already made, he couldn't account for the tendency of the skin to slide over the underlying soft tissues. Effectively the skin slipped upwards and over the soft tissues beneath and compressed a different area."

He put his forefinger and thumb against his throat and moved the skin upward to illustrate.

"There was no evidence of a struggle?" asked Johnson.

"No. The Midazolam, I would guess."

"So do we know exactly what happened that night?" asked Helena.

They both looked at Eisenmenger. He took in breath, hesitated and then said, "Yes, and no."

They both looked despairing and Johnson groaned. "What does that mean?" he asked.

"I think we can deduce some of what happened, but certainly not everything." He frowned, then said, "How about if you recap, Bob? Take us through what we think we know."

Johnson had been the only one taking notes. He frowned. "Correct me if I go wrong but I think the sequence of events was as follows:

"Nikki Exner and Jamie Fournier met Bilroth in the museum at just after six where Bilroth gave her some drugs."

"And yet she had no money," pointed out Eisenmenger. "Isn't that what Fournier said?"

"Bilroth wasn't happy but eventually agreed to hand them over," confirmed Johnson.

"On tick? Does that sound reasonable?"

Johnson shrugged. "He knew where to find her. Knew that she wasn't going anywhere."

But Eisenmenger still looked unconvinced. Then Helena said, "But we have evidence that Bilroth had sex with her that night, don't we? Perhaps that was the price."

Eisenmenger's face broke into a large smile. "Yes! That's exactly what happened. That's why she didn't want to spend the rest of the night with Fournier, because she had to go back at ten to the museum and pay for the drugs."

"Which puts Bilroth back at the murder scene," said Helena, "And it puts him there within the time frame of 10 p.m. to 2 a.m."

"We always knew that he was there or thereabouts. This doesn't change anything. The identity of the third person who had sex with her that night is the crucial thing to discover."

Johnson continued, "So we have Nikki Exner returning to the museum at about ten o'clock to meet Bilroth. We assume that they had sex and that the sex was with her consent and in payment for drugs."

The waiter offered more coffee, only Eisenmenger having some. Helena asked, "And then what?"

"Then Bilroth leaves and a third man comes on the scene. The murderer. His motive for killing is blackmail, his motive for the desecration is to remove the evidence of a pregnancy."

"And just as a final flourish, he commits necrophilia." Eisenmenger's tone was dry enough to open sores.

"But it leaves us with only two suspects," Helena said eagerly. "Russell and Hamilton-Bailey."

Abruptly Johnson said, "No, it doesn't. It leaves us with thousands."

They looked at him in surprise. "How come?" asked Eisenmenger.

"If Bilroth let Nikki Exner into the museum, then she could subsequently have opened the door to anyone. Anyone at all. The suspects are no longer restricted to the keyholders."

Helena looked momentarily shocked, then anguished. As she groaned, Eisenmenger was silent. Johnson was right, but he knew with deep certainty that it hadn't been just anyone who had been in the museum so late that night with Nikki Exner.

Helena returned to the office in a profoundly pensive mood. So much information, so rapidly given. Her reactions to it were confused, though. Clearly the simple picture of rape, murder and dismemberment that the police had constructed was too simple, but they had as yet made little headway in showing that Tim Bilroth had not been responsible, and they were far from proving Beverley Wharton incompetent.

And then there was John Eisenmenger. Even knowing where to start with her feelings towards him was beyond her. The more she saw of him the more he infuriated her, and yet the angrier she felt, the more something inside her found things to like about him.

Since her return from the destruction of her family, since she had rebuilt herself, she had had a few affairs, but none had had significance. None, indeed, had included any form of sexual intercourse, as if none of her would-be suitors had met whatever criteria she now held inside. They had all been reasonably good-looking, all quite personable; 'suitable' would have been the word her parents might have employed. Most of them had been more athletic and attractive than Eisenmenger, yet none had interested her quite as much as he did. He had qualities that somehow seemed to insinuate themselves beneath her defences, within her citadel.

Yet try as she might, she could not define them. She could see within him intelligence, wit, capriciousness and insight; she could sense also deep vulnerability allied to unworldliness. Any of those on their own would not have been enough, surely, to make him so curiously engaging – indeed, some of them (the vulnerability for a start) ought to have repelled her – yet somehow their combination was a gestalt. The sum was greater than the parts.

She was forced to concede that John Eisenmenger, whether he knew it or no, was working some sort of charm.

Sighing, she let herself into the front office and walked through to the back. She felt tired and somewhat sleepy but she had work to do.

Eisenmenger and Johnson parted, Johnson to drive back home, Eisenmenger to catch the Tube into town. He had a new wardrobe to buy, what with Marie's assault on his sartorial stock. It was raining again and the light was bad, the day nearly over. He had his head down against the wind, thinking thoughts of nothing in particular, mostly about Helena. Why was she so difficult? Was this prickly behaviour reserved solely for him? Certainly she didn't seem to find Johnson so provocative. Did she honestly believe that to give an inch would be to invite some terrible fate – sex, violence, degradation and an untimely death? What was wrong with the girl?

237

He had to cross the road, passing between two closely parked cars. As he did so his raincoat caught on a jagged piece of metal that was sticking out from the wing of one of them. He swore, pulled it away and then stopped.

It was a red car.

Helena had settled to some work but the last will and testament of Mrs Angelina Dieulafoy was proving less than adhesive reading. The wind was throwing rain against the glass of the sash windows as if people were chucking it with buckets. She had spoken with Mr Morton, the senior partner, on several occasions about the amount of draught that came through the windows, but as ever money was tight when it came to such indulgences. She had put the electric fire on and that at least made a semblance of cosiness, what with its glow and the single circle of light cast from her desk lamp.

Abruptly she was back at home – her real home, the childhood one – with her parents and her brother. Theirs had been a large, old and draughty house, and in the winter's night the lamps and lights had never been strong enough or eager enough to chase away the shadows. The Christmas lights and the feelings of love and kinship had been all the brighter for it.

The wind blew suddenly hard and the memory was whisked into shreds before its coldness. She was back in her office.

Maybe it wasn't her car – there must be hundreds of red cars with crumpled front wings out there. Except that he knew it was Marie's.

Maybe she was just here shopping. Except that it wasn't a shopping centre.

Well, maybe she was here to meet someone. Except that she had chosen to meet someone a few hundred metres from Helena's office.

He began to walk quickly back along the street. Then he began to run.

Helena had read through Mrs Dieulafoy's will four times and it still made no sense. She wanted to leave her estate to the milkman, it appeared; that is, all except the refrigerator which she wanted to leave to the postman (presumably because the milkman would already have a refrigerator). No wonder the family were contesting the will. The question was, was she openly a lunatic or one of the quiet ones? Could she prove that Angelina Dieulafoy had been of the kind that believed she was Joan of Arc, the government was infiltrated by aliens from the planet Oobijoobi, and the standard lamp in the corner of the sitting room was talking to her?

Suddenly there was a loud banging on the door that made her start. What the hell was that? The banging stopped but started again, more loudly and this time accompanied by shouting. It sounded as if the lunacy of the will had escaped into the real world.

Helena rose and walked to the door of her office. She felt it wise to find out who was out there before betraying her presence. At the door she paused, then slowly opened it, to peer round carefully.

John Eisenmenger, cold and very wet, but screaming and shouting, hitting the toughened glass again and again, a look of panic on his face. What was wrong with the man?

She opened the door of her office wide and was already framing questions for him.

The glass of the window to her left shattered. Helena started to turn at the sound just as the half-brick struck her temple.

Eisenmenger hated A&E departments. Here was where humanity met the medical profession without quarter given, where the bloodier, the more violent and the more soulless aspects of mankind came for succour and aid, and where gratitude and regret were all but driven from the face of the world. He had spent the last few hours sandwiched between a drunken woman who kept retching into a cardboard kidney dish, and a small boy and his mother, the former with a large boil on his neck that was in imminent danger of spurting forth.

Helena had not been seriously hurt. She had been knocked sideways, stunned and all but unconscious. He had been forced to use a brick himself in order to break into the office, then, when reasonably reassured that she hadn't sustained a serious head injury, he had called the police. He had brought her to the Casualty Department as much as a precaution as anything, and in defiance of her protestation. She was shaken and bruised but, he thought, little else: the three-hour wait had probably done as much harm as the actual incident.

A small, dapper man came hesitantly towards the reception desk, not far from where Eisenmenger was sitting. He had an expensive suit and a balding head decorated with scattered solar keratoses. His manner was diffident.

Eisenmenger would have ignored him but for catching the name 'Flemming' as the little man talked to the receptionist. On being told that she was in treatment, the little man looked around for some-where to sit. Wondering who he was, Eisenmenger rose and made his way over.

"Excuse me. Are you here for Helena Flemming?"

The man nodded warily.

"I'm John Eisenmenger. I was with Helena when it happened."

The man's face showed enlightenment and then concern. Shaking him by the hand, he said, "Morton. Christopher Morton. I'm the senior partner in the firm."

Eisenmenger led him to a corner of the room that was slightly less heavily infested with wounded.

"What a terrible thing!" began Mr Morton. "What a terrible, ghastly thing! Are you all right? Is Helena all right? I came as soon as I was told. The police are there now . . . "

On and on he went, only pausing for oxygen after a seemingly infi-nite number of questions and expressions of horror. Eisenmenger was then able to reassure him that Helena was not badly injured.

"It was those travellers, of course."

Eisenmenger didn't follow.

"Travellers. You know, gypsies. We had a case a few months ago. Helena took it on. One of their young women was charged with reckless driving – a man on a bicycle was knocked off and killed. Helena defended her but there was little she could do: the girl was convicted. Ever since then we've had death threats and goodness knows what else. One night we had all the front win-dows broken."

Eisenmenger listened, unsure of what to think or say. He had been convinced that Marie had been responsible, at least in his own mind. He had been debating the wisdom of confiding his suspicions to the police, yet now this little man was suggesting another possi-bility. Could it be that this was nothing to do with Marie?

"I told the police at once. They were very interested."

Now that he thought about it, Eisenmenger was forced to recon-sider. Perhaps it had been mere coincidence that Marie's car was nearby – and not even that near. He hadn't actually seen Marie in person and, as far as he could tell from what she had said thus far to the police, neither had Helena. Certainly it would be completely out of character for Marie to be so aggressive and violent . . .

But then, he remembered, she had been behaving in a fairly aggressive and violent manner a few nights before.

He was now acutely aware of a dilemma – should he say any-thing, or should he remain silent?

Mr Morton, while not exactly wringing his hands, prattled on beside him.

When she emerged from the treatment cubicle Helena looked nauseous and grey. Although the gash on her forehead had been dressed and steri-stripped, the traces of the blood that had flowed freely from it were clearly to be seen on her normally perfect attire. Her eyes found Eisenmenger, slid off him and stayed on Mr Morton. For him she tried a smile and a lift of the eyebrows that made the steri-strips take a tiny bow.

"Helena! Are you all right? You look awful!"

Mr Morton's arms were out and, if she didn't exactly rush into them, she did at least allow herself to be held by his hands around her shoulders. "Not too bad, thanks."

"Those wretched travellers! I knew we hadn't heard the last of them."

"Travellers?" She looked surprised, as if this was a novel concept.

"Why, yes. Who else would be likely to do a thing like that? The police have the file and I've told them of all the trouble that we've had, but I doubt that anyone will ever be caught. The family probably isn't even in the country at the present. Friend of a friend, that kind of thing."

While Morton had been solving the case, Helena's eyes had briefly returned to Eisenmenger, then down.

"I think I'd like to go home," she said.

"I'll take you." Eisenmenger just managed to beat Mr Morton in the sprint finish. For a second it looked as if she would prefer her employer, but then she nodded. Mr Morton accepted gracefully.

"You're not to come into work for a few days," he commanded her. "A week at least."

She took these blandishments with thanks but in a way that suggested to Eisenmenger that she was overused to them: a spoiled daughter, almost.

It was only when they were in his car and driving past ambulances queued outside Casualty that she spoke again. "He looks on me as a lost orphan. He's very kind."

"I can see that."

He thought that she was concussed and drowsy, for her eyes were closing when she asked, "What did you want?"

Lost without context he didn't answer.

"When you came back to the office. You were hammering on the door. What did you want?"

Thrown, he opened his mouth but the lie took a while coming. Perhaps she didn't hear the falsehood. "My mobile. I mislaid it. Thought it might be on your desk."

She said only, "Was it? I didn't notice it."

"I've found it since. It was in my pocket."

Her eyes still closed she said, "Well, I'm grateful you thought you had lost it."

He mumbled agreement with a laugh.

More silence and then she said, "I seem to be jinxed."

"How come?"

She paused. Her voice was soft and dreamy but there was an undertone of something. "First your ex-girlfriend tries to knock me down. Now this."

He didn't say anything: he could find no words and no tone to say them in.

"I wonder if there'll be a third thing."

He had stopped at traffic lights. Looking across at her he said, "You'd better be careful. Just in case."

The Hamilton-Baileys' attendance at the Dean's luncheon party that Sunday was not, for the Dean, opportune. Despite his remarks to the Professor, he had had no intention of inviting the beastly little man to any form of social gathering, and the thought of having social intercourse with a woman with whom he had once had sexual intercourse left him positively nauseous.

However his wife, Sally, was of a different persuasion. She liked, she told him, Irene Hamilton-Bailey. Moreover, the pointed omission of the Hamilton-Baileys from the Dean's social agenda could not continue: he knew as well as she that it was expected that senior academics from the medical school would be invited to attend at least one social gathering over which the Schlemms presided. It had, she said in a tone that suggested this was heinous, been three years since the Hamilton-Baileys had been so blessed. The Dean reflected that it must therefore be three years since Irene Hamilton-Bailey had lain with him, a thought that was swiftly followed by discomfort at the thought of seeing her again so soon.

Unfortunately his wife, although small of stature and appearing to have the characteristics of the meekest of the mild, in fact possessed the inclination of a dictator. The Hamilton-Baileys were invited and Dean Schlemm was forced to rely on Irene Hamilton-Bailey's finer feelings and sense of propriety. He was not to know that there were greater considerations on her mind, and thus he was externally delighted and internally irritated to find them at his imposing, oak front door.

Pleasantries were exchanged, the two wives kissing and then walking away together, conversing and laughing as if they really did know and like each other. Schlemm watched them with some wonder, some distaste at their ability to rise by convection above any other consideration. He turned to Hamilton-Bailey who was also looking at the women, although his expression was one almost of detachment.

"Good of you to come, Alexander. Shall we go into the library? I think you know most people here."

There were about thirty guests present and the Dean had not lied in his estimation that most of them were known to Hamilton-Bailey, although his demeanour over the next two hours might have suggested otherwise. He kept his head down most of the time, apparently regarding the carpet and the polished oak of the dining table as of more intrinsic interest than the erudite ramblings of his fellow guests. On two occasions he visibly jumped when remarks were addressed to him, and Dean Schlemm did not fail to appreciate this. Nor did he miss Irene Hamilton-Bailey's covert and continual glances at her husband from across the silver plate. The diminutive Professor ate nothing, drank very little.

It was after the light luncheon that Irene Hamilton-Bailey approached him as he came back from issuing orders to the catering staff in the kitchen. "May we talk, Daniel?"

His smile was a paragon of courtesy as inside he felt a tired foreboding. Did she want to retread old ground? He looked around. Most of his other guests were happily ensconced in conversation around the room and all seemed to have sufficient of their beverage of choice to allow him to escape for a few minutes. In particular his wife was happily talking to the Chief Constable and Alexander Hamilton-Bailey was staring out of the window at the French garden.

"In here," he said and led her into a small back sitting room that his wife used for sewing.

Expecting some sort of embarrassed declaration of not quite fully requited love, he was considerably surprised when with a superior calm she said, "I want to talk to you about Alexander."

"Alexander?"

"You won't have failed to have seen his state."

He shook his head, hiding relief but also aware that she was obviously going to ask him for a 'favour'. Schlemm disliked the concept, preferring instead to deal in direct quid pro quos. "He seems distracted," he admitted.

"It's this ghastly murder business. It's affected him dreadfully."

"The murder?" and he could not keep surprise from his voice. "But why? It was weeks ago, and he wasn't involved, not directly. I remember the police interviewed him, but that was only because . . . "

He stopped because she was just looking at him. Her eyes were large and looked dreadfully meaningful. "Oh, my God!" he said involuntarily but she held up her hands and said immediately, "Alexander didn't do it, Daniel. He assures me of that."

She actually took a couple of steps towards him and he found himself edging backwards, as if they were performing a peculiarly English version of the tango. She stopped and that allowed him to regain some composure while he tried to decipher what she was telling him.

"He didn't? Well, thank God for that. But what is the problem, Irene?"

She was suddenly shy and Schlemm found himself wondering at women yet again. What could possibly be worse than murder?

"He has told me that he was . . . involved with the girl," she admitted at last.

Schlemm stared at her. He had the grace not to laugh, although the struggle to suppress it was titanic. Imagine! Alexander Hamilton-Bailey – small and seemingly asexual – had had sex with the Exner girl! The tableau conjured in the Dean's mind was surreal.

He retreated into high-minded disdain. "Involved? Alexander?"

She nodded. "He is terrified that it will become public. It is killing him, Daniel."

That was clearly no great exaggeration, but the Dean's concentration was filled with thoughts of Professor Hamilton-Bailey; improper thoughts and thoughts, moreover, that were not untinged by envy, for he had seen pictures of Nikki Exner and had been struck by her beauty. Incredulity was the offspring of this envy.

"Alexander had . . . a relationship with the Exner girl?" he enquired for full clarification. She nodded silently. At least, he reflected, she was keeping disapproval from her voice: he would have found such hypocrisy a difficult dish to consume.

Then she said, "She offered him her . . . services in return for which he had to promise her the Anatomy prize."

Schlemm was greatly surprised. A dalliance with an attractive student was bad enough, but selling academic prizes was heinous.

At the same time he wondered who precisely had made the first advance, on whose terms the bargain had been contracted.

"He is truly repentant, Daniel."

The Dean considered. His shock at this news had to be weighed against the need to protect the medical school. And yet . . .

He allowed her anxieties to mature in silence before addressing the ramifications. "I can see the cause for Alexander's discomfort," he said carefully, "but I cannot see what I can do."

She hesitated and at the same time her face and body took on a tense, slightly supplicating attitude. They were close to the crux. "I felt that you have influence – "

"But the case is closed," he interrupted. "The young man who committed this atrocity is dead."

"There was talk of reopening the case. Is that true?"

The Eisenmenger business.

He smiled reassuringly. "The Bilroth family. I'm sure that there is nothing to worry about, Irene. The police seem fairly confident that it's doomed to fail."

But she was not reassured and, in truth, he wondered about Eisenmenger.

"If people are digging about, it's possible that they may stumble upon something." And she then seemed to stumble upon something herself for a look came into her eyes that was not without guile. "The last thing that Alexander and I would wish to see would be embarrassment for the school."

The Dean's head jerked slightly. A threat? No, he decided, not that. Just a reminder of mutual concerns. He stared at her for a short while, then nodded slowly. "I appreciate that. The little that I can do will be done."

He smiled and she responded in kind briefly then looked down.

"Come," he said, ushering her out of the room. "Let's forget the matter for the moment. I will do my utmost to see that such irrelevancies are kept out of the public eye, and you may have my word on that."

"Thank you, Daniel." She said it quite formally but then she glanced up and there was a moment when they were looking at each other directly and the Dean was forced into a past he had thought dead. Then she looked down again, turned and walked before him out of the room.

At about eleven-thirty on the Sunday morning, just as she was returning from the short walk to the newsagent on the corner with three broadsheet newspapers under her arm, Helena began to feel nauseous and the world around her head commenced a stately, groggy whirl. By the time she had reached her flat, she could feel a membranous perspiration on her skin and the colours of the universe were fast bleaching to a sickly hue. It was as she slammed the door behind her that she fainted, falling heavily to the carpet, her fall at least partly broken by the bulk of newsprint that hit the floor just before she did.

When she came to, the nausea was still present but thankfully she had not vomited. When she tried to pick herself up, she found that her muscles were belligerently refusing to co-operate, preferring to shake uncontrollably rather than do her bidding. Leaving the newspapers where they were, she made her exceedingly unsteady way back to her bed, thinking, *It must be a virus. One of those things that are always going around.*

She did not bother to undress as she lay on the bed. A glance at the clock by her head told her that she had been unconscious for perhaps fifteen minutes, although she felt as if she had been in a coma for months, perhaps years. Everything around her was still curiously drained, almost pathetic in its colouring, and it still insisted on moving, although only when she was not looking directly at it. Her head was beginning to ache, too.

She drifted off into sleep, but it was not a restful state, rather a strained, tortured ordeal, full of awareness, although awareness of what she could not say. Twice she was roused from this state to be sick.

By three o'clock, and no better – she was shivering now, whilst her head beat heavy cast iron to a thudding pulse – she decided she should call for help, but therein lay a problem. She had never registered with a general practitioner. Usually sickness passed her by (the worst she suffered was usually a heavy cold and once she had had influenza) and there had always been better, more productive things to do.

She refused to believe that she was ill enough to warrant an ambulance and considered, as she lay upon her bed and looked at the ceiling, whether she could try NHS Direct. She rose warily from the bed and walked unsteadily into the sitting room. She sat herself in one of the armchairs – the one by the phone – and searched through the directory. She signally failed to find what she required, realizing only tardily that her directories were probably out of date.

Angrily she threw them to the floor, turning with little hope to her personal telephone notebook. Perhaps, she reasoned, one of her friends or colleagues might be able to assist her.

Thus it was that she came upon John Eisenmenger's phone number.

Sunday afternoon had come with Eisenmenger stretched out on the sofa in an attitude that would have caused Marie an apocalyptic apoplexy. On the coffee table was a quarter of a pizza in a greasy, tomato-smeared box, beside which were an empty bottle and a full glass of red wine. The television was on but Eisenmenger was not concentrating on it.

He had tried on numerous occasions since Saturday afternoon to contact Marie but without any success. He left messages on the answering service of her mobile phone asking her to ring, but if she had heard them she hadn't responded. Not that he wanted to talk to her but for all Mr Morton's conviction that the brick had been thrown by a disgruntled gypsy, and for all Eisenmenger's disbelief that Marie would be capable of such an act, he wanted to hear shocked denial from her own mouth. And of course, as his luck played the fool with him, now that he wanted to communicate with her, she was silent and invisible.

And as if all that were not enough to occupy him, there was still the death of Nikki Exner to ponder. He felt instinctively that his analysis of the findings was correct, even if he would not be able to prove it by strict Socratic means. The problem came with the corollary of his reasoning: that either Hamilton-Bailey or Russell was the murderer. Not only murderer but also sodomite, necrophiliac and dissectionist. It seemed a heavy burden for any man to bear, although so traumatic had been his relationship with Russell and so underhand had the man's behaviour been on occasion that he was inclined to believe him capable of anything.

Even though . . .

Something was missing. This thought kept gnawing at his tiredness and his concern for Helena.

The doorbell rang and, completely without rational foundation, he knew at once that it was Marie. He hurriedly got to his feet and went out to the hall. Through the frosted glass panel beside the front door he could see a female shape and he felt suddenly confused by the contradictory emotions he felt. The relief he had felt since she had gone and taken with her the obsessiveness, the emotional brittleness and the hysterical undertones had been wonderful, and he didn't want to be immersed in them again. Yet he had once loved her, found her attractive and good to be around; not all her character traits were negative. Anyway, he had to talk to her, find out whether she could possibly be undertaking some sort of vendetta against Helena.

He opened the door.

"Dr Eisenmenger – John? May I come in?"

Without actually waiting for an answer, Beverley Wharton moved inside past a startled pathologist. She stopped in the hall and turned to him. The surprise must have shown on his face for she frowned slightly and said, "Were you expecting someone else? Is it not convenient?"

He rearranged his face. "It's fine. Just a bit surprised, that's all."

She smiled. "I thought we should talk."

She was wearing a tailored navy blue overcoat and this she now took off. Beneath she was wearing a tight, cream-coloured top and a skirt that had clearly been cut from some cloth the size of a face flannel. If Eisenmenger's eyes did not exactly start from their sockets like quills upon the fretful porpentine, they certainly widened both appreciably and appreciatively. She made no sign that she had noticed this reaction. In turn he made no sign that he thought she was sex on a stick.

He took her coat and she went into the sitting room. By the time he had hung up her coat and followed her she was looking in admiration around the room.

"You have very good taste."

He smiled for a second but said nothing. What did she want? He was wary but intensely curious. "Can I get you a drink?"

She indicated the wine. "I'll have some of that, if you have any more."

When he returned with a second bottle and a glass, she was sitting in an armchair, her knees bent and her legs angled slightly obliquely as if they were too long to sit comfortably in the space available. The attitude showed them to good effect and he tried not to look at them.

"We've worked together off and on for quite a while. I thought that it was about time to get to know each other a little better."

But he hadn't, until now, done forensic work for a long time, and on the few occasions when they had chanced to meet in the past she had shown no desire to 'get to know' him.

"Really?"

She took a sip of wine.

"I remember you from the Pendred case. I don't suppose you noticed me. I was just a beginner. It was my first big case."

But he did remember her. Remembered thinking at the time that she had been remarkably attractive. Of course, things were different then.

As he found himself wondering what she wanted, he was also pleased that she was there. He said cautiously. "Of course I remember you."

"You don't seem enthralled."

"I'm slightly surprised, I suppose. Most of the police officers I've worked with haven't seen socializing with me as a priority."

"Most of the police officers you've worked with have probably had trouble putting on their underpants. I'm different."

And from where he was sitting, Eisenmenger could appreciate how different.

"This wouldn't have anything to do with the Exner case, would it?" he enquired.

She stared at him for a moment, as if making a calculation, then smiled broadly over another small drink of wine. "The Exner case is closed," she pointed out.

"Is it?"

Her eyes as they stared at him were dark and grey. There was lipstick on the rim of her glass, like cherry-red crayon. "Closed and dead. Gone for ever."

"Then why do you want to know what I found at the second autopsy? That is why you're here, isn't it?"

She took a long time and a fair amount of wine to answer that one.

"I admit that I'm curious."

Perhaps it was the wine, perhaps it was the feeling that he had the measure of her, but Eisenmenger found himself enjoying the situation.

"You know that I can't tell you that. The defence is not required to divulge its evidence."

"Defence? But as I've said, the case is closed. Tim Bilroth murdered Nikki Exner. There's nothing *sub judice* about this; you have no client who will suffer if you tell me what you've found."

He considered this. What she said was true, but he had sided with two people who were her enemies. Helena clearly hated her with corrosive passion for what she believed she had done to her brother: Johnson claimed that she had framed him because he had threatened her ambition. He, however, had no such animosity towards her.

She continued, "I know that Tim Bilroth committed those crimes: I know that he raped her and then murdered her in a vile and appalling way. But if you have evidence that you believe may contradict that, then you have a duty to make it known to the police as soon as you can. If there's the slightest chance that we were wrong, we need to know as soon as possible."

It was a persuasive speech. Her glass was empty and he refilled it for her. She said, "Look, John. I admit that I would like to know what you found, but that's not the only reason I came here this afternoon."

"No?"

She leaned forward. It was only then that he realized she wasn't wearing a bra. "I do find you attractive. Perhaps we can work together. We'd make a good team, I think."

For the first time Eisenmenger could feel the wine's effects. Her words swirled slightly through his head. She went on, "If there's a suspicion that Tim Bilroth was innocent, we need to act fast."

She was right, perhaps. They were playing at detectives and she, for all her faults, was a professional. Whatever Helena's dreams of seeing Beverley Wharton destroyed, their first consideration had to be to the Law.

He hesitated and to hide it he finished his wine, refilling it as he topped her glass up. She leaned forward to take the glass. He noticed that her wrists and fingers were almost painful in their thinness. She wore a slender gold neck chain and bracelet to match. Her nails looked manicured.

"This wine is delicious," she said. "I hope you've got some more."

The implication shone and sparked. The smile that grew on his face was autonomous and not about to listen to any instructions he might give it to fuck off. She looked again around the room. "Is there no Mrs Eisenmenger? No helpmeet?"

No, unless you count the psychotic one who was stalking Helena with a knife of pure poison stuck inside her suspenders.

It occurred to him that he should tell her about Marie, but he knew that he couldn't. In the deepest part of him there was still only fear not conviction that she was guilty. Anyway, he was enjoying the flirting too much to spoil it with reality.

"Not at the moment."

She looked surprised. "No? What about little Helena? Surely you and she . . . ?" If condescension were made solid, it would have been indistinguishable from Beverley Wharton.

He shook his head and tried sophistication as he replied, "Not in the least," as if it were a question testing his maturity.

Perhaps he passed because having finished the glass she leaned back with a sigh, her head stretched over the chair back, her eyes closed. "I can't believe a good-looking man like you will be on his own for long."

He got up. He felt drunk but it wasn't all wine, he was sure. "Another bottle?"

"Why not?" she asked.

From the kitchen he said, "Look, about the Exner case. I see what you're saying, but I can't let you see the report without talking to Helena Flemming first. It is hers, technically speaking."

He didn't see her reaction. He heard a languid reply though. "Of course. I understand."

He returned to the living room, an opened bottle in his hand. She was smiling, she was relaxed, she was suddenly the only thing within his field of view. He brought the bottle back to her, trying to tell himself that he wasn't drunk, that he was in perfect motor and emotional control. That the bottle neck knocked against the rim of the glass gave the lie to the first and thus destroyed hope for the second.

But he wasn't about to let reality intrude on what he wanted to believe.

He sat down beside her and somewhen, somehow he had become part of an intimate, private party, a dance towards copulation. He saw Beverley watching him, saw in her eyes that she, too, knew where they were bound, saw also (he fancied) excitement.

He robustly thrust to one side the concept that she was using him.

She moved closer to him, personal space joyously a thing of the past. He could feel how warm she was, how soft and warm and fragrant. Her lips were shiny bright, her eyes were large. He didn't need to eye her legs or her breasts or her waist to appreciate just how arousing she was, and how pleasurable it would be to caress her and to have her caress him in the intimacy of his quiet bedroom . . .

His phone began to ring, a bastard cuckoo.

"Shit," he murmured. For a moment he considered ignoring it, and he even looked to Beverley for advice, but her face was expressionless, as if daring him to answer it.

"Sorry," he said. A brief look of irritation passed across her face as he pulled away from her and picked up the phone.

"John Eisenmenger."

"I'm sorry to bother you."

Helena didn't sound bothered, just slightly detached. Anyway, the irritation he had felt when she had rung had dissipated at once when she had opened the door to him and large eyes had looked at him from a grey, pasty face. That she had almost fainted in front of him had also helped.

He smiled. "No problem."

He had helped her back to her bed, and was now feeling her pulse, checking her eyes. He had brought with him an old sphygmo-manometer and stethoscope (from an ancient time in his career) and had discovered that her blood pressure had dropped significantly.

"A virus, I suppose."

"Maybe. But I think it's more likely to be delayed concussion."

She frowned. "But I feel awful . . . "

He smiled. "People with concussion do, Helena." He stood up. "You need to sleep. It may take a day or two to get over it."

She nodded slightly. For a moment she said nothing, then murmured, "I hope that you weren't doing anything."

The smile that he produced was outwardly reassuring, inwardly ironic. "Nothing. Nothing at all."

She closed her eyes. He moved out of the bedroom, returning with a jug of water. "Drink lots. Paracetamol for the headache. Eat when you feel like it."

She was almost asleep. "I'll go now. I'll call back tomorrow. If you need anything else, let me know."

But she didn't reply.

Beverley Wharton was long gone when he returned, although not as long gone as Eisenmenger imagined, for she had returned to his apartment as soon as his car had turned out of sight. It hadn't taken her much trouble to enter, using skills and tools picked up in her police career, and it had required only five minutes to locate what she wanted. She had then spent a further twenty minutes making detailed notes of Eisenmenger's autopsy report.

She had replaced everything neatly, then had left at once.

She made only one mistake, leaving the door to his study wide open, when he had left it only slightly ajar.

Thus it was that Eisenmenger looked into the room, the faintest of suspicions aroused. Even then he might well have ignored the incident – after all, he couldn't be certain that he wasn't mistaken or that a draught hadn't blown the door open – but that when he went into the study and looked through his papers, he caught the faint but unmistakable scent of Beverley Wharton's perfume.

He sat back in the chair before his desk and began to wonder.

Monday brought a slight warmth in the air but that merely high-lighted the dampness. Walking along the streets produced only a feeling of moist depression, the atmosphere unable to decide whether it was gas or liquid and settling for an unsatisfactory emulsion of the two. Only the wet-distorted cobwebs drooping from gateposts and bushes lent a hint of sparkle to the vague mistiness all around.

Professor Russell's attitude that morning was not exactly euphoric but he did feel slightly more content than he had done for several weeks. Thus his entrance into the Department of Pathology was not accompanied (as it frequently had been) by a crescendo of caustic put-downs, explosive dismissals and obscenities, but by a relative calm that allowed the customary antemeridian tension gradually to ebb away.

He even smiled at Gloria, an experience which she later claimed in a loud whisper to Belinda to have brought on her period.

After passing through the secretaries' office Russell shut the door and was therefore unaware of the looks that were exchanged by all those who had witnessed this miracle.

Thus the morning began; alas not to continue so.

Eisenmenger had arrived early but without achieving anything productive. He had already telephoned Helena, discovering with a surprising amount of relief that she was feeling much better. He had advised her to continue to rest as much as possible.

His offer to come round had been gratefully acknowledged, gracefully refused.

Which left him to contemplate events that had come to pass and those that might have done, a process that left him listless and depressed. He tried to analyse his guilt – after all he had not actually had sex with Beverley Wharton – but this lack of action did not comfort him. He knew that had Helena not called when she did, he would have happily fucked Beverley Wharton as much as and in whichever way she wanted. He still felt that he had committed a mortal sin, that there had still been betrayal, a feeling that would not yield to rational argument. He knew that he owed nothing to Marie and he hardly knew Helena, that he had no history of significance with Beverley Wharton, and all of this knowing made no difference whatsoever.

There was also the matter of whether Beverley Wharton had merely been trying to generate an opportunity to get a look at his autopsy report. His self-respect vehemently proclaimed this as rubbish but there was enough insight within his soul to admit that this was possible, perhaps even probable. He had little in the way of tangible proof, but he *knew*, just as he knew without proof that the sun would rise again tomorrow, that she had been back, that she had been in his study.

What to do? He fretted this question out for a long time, during his journey in and while sitting, absorbed, at his desk, although in truth he knew that confessing his actions to Helena was beyond him. He would have to live with it, drawing comfort (perhaps falsely) from the knowledge that he had probably acted in a legally correct manner, even if the ethics were moot.

It was at this point that there came a knock on the door and, without pause, the Dean entered.

Eisenmenger was so surprised he didn't speak for a second. Seeing the Dean out of his office was like seeing a snail out of its shell or, perhaps more aptly, an alligator in the living room.

"Dr Eisenmenger." Not a question and not a smile. This was an alligator with prolapsed piles. Somewhat belatedly Eisenmenger stood, indicating with a gesturing hand that his visitor should take a seat. The Dean remained standing and merely stared at Eisenmenger as if he had just caught him mooning out of the window.

"It has come to my attention that despite friendly advice to the contrary you have persisted in your pursuit of the Exner business. Is that correct?"

The phrasing was not quite as he would have wished, and the tone was definitely not to his taste, but Eisenmenger had to concede that there was a nucleus of truth within the Dean's words. "What of it?"

The Dean's expression suggested that by this remark Eisenmenger had shown himself to possess the intelligence of an earthworm with learning difficulties. "The Exner case was a most unfortunate occurrence that brought unwelcome publicity to this institution. It was bad enough that it happened at all, let alone that the circumstances should have been so . . . macabre: the fact that it should have been committed by an employee of the medical school – albeit one in an extremely junior position – only served to increase the damage done. I had at least hoped that we had seen the worst of the affair through and that the medical school could begin to forget about the incident.

"You, however," and he used an intonation on the personal pronoun that was little short of venomous, "clearly have a different agenda."

Eisenmenger felt himself to be mild-mannered, but he wasn't inclined that particular Monday morning to bend over invitingly so that the Dean could plant one on his arse.

"My agenda," he said with a tight, not to say linear, smile, "is to find out who really killed Nikki Exner."

"That has been established. The only purpose you serve in continuance of this matter is to destabilize this department, indeed the medical school as a whole, and to risk further damage to the reputation of one of the most venerated medical academies in Europe."

Eisenmenger was so surprised by this charge he didn't have time to respond before Schlemm continued. "Since as an employee you are charged with upholding the high reputation of the medical school, I believe that you can be considered to be in breach of contract by your actions. Accordingly, I will be bringing your case before the Academic Board tomorrow. If they agree, as I believe they will, and if you do not immediately desist in your actions, you will be suspended as from 5 p.m. on Friday."

Eisenmenger didn't know whether to be happy or angry: certainly sadness wasn't among the options.

"I don't believe that Nikki Exner died at the hands of Tim Bilroth, " he said. "I think that someone else killed her and whether or not I'm employed here will make no difference to that."

Schlemm just stared at him for a while. He then turned and walked to the door. "I have talked personally with the Chief Constable. The police are entirely convinced that Bilroth was responsible for the murder. They do, however, believe that by your actions you are hampering any subsequent investigations into the role played by any accomplices."

He opened the door. "You have until Friday."

Eisenmenger's shock at the Dean's news had rendered him silent. The Dean left and Eisenmenger just stared at the door. They were looking for accomplices? Was that connected with Beverley Wharton's sudden interest in him? He felt that it ought to make sense, but he could see only swirling patterns. They were so mesmerizing that he hardly bothered to consider his own impending dismissal.

Just then he felt pinned, ready for dissection, by guilt, uncertainty and the suspicion that deep forces were moving stealthily around him.

On Monday morning Stephan Libman waited until his mother had been gone on her shopping trip for ten minutes before beginning to write his letter. He emerged from his room, whistling slowly and quietly, the picture of a young man who had decided on a course of action and who was going to follow this resolution through with determination. He descended the stairs, one hand holding the banister, the fingers of the other running over the rough surface of the wallpaper as they had many thousands of times before. Then he swung around the newel post, leaping off the last three steps as he did so, to land in the hall facing the kitchen. He then turned left through the closed doorway to enter the sanctum that was the front sitting room.

It was cold and it was musty, more sensations that he knew so well that they had solidified into foundation bricks for his life. Never disturbed and hardly ever used, it represented for his mother a symbol of a gentility and financial comfort that had long since passed into fragmented memory and nostalgia.

Poor old cow.

There was a bureau in this room; one of his mother's many heirlooms. It was a tattered thing of scratched walnut veneer that she fondly believed was valuable but of too much sentimental worth to sell. Stephan thought it was probably worth shit but also thought it wouldn't do any harm to test the market when his beloved mother croaked. For now, it served as a desk whenever his mother had to write letters on the small, clackety portable typewriter that lived between its squat legs. It was to this that he turned having pulled the bureau open.

In one of the drawers there was a half-empty box of typing paper that had been purchased in 1962, and he now took a sheet of this and put it into the typewriter. In the end he had to put it in three times because he couldn't get it straight, but eventually he was ready.

What to write?

Stephan was not experienced in writing. He had left school with eight GCSEs, of which one had been English, and he enjoyed reading, but composition was not a strength. Certainly not the ability to construct a letter of this type. Thus he had to ponder things before commencing. Businesslike, he decided after much thought, would be best. Pithy and without melodrama. The facts presented, the possible consequences made plain, the solution written without emotion or hint of hesitation.

Even then, three more pieces of his mother's yellowing typing paper were required before he felt reasonably content with his labour. The envelope also proved problematic, both to feed through the machine and to orientate correctly. After nearly an hour's work he was finished and reasonably satisfied. He then took from his pocket a photograph and folded the letter around it before putting it in the envelope. It only remained to find a first class stamp and this was easy since he knew that his mother kept a small supply of them under a china shepherdess on the mantelshelf.

256

At last he had completed his task and it was with no little happiness and anticipation that he contemplated the result of his labour but, aware that he could spare no time (his mother was due back in the not too distant future), he felt that he could not rest. Accordingly he put on his beloved black leather jacket (his mother, he knew, silently disliked it but never once had she openly criticized it), checked that he had his house key and pulled the front door closed behind him.

The nearest post-box was a five-minute walk away. He had debated the wisdom of posting this particular missive at a more distant place – even the other side of the city – but he had decided against this. He was not planning, after all, to maintain absolute anonymity throughout this particular transaction. There was no point. No point at all.

He smiled as he turned the corner, the post-box now invitingly red in the distance. He considered that he had been patient: his mother was always telling him that patience was a virtue, that he was too impatient, and now (had she but known) he had demonstrated such moderation, such restraint he felt sure that she would have been proud (had she but known).

Still it would be well worth it. The kind of chance, he was convinced, that would come only once but, if grasped, would lead on to fortune. Stephan had read *Julius Caesar* at school for his English GCSE and he often liked to use its wisdom to lead him through life.

He reached the post-box and paused. So great was the significance of this moment that he paused. It should not pass without some slight ceremony, he felt. Accordingly he took the envelope from his inner pocket, regarded it, kissed it and then flourished it with a quiet verbal fanfare before finally consigning it to the lips of the box.

Then he turned round and discovered Johnson standing behind. He was so close Stephan almost bumped into him.

"Hello, Stephan." There was a look around the eyes and there was a tone in the voice that Stephan didn't care for. What had he seen?

"Nice day for a walk," continued Johnson. It wasn't actually. It was cold, blowy and grey, and there was a faint touch of drizzle around them.

"Yeah." He kept his head down as if embarrassed. There was a wait, then he said to his shoes, "I'd better be getting back."

"Mind if I walk with you? I've got a few more questions to ask you."

Accepting this as inevitable, Stephan only shrugged. They moved off, away from the post-box.

"Posting something, were you?"

"Yeah."

Johnson marvelled at the utility of that monosyllable. "Found another job?"

Stephan shook his head.

Johnson nodded understanding. "Plenty of time. Young man like you shouldn't rush headlong into something that you'll later regret. As long as your mum doesn't mind you lazing around the house all day, eh?"

Stephan said, "She's okay with it."

"Good."

They walked on. Then Johnson said, "The night of the murder. What time did you leave the museum?"

Stephan's eyes flicked up then back to their station on pavement watch. It was a movement that Johnson caught. "Just after six."

"And then what?"

"I went home. Had my tea."

Johnson puckered his lips and nodded as if this cosy domesticity met with his full approval. "Then what?"

Stephan's response to that one came along a second's fraction later than his previous replies. "I went out. To a club."

"Which one?"

"Casey's."

Johnson knew it. Knew also that it would be impossible to verify the story. "What time was that?"

"'Bout nine."

"And you got back?"

"'Bout midnight."

"Your mum could support what you say?"

For the first time Stephan showed more than just grumpy indifference. "Of course she could!" he protested and Johnson didn't doubt that she would.

They were nearly back at Stephan's house and Johnson didn't particularly want to meet Mrs Libman, or her teapot, again. He parted from Libman and walked back to his car. He hadn't learned much but he had again felt a hint that Stephan was hiding something. And it was interesting that Libman had been out from nine until midnight. From here the travelling time to the museum was thirty minutes, which meant that Stephan could have been there between nine thirty and eleven thirty, overlapping with the time that Nikki Exner might have been there, and also coinciding with the likely time of death.

He got into the car. He couldn't believe that Libman was the murderer, but he'd been wrong before. He started the engine and moved off. As he drove past the post-box, he again found himself wondering what Libman had been doing as he had walked up behind him. The address had been typewritten but Johnson had unfortunately not been able to read it.

Beverley Wharton had worked quickly that morning. Her perusal of Eisenmenger's autopsy report had been well worth the risk of illegal entry. It was a pity, she decided, that she had not had the chance of a night spent in his bed. She suspected that there would have been much mutual satisfaction . . .

Perhaps another time.

She drove straight from his flat to the station. She was well aware that Superintendent Bloom was an early riser and the fewer people around the better. She was going to have to do a lot of explaining, a lot of 'reinterpretation'. She had no doubt that this would cost her a few nights of moist, sweaty boredom in the weeks ahead.

Eisenmenger's report was a strong, possibly fatal, blow against her interpretation of what had happened that night. She had enough respect for his abilities to prefer his findings to Sydenham's and she knew that others would as well. Now, therefore, she had to reactivate the case but do it on her terms: she felt confident that if she managed the situation calmly she could come out of it with her standing intact. The trick was to use what she had gleaned to her own advantage but it would only work if she acted quickly.

She was right in expecting a hard time. Her request did not go down well.

"You want what?"

"I want to reopen the Exner case."

The Superintendent looked at her for a long time. His expression was opaque but his accent began to show slightly.

"But I don't understand, Beverley. You have reassured us that the case is closed. Bilroth killed her and now he, too, is dead. He had form. He had her possessions in his flat. Very neat."

"Yes, sir . . . "

"But now you want to reopen the case."

"Yes, sir . . . "

He held up his hand to silence her. It was a nice office; neat, tidy and, she now noticed, silent. Abruptly, he sighed, smiled and leaned forward, forearms on the desk. "Just what the fuck are you playing at, Beverley?" he enquired in a deceptively plaintive tone.

"I'm still convinced that Bilroth was involved," she said quickly, "but further information has . . . come into my possession."

The smile remained but his eyes closed. "Meaning?"

"Look, Bilroth killed her. He raped her and he killed her – the evidence is still incontrovertible on that – but I think that there may have been someone else involved."

"Why do you think that?"

She was having to go further than she would have liked but her options were limited.

"The second post-mortem . . . "

She was interrupted with a soft sigh as if he had known that no good would come of it.

" . . . indicates that she may have been sodomized; there may even have been necrophilia. That would indicate serious sexual perversion."

"And Bilroth wasn't a pervert?" he asked tiredly.

"I think it would be prudent to assure ourselves that no one else involved in the case has such a history."

He considered. "Why didn't the first autopsy show this?"

She certainly wasn't going to take any crap about that particular cock-up. She shrugged then added, "There's more."

Bloom jerked his head up. "What now, for Christ's sake?"

"It's possible that she was pregnant, that the uterus was cut out and substituted."

For a long moment he just stared at her. "Fucking hell!" he said at last. "Fucking, bloody hell! Didn't Sydenham get anything right?"

She let that one go as well. She had, she felt, done enough to ensure that Dr Sydenham would not be called in again.

The conversation moved on. Warily she was asked, "Anything else?"

She shook her head. "You can see why I think it prudent to reopen the case, can't you?"

Again he was looking hard at her as he replied. "I agree that it would be unwise to ignore this new evidence." Then, "How did you come by it, Beverley?"

She kept her face passive. "I know John Eisenmenger quite well, sir."

He nodded slowly. *I bet you do.* "This could turn out to be very embarrassing," he said slowly but it was as much to himself as to her. Then, almost as if he were changing the subject he said, "You've impressed a lot of people, Beverley. The right people. We have high hopes of you . . . "

The dying fall was like a disappointed sigh.

"If this autopsy evidence had been available at the time, sir . . ." she pointed out and he nodded sadly in agreement. Perhaps he did not recall that she made the arrest within eight hours of the crime being discovered: certainly he did not bring it to her attention. She added, "It doesn't alter the fundamental facts implicating Bilroth."

Another nod. Then a pause, then a decision.

"Okay. Take Wilson and one other."

She expressed gratitude but didn't make a move to go. He raised his eyebrows. "Is there something else, Chief Inspector?"

This was even more delicate. "There's still the problem of Bilroth's family and the lawyer they've employed. Johnson's been employed to snoop into things for them . . . "

"He's resigned. I can't touch him unless he breaks the law."

"I realize that, sir. But their activities may hamper my investigations."

Bloom's face told her the answer before he spoke. "Hard luck. If the law's broken, feel free to drop on him and flush the toilet. Otherwise, leave him alone."

His tone was final. She stood. "Thank you, sir."

He got up and went to the door, ostensibly to open it for her. His hand remained on the handle.

"You're certain that Bilroth did it, aren't you?"

Their faces were close. She could see that he had scratched a spot on the side of his nose and made it bleed. "Oh, yes," she said simply. She didn't blink and she didn't swallow. Another long pause while he stared at her.

"Don't cock it up, Beverley." Then the smile again. As he opened the door he said into her ear, "You owe me, Chief Inspector."

She didn't doubt that the debt would be called in. Taking a deep breath she tried to put the thought out of her head as she went looking for Wilson. The canteen seemed the likeliest place but in the end, and somewhat miraculously, she found him sitting at his desk. As usual he looked pale, ill and dyspeptic. His tie had once been pale blue and tie-shaped: now it was a stretched cord and its palette of topaz shades – streaks, blotches and distorted circles – caught the eye, much as a drying pile of vomit on the pavement might. His desk was piled high with paper on which she could see his scrawled misspellings, and around him, on the dirt-streaked nylon carpet, there was a confectioner's assortment of chocolate wrappers.

He straightened slightly as he saw her. "Morning, sir," he said. It had taken him some time to stop reflexively calling her "Sarge".

"Where's Lockwood?"

He shrugged and it was clear this meant not only that he didn't know but, more significantly, that he didn't give a shit.

"Find him. In my office, ten minutes."

Eisenmenger felt the need to return as an instinct. It had tugged at him throughout the day – a calling, a yearning, as if he were a bird hearing the call to migrate home. His journey through the coldness of the dusk was an automaton's, his thoughts flowing through him and gone without trace as he walked.

Tamsin's grave.

The old man had gone. All humanity had gone, leaving only the ghosts and the disregard, the chill and the sorrow. The grass was wet and it took no time to soak through his shoes and to saturate his trouser legs. There was nowhere to sit – why should there be?

And as he stood there, the darkness as much a tomb as the ground beneath, he at last knew why he had come.

To ask forgiveness.

The guilt with which he had awoken would not leave him, had actually grown with the day's ageing. It had come as something of a shock to realize why.

Helena.

He was falling in love with her.

And this had caused him yet again to try to analyse his feelings towards Helena, this time with added data. The conclusion was shocking to him, for he had understood himself so poorly. He had thought that he felt attraction towards Helena, that she was an attractive, intelligent woman with whom he desired a relationship; now he discovered he was deeply in love with her.

Incredibly, Helena had infused into him, completely beyond his detection, so that now she was part of him.

Hence the intensity of his pain at his action.

Hence his presence here, at Tamsin's side. Tamsin was the one person who, through her innocence and incorruptibility, could allow him exoneration.

But he knew that such absolution would not come without price, that exculpation would be just that – an extraction, an exhumation, an elimination. Without pain, it would be meaningless.

He felt the coldness of the air and the dampness of the grass through his feet. He began to pray and, not long after, he began to cry.

That night Helena was in a hurry and she dropped her keys as she came through the lobby doors and entered the vestibule of her block of flats. If she hadn't done that she might never have seen the figure sitting in one of the easy chairs of the waiting area. It was late and only the uplighters were producing any illumination, but there was something about the outline that caused her to pause. Was the figure staring at her? She could make out no details but its posture conjured the impression.

Helena was tired and wanted only to relax in the comfort of her flat, but she was not the kind of person just to ignore something like this. If she was being stared at, she wanted to know why and by whom. She approached the figure.

"Can I help you?"

The first detail that became apparent was the eyes. Eyes that were large and both impassive yet beseeching. It was then that Helena realized who it was.

"You're Marie, aren't you?"

Still the figure did and said nothing.

Helena moved closer, so that the shape of the face became clearer. Of the body she could see nothing, for it was hunched and enveloped in some sort of encompassing dark clothing. "It is you, isn't it? What are you doing here?"

But the eyes said nothing, and Helena found the figure's impassivity becoming threatening in itself.

The brick through her office window came back to her. The assumption that it was the travellers was widely held and it was the main theory of the police, but as far as Helena could tell it was without supporting evidence. It was likely because they could think of no other explanation, but this to Helena showed the limitations of Occam's razor: the simplest explanation was only the likeliest if you had the wit or the knowledge to exclude all else. Her perspective on the crime was different because she knew that someone had recently come close to running her down. Was that connected?

She had worried at this for the last two days, swinging between suspicion and disbelief – it was plainly absurd that someone would want to throw bricks at her head – but never settled on an easy conclusion. She had half suspected that Eisenmenger, too, had wondered, but she had not dared to question him on the issue.

And also there was the problem of why she had not told the police of the possibility. That question was even harder to answer.

Now here she was, closer still to Helena's personal space. Not screaming, not spitting, just contemplating: the passivity far, far scarier than histrionics.

She tried again. "Look, Marie, I don't know what you're doing here, but I might as well tell you that you've got hold of completely the wrong idea, okay? John Eisenmenger and I aren't . . . lovers. We just have a professional relationship and – "

Abruptly she was interrupted.

"I don't know what you're talking about."

Taken aback, Helena said, "What do you mean? Of course you do!"

The other just sighed. Her face was laden with concern and worry but it was focused elsewhere, as if Helena was just a distraction. A couple came in through the entrance doors making for the lifts when Helena said, "Don't act the innocent. I'm fed up with this harassment. I'm going to the police if you don't stop."

She hadn't intended to speak loudly but there was sufficient volume for the couple to glance across as they waited for the lift.

"Really, I don't know what you mean. I'm just waiting for someone."

"Who?" demanded Helena. "Who are you waiting for?"

Her eyes were on the distance over Helena's shoulder as she replied, "My boyfriend."

"You mean John, don't you? He's your boyfriend, isn't he?"

The lift, as ever, was taking ages, but the couple no longer cared. No popcorn but free admission.

"I think I'd better leave."

She began to push past Helena, but Helena resisted and for a moment there was a slight scuffle. Then abruptly the woman called out, "Please let me go! Stop pushing me! I want to leave now!"

The lift doors opened but no one cared. With sudden strength the woman pushed hard and Helena staggered, then fell on the marble floor. The other was gone before she realized, shouting, "Leave me alone!" into the night. The lift doors were closing but the man stopped them and forced them open again. Then the couple got in. Helena's last sight of them was as she stood up and brushed herself down. Their expressions were mingled pity, amusement and disdain.

On Tuesday morning Gloria took Professor Russell's post in to him at about half-past ten, as per usual. According to custom she had first separated the cases referred to him for his expert opinion and given these to the laboratory staff for registering and processing. The remainder consisted of the usual assortment of memos from the Trust management, generic, photocopied letters from regional pathology groups and committees, polythene-wrapped journals and flyers from medical book publishers. Very occasionally there was a letter that was marked 'Private' or 'Confidential', and these she left unopened since the one time that she had not done this (it was her second day), Professor Russell had emerged from his office puce, eyes staring and flesh actually quivering. He had then demonstrated to her the full range of his considerable biological vocabulary, using a voice that alternated between a menacing snarl and a jowl-wobbling shout. Someone more timid would have crawled, broken, to the door never to return: Gloria sat there, took the shock wave without a backward stagger, then made a mental note not to do it again.

Thus it was that the letter marked 'Private and Confidential' passed through her hands unmolested.

And thus it was that he slit open the envelope and pulled out the letter. The photograph fell out on to the desk, face up. His curious glance at it petrified into a stare. Horror subsumed him and he stared at it, paralysed. Then the letter re-entered his consciousness and he turned to it with an awful certainty in his heart.

He read it through, then read it again. His face collapsed as if every muscle had vanished, the skin paling quite suddenly, taking on as it did so an instantaneous sweaty moistness. It was as well that he was sitting, but even so his whole frame collapsed back into the leather of the chair.

He began to shake. Shake with fear.

There was really no alternative, although he had taken many hours to decide it. And the decision, once made, served to relieve him, to liberate him. Indeed, so liberated and relieved did he feel that he felt emboldened to ring the Dean.

"Yes?" The question was posed as if he could not imagine why Eisenmenger should be bothering him, as if he had not so recently appeared, mean and lean, in Eisenmenger's office.

"It's John Eisenmenger. I've come to a decision."

There was a short pause and Eisenmenger couldn't be sure if Schlemm was distracted or merely uninterested. "And?"

"You will have my resignation by tomorrow morning."

He had expected more than he got. "Really?" was the reply. Then, "It occurs to me, Dr Eisenmenger, that given your obviously . . . " He had trouble with the *mot juste*, "heterodox views, your continued presence in the department would be unhelpful."

Eisenmenger once more found himself trailing Schlemm's loquacity, bobbing in its wake and out of control. The Dean, God bless his soul, decided to help. "You need not work out your notice."

Eisenmenger's feeling of relief was gone, washed over by incredulity. It didn't seem to have occurred to the Dean that this decision might prove difficult for Russell.

"But . . . "

But, indeed. The Dean had put down the receiver.

Stunned, Eisenmenger went from disbelief through anger, incandescence, resignation and then amusement. Very well, if that was what the Dean decreed, so should it be. He wrote at once his letter of resignation to Personnel, making quite sure that it included Schlemm's suggestion that he need not work out his notice, and copying it to Russell and Schlemm.

He had just finished when Sophie came in. Coincidentally it was her last day as well. "I've just come in to say goodbye and thanks." She looked, he thought, the happiest he had ever seen her.

"I'm sorry it had to end this way, Sophie."

She shrugged one shoulder as if the other were frozen, a curiously lopsided gesture fully in keeping with her lopsided yet appealing character.

"What are you going to do?" he asked.

"I'm thinking about Public Health Medicine."

PHM was the medical equivalent of a nursing home for the mentally incurable. He wasn't surprised by her inclination but it dismayed him nonetheless. "Are you sure about this, Sophie? Don't rush into it."

She nodded as if taking his words seriously: perhaps she was. She left him to his letter and then Belinda came in with some work and the next two hours were thus consumed. As she left he asked, "How's Russell? I've got some bad news for him."

She laughed. "I doubt whether he'll notice. He's in a terrible state. Couldn't even be bothered to shout at anyone today. Wherever his mind's gone, it's left his blubber behind."

Ten minutes later, when he knocked and went into Russell's cavernous office, he saw this for himself. The man was sitting and staring abstractedly at a pile of research articles, the one on top folded over but sadly neglected. When he focused on Eisenmenger, his eyes seemed to travel a million leagues to find him.

"I'm telling you right away as it's only fair. I'm resigning with immediate effect."

He held out the letter and Russell's gaze tracked slowly down to it. Only slowly did he take it, and then all he did was hold it in two hands and look at it.

Eisenmenger had expected shock certainly, anger probably, a hint of consternation possibly, but not blankness, not incomprehension. Russell reacted, or rather failed to react, as if this was an irrelevancy.

Then Russell frowned slightly, looking at Eisenmenger with a face that seemed to cover inner torment. It wasn't warm enough to perspire but Russell's face was damp.

Eisenmenger asked, "Did you hear what I said?"

Russell only slowly cranked up his nodding gear. "Fine. With immediate effect."

Eisenmenger didn't know what to do. It wasn't, he felt, fair. The bloody man ought to have had the grace to at least look out of sorts. From tomorrow he was going to have to run the department single-handedly. Dismayed he turned and walked from the room.

Russell put the letter down unopened.

The porter was dressed in a sort of uniform, although it looked more dirt than fabric. He looked as if he smelled and close proximity did nothing to dispel the notion. He was bad-tempered and clearly going to be uncooperative but Beverley was in no mood to accommodate him.

"Mr Leyden?"

"Who wants him?" Wilson showed him a warrant card that he took in a hand protruding from a frayed cuff and then proceeded to scrutinize.

"Police?" This was in a tone she knew well. "What do you want?"

Beverley Wharton had been looking around the marble and chrome of the art deco entrance hall. She decided that she liked it and was wondering what she would have to pay for a flat there. Turning to Leyden she asked, "You're the porter. Is that right?"

"I am."

"Been here long?"

"Seven years."

"Know the residents well, then, I expect."

"A bit."

She nodded in sympathy. "Get to see a lot, I bet."

"I see it all. I don't miss much."

More empathy was applied. "Good to you, are they? Treat you well?"

He scowled. "You must be joking. Most of 'em treat me like dogshit. Ignore me completely until they want something, then they scream for me as if I was a nigger."

She rode over this breach of the Race Relations Act in the interests of a higher justice. "It's not as if they're better than you . . . "

He nodded vigorously. "Too bloody right. Toffee-nosed bastards. I've seen what some of them get up to. Drunk-driving, mistresses . . . "

Suddenly Beverley asked, "How about Professor Russell?"

The wariness was clicked back into place, exponentially increased. She could almost see it solidify into a carapace.

"Professor Russell?"

"Yes. Professor Russell. Flat seventeen. Know him, do you?"

He made a face that was hard to read. "A bit."

"What does he get up to?"

"Dunno," he mumbled but there were flags above his head fluttering in the breeze and they were telling a different story.

She waited a second, just staring at him, then, "Let me put it this way. I know what he gets up to. I want you to confirm it."

His eyes were wide, exposing whites that were singularly misnamed. His mouth moved, slightly open. He had halitosis.

"Well?" she pressed.

At last he said, "You mean the girl?"

She didn't know what she had meant but she smiled and nodded and said, "That's right. Tell me about her."

He didn't know what to say again and eventually decided on the factually correct but unexpansive, "He has a girl."

There was something about the way he used the word 'girl' that implied this was more than a fiancée.

"A prostitute?" she asked just to ensure that there was no misunderstanding. Too late he realized that he had been fooled.

"Yeah." He looked like a gargoyle.

"Just the one?"

He nodded.

"Always the same, and only ever one?"

He sighed. "Same one, same time, same day."

This was interesting. This was very interesting indeed.

"Do you know her?"

"Sorry," he said, although his look of innocence wouldn't have fooled a two-year-old. It was people like this behaving in this way that she found worst about the job. She leaned as close as her sense of well-being would allow her and said, "I want her name and address and I want them now. You know as well as I do that you were the one that found her for him, and if you don't tell me what I want to hear right now, we'll take you in for procurement, for obstructing the police, for resisting arrest and for having shit for brains." She smiled. "Okay, Mr Leyden?"

Wilson moved behind him and just stood there. Wilson was a crap copper but he could stand menacingly along with the best of them.

Leyden peered behind him for a few seconds, then picked a scrap of paper off his desk and found a pen under his tabloid newspaper. He scribbled just the name *Linda*, followed by an address.

"No second name?" she asked.

Apparently not. It was an occupational hazard, this loss of the surname. The address was quite near.

She passed the paper to Wilson who shook his head. She turned her attention back to the porter. "And this has been going on for how long?"

"Years. Every Wednesday."

"Wednesday? You're sure?"

He looked bored now. "It's been every Wednesday for years. The only time he's ever missed was a few weeks back."

She didn't believe that there was a God, but she prayed to something. "Which Wednesday? Can you remember the date?"

More irritation, but eventually he engaged the neurone and decided. "Same day that student got cut open. I remember because – "

But Beverley didn't care. "You're sure?"

He took offence. "Of course I'm sure."

She wanted to do a little dance but this time she was going to make one hundred and one per cent certain. "Has he ever hurt her?"

He shook his head at once and with great conviction. Either he knew to the contrary or he didn't know at all. That wasn't what she wanted to hear but the coincidence was too much. Far too much. Deciding that she wasn't going to get anything more out of him, she said, "Okay, Mr Leyden. Thanks for your co-operation. I'd advise you to keep this conversation to yourself. Understand?"

He understood. He scowled but he understood.

As they walked out of the building, she instructed Wilson, "Get one of the girls and go and pick her up. Take her to the station, but don't make a big fuss about it. Okay?"

They got into the car, missing Johnson who, having seen them emerging from the building, had hurriedly gone into a pet shop trying to look interested in budgerigars. When they had driven off he left the shop, the shopkeeper eyeing him suspiciously.

What the hell were they doing here?

He crossed the road and went into the mansion block. Mr Leyden was still scowling. Johnson smiled. "Mind if I have a word?"

Leyden glared at him but Johnson was not to be deterred. "I'm after some information."

"Oh, yeah?"

Sensing that there were barriers to be climbed, Johnson changed strategy. "That was the police, wasn't it?" He asked this in a tone tinged with hostility. The porter just continued to glare and so Johnson continued, "What did those bastards want?"

For a moment he thought he had guessed wrong but then the porter's expression changed and he said, "Making fucking trouble, as usual. That's what they always fucking do."

Johnson decided that now he knew his quarry. He pulled out his wallet and found within it some twenty-pound notes. "How would you like to earn some pocket money?" he asked.

The report from the molecular biology lab came through late that afternoon. The first thing that dropped out of the envelope was an invoice for two hundred and seventy-three pounds – money that Eisenmenger would have to find himself – the next was confirmation of what he already knew. The uterus had not been Nikki Exner's.

He had been in his office packing stuff away in boxes. Now he stopped and put this report carefully in his briefcase with the report he had written that morning on the histology sections (he had been informed by the hospital Finance Department that the preparation of the slides was going to cost him one hundred and ninety pounds) he had taken from the corpse: the histological appearances confirmed that the vulval and anal abrasions had most probably occurred after death.

Some hours later, Lockwood's arse was itching fiercely and consequently he was bad-tempered. He sat in the car with Wilson and tapped his fingers on the steering wheel in irritation. Wilson had on his personal stereo and was enjoying some thrash metal but the tinny squawks that reached Lockwood were not conducive to a calm acceptance of his situation.

"Shut that bloody thing up, will you?" he said. Wilson's eyes were closed, his head jerking slightly: it wasn't obvious whether this was a conscious count of the rhythm or a decerebrate spinal reflex induced by the volume of the noise. Lockwood figured once was enough and, reaching out with a perpetually sweaty paw, tugged fiercely on the headphone cord.

"What the fuck did you do that for?"

"It's too loud. Anyway, how can you keep obbo with your eyes closed?"

Not that there was anything worth observing. They had been outside Russell's mansion block for three hours now, having waited for nine hours outside the Pathology Department. It was late and it was cold and it was, in Lockwood's opinion, a waste of his precious time.

"I don't even know why we're bothering with this," he declaimed.

"Cos Bev told us to," was Wilson's accurate but simplistic response.

"But what's the point? We all know that Bilroth topped the girl. What does it matter if Russell likes a bit of fun with a prozzy? Does that make him Jack the fucking Ripper?"

Wilson replaced his headphones and turned the volume down a tenth of a decibel. He had no answer to questions like that, a position he held on all matters of debate, large or small.

Lockwood warmed to his theme. "She said she'd never been hurt by him. He's never so much as cuffed her, let alone got out a knife and threatened to fillet her."

There was no reply to Lockwood's criticisms of his superior's strategy.

In truth, he was not being unreasonable. Beverley Wharton had hoped for considerably more from the prostitute, but had been forced to draw sustenance from scant provender. Russell used a prostitute, once a week, every week. First she performed fellatio on him, then he wanked himself over her then, bizarrely, she was given Madeira wine, paid and sent home. That didn't make him a serial killer but it did (Beverley decided) make him a sexual deviant.

Which was better than Hamilton-Bailey who, as far as she could establish, was completely asexual, even with regard to his wife. There was no hint of impropriety and, it appeared, he and his wife lived separate sexual lives.

She therefore decided that while she continued to dig into Russell's and Hamilton-Bailey's past lives, it would not go amiss for Lockwood and Wilson to keep Russell under close observation.

And so they sat in their untidy, litter-strewn car and watched the blank of the building.

Lockwood farted noisily but Wilson was only aware of this when the stench hit his nostrils. The profanity and distress elicited caused Lockwood some small, compensatory pleasure. He began to chuckle and the more his colleague abused him, the funnier it became.

Thus it was that they almost missed the exit of Russell's overlarge black Mercedes from the building's underground car park.

"Shit!" said Lockwood. "He's leaving!"

Hurriedly he started the car while Wilson again removed his headphones.

They only just managed to keep Russell's car in sight.

Johnson was pissed off, although he wouldn't have used that particular vernacular. He had gone at once to the address that Leyden had given him but was a few minutes too late, arriving just as the police car containing Lockwood, a female uniformed PC and a young woman had driven off. His frustration was alloyed with curiosity. How come the police were suddenly interested in Russell and his sex life? How come, effectively, they were thinking along exactly the same lines as he, Helena and John Eisenmenger were?

He wondered what to do. There was nothing he could do about Hamilton-Bailey – he had initiated several lines of enquiry using contacts who were already becoming tired of hearing from him, but so far there was nothing: not even a suggestion that they might prove productive.

He felt almost juvenile as he was coerced by his indecision to ring Helena.

She did not take his news well.

"She knows, doesn't she? Somehow she knows about the report."

It was difficult not to reach that conclusion.

"Well, I didn't tell her. Did you?"

He declined to offer culpability.

"So it was John," she concluded. She tried to sound objective, but failed. Disappointment was written through in fading letters.

"I can't believe that John would have leaked his findings, Helena."

She looked at him, hoping he was right. "That can wait. The question is what do we do now?"

Russell had been his main hope. Doubtfully he said, "Well, there's still Libman. He's lying; I can feel it. And I haven't spoken yet with Goodpasture."

For a few moments she was silent, then, "Can you find out what the police are up to? You must have some contacts."

He winced. He had been afraid that she was going to ask that. "I don't know. I can try, but people are quickly forgetting that they ever knew me, Helena."

"Try anyway. Then we might as well go and talk to Goodpasture."

"We?"

It was after five and she was at home and bored, feeling left out from the exciting side to all this. "Yes, we. Got a problem?"

He knew better than to have a problem.

The area wasn't a slum but it wasn't good either. Depressing and monotonous, the houses merged into terraces, the terraces into streets, the streets into panoramas, the panoramas into oblivion. Some of the houses were disregarded and neglected, others neat and trim: some were tastefully decorated, others were kitsch: all were indubitably the same however.

In the car, Johnson said, "I've talked to the ITU staff who were on that night. All of them claim to remember clearly, and all of them state quite categorically that Goodpasture was in or around the department until the next morning."

"Then why are we bothering?"

Johnson heard exasperation in her words, as if she was starting to fear they had lost the game; perhaps also he heard hurt that John Eisenmenger had apparently betrayed her.

"Because all of them *know* that he was there, but not one of them could be certain that he was there *all of the time*. There were times when he was gone from her bedside but it was assumed that he was in the relatives room, or in the toilet or on the public phone, and no one could say quite how long these absences were. I would estimate that he could have been gone for perhaps as long as an hour, maybe even longer."

"Long enough?"

He shrugged. "Maybe."

"But why? Why should he have done it?"

But again Johnson didn't know. Didn't care really. He was only asking questions because he knew that was how you found out the truth.

The house was bang in the middle of the terrace. Neat and tidy, but with an air of early neglect. They got out and there was a faint tang of malt in the night air. When Helena made a face Johnson commented, "Brewery. Biggest in the city."

Outside the door was a pile of papers, the free local ones that no one reads. Johnson said, "Perhaps he's away."

They rang the bell and waited. Nothing. Johnson rang the bell again but it was the sound of an empty house. They were about to go when they were suddenly confronted by a woman who in Johnson's mind conjured the word 'fat' and in Helena's mind produced the word 'unfortunate'.

"Do you know Mr Goodpasture?" Her voice was thin and reedy but overlain with suffocating curiosity disguised as concern.

Helena wasn't sure what to say but at once Johnson said, "That's right. He hasn't been to work and we were worried out about him."

"He's not well, you know. He's become very depressed following the death of his wife."

Neither of them had known that Mrs Goodpasture had been struck from the electoral register. "We didn't realize," explained Helena.

Delighted to spread bad news, this paragon of neighbourliness elaborated. "Oh, yes. You know she had the stroke . . . ?"

They knew.

"Well, she hung on for weeks. Seemed to be getting better. I visited her regularly, and I thought she was going to be all right . . . Course, it was a bad stroke. Stiff all down one side. Couldn't speak or nothing . . . Then she just died."

Johnson had a feeling that medical opinion might piece things together a little more cogently but he grasped the gist.

"So he's gone away, Mrs . . . ?"

"Bell. Mrs Bell."

"And Mr Goodpasture has gone away, has he, Mrs Bell?"

Mrs Bell intimated that she didn't know. "My Dick says that he has," she said (neither Helena nor Johnson choosing to play up to the double entendre), "but I'm convinced that he's in there. Pining."

Helena said, "What makes you think that he's in there?"

Mrs Bell hesitated. "Well, I don't know for certain. He might have gone to his stepson's but he never said that he was going, and they used to tell me when they were off somewhere." She paused for breath. "Still, who knows? He might have gone there and forgotten, what with his sadness, mightn't he?"

This vacillation made them unsure what to think. Helena glanced at the front door. "There's no milk outside."

"They never had it delivered," Mrs Bell assured her. "Nor the newspapers."

Suddenly Johnson tried to break this impasse of indecision.

"Well, if he's not answering the door, I'm sure there's nothing to worry about. He must, as you say, have gone away."

"Yes," she agreed but there was so much doubt in this syllable it seemed too strained to bear the weight of belief. As if spurred by her fears, Johnson again rang the bell, but again without result. He made a face of helplessness. Mrs Bell cast a look of concern at the pale blue paint of the front door and sighed.

"You don't happen to have the stepson's name, do you?" enquired Johnson but Mrs Bell didn't. Nor did she have his address.

It was at this point that Mrs Bell bade them goodbye, retreating with what the unkind might have called a waddle.

"What do you think?" asked Helena.

"I think he's gone away. Why shouldn't he, if his wife's just died?"

"What do we do now?"

"Well obviously we'll have to wait until he returns. Meanwhile I guess we should call on Mr Libman."

They returned to the car. "It's just a formality, anyway. I can't imagine Goodpasture's got anything useful to add."

Inside the house, Goodpasture sat and stared, breathing the vacuum of his wife's death, barely aware that the doorbell had rung three times.

Feeling nervous and exhilarated, Stephan Libman closed the door to his room quietly. He stood and listened for a few moments, just to ensure that his nosy mother wasn't lurking in the vicinity, then turned to his desk. The bottom drawer was locked and inside it was a small metal cashbox, also locked. Inside this were eleven Polaroid pictures, ten of which he now put in his pocket. Then he returned the locked box to his drawer, made it secure and left the room.

"Are you going out, dear?"

Inevitably his mother was there and asking questions. God, he was so tense he thought he might explode! It was only with a huge effort that he stopped his tongue from telling her what he really thought of her. Patience, he told himself. Soon he could unleash years and years of pent-up abuse, but not yet.

"Cinema. With Mark." *What the fuck does it matter to you?*

"Have you got enough money, dear? Would you like me to give you some?"

"I'm fine." *Just fuck off, will you?*

"When will you be back?"

"'Bout eleven." *In a day or two, I'm never gonna come back.*

"Have a nice time."

He didn't reply, but went out, slamming the front door behind him.

"Going out, Stephan?"

He couldn't believe it. That fucking copper again. Popping up from the undergrowth every time he left the house. Was he watching

275

him? The thought was suddenly the truth and with it came terror, but then he realized he was being stupid. He couldn't know . . .

"Yeah."

"Somewhere nice?"

He looked from Johnson to the woman with him. Somewhere deep inside him he registered that she was very, very shaggable, but he was panicking again. Something about the guy's tone, the look on his face . . .

"Just out."

"Mind if we come with you?"

But Stephan did mind. "Why?" he demanded. They knew something.

"Why not? You're not doing something illegal, are you?"

Stephan heard the words and the panic swelled.

"Of course not," he protested.

"Then where are you going?" Johnson's voice didn't rise or show anger, but it did consist entirely of relentless implacability.

"To the pub," mumbled Stephan. Johnson didn't look as if he believed him but then the front door opened and Mrs Libman peered out. The distraction allowed Stephan to push past them and down the garden path. Mrs Libman was staring suspiciously, then recognized Johnson.

"Mr Johnson! How nice of you to call!"

Johnson tried a grin but the thought of Mrs Libman's refreshments tarnished it. Mrs Libman continued, "What a shame Stephan's going to the pictures tonight. It was him you came to see, I expect?"

But Johnson had caught the discrepancy and it crystallized his certainty that Libman was up to something. He exchanged glances with Helena and they turned around, hurrying for the car.

"You little shit."

Russell's bulk seemed even greater in the shadows of the street lamps but Stephan wasn't about to be intimidated. Not now, not with what he knew.

"Less of the nastiness, Prof," he advised, hoping that his tension was not betrayed by a tremor. "The days when you could boss me around have gone."

Russell looked angry enough to burst but he said nothing more. They were standing in the doorway of a derelict synagogue, the late evening traffic rumbling past them.

"Brought the money?"

Russell didn't respond directly. "That thing you sent me . . . "

276

"Just a Polaroid, Prof. Just a Polaroid."

Russell looked ill. Libman was starting to enjoy himself, the nervousness fading and being replaced by cockiness. He continued, "Goodpasture's office, you see. That beautiful window gave a wonderful view of Nikki's performance."

If he had hoped to reassure the good Professor, he was forced into disappointment; Russell just looked worse than ever.

"What were you doing there?" he asked, his voice husky.

"That used to be Tim's treat. He'd tell me when Nikki was going to perform and he'd let me watch. Sometimes it was with Tim – she paid him for drugs that way. Yours was an unexpected extra. She'd done the business with Tim but instead of leaving with him she stayed behind. Must have told him she was going to meet her boyfriend or something. Anyway, imagine my delight when you walked in."

"But you had a camera."

"That was Goodpasture's. He took Polaroids of his specimens, kept the camera in his office. Luckily there was a film in it."

Russell nodded vaguely as if he, too, thought it had been astonishingly good luck.

"I thought a picture would come in handy," Stephen continued.

Russell said hesitantly, "What else did you see?"

Stephan leered. "Wouldn't you like to know?" Then, with what he believed was a superior smile, he continued, "The money. Five thousand pounds."

Russell found something of his usual condescension. "There wasn't much time."

"Have you got it, or haven't you?"

Russell stared at him but didn't say anything as if considering.

"Come on, Prof. Five K isn't much for someone like you. I'm not being greedy."

For a few seconds Russell continued just to stare. Then, "What if I don't have it?"

Libman fabricated mock concern. "Don't say that, Prof, not even as a joke."

Russell continued his intense scrutiny, as if here was a cadaver that defied even his distinguished consideration. He licked his lips, a peculiarly revolting gesture. "How many photos are there?"

"Including the one I sent you? Eleven."

"How can I believe that that is all there are?"

Libman was affronted. "You can trust me, Professor. Just one payment of five thousand pounds – less than five hundred a shot – and you'll have no more need to worry."

More scrutiny. In the half-light Libman wasn't sure but he suspected that the obese man was sweating profusely, then Russell said, "I didn't kill her, you know."

Stephan almost laughed with contempt, but he had the sense merely to say, "Yeah, right." Then, "To be honest, Prof, I don't give a shovelful of shit whether you sliced her open or not. All I want is a bit of ready cash."

Another pause. "Where are they?"

Stephan reached into his pocket and produced a bundle of small, square photographs. It was at this point that, unwittingly, he produced a masterstroke of psychological manipulation.

"Would you like to see them?"

Russell could fairly be said to shudder at this. "No!" he said quickly, then he seemed to lose some of his bulk as if a safety valve had released some obesity into the coldness of the night. In a more measured tone he continued, "No, that will not be necessary. I have the money here."

Lockwood and Wilson sat in their car and observed the meeting with rising excitement. As soon as Russell had stopped in this anonymous, rather dingy high street, they had realized that something odd was happening, but the appearance of Libman had been as intriguing as it had been unexpected.

"Fuckin' hell!" remarked Lockwood, his usual response to things odd, significant or spectacular.

They had then debated what to do. A call to Wharton seemed the safest, if most minimal response.

"What are they doing? Can you see?" she asked.

"Just talking." It was at this point that Libman produced the photographs. "Libman's showing him something. Cards or something."

Wharton's mind was working furiously. How did this fit in? Blackmail? Could Libman be blackmailing Russell? But about what?

Lockwood interrupted her thoughts. "Now Russell's taken something from his breast pocket. They're doing some sort of exchange."

So it was blackmail – about the murder? How did Libman fit in? Intriguing as these questions were, they would have to wait.

"You continue to follow Russell. I'll go to Libman's house."

Helena and Johnson had had some trouble locating Libman but they spotted him after about ten minutes. Johnson had then had the problem of following a pedestrian in a car – the hardest form of surveillance – but Libman had been too immersed in his own thoughts to prove a difficult quarry. When he had stopped and loitered by the synagogue where Russell had then emerged from the shadows, Johnson had been forced to drive past and then park the car some twenty metres further on.

"Well, well."

"Who's that?" asked Helena, who had never seen the fat Professor.

"Russell."

"What are they doing?"

"Well, I hardly think that Russell and Libman meet socially on too many occasions, and this is hardly the type of neighbourhood Russell would normally inhabit, so presumably this is pre-arranged and clandestine."

They watched the two of them talking, then saw Libman produce something from his pocket.

Helena said, "Photos?"

Johnson didn't say anything. He kept watching intently. When Russell brought an envelope from his pocket he muttered, "Blackmail."

Helena frowned. "But how does that fit in? I thought Nikki Exner was the blackmailer."

"Maybe young Stephan found out what was going on and decided that he too should make a little money out of the situation."

"He should be careful then, in view of what happened to Nikki."

The mismatched pair were parting. It was then that Johnson's eyes wandered up and down the street.

"How very intriguing," he said.

"What?"

He pointed at a blue car on the opposite side of the street, about fifteen metres away. "That's a police car and, if I'm not mistaken, Constables Lockwood and Wilson are sitting inside it."

For a moment she was lost, then she understood. "They're following Russell!"

"Presumably."

She lapsed into renewed irritation at having the investigation stolen from them. It was at that point that Libman and Russell parted. "What do we do?"

"We can't follow them both. You tell me. Libman or Russell?"

Was he joking? But they were disappearing and she didn't have the time for an intellectual discussion. "Libman."

He didn't argue, didn't even show approval or otherwise. He just started the car and waited for Libman to walk a decent distance away.

Russell was shaking as he climbed into his car. He felt sick, revolted, as extreme a feeling as he had ever felt. Dirt seemed to cloak him and cling to his corpulent perspiration, horror to suffocate him, despair to bury him under a mass of recrimination. For long minutes he could do nothing but sit, breathing heavily as if he had just run up the steepest hill in hell to find that the only view was in the devil's smile.

He knew, though, despite all the loathing and dread, that it had not ended. He had eleven photographs but he did not have reassurance. If eleven, why not twelve? Why not twenty, thirty, a thousand? And what of Libman himself? Even without the photographs, he *knew*. Just a word or a letter from that little shit could serve to annihilate him. Not only was there the question of an improper relationship with a student, there were other matters. There was the question of her rather good examination results, considerably improved by prior knowledge of the questions obtained with his help. Such a shame that she had decided to renege on the deal, demanding money for her silence.

What had Libman seen that night, other than Nikki Exner earning some extra money on her knees? Had he seen him offer her the customary glass of Madeira? Not, of course, that he could have known that it was laced with Midazolam. Had he seen him exploring her when she had succumbed to the drug?

But he hadn't done that thing to her! Someone else had done that hell-bound thing. Surely, whatever the little shit knew or didn't know, guessed or might come to guess, he couldn't say that he had done such a terrible thing to the girl?

But supposing he did? Supposing for some reason he told the police not only what he knew, but what he perhaps thought had happened?

He could not allow that to happen.

Libman had then to die. Why not? Russell was well versed in the subject. It was a risk – should Libman have more photos and should he have made arrangements for them to become public in the event of his demise, all would be for naught – but he knew that he could not live under the threat of Libman's manipulations. The chance he would have to take was that Libman had told him truthfully that there were no more photos or else that his hiding place for them would remain undiscovered after his demise.

Suddenly his mind cleared and the portentous feelings were gone. *He shall not live.*

It was ironic that it was with this thought Russell decided that he was going to kill Stephan Libman. He had made careful note of Libman's home address before coming out to the rendezvous.

He would do it that very night.

"We might as well go and wait for him at his house."

They had been following Stephan for about ten minutes. He was retracing exactly his path from his house and Johnson could see no reason why he wouldn't go back home.

"Supposing he takes a detour close to home?"

Helena's question was reasonable. He sighed. "Point taken."

They continued their jagged pursuit of Stephan.

The Mercedes moved off, smoothly and almost supernaturally.

"Beautiful motor," remarked Wilson. In fact it was so beautiful Lockwood had trouble keeping up with it.

Wilson said, "He's in a hurry. I wonder why."

Lockwood silently wished his colleague would shut the fuck up.

Beverley Wharton had moved quickly following Lockwood's call. She had commandeered a driver and a car and had gone at once to Stephan Libman's address. Then she sat and waited.

Stephan came along the well-lit street about six minutes later. As soon as she saw him she felt excitement and apprehension; Libman clearly knew something about the murder, knew too about Professor Russell. Handling that knowledge, once she had it, would require great delicacy if she was to come out of this with reputation intact.

Then she saw that Libman was being followed.

"Shit!"

Her driver looked across at her, surprised by the vehemence, but Beverley Wharton didn't notice. She recognized Johnson's car, although it was too far away to see who was in it. The car was parked about a hundred metres from Libman's house.

A black Mercedes turned into the street, travelling slowly. Missing its significance, she paid it little attention.

Having parked the car, Johnson said, "Well, he's going home," as if to mark up a point scored against Helena. She didn't say anything. She was aware that a car had just turned into the road behind them, although she didn't bother turning to look at it.

Stephan was walking slowly, apparently lost in thought, perhaps planning how to spend the money that was swelling his pocket.

Lockwood didn't know Libman's address and so he wasn't alarmed by Russell taking that particular route. He was somewhat exercised by Russell's sudden transformation from speed king to old age pensioner, a change which required him to apply his foot to the brake pedal with such alacrity that Wilson (without seat-belt) hit the bridge of his nose on the dashboard.

"You twat!"

Lockwood would normally have found this hysterically funny but he was concentrating on finding somewhere to put the car that was not too obvious. Ignoring Wilson he muttered, "What's he playing at?"

Wilson, blood peeping shyly from his right nostril, betrayed less than professional concern. "How should I know? Perhaps he's had a heart attack."

Lockwood had no evidence to refute this but he had a strange feeling that the occupant of the large black Mercedes some fifty metres ahead was watching and waiting.

Russell didn't know the area, would not normally have allowed even his corpse to be seen in it, and he certainly had no idea where in the long dark road Stephan Libman's house might be. He was forced therefore to slow quite abruptly when he realized he had arrived at his destination. Although there were street lamps the road was lined by large lime trees and it was relatively broad, the consequence of which was that there were extensive areas of shadow into which Russell could not see. In any case, it was entirely possible that Libman had managed to get home already or even that he had not gone back to his house.

He searched around, the car in the middle of the road softly growling out exhaust. Nothing.

He wondered what to do, but there was no other course for him to follow. His road to hell was plotted, the compass fixed. It had been fixed, really, for some time now, and he had thought only wrongly that it was otherwise.

Yet only now did he realize this, only now was he having to commit himself totally, without revocation.

It was not the act that frightened him, it was the finality of his action, his commitment to a course.

A tiny sliver of doubt and question sliced into his mind and might even then have had some effect but it was at that moment that he saw Stephan Libman walking towards him.

How was he going to do it?

The question reared up in front of him, absurdly silent until that moment. How precisely was he going to commit this murder?

But Stephan, ever helpful, gave him an instant answer.

He stepped out then between two parked cars, crossing the wide road in a long diagonal.

Beverley saw Libman begin to cross the road and decided that she would intercept him before he reached his house. She got out of the car and heard, as you might hear a distant aircraft overhead, the sound of a car's engine revving.

"Stephan Libman?" she called.

"He's on the move," said the ever-perspicacious Wilson.

"Bloody fast, too," was Lockwood's contribution as he, too, accelerated.

Johnson and Helena saw Libman beginning to cross the road, then saw him stop and turn. Suddenly, too, they heard the car.

Stephan had been lost deep in wonderful, joyous thought. He had in his pocket more money than he had ever before possessed, and now he could express countless years of suppressed emotion to his mother. He could at last inform her, in great, graphic and intimate detail, just where she could insert her mother love, her constant concern, her blindness and her sodding jam sandwich biscuits. Now he could walk out of that house and know that he need never come back. Now he could lead a life.

The first thing he would do would be to hire a prostitute. He knew just the one, had had her for a quick fuck about a year ago, but this next time it would be for an entire night, and he would make her do the things that he wanted, the things that he sometimes dreamed about at night . . .

"Stephan Libman?"

A female voice that he faintly recalled. A voice of authority. Suddenly he was very, very afraid. The police, he knew at once.

He stopped, caught between the desire to run and the desire to bluff it out. Surely they couldn't know. How could they?

He began to turn. He noticed the big black car that was travelling down the road towards him but he thought it was a police car. He thought that it would, in the manner of all good cinematic police, screech to a halt, its fender no more than a few centimetres from his legs.

These thoughts were wrong.

Russell had never really used the full power of his car before. Living where he did, with its constant traffic and small, interlocking patterns of street and mews, it just wasn't possible. Now, as the rev counter climbed steadily and he felt the acceleration forcing the parked cars on either side to squeeze faster and faster behind him, he was suddenly terrified. Terrified but capable of nothing but heading for the young man who stood in the light of his headlamps. Terrified but capable of nothing but killing.

He didn't see the car behind him, desperately trying to catch him.

He didn't see the attractive blonde woman to his left.

He didn't see the couple in one of the myriad of parked cars that rushed past him.

Seeing only Stephan Libman, he accelerated even harder.

Stephan at last realized that the car rushing towards him was not going to stop.

Beverley had the perfect vantage point, as if placed there by God, a singular audience for a singular playlet. She had called to Libman across the roof of her car and when he stopped and stood there, as if paralysed, she began to walk along the length of the car while they looked directly at each other.

She heard the car for perhaps three seconds before its crescendo registered and she realized that it wasn't irrelevant and it wasn't going to stop. She glanced back along the road, saw the car and then stepped forward between the parked cars, her mouth open to shout a warning.

She didn't get the chance.

Russell was fixed upon Libman, but the figure that his car hit was a different entity. The thump that was so loud and yet so dissociated from the fat Professor changed Libman from a young, rather stupid young man into a side of meat cast from the devil's abattoir. It was merely a carcass that was flicked into the air, its face impassive, not even surprised, its arms and legs moving independently of the torso.

The shoulder of this thing clipped the side of the windscreen directly in front of him, causing Russell to flinch, then, all dead limbs and slack head, it was pushed away to his right in the wake of his car, crashed down on to the front of a parked car, skidded across it and came to rest on the slabs of the pavement.

"Christ!"

Lockwood had not been able to see Stephan until he was tossed briefly into his line of sight, immediately to vanish again into the peripheral darkness. Wilson didn't say anything but his expression was an unusually eloquent one of horror. The car ahead of them hadn't slowed and Lockwood was caught between the desire to get the bastard and the feeling that he should stop and help.

He slowed the car but almost at once Wharton was there on their left-hand side screaming, "Get after him!"

From their viewpoint, Helena and Johnson saw Stephan Libman from some way further up the road, Russell's car accelerating towards them. As the car came closer and closer they saw Libman turn from poorly seen, through brightly lit to silhouette. They saw too – felt almost – the car smash into him, then flip him up so that the forward moving windscreen clipped him and flicked him away to the right.

"Oh, my God!" breathed Helena as the car shot past them. Johnson didn't say anything. He started the car at once, a look of ashen shock on his face. They were facing the wrong way but he at least had to attempt to make chase. Then he saw another car race past them and, glimpsing Lockwood's face within it, he knew that there was no point.

Beverley had run across the road and was kneeling by the body as they ran up. The legs were at a strange angle and were clearly broken. The arms were stiff and the head rested on the pavement, facing the hubcap of a parked car. The eyes were open but he looked godawful. His face was a smudged network of laceration and graze, blood appearing, almost miraculously stigmatic, as she watched. His left leg was angled oddly and there was a jagged protrusion under the cotton of his jeans that was patently bone; from the way his shoulder was humped forward she suspected that it was either broken or dislocated.

Helena and Johnson ran up and Beverley didn't seem particularly surprised to see them. In truth she looked more shocked, more sober than Johnson had ever before seen her. She didn't even bother to adopt a tone of condescension as she looked up at Helena and said, "Get an ambulance. Get it fast."

Front doors were opening, people looking out. One of them was Mrs Libman.

Johnson suddenly felt very, very sorry for Beverley Wharton.

Lockwood was a slob and a shite copper but he was a good driver. The car in front was fast but it was being driven by a tyro, and Lockwood had no trouble keeping up with him through the side streets and, a few minutes later, the main roads. It was while they were hurtling down one of these, Lockwood clocking the speed at one hundred and seventy kilometres per hour and Wilson screaming instructions into the radio, that Russell eventually was brought to a halt.

Russell found himself thrilled by the chase. For decades his life had been without the ancient feelings engendered by the adrenaline rush of the race, his only excitement emanating from his weekly appointment with Linda and from the increasingly sporadic occasions in which he achieved some successful research. Suddenly the atavistic pleasure of charging at speed, chasing or being chased, was reborn to him and, like a child finding delight in some new and previously undiscovered talent, he was screaming with terrified joy as he drove.

Cars, lights, shadows and buildings were blurred as they sped past his eyes, the sounds of the engine competing with his own panting within the car, and with the scream of the siren behind him. So fast was he going that the orange neon lights flicked on and off in the car, almost strobing the world into a series of stills drawn from art.

And then he saw that he had reached a major junction, the lights set red against him. He didn't think to stop. Almost as if he had become inured to the stimulation of the pursuit, the thought of risking all as he crossed the traffic lanes ahead seemed too good to miss. He accelerated, the engine whining with pain.

He almost made it. He crossed the first half of the road, narrowly missing a bus by twisting the wheels hard to the left so that he passed just in front, the driver's terrified expression frozen into time. On the other side, though, there was an articulated lorry. It was nearly half-way across the junction and there would have been plenty of space had he not had to avoid the bus. All he could do was to try desperately to steer the car to the right so that it would hit the front axles rather than between the wheels.

He had time just to scream one, rather unprofessorial word – "Shiiittt!" – before the car hit, the front end crumpled almost to nothing, the airbags around him exploded and he found his legs being encased in sudden anguish. He knew no more of pain after that.

Eisenmenger had only just returned to his flat when the phone rang. He had been to Marie's parents' house, there to be received with coldness. They appeared to have a somewhat different perspective on the situation to Eisenmenger and did not feel inclined to tell him where Marie was living, or even how he could contact her. He suspected that she had returned home but short of locking them in the lounge and ransacking the house he didn't see how he could prove it.

He picked up the receiver expecting it to be Marie, finding it to be Johnson.

"What is it, Bob?"

"We've had a few developments." He sounded shocked, dazed. He went on to tell Eisenmenger of all that had happened. "Libman's still alive but in a bad way. May or may not make it. Russell hit an HGV but amazingly he survived. They had to cut him out, but he should make it. "

Eisenmenger had sat down on the sofa, listening intently. Libman blackmailing Russell? Russell trying to run him down? Had the world's madness grown so huge?

"Are you still there?" Johnson demanded.

Eisenmenger hadn't realized that he had been quiet for so long. "Yes, yes."

"We're at Helena's flat. She's pretty shaken up by it all."

Where did this further quantum of insanity fit in? What did Libman have to do with it?

"John?" Johnson asked this in a different tone. Not suspicious but certainly wary.

"What?"

"Did you tell Beverley Wharton of your suspicions?"

He began to deny it – of course he hadn't – but then he stopped. He thought of his suspicions concerning Beverley, of his unsupported conviction that she had been in his flat and seen his report of Nikki Exner's second autopsy. Then he thought of how close he had come to betrayal that afternoon and guilt flooded him again, and it almost paralysed him.

"No," he said at last. It wasn't a lie but was it the truth? In any case it achieved a degree of success for Johnson could be heard to relax with relief.

"She seemed to be thinking along the same lines as us. She was having Russell followed, that's how they got after him so quickly when he ran Libman down."

"What do we do now?"

He heard a whispered conversation then, "Helena thinks that we need to meet to try to sort out what this means for the Bilroth family. When can you make it?"

Well, actually he could make it any time they liked, but perhaps there was no point in being precipitous about things . . .

"Give me a couple of days," he said, "I've got to think about all this. I'll let you know when I've come up with something."

He put down the phone before he could hear the protests.

The next day found Johnson angry and despondent. Sally had suddenly disappeared, gone to her mother's leaving only a note and he didn't know when she'd be back. He hated uncertainty and change, and was slightly disturbed by this uncharacteristic behaviour. She had been increasingly sullen and secretive, ever since the night of their anniversary, her mood brittle and prone to flare. He had thought about ringing, then thought better of it. His mother-in-law was old and frail, but she was also spiky and critical of him: he had had too many spats with her to welcome another one.

He had spent the afternoon visiting old haunts, sometimes alone but often in the company of old friends, old allies, even old enemies. He could sense in many an undertone of suspicion, even hostility, but this was expressed overtly only once, when the land-lord of a particular public house refused to serve him with a curt and clear "Fuck off, cunt." For the most, there were wary greetings and idle, unimportant chat, the catching up with news and the recharting of all stories, all the while avoiding the obvious and ever-present questions about just what had happened to Detective Sergeant Johnson.

He returned home at seven, slightly drunk, no happier.

"Sally?"

The house was silent but he knew that she was in. At once he was worried. Sally loved noise – the radio, the television, a CD – and she was never without it.

"Sally."

And then he heard the sound of water running in the pipes and with the sound came certainty, fearful certainty. He ran upstairs calling, "Sally? Sally?"

She was in the en suite. She wasn't trying to hide away – the door was unlocked – for she was too intent on what she was doing. The harsh, white noise of the water was made louder by the gaunt echoes of the bathroom, so that she wasn't aware of Johnson's presence for several long minutes; long minutes in which he stood at the door, tearful despair cascading down him, watching her back as she hunched over the sink, scrubbing, scrubbing, scrubbing her bleeding hands into red-raw lumps of flesh.

Not surprisingly Libman looked bad, but not as bad as Beverley had feared immediately after she had seen him cartwheeling through the neon-lit night air. His head was bandaged, both eyes were black and there were stitched lines running haphazardly across his face; his left wrist was bandaged and his left arm was in a sling, while beneath the bedclothes was the cylindrical shape of the cast on his left leg. At least he was down to one intravenous drip from the three he had earned immediately after the ambulance had arrived.

She had had to evict with considerable force the ever-loving Mrs Libman, but not before she had been harangued about the disgraceful fact that her son merited a police guard and the poor standards of nursing care.

Now, at last alone, Beverley tried to assess where her best interests lay. She had a shrewd idea what had happened the night Nikki Exner died, but she had doubts that Libman would see matters the right way; at least, not at first.

Entirely predictably, for the first ten minutes, Stephan Libman was sullen, uncooperative and inclined to play on his injuries. Then Beverley leaned across to him, put her hand gently on his broken wrist, pressed hard and said into his wincing face, "Listen, you little shit. I'm completely fucked off with wankers like you jerking off all over this case. If you don't want to go down for blackmail and accessory to murder, you're going to co-operate. Got that?"

She continued to smile and those who walked past the windows of the cubicle would not have guessed that she was doing anything other than chatting quietly to Libman. He stared back at her, his mouth open, saying nothing. Then she released the pressure, sat back and smiled. "We're alone, Stephan. Nobody's listening.

Let me explain to you what I think happened. Then you can tell me if I go wrong . . . "

"You've nothing to blame yourself for, Bob."

The general practitioner's reassurance was well meant, perhaps even genuinely believed, but it did nothing to assuage his feeling of culpability. Not that he could think straight: memories kept obtruding through from nightmare.

"She's better off in hospital for the time being."

These platitudes, fired off like torpedoes in his general direction, loaded with emollient, missed their target, sailing past him and travelling on into dissolution.

How had it happened so quickly? Had there been signs that he should have seen? Had he precipitated it?

It was this last question that caused him most pain.

"I'm sure it won't be long before she's home again."

Last time it had been four months. Time in which he had learned of a new disease, a bizarre affliction that was as close to insanity as a sane person could come – Obsessive-Compulsive Neurosis.

Ever since he had first met her, Sally had been fastidious in everything but not, he thought, abnormally so. Only with hindsight had he been able to pick out a change, a deterioration, from normal worries to abnormal neuroses, from passing fancies to incarcerating convictions. Even now, there were still times when he recalled some incident early in their marriage that, for the first time, he saw with novel, sinister significance to have been a harbinger.

She had started to clean the house more and more often, taking longer and longer each time. First once a week, then twice, then thrice, then every night, she would vacuum and dust, polish and spray, rub and scrub. They had joked about it at first but that had soon proved an ineffective camouflage and they retreated into silence. Then, the cleaning done – perhaps at eleven, perhaps at midnight – she would turn her attention to her own ablution.

And that, gradually but inexorably, came to take longer and longer over the months, until at the end she would be scrubbing her hands and her face, her feet and her armpits, time and time again, never satisfied that she had removed the dirt, never happy that she wasn't contaminated, that she was whole and pure and not defiled.

It came to destroy her life, forcing her from work when she was spending more time in the washroom than at her duties, when she refused to shake hands, when people refused to shake hands with *her* because she was wearing gloves indoors to cover the raw flesh.

It came close to destroying his life, because she couldn't bear to touch his filthy, unclean flesh, when she started to sleep in the spare bedroom and he would lie awake in the night and listen to the water running and running and running . . .

"I expect something was preying on her mind, something quite trivial. It'll soon be sorted out."

He didn't know how those words made Johnson cringe inside.

It took numerous telephone calls and much, much patience for Eisenmenger finally to get to talk to Beverley Wharton. It was late in the evening some one hundred hours after the incidents when she returned his numerous calls.

"John? It's Beverley. You wanted to talk to me."

Her voice could have been full of innocence or full of knowingness, he couldn't tell. How could two such extremes be so difficult to distinguish?

"Yes." He didn't feel that he wanted to launch straight into direct questioning. "You're a difficult woman to get hold of."

"Am I?"

She sounded amused and while he was wondering if she were laughing at the secondary meaning she continued, "Things have become a little busy of late. But then, I would guess, you already know that."

"Well, actually . . . "

"Actually you want to know what's been going on."

Why did he feel like a supplicant?

"Actually I want to know why you suddenly found Professor Russell worthy of so much attention."

She laughed. A provocative sound, he was forced to admit. "I haven't been home for three days and now at last I've got here I'm damned if I'm going to trek out again."

In the silence that followed he thought that perhaps he heard her grin.

"Could I . . . come to you?"

She sighed. "I suppose so. If it really is that urgent."

She didn't laugh, not until he had put the phone down.

He had half expected – half hoped? – that she would be pretty well undressed when she opened the door to him some forty-five minutes later. Instead she was dressed in jeans and a white T-shirt. She wore a large smile that made him feel inadequate, as if she knew all the answers and he knew nothing.

"Come in."

He walked past her and looked around. "Spacious," he remarked. "Minimalist. Easy to clean, plenty of light."

He walked around the lounge, stopping at the window. "I'm impressed," but he was wondering how she afforded it.

She seemed pleased by his appreciation. "Drink? I've got most things."

He opted for wine and they sat on the sofa.

"You wanted to know what's been going on," she said.

"I think you owe me that."

"Do I?"

"Yes."

She didn't appear to follow his logic. At a loss she drank some wine and then said, "You don't understand, John. I can't go around divulging details of ongoing investigations to all and sundry."

"But I'm not 'all and sundry', am I? I'm the one who put you on to Russell in the first place."

A smile was trying to make itself seen around her lips. "Are you?"

He leaned back against the yellow leather of the sofa, suddenly enjoying the contest. "As I recall, the case was closed. You had your killer, or rather the killer was dead. Yet suddenly you begin looking into Russell's private life, you then devote precious resources to following him."

"And how does this legitimize your curiosity?"

He picked up his glass and drained it, then put it down next to the bottle, at the same time moving closer to her. "This happened less than twenty-four hours after you visited my flat where my autopsy report and conclusions were left open and easy to see."

She frowned. "You're not suggesting that I snooped around your flat, are you?" She poured more wine anyway. "As I recall, you were with me the whole time."

"And then I left."

"And so did I."

He raised his eyebrows. "Did you?"

The expression on her face could have meant so many different things. "What are you implying?" she enquired. There was no indignation in the question.

He took the glass and put it down on the table. She smelt strongly of perfume that she must have put on for his visit. "I'm suggesting," he said, "that you could at least tell me what you've found out about Russell and why Libman was blackmailing him."

She was surprised, he could see, that he knew as much as he did, then she murmured, "Bob, of course." She considered what to say, then, "Bob was a good copper. It was a pity he had to resign."

There was a whole debate to be had about that remark but Eisenmenger kept quiet. Beverley paused, then asked, "Do you want to fuck?" The question was not asked in a sensual way, but with curiosity, almost naivety. When he smiled sheepishly and shook his head, she said, "No. Maybe not."

"About the case . . . "

She sighed.

Both Russell and Libman were lucky to be alive. Russell was in danger of losing one or both of his smashed legs but the airbags had absorbed much of the impact. Libman had come through both neurosurgery and orthopaedic repair with relatively little lasting damage. Beverley had managed to speak to him only a few hours before.

"Stephan has been wonderfully co-operative. Told us all we need to know."

Warily, Eisenmenger, murmured, "Really?"

"Oh, yes. Explained it all."

He could sense the satisfaction, sense too the stench of a dirty little deal. She continued, "Russell did it. She was blackmailing him for drug money. He couldn't afford to let that continue."

"So he killed her?"

"Russell denies it, of course."

"Of course." Eisenmenger murmured this and she did not detect the tone.

"He says that he was paying Nikki Exner for sex, but that was all."

"You don't believe him," he stated flatly.

Surprised, she asked, "Do you?"

He shrugged. She continued, "From what Stephan says and what we already knew, I think I can work out what actually happened."

"Which was?"

"Russell was sexually inadequate big time. He employed a whore on a weekly basis."

That didn't mean much. "To do what?"

She said at once, "To do anything he wanted, basically. Usually it was just a blow job."

"So? Does that mean he killed Nikki Exner?"

"Not of itself, but it does give us an indication of habits and possible motives."

"And what? She sucked him off but accidentally dug her teeth in so he killed her in an insane rage due to a sore dick?"

She sighed. "Hardly. Most men seem to like having a sore dick – shows they've done the job properly."

"Then why did he kill her?"

She snorted, suddenly leaning forward. She implied impatience with his scepticism. He noticed her breasts again, felt temptation and shame, tasting like a mix of chocolate and salt.

"As I said, she began to blackmail him. She liked a good life, did Nikki."

Don't we all? he thought, as she went on, "She pushed him too far, he objected. End of story."

"Blackmailing him? About what?" He stared directly into her eyes, trying to see if she would admit what she knew, what she had stolen from him; he thought he handled it pretty well, innocence and ignorance oozing from him. Yet when she answered her face was full of teasing amusement.

"Isn't it obvious, John? Can't you guess?"

So there it was. Short of admitting that she had read his notes and acted upon them, she couldn't have signalled it more clearly.

"It's not a question of guessing, is it? More one of knowledge and how it was acquired."

She widened her eyes, her pupils already full in the half-light. She looked long and hard at him, before saying in a low voice, "I think he made her pregnant and that was what she was using for blackmail."

He raised his eyebrows but didn't return her gaze. "Now there's a thought."

"The desecration, the removal of the uterus, always bothered me. Unnecessary, almost. But perhaps it had another reason. Perhaps what we found at the scene wasn't the original uterus."

Ironically, now he heard Beverley Wharton expound his theory the obvious objection came to him with insulting ease. How had a man who was apparently only interested in fellatio made her pregnant?

She moved slightly so that their arms were touching softly. It was a wonderfully warm sensation. "Was it a substitute?" she enquired in almost a whisper.

He waited a long time before saying anything. The feel of the touch of her was charged with so much; he could hardly breathe, knowing that to inhale was to take in her perfume, perhaps even the air she had respired.

He knew she was wrong, knew that Russell hadn't made Nikki Exner pregnant. "Yes," he said at last.

She let out a long breath. He almost heard her pleasure at his reply. He asked then, "So where do Libman and Bilroth come in? What were the photographs Libman was showing to Russell? Presumably he, too, was trying to blackmail him."

"I think it's fairly obvious Russell needed an accomplice. All that manual labour, not really his style, is it? Can't see that fat bloater hoisting her up on a rope, running up and down those steps."

"Then who?"

"It's pretty obvious, isn't it? Russell asked – employed – Bilroth to do it."

He could see then. See how things were going to be spun so that despite all that had happened, Bilroth had still been guilty (if only in part) and therefore she would be vindicated.

"Don't tell me," he said. "Libman had nothing to do with the murder. Just found the photographs somewhere about the house. Thought they might come in useful."

"Really, John. Such sarcasm is beneath you."

"I can't imagine where it springs from."

The sparring done she continued, "Stephan has been very co-operative. He admits trying to blackmail Russell – and that, of course, cannot be ignored – but he has admitted that he witnessed the murder and mutilation of Nikki Exner. He has signed a statement to the effect that he saw from the curator's office Bilroth and Russell commit the crime."

"Very neat."

She chose to take it as a compliment. "Thank you."

Eisenmenger was running it through his mind, trying to decide that it was a good fake, but it was a fake. "Tell me, how come Stephan had pictures of Nikki Exner with Russell, but none of the actual murder?"

At once she came back, "He ran out of film."

"Shame."

"Wasn't it?"

"That makes it Russell's word against Libman's," he pointed out.

"Russell's word will mean no more than shit after it's been pointed out in court that he used a prostitute for oral sex, that he used one of his students for the same, and that he tried to kill Stephan Libman."

"Stephan Libman is still a fairly tainted witness."

"It fits the facts."

"Maybe," he muttered.

He thought of Stephan whimpering in the library the morning after it happened. When he brought this up, Beverley said dismissively, "He was acting. Couldn't very well shrug it off, could he? He had to react with some sort of shock."

He missed his vocation then. Hollywood needs actors like Stephan Libman.

Changing the subject, he said, "Don't forget that there are other suspects." The effect was immediate.

"Oh, come on, John! I know you and Bob and Miss Fridgidaire have been desperate to prove me wrong, but it isn't going to work because I'm a fucking good copper."

She was bright and she was beautiful, but Eisenmenger wondered whether she was as wise and wonderful as she reckoned. She continued, "Hamilton-Bailey has his wife's alibi for one thing; for another we've got Russell in the library at exactly the right time while Nikki Exner chomps her way through sausage and sprouts. I don't really see that we need two Professors for one murder, do you?

"As for Goodpasture, you may have forgotten but his wife was in a coma on ITU at the time. Not only does that give him a pretty good alibi, but it's difficult to think of a reason why he might have nipped out for a bit of murder and dismemberment at that particular time."

Sound reasons, and yet the lack of definitive proof still bothered him.

She got up, a clear signal that she considered the discussion finished. "You can go back to the lawyer-lady and tell her that she's failed. She'll never prove that Bilroth wasn't involved, and as far as we're concerned the case is solved. If she doesn't believe me, she can discuss the matter with the Chief Constable."

On his way back home, Eisenmenger called into the off-licence and bought a bottle of malt whisky. It was a spontaneous purchase and his precise motives eluded him. Partly, he supposed, it was the feeling of guilt and despond that still clung stubbornly to him but mostly he suspected because Beverley's story, although it had explained much, nevertheless did not yet convince him. There was truth in it, he had no doubt, but it was adulterated truth.

His journey home took him past the site where Tamsin had died. Over the years he had trained himself to treat this place as no different, but it had been a long, gradual process. Now he barely looked whenever he passed, this forbearance helped by the recent development of the site so that now there was a nice, square and convenient three-bedroomed house; just right for a family of four to be boxed in.

Thus his head did not move at all and it was only his eyes that glanced across as he drove by, catching the slightly stooped figure that stood just inside the garden gate.

Marie?

He braked at once, irritating a van driver behind him who showed considerable skill and ingenuity in the construction of his abuse. Having found somewhere to park that was only slightly illegal, he ran back to the house, perhaps two hundred metres.

There was no one there.

He searched for several minutes but without reward. Returning to his car, he began to wonder if he were going mad.

Part Three

Goodpasture's eyes saw the dawn but their uncomprehending, leaden gaze did not react. They were filmed, and crusted yellow mucous stuck to the lashes and extruded from each inner canthus. His skin was almost leathery in its oleaginous saffron sheen and his hands held a fine tremor. He sat at the small kitchen table unable to sleep: the makeshift bed on the dining-room floor – an old and dirty sleeping bag and a cushion – had not been used now for three nights. The silence that surrounded him condemned him.

He had not eaten for a long time, but he could not have said precisely how long. He had drunk only water and that without thought: indeed all the necessities of living he had performed without higher reasoning, allowing them to be dictated by the more basic, more primitive parts of his brain, for his higher mind was occupied.

And, though it filled his consciousness, it was, in essence, a simple thing.

Grief.

Grief that his wife had died, desolating his existence. Grief that she had gone without forgiving him. Grief that he had done what he had done.

A simple phrase repeated endlessly wherever he looked; *why didn't I tell you?* He felt that if only he had managed to tell her everything and thereby allowed her to absolve him, he could bear the loss that he now felt. The possibility that this was no more than a dream could not be allowed to enter his reality, was kept an aborted, sickly thing in a room beyond.

He turned away from the window but it was not with purpose: his mind was incapable of anything beyond impulse and reaction. He looked around the kitchen and saw disjointed objects, each with disjointed characteristics. He saw a cooker, a fridge, a sink, a cupboard, but not a kitchen: when he concentrated on any individual thing such as a chair he saw wood, he saw brown, he saw a shape but he did not see the whole. He tried to concentrate but he couldn't. It was as if his mind were dying.

"Please, God."

A punishment. At once it was decided and thus set, the truth, the inescapable.

He sat suddenly down on the chair, partly relieved that it was real. Why couldn't he cry? Why couldn't he crumble into complete and utter loss?

Suddenly he knew that she was in the next room, that she was moving through in her dressing gown, round and warm and comforting as she had always been. He rose at once and strode to the doorway and through it.

No one there. There never was.

He half sighed, half sobbed as his head came to rest against the wood of the door jamb. It was as it always was. A ghost, a memory, a tantalizing sense. He knew that she was there but he never saw her, never heard her. Perhaps she was trying to contact him, tell him that he was, truly, forgiven but how could he know if he could never see her? The frustration was sending him into madness.

And still he could not cry.

Why couldn't he see her? If only he could see her he could perhaps talk to her, explain what had happened, why he had done what he had done.

The knock at the door came and went and he only realized when it was repeated. It left him perplexed. It was just a noise. What did it mean? Was it something that required him to act?

Only gradually did he manage to make sense of the sound. He moved out of the kitchen into the hallway. A pixelated shape could be seen through the small frosted panel in the front door. He did not recognize it as a human face.

And then, the thought born whole and formed, he knew instantly that it was Janey standing there. She had come home at last . . .

He jerked the door open and peered out eagerly, his mouth open, ready to smile and cry and hug his Janey.

He saw a large woman dressed in a sweatshirt and leggings that were clearly stretched beyond endurance around her rump. She wore too a look of concern that broke into a smile of relief as his face appeared from around the door.

"Oh, Mr Goodpasture! You're all right!"

300

The intense disappointment left him unanchored. For a long while he felt winded and just stared at her. She knew him. Did he know her? Perhaps he did.

"I was a bit worried," Mrs Bell went on. "What with the tragedy with your wife and all. I said to Dick, 'I hope Mr Goodpasture's all right. I haven't seen him for three days.'"

What was she saying? She had mentioned his Janey but the words were gone before he had understood.

"I hope you didn't mind me knocking. Just to make sure. Is there anything I can get you? My Dick and I, we're off down the high street in a minute."

Already he was shaking his head although he had hardly understood the question. The door was closing as his hand pushed it and she was twisting her body to look into the narrowing gap.

"You're sure you're all right?" Mrs Bell asked but the door clicked on its latch and she was excluded. He hadn't looked well, she decided, but at least he was still alive. She shrugged slightly. Some people just wouldn't be helped. Still, no one could say that she hadn't offered.

Inside Goodpasture leaned against the door and his eyes were again closed. Only then did he realize that it had been one of his neighbours, although her name eluded him. She had mentioned his wife . . .

A voice from upstairs. His eyes jerked open. Had it been real or in his head? He called out, "Janey? Is that you?"

No answer.

He sighed. Too many times he had chased phantoms. He walked back to the dining room and sat again at the table where they had eaten so many meals together. Why hadn't he been allowed the chance of forgiveness? Why had she gone from him? Why couldn't he cry?

The questions, mired in grief, recurred endlessly until they shouted down the silence. If only he could cry; that was all he needed.

Another sound, this time from the kitchen.

"Janey?" He got up and went out, but he knew before he got there that it would be empty of her, empty of his life.

Was she tormenting him for what he had done? He could not accept that.

And then, quite without warning, the truth was in his head and a decision made. Janey was calling him. Calling him to join her and then she would forgive him. Of course! She had gone beyond but she could see his misery and now pitied him. She wanted him to be released from his agony, she wanted him to be happy again.

Above all Janey wanted him to be with her.

He knew then what he had to do. With a deliberation that had been entirely absent for the past days he rose and searched through the drawers in the sideboard for some paper and a pen. Then he sat down to write.

He wrote for two hours, but after that time, he had managed no coherent account. The monster that was within writhed too much, was too horrible to look at. As frantic as he was to place down in writing what had happened, the words would not be mastered, the sentences rebelled. Ten times he had started, and ten times he had written only scraps. Words were not his friends, never had been. Words had betrayed him all his life, coming slowly and rarely, usually to trip him. It had been his hands that he had relied on, his hands that had given him what dignity he had pulled in for himself.

At last he gave up. He looked down at the pieces of paper, knowing that it wasn't good but knowing also that it was all he could do. He found an envelope and addressed it in barely legible letters to Dr J. Eisenmenger. It was only after he had put the papers inside and sealed it that he remembered he didn't have a stamp.

He was beyond laughing at this irony.

He began to search through all the drawers of the sideboard, in china pots on the mantelpiece, in pockets of coats, but there was no stamp either old or new, first or second class. Rage flared within him, his frustration at this minute, insignificant thing completely engulfing him as it assumed the symbolism that here was his entire life in one example.

No! No! No!

In his fury he was about to screw up the envelope and throw it into the wastepaper bin when a floorboard creaked in the room beyond and his head jerked upwards, his eyes widened into round white-rimmed pits.

"Janey?" he called querulously. Sobbing. For a moment he thought that it was his, but then he realized the truth. He got up, almost running to the doorway.

"Janey?" he called again as he entered the kitchen, but it was empty.

He stood for a moment staring into nothing, listening for her voice but hearing nothing.

He started to weep.

Returning to the table, he picked up the envelope no longer caring if anyone heard his voice. He put it on the hall table under a large and spectacularly ugly pot, a 'present from Yarmouth', where he and Janey had always put the things they were going to post.

They were back in the same place, the same waitress dancing inattendance upon them, the same music tape looping through the air between them. It was as if the tape had always played, as if it would go on playing for ever, always there whether humanity listened or not. It lent an air of eternity to the proceedings but it was a funereal air. The music might not end, but something certainly had.

Helena looked ill, as if some wasting disease had finally overcome her, turned her into nothing more than a substrate for a pathogen. Johnson, too, looked tired although not unduly despondent, but then he didn't know what Eisenmenger had said to Helena last night.

"Tell him," said Helena, a mix of command and suggestion, her voice nearly drowned in melancholy.

The waitress looked at them, or rather she looked at things upon their table, saw that they weren't spending money and moved on. They had decided against the wine list and were drinking coffee.

When Eisenmenger had completed his account of what he had been told by Beverley Wharton, Johnson said disbelievingly, "That is breathtaking. Absolutely breathtaking."

Helena was already nodding but Eisenmenger said, "Is it? Can you prove she's wrong?"

"Can she prove she's right?"

"Bob, she has a witness."

"A witness who's done a deal with Beverley Wharton."

"You know as well as I do that we'll never be able to show that."

Johnson turned to Eisenmenger. "Leaving aside Bilroth, do you think Russell did it?"

Eisenmenger had been wondering that. He said after a pause, "It's possible . . . "

"But?"

"But I rather think not."

Johnson turned back to Helena. "Beverley Wharton's doing it again. She's twisted the evidence to show that Bilroth was involved when he almost certainly wasn't. And hell, much as Russell's a loathsome slug, he does at least deserve a fair trial."

Johnson was becoming almost angry the more he argued. Helena had never seen him like this. She pointed out, "We have no evidence that he didn't do it. We have only an opinion."

"And I'm afraid the same goes for showing that Bilroth wasn't involved." Eisenmenger felt that he was mugging Johnson. "We have not one fragment of evidence of his innocence. I believe that he wasn't the murderer, but I can't say why exactly. You believe he wasn't involved, but that's only because you hate Beverley Wharton and because she never got around to proving her case. Helena also wants to prove Beverley wrong, but how do we know that Bilroth wasn't actually a part of all this? He was a rapist, after all."

Johnson couldn't believe what he heard, and for a few moments Helena stared at Eisenmenger as if she had just heard him condone bestiality. Then, abruptly, she dropped her eyes and he saw acceptance.

Johnson opened his mouth but then appeared to think better of rebutting the gibe. Eisenmenger explained, "I'm just trying to make you see the realities and how others are going to view the situation."

"It doesn't matter if he was a rapist," persisted Johnson. "It doesn't even matter if he was a mass murderer. It only matters if it can be proved that he committed this particular crime."

Eisenmenger was shaking his head. "This has gone beyond a formal criminal trial, Bob. Balance of probabilities is all that matters now."

"So all we have to do is keep digging. Change the balance."

Eisenmenger saw something novel in Johnson, the first time he had suspected real desperation at the base of his motivation. When he looked at Helena he expected to see a similar hunger but there was only blankness.

Eisenmenger said, "I think that we've fed enough on the corpse of Nikki Exner."

"What does that mean?" Johnson demanded.

"Isn't that what we're all doing? Picking over her body? Using her death for our own needs and desires?"

Johnson looked outraged but Eisenmenger thought that Helena at least was uncomfortable with the notion. She continued her silence while Johnson said in an offended tone, "I can't speak for you, John, but I've gone into this to correct a misjustice, nothing more."

Eisenmenger didn't feel like continuing the argument. Let Johnson believe that his motives had been entirely pious; for himself, he couldn't quite find such conviction. From the way that Helena was now frowning he was inclined to suspect that she too now had her doubts.

"Well," he said in a conciliatory tone, "whatever our motives, we didn't exactly shine, did we?"

"That's why we shouldn't give up. We know that Russell was involved, even if he didn't actually do it, as the police say. We should press on to uncover the truth."

Tiredly, Eisenmenger asked, "How? Where do you look now?"

Perhaps he had the answer ready, the next phase of the investigation mapped out, but he never got the chance to reply because Helena said in a low voice, "It doesn't matter. We're not continuing."

Surprised, they both looked at her. "What do you mean?" asked Johnson. "Of course we are."

But she was shaking her head. "I spoke with the Bilroth family this morning. They have specifically requested us to stop."

"Why?"

Eisenmenger could guess but he let Helena explain. "All we've achieved so far is to stoke it all up again, and to what end? Bilroth is still involved. We haven't amassed any evidence to show that he couldn't have been involved, have we? The family has had enough. They want us to let things lie, let them get on with their lives."

"But we can keep digging," persisted Johnson. "It's not as though they're paying us. We just don't have to be too conspicuous about it."

"And if we find something?" asked Eisenmenger. "What then? You can bet that Beverley Wharton wouldn't roll over without a fight. A very public fight."

"But if it was convincing enough . . . "

"The smoking gun?" enquired Eisenmenger. "Do you really think there is one?"

Johnson turned to Helena. "You can't really be thinking of just giving up?"

Helena looked almost ashamed, her eyes on the pale cream of the tablecloth. "My call to the Bilroths was made following one I received from the Exners. They, too, want an end to it. Poor Nikki's been dissected enough."

Johnson looked as if he wanted to argue but the weight of Helena's depression was too heavy to lift. He remained dissatisfied but silent.

The waitress orbited them again. Beethoven's genius filled the atmosphere, unregarded by everyone in the room.

"So that's it, is it?" asked Johnson, drinking the last of his cold coffee. "We just give up?"

"I don't know where else to go, Bob. I've spent long hours trying to break this, but I can't."

"But we can't let Beverley get away with it! We can't!"

When neither Helena nor Eisenmenger answered him, he felt despair; almost enough despair to tell them about Sally, about the price he had paid for this investigation. He put his hand on Eisenmenger's sleeve and said, "Please?"

Eisenmenger didn't understand why it was suddenly so important to Johnson, but he did understand the magnitude of the other's emotion. He found himself remembering just what Johnson had done for him in the past.

"All right," he relented. "If you can suggest where else we should look, I'll give it one more go."

The emptiness of the house accused him. Johnson heard its mute condemnation even before he walked through the front door, saw its tears of recrimination in the darkness of the hallway. He tried to tell himself that it was his fancy, but he was not fooled: he knew that it was real because he knew that it was merely his own guilt staring out at him from the shadows, and whispering to him from the emptiness.

He had visited Sally that morning and she had looked out at him from large, red-rimmed eyes, frightened by her illness, frightened by the demons that drove her, frightened to be once again in the pit. It would be several days before the medication began its work, days in which only therapy and counselling would be offered. Her room was bright and clean, the medical and nursing staff attentive and caring. There were some flowers in a vase by her bed, sent by friends of theirs, while already three cards had arrived.

She had been uncommunicative, a mood which he knew well from old. He had spent three-quarters of an hour trying to make her produce conversation that was in some way animated, or interested, or even undisjointed, but he had been forced to concede to failure. When he had left he had kissed her on the cheek, but it was the warm, soft flesh of a living corpse that his lips brushed against.

And now, at the house that was his home, he had to endure not only the guilty knowledge of his wife's illness, but also the frustration that it had all been for naught. He found it intolerable that the case should end like this, complete capitulation to injustice, fabrication, laziness and corruption allowed to succeed. The sheer unfairness of it was caustic within him. He told himself that this was a thing of ideals, that he wanted justice because justice should always be desired, for its own sake, unsullied by personal considerations, but somewhere in his mind the insistences became tarnished. Eisenmenger had seen a desire for vengeance in their actions and he had vehemently refused to acknowledge this, but no matter how strongly he reiterated this denial, the suspicion that he was lying to himself kept growing.

He stood in the front room window, looking out on the long front garden. It was a good neighbourhood, full of people who cared. He cared. That was the problem – he cared too much.

Fuck Eisenmenger! Why did he have to articulate what should have been left unsaid?

So what if he did want to see Beverley Wharton brought down? A small dollop of personal satisfaction was not incompatible with higher matters, was it? Why shouldn't he be allowed to exult in her failure?

Nor was he using the Exner girl – at least no more than any other investigation 'used' a corpse. Doctors 'used' sickness, firemen 'used' conflagration, lawyers 'used' crime. Why shouldn't he 'use' the irrevocable fact of this girl's slaughter? Use it to achieve something both for himself and for all the other poor bastards Beverley Wharton had stabbed and slayed on her way to the top.

But, the fact remained, things were apparently hopeless. They had no mandate to proceed, nowhere to go anyway.

He sighed and turned away from the window, but looking into the house only brought back Sally's absence. He had to get out, to walk it off.

He didn't want to drink so he opted to go into the shopping precinct, the vague idea to buy something for Sally hovering in his head. It was there that he met Alport, who happened, in the course of the conversation, to mention that Goodpasture had just committed suicide.

Schlemm was enjoying his coffee and biscuits for the first time in several weeks. He had just put the phone down after a conversation with a fellow member of his Royal College. Nothing had been said openly but the subtext had been clear: the College was looking for its next President, looking in his direction. A smile of small satisfaction pulled at the corners of his mouth as he bit into some shortbread. At least the distressing publicity about the appalling happenings within the museum had not reflected upon him personally.

It had, however, reflected on the medical school, and this was a source of considerable discomfort to him. The police had been very supportive. Several conversations with the Chief Constable had kept him informed of their conclusions, of the connections between

Libman and Russell, of Russell's role in the death of Nikki Exner. What he heard worried him greatly, but it was not so much the acts themselves that caused him such distress, as the possibility that they might become public.

Delicate discussions had followed. It was not in the best interests of either the police or the medical school to allow all the facts to become widely known, it was decided. In particular, Russell's role in the death was, they both felt, worthy of careful handling. There was no doubt in the Chief Constable's mind that Bilroth had still been involved in rape, murder and quite possibly blackmail: any mention of Russell in this connection would only cloud issues that were otherwise of absolute clarity. His involvement in the attempted murder of Libman was another matter, but the Chief Constable had spoken personally with the officers who had witnessed the event and none of them were willing categorically to exclude the possibility that it had been an unfortunate accident.

The Dean had listened and agreed. He knew that he was spending favours – many large favours – but if it achieved a desirable result, he calculated it worthwhile.

But the press had been a different matter. For several days following Russell's car crash there had been constant enquiries, some clearly implying that the police version of events was dubious. Connections were suggested between the accidents of Libman and Russell, so close were they in time and place. More connections were made with the death of Nikki Exner, not surprisingly given their links with the museum.

And then the devastation of the news. Russell charged with the Exner girl's murder and the attempted murder of Stephan Libman. The public furore and the private incredulity had proved a formidable combination, yet he had handled all the intrusions with courteous blankness. The police, not the medical school authorities, were the correct place at which to make enquiries on the matter; the medical school knew nothing. Gradually the calls had decreased, then ceased, leaving only the problems of what to do about Histopathology and, inevitably, the museum.

With no consultant staff, the question of the Histopathology Department was effectively answered for him. The everyday work of the department had been spread around Histopathology Departments in surrounding hospitals, the staff following the work in order to alleviate the strain. He had ordered the Personnel Department to dust off the job description for a new chair in Histopathology, while he and his colleagues on the Academic

Board had begun the customary task of informally canvassing likely candidates. True, Russell had not yet been found guilty, but everyone accepted that it would not do to have someone *like that* on the Academic Board. It had not occurred to him to ask Eisenmenger to return to his post.

The museum, however, had proved a harder dilemma to solve.

It had been Schlemm's first instinct to close it for ever, feeling that its associations were now too macabre and too unedifying to allow it to continue. His colleagues, however, had counselled against a precipitate action and he had listened to this advice, naturally wary of rashness. When he had consulted more widely – fellow Deans and their like – their responses had been unanimous. The museum was too important, too venerated and important to lose because of what one of them called 'tasteless antics'.

This laudable aim, however, raised another difficulty. He had no staff to run it. Not only did he no longer have a Director or any assistant curators, he had now lost his head curator. Goodpastor, Greenpasture – whatever his name had been – had committed suicide some few days before. On first hearing the news, Schlemm had been struck with concern: surely not another twist in the Exner affair? Once again, however, the Chief Constable had proved an unlikely source of comfort. The curator had taken his own life by hanging because of overwhelming grief at the recent death of his wife. No note but often they didn't. There were no suspicious circumstances.

Clearly he had to appoint a new Director as the first step and the obvious choice was Hamilton-Bailey. The little Professor had returned to work and had clearly begun a recovery from his mental collapse, but Schlemm was still unsure. He had telephoned Irene Hamilton-Bailey partly in order better to gauge Hamilton-Bailey's mental state, partly to point out that he had done as she had begged. Her assurances that her husband was far better and still improving had been met with acclamations of delight and pleasure; however he had been more interested in her fervent expressions of gratitude for his help.

He pointed out that, given the present situation, he had been considerably inconvenienced by the loss of Eisenmenger. He pointed out too that Hamilton-Bailey's name had not once been mentioned in connection with the murder.

"You know that I'm extremely grateful, Daniel."

He paused. *How grateful?* he wondered, although something in her tone suggested that it was an easy question to answer. He also wondered if he wanted to grasp this opportunity: could he be bothered to ignite this particular fire?

"Perhaps we should meet, Irene," he suggested carefully. "It has been a long time."

She had thought so too.

But after this he had then wondered about the wisdom of putting the small fat Professor in charge of the museum. Its direction would need much work, much stamina, much concentration. Would Hamilton-Bailey be able to cope with such onerous, extra responsibility? Even if he was truly recovering, was it fair and wise to ask him to take this on? One of the most pressing issues was the question of the origin and legality of many of the specimens, an issue that the Dean had known full well from the first was going to be an exceedingly delicate, complex matter.

And he had wondered also about Hamilton-Bailey's 'relationship' with Nikki Exner.

He had decided eventually that Hamilton-Bailey should at least be approached and thus he had invited him to a meeting the day before yesterday and had presented him with the proposition. Hamilton-Bailey, looking better but by no means as if he was peaking in the physical fitness stakes, had hesitated but had agreed fairly readily. Schlemm had in fact been taken aback by this relative, restrained eagerness, but he could not now retract. The deed was done.

Still he wondered, only partially enheartened by the knowledge that he had little other option.

Johnson had called Eisenmenger at once, telling him to meet him at Goodpasture's house. Then he had gone straight there, but it was while he was waiting for the pathologist that he began to wonder what they should do next. He hadn't even analysed why he knew that it was a significant event, why he was certain that he wanted to get into that house and look around. Now that he had arrived, however, the practicalities soon became obvious.

The house was empty, so how to get in? He looked up and down the street. It was possible that one of the nearby householders had a key, but he didn't fancy having to knock on perhaps ten front doors, lying to each face he saw about why he might want to get in. The alternative, though, was to break in. He looked up and down the street; still no Eisenmenger.

He weighed up the immoralities, finally being decided by the immediacy of breaking and entering: he was feeling impatient.

To attempt illegal entry at the front was clearly impractical, given the number of windows reflecting the cloudy sky down on to him, but the back, he soon discovered, was different. As long as he could get close to the back door unseen – and there was a liberal sprinkling of large shrubs on the Goodpasture estate to provide the cover – it was essentially a very fine and very private place for breaking and entering. Within ten minutes he was in the kitchen, pocketing the penknife with which he had forced the lock.

It stank. In the few short weeks since Goodpasture's wife had collapsed into a coma, the house had taken on an air of abandonment, decay and sorrow. Goodpasture's own black depression had added to the atmosphere, his death and subsequent early decay gilding the dark vapours. Even though the body was gone, undertakers having removed it a day or more before, the sense of despair clung to the building like rot and it made Johnson at once sorry that he had come.

But he had come, though what now to do?

He looked around, saw the few dirty dishes on the table, the fine layer of city dust on the surfaces: saw Goodpasture's slippers by the door to the hall and his wife's knitting bag next to it. He felt sordid just standing there.

He moved into the hall, keeping away from the frosted glass of the front door with its pile of mail beneath. A barometer was on the wall, an old telephone on a small table next to a souvenir from Swanage. Outside a car, casting a brief, squirting shadow on the wall, went past, then stopped. He cautiously opened the door. It was Eisenmenger. When Eisenmenger got out and look around, Johnson decided to risk discovery. He pulled the door open more widely and hissed at Eisenmenger.

Inside, the door closed, Eisenmenger said, "Should I ask how you got in, Bob?" His tone was laced with curious amusement.

"If we get caught . . . "

"Let's try not to, then." He looked around, wrinkling his nose at the same, half-imagined, half-detested emanations. "What are we looking for?"

To which Johnson could only shrug.

"Well, then. Where do we start?"

The front room was on their right and they entered it cautiously, aware that there were net curtains but still aware that neighbours – all the neighbours on God's green earth – have sharp, poky eyes.

The feeling of gloom deepened. Johnson felt as if his large dirty boots were treading mud into the lives of these people. Here, where the mementoes and ornaments, the photographs of holidays and weddings, birthdays and Christmases were clustered together in cheap, mute company, the feeling of despoliation was even more acute. Abruptly the sense of self-disgust flared again, hotter than ever. He recalled Eisenmenger's words about scavenging, being a thing of carrion.

And then he looked again at the photographs and he forgot to loathe himself any more.

"Well, well," he said, picking up the largest one, the one that had the central location. He showed it to Eisenmenger, who raised quizzical eyebrows. "Who's he?"

"James Paneth."

They continued their search in the back room. Silence, cheapness and sadness. There was nothing of light here, nothing to show the heights to which man aspired. They began to pick at the leftovers of two lives, opening cupboards, pulling out drawers, moving ornaments. Eisenmenger found a bundle of bills – all paid – and leafed through them; Johnson read through a pile of old Christmas cards.

"Where did he hang himself?"

Johnson wasn't sure. "In one of the bedrooms, I think. From the light fitting."

They moved on, Eisenmenger to the kitchen, Johnson to the sideboard. Eisenmenger spent ten minutes finding nothing while Johnson went through more old bills, older photographs and certificates telling of events that now mattered for nothing. There was nothing of significance. Eisenmenger went out into the hallway, saw nothing and went upstairs. It was a further ten minutes before Johnson moved to the hall.

Like Eisenmenger he would have missed it had his mother not had a similar illogical habit.

"John?" he called.

Professor Hamilton-Bailey sat in his familiar office, trying to find some of his old confidence and calm. He knew that he was better but with that knowledge came the realization that he was far from right. True, he had started work on Gray's again and he was picking up other, long-neglected academic duties, but he did so with feelings of trepidation and depression. There was still something deep and dark and black about the future, perhaps a reflection of the recent past, perhaps a prescience of his fate.

And now he was being pressed by the Dean to take on the added burden of Director of the museum. How surprised he had been, and how he had struggled with the dilemma of whether or not to accept the post. The thought of the extra responsibility had urged him strongly to decline but the possibility, however remote, that someone else in such a position might discover something . . .

The very idea made him feel ill. The spider above him stared sightlessly ahead.

Yet now, having accepted the position and being faced with a tottering pile of correspondence, he questioned whether he had done the correct thing. Sighing deeply he began to open and read the letters, leaflets and brochures.

Again they met, Helena starting to feel that they were little better than ineffectual conspirators in a play. This time they were in her flat. She had a lot of work to do – real work, as she now considered it – and she had little hope that this would prove fruitful.

"What's all this about?" They all heard the slightly peremptory tone in her question, as if she were a teacher being interrupted yet again. Eisenmenger indicated that Johnson should start.

"Goodpasture, the curator, committed suicide."

"I know that. His wife."

"So everyone believes."

For the first time, she caught a whiff of interest. "It wasn't his wife?"

"John and I paid a visit to the house. We found this on the mantelshelf." He produced the photograph, still in its brass frame. At the bottom was the signature, *Jem*.

"Should I know him?" she asked.

"Jem. James. James Paneth. Her son, his stepson."

She forgot her work. "The medical student? The one she tried to blackmail?"

"That's him."

She was thinking hard. "A motive. Paneth's got an alibi, hasn't he?" Then she paused, "But so have the Goodpastures."

"That's not all." Johnson nodded to Eisenmenger, who handed round photocopies of sheets of A4 paper.

"These were in an envelope we found in Goodpasture's house. The envelope was addressed to me, so I guess he was thinking of posting it to me. Events intervened, apparently. It's disjointed and fairly incomprehensible, but I've managed to get some sense out of it."

313

Helena looked through the sheets. The handwriting was bad, the spelling worse, the grammar appalling. There were very few intact sentences, and the fragments and phrases she could make out seemed either fantastical, nonsensical or incomprehensible. Some pages had only a single phrase on them.

. . . Janey's hear I can feel her . . . . please god please give me hope give me strenth to do this

She desserved it the bitch . . . . the proffesor said he didnt kill her but I think he must have . . . he

I didn't want to leav her . . . . Id seen her from my window and hated her more and more and more and more . . .

She was naked . . . . He was angry when I said no and threatened to tell evryone

He called while janey was ill before they arrived before I new what was wrong . . .

He told me he had just found her . . . . the doctors said she might not live

Sucked her brests

Then back to janey praying she hadnt died

Im a madman now . . . . he said she was going to have a baby

Strung her up round her neck

It wasn't till I was going to start I saw who it was

Im sorry janey

She was already dead strangled I only cut her up like he said . . .

. . . . i couldn't help it couldn't stop myself . . .

The bitch who had ruinned Jems life . . .

Janeys cross but now shell be happy . . . forgive me janey . . .

The proffesor was waiting for me still angry . . . . I cut her open laughing . . . chucked the uterus cross the room . . .

He left me to do it and I took her took her as she desserved took her and made her mine

It doesn't matter now . . . . he said I was to take her uterus . . . I was to make it look as if a madman . . .

. . . . at first he made me do it but then I saw who it was . . .

I had to do it he knew

. . . . my lovers

. . . . im going mad . . . .

She looked up. "Is this supposed to be a confession?"

"Believe it or not."

Johnson had reservations. "It doesn't actually make sense. Most of it's just ramblings."

"It's disjointed, I admit, but it actually explains most of what happened. The secret is to read it without having the usual linear narrative in mind. If you do that, there is something here that makes sense. I've checked as far as I can, and it fits."

She put the photocopies down. "Perhaps you'd better interpret it for us."

"Janey is – was – Goodpasture's wife. On the evening of the murder, she had a stroke, a cerebrovascular event. Judging by the timings, I think that it happened at about ten in the evening. Naturally enough, Goodpasture called an ambulance and it was while he was waiting for it to arrive that he received a phone call.

"That phone call was from someone who wanted him to come at once to the museum."

"'The Professor,'" interrupted Johnson.

"But which Professor? Without knowing that – "

Eisenmenger put a finger to his lips. "Later," he said. "Goodpasture talks about being made to do it, by which I assume that the compulsion was to both attend and to do something. Goodpasture went to the museum, but only after he had made sure his precious Janey was in ITU. He was devoted to her and no matter how strong the compunction to do as he was told – and I think it was very, very strong – he wasn't about to put her second.

"When he arrived at the museum, Nikki Exner was already dead. That night, I think she had probably had sex with Fournier and with Bilroth, the first for pleasure, the second for business. We know also that she had given head to Russell, watched and photographed by Libman. What we don't know is what happened then, but I suspect I can work it out.

"In any case, 'the Professor' was there and in the presence of the dead body of a young girl. She had been killed by strangulation, first being drugged. Because she was pregnant, she was to have her uterus dissected out, a substitute being supplied from the Department of Histopathology; the assumption must be that 'the Professor' thought that he had fathered the child, although I think it is entirely possible that he was being deceived. In order to disguise the motive for the hysterectomy, the young girl was to be mutilated. Clearly 'the Professor' didn't fancy the manual labour involved in all this, but he didn't need to do it. He had Goodpasture."

Helena interrupted. "But why should Goodpasture get involved?"

"Because he had no choice. Because, I think, Goodpasture had a secret known only to our friend, 'the Professor'. Not even Goodpasture's wife knew it. I suspect that when he died, he developed a

315

delusion about her. I think that he began to believe he was haunted, that her spirit possessed some form of knowledge of what he had done. That, I think, was what forced him to confess and what forced him to suicide."

"Do you know what the secret was?" asked Johnson curiously.

Eisenmenger nodded. "I think I can guess." He continued, "Understandably, Goodpasture wasn't keen; at least not until he saw who it was. Nikki Exner, the girl who had ruined his stepson's career, and thereby ruined the lives of all who were important to him." He looked up. "I talked to Paneth yesterday. Paneth and Goodpasture were never close, but Goodpasture doted on his wife and she, in turn, doted on Paneth. Goodpasture saw the effect that Nikki Exner had indirectly had upon his wife; he may even have blamed her for his wife's stroke. His hatred had grown in proportion to the increasing devastation that was being wrought in his own life. What does he say? *I'd seen her from my window and hated her more and more and more and more . . .* So, as soon as he saw who was to be mutilated, he agreed readily enough. He wasn't just willing to be involved, he insisted.

"I think that it was then that he was left alone to complete his task; presumably it was considered somewhat too 'unappetizing' for the refined tastes of 'the Professor'. I'm pretty much speculating now, but it's speculation that makes sense and fits the available data. It's also speculation that's pretty distasteful."

He looked meaningfully at Helena who said, "Go on."

"It relates to Goodpasture's secret, the means by which he was coerced to come to the museum, even though his wife was seriously ill in ITU. It also relates to the state of Nikki Exner's body.

"Nikki Exner's body bore the marks not only of forced vaginal intercourse, but also of anal intercourse. Don't forget that there was always a problem of forced intercourse when she had been drugged with Midazolam. And, of course, it's possible that sodomy was one of her pleasures, but the tissue samples I took from her corpse suggest that the vulval and peri-anal lesions were made post mortem."

It was Helena who got it first, followed quickly by Johnson. She said, "You mean . . . ?" and this was followed by Johnson breathing the word, "Christ."

"The third semen type came, I think, from Goodpasture. I think that he was a necrophiliac, and it was this secret that was used to make him comply with the grisly business of dissecting Nikki Exner."

Helena looked ill, Johnson merely thoughtful.

"He had sexual intercourse as a means of revenge. Then, in continuance of that revenge, he sliced her open and removed the uterus as requested. Then I assume he showered, changed (I think he must have worn the clothes usually worn for autopsy work) and went back to the intensive care unit. He was not missed, although we know that nobody can account for all the time that he claimed to have spent there."

For a few minutes after he had finished, they looked down at the disjointed phrases Goodpasture had written before he died, verifying Eisenmenger's interpretation with what was before them. Then Johnson asked, "You haven't said which Professor it was."

Eisenmenger sighed. "Poor old Goodpasture. I suspect it never occurred to him that there might be uncertainty as to whom he was accusing."

"Do you know?"

He nodded, but then said, "Although as with so much of this benighted universe that may not be enough."

"What does that mean?"

"There are curious occurrences that suggest a name. The first was Russell's penchant for fellatio. There is testimony to the effect that for years Russell had been employing a prostitute on a weekly basis and never once did he want vaginal intercourse. That, added to the Polaroid photographs of Nikki Exner, must make one ask how and why he made her pregnant. It suggests to me that whoever was the father, it was exceedingly unlikely to be Basil Russell.

"The second is a quirk of Goodpasture's. Goodpasture didn't like change, a not unsuitable trait in a museum curator; not only did he not like it, he actively rebelled against it. The most overt manifestation of this in his day-to-day working life was in his interaction with Russell. Russell had been a mere senior lecturer when Goodpasture first knew him and his elevation to Professor meant nothing to Goodpasture. Either through inability or disinclination he never called him 'Professor', to Goodpasture, Russell was always just 'Doctor'."

Helena asked, "You think it was Hamilton-Bailey?"

Eisenmenger didn't answer for a few moments. "I think it was," he admitted, "Although even if that turns out to be the case, the problems don't end there."

"Why not?"

It was Johnson who answered, "Because Goodpasture's own confession, such as it is, states that Hamilton-Bailey denied actually killing her. Presumably he would claim that someone else – possibly

Russell – actually murdered her. He only took advantage of her death by destroying the evidence of her pregnancy."

Eisenmenger said, "And Russell will say it wasn't him."

"So there's nothing to convict either of them." Helena sounded suddenly depressed. "Have we made any progress at all?"

At once Johnson said, "Oh, yes. This destroys Beverley Wharton's story. It discredits completely the account that Tim Bilroth was in any way involved. There is nothing to connect him with this crime.

"From that point of view, this is a complete success."

Beverley Wharton was quite happy with life until the day that she saw Helena Flemming and John Eisenmenger at the end of the corridor outside the Superintendent's office. They were in the distance and were soon gone down the stairs that led to the front entrance, but she knew then that here was trouble. She waited for some sort of sign of its coming but first one day, then another, passed and nothing came. She forgot about the incident.

Beverley didn't think that the call into the Superintendent's office was that sign, not at first anyway. Just another day, another summons into the presence. She thought that it was about a case involving a paedophile ring; it was high profile and therefore she was constantly being requested to attend to her superiors' fears and anxieties about progress and PR. Not that she was fussed, since progress was gradually being made.

Nothing to suggest, then, that this meeting was not about paedophiles, or expenses, or an invitation to intercourse.

She knocked and waited. Waited a long time. When the permission to enter came, it was in a voice that was noticeably angry.

"You wanted me, sir?" She kept her face set, her tone level, as if she was confident and ignorant, both at the same time. He was reading something, although she couldn't see what. He kept reading it as if he hadn't noticed her presence. It was only after three long minutes that he had sucked all the interest out of it and therefore could afford to look up at her. His eyes were angry, his face almost white.

For another thirty seconds – seconds that crawled slowly to their grave so that she felt her heart beat a hundred thousand times – he stared at her, then, "Do you know what this is?"

He gestured at what he had been so avidly perusing. Of course she didn't, and she wasn't meant to essay possibilities to him. She was supposed to shake her head and wait for damnation.

"These were found in Goodpasture's house. It is in effect a confession. It is not signed but the handwriting has been verified. It describes his part in the death and mutilation of Nikki Exner. It makes no mention of Bilroth's involvement."

An image came unbidden into her mind *Eisenmenger. Helena.* She felt as if she'd been groped by a leper.

She held out her hand. "May I?" she asked.

He picked it up and flicked it over to her, as if it were detritus to be disposed of. She caught it and began to scan it. For a long while there was silence while she stood and read – he had not offered her a seat – and he sat with his chair turned away from her, his face scowling.

When she had finished, she put it back on his desk and he turned to her and demanded, "Well?"

How to play it, that was her dilemma. How, in effect, would he want it played, was her question. Would he be happy to massage things again, or would he demand a rigorous reinvestigation?

"It's pretty incoherent, sir."

He grabbed the papers from her hands. "*She was already dead strangled I only cut her up like he said* . . . I can understand that one, can't you?"

"So Russell killed her and made Goodpasture help him. It doesn't fundamentally change – "

"One: Eisenmenger has pointed out that it could easily be Hamilton-Bailey; in fact, he's given me some pretty good reasons why it probably was. Two: you've pinned your entire investigation on implicating Bilroth." He waved the papers at her. "I don't see much room for him here, do you?"

For a second she thought about arguing, but only for a second. She said quietly, "No, sir."

"This has been a fucking gold-plated fiasco, Beverley. A complete and utter fucking cock-up."

"I know, sir, but – "

"But nothing. First you say it was Bilroth, then you say it was Bilroth and Russell. Now what are you trying to say? That it was Bilroth and Russell or maybe Hamilton-Bailey and then Goodpasture? What is this? Some kind of fucking relay race?"

She took some breaths, riding his anger. Then, into a space of calm, "Maybe we were wrong to connect the Libman-Russell business directly with the murder. Maybe that was an entirely separate affair. If so, we still have to ask who actually killed her, assuming this confession is correct, and assuming it wasn't the result of some sort of insanity – "

He snorted. "Believe in the fairies, do you, Inspector?" Bad sign – effective demotion. She found herself panicking slightly and not enjoying the unfamiliar feeling.

"We've got to talk to Hamilton-Bailey, sir. Find out what he has to say."

"Naturally."

"And we still don't know for sure who killed her. It's possible that Bilroth – "

She knew at once that she had made a major tactical misjudgement. His anger was white and hot and sudden.

"Don't give me that fucking crap, Wharton! That's gone, dead, six feet under. You made a mistake for which you'll have to answer when the time comes. For now, we take this confession as the basis for a new investigation into what happened. Understand?"

She felt herself hot and red, her heart beating fast. She nodded and said at once, "Of course, sir."

Her hands were wet with perspiration and she surreptitiously wiped them down her skirt. He said, "I'm going to take personal charge of this one, Inspector. You will answer to me."

"Yes, sir."

He indicated the confession. "Take this and get going."

She left the office swearing under her breath. Outside she leaned against the wall, her eyes shut tight. Through her mind ran emotions of discomfort, shame and fear, yet already she was planning how to escape, or at least minimize, the damage.

It depended on the Superintendent. If he calmed down enough, if he saw himself as safe from danger, if he was keen on a few nights of sexual athletics with the best lay in the constabulary . . .

After all, she reasoned, calm returning slowly, the arrest had been made when Chief Inspector Castle had been in charge of the investigation. Technically speaking, he was the one who would have to answer for any tragic mistakes.

She felt slightly better, but only slightly.

The Bilroth family informed, Helena had intended to return to her flat and there to revel in her victory, perhaps with champagne: not too much, but a small release from her constant, driven tension. This she had decided as soon as the shock of Eisenmenger's news had subsided and the implications had bedded in. For a few days she had experienced a purity of intense joy the like of which she had not known for many years.

320

But then it had faded; reality had asserted its bullying supremacy over her imagined pleasure.

What, precisely, had been achieved?

True, Tim Bilroth would be exonerated of guilt in the death of Nikki Exner, but that, it seemed to Helena, was the limit of their supposed 'victory'. After all, Beverley Wharton had been shown merely to have been incompetent, certainly not corrupt. The Superintendent had even implied that as she had not, officially, been the Senior Investigating Officer, it was possible she would carry no blame for the error.

Helena was cynical enough to listen to the word 'possible' and hear the word 'probable'.

And if there was pleasure in the hearts of the Bilroths, she knew that there would also be pain a thousand times worse in those of the Exner family. In uncovering the truth of her murder, they had defiled her. They had shown the world that she was a scheming bitch, a drug-abuser and a whore; they had destroyed her family's innocence. Her parents would have to live for ever with the knowledge of what Nikki Exner had really been, not what they wanted her to be.

Her motives, too, worried her. Since Eisenmenger had brought up the subject she had found herself worried about what she was doing and why. His description of Nikki Exner's corpse as carrion had stayed with her, wouldn't be budged. The more she denied it to herself, the more truth it seemed to contain.

Thus her return to the flat was in a sombre, curiously dissatisfied mood. There was a message on the answerphone but its content only served to deepen her mood. Mr Morton was wondering how she was. Would she, he wondered, be returning to work soon? If she felt up to it, he had several very interesting cases for her . . .

She switched off the hesitant, kindly voice and sighed. She had a feeling that she would never feel up to it again.

She went into the lounge and stood for a long time looking out into the road. She felt slightly odd and for a while she couldn't place the sensation. It was with detached sense of surprise that she came to realize what it was – loneliness. For the first time in many years she appreciated the fact of her aloneness and, like a kitten finding flame, she did not at once associate the experience with pain: indeed, the first question she asked was why. Why should she feel alone, now of all times? It was so far in terms of time, distance and emotion since the tragedy that had sculpted her, why should it be this concatenation of circumstances that evoked loneliness?

Was it the failure? The wounding but not the slaying of her enemy? Was it the hurt done to those she had wanted to help?

Or was it John Eisenmenger?

Had he betrayed her? He denied it, but somebody had.

She found herself hoping vehemently that it had not been John, that here was someone at last whom she could trust. Before she knew it there was a moistness in her eyes, a moistness that at once she cursed. She turned away from the window, reaching for a tissue from the box on the little occasional table. The table on which were photographs of Jeremy and photographs of her parents.

"Damn," she whispered. "Damn."

The room was pleasant, the view from the barred window inviting, but it was a *barred* window and it was a view of the rest of the psychiatric unit. Sally sat in the chair by the bed and played a kind of chaotic cat's cradle with the cord that the nurse had given her. She did this with absolute concentration, so complete that it allowed for no other thoughts, no other people.

Certainly not Johnson.

He knew that the drugs and the therapy were helping her, that she was in the best place, but the knowledge was an abrasive reassurance. He had been there now for an hour and a half and his attempts at chatter had been met with a dull indifference. Even his announcement that the Exner case was resolved had failed to result in any uplift of her spirits.

He decided at last to go and announced the fact as he stood. He felt awkward, unsure of whether she would want him to kiss her. In the difficult silence she looked up at him – for almost the first time – and said, "I'm sorry, Bob."

A smile flitted across her mouth, almost a spasm, then she looked down.

He felt as if he had been holding his breath since the beginning of time. He opened his mouth, let out a low, joyous "Oh," then moved at once to stand in front of her, take her by the arms and bend to hug her. She allowed him to do this, but didn't respond in kind. Her hands were still scabbed and sore.

He knelt down beside her. "There's no need to be sorry, love."

She was not looking at him and was still toying with the cord. "I'm scared," she said.

He didn't know what to say to reassure her. Then he decided on the truth.

"So am I, Sally. So am I."

Eisenmenger had talked to no one other than occasional shop assistants and his television for a week. He had given up trying to contact Marie, both because he had been thus far spectacularly unsuccessful and because he no longer knew what he could say to her. The fear of reigniting some sort of relationship with her – or rather her delusion that there still existed some sort of relationship – terrified him into inaction. The acts, real or imaginary, for which she had been responsible over the past few weeks now seemed less important. She was becoming less real to him.

Yet the flat was lonely, and not because he was alone. It remained very much Marie's flat and it was therefore full of Marie's absence. He would, he had decided, have to move, both because of this and because of his present state of unemployment. His relief at leaving his job was now ebbing before the reality of being without an income, and there was only so much pleasure to be had from not having to go to work in the morning.

On one or two occasions he had tried to contact Beverley Wharton but she was always unobtainable and had not returned his calls. It had not surprised him, nor really disappointed him.

And Helena. God, how he had wanted to talk to Helena, yet he had not had the strength, afraid that something had gone sour, and that to see her and hear her would only destroy them.

Even Tamsin had gone, though he didn't know if that was through release or suppression.

He had heard nothing from either Johnson or Helena and he had therefore assumed that they had gone from his life for ever, but at about six in the evening on the Friday he heard someone at the door and found to his surprise that it was Helena. She looked no less wary or severe but at least, he reflected, she was there.

"Helena! Come in."

He had a feeling that he looked less than spruce and this was strengthened by the covert glance from head to foot that she gave him. She gave him a smile as if they were too expensive to be careless with and preceded him to the living room.

"Can I take your coat? Would you like some tea or coffee?"

She declined the offer of a drink but she did consent to take off her black woollen overcoat. She sat on the sofa, he in the armchair.

"How have you been?" he asked.

"Busy."

"Any news on the Exner case?"

She said, "Hamilton-Bailey's been arrested but released on bail. He denies the murder, as does Russell. Libman and Russell are still in hospital. That's all I know."

"And Beverley Wharton?"

She frowned, suddenly sullen. "Nothing," she admitted.

He didn't say anything and it was as if this was a deliberate provocation to her, for real fury abruptly welled up within her. "It's so unfair! It's obvious that she was responsible for Tim Bilroth's death, yet no one's going to do anything about it."

"It's difficult – " he began.

"To hell with difficulty! This is about people's lives, not about protecting people's feelings and comforts."

He was trying to calm her down but not for the first time he found that he was having the opposite effect. "Things aren't always that clear-cut," he suggested.

"So we just leave things alone, because that's the easy way, do we?" she demanded.

"No, not at all . . . " He paused. "Look, Helena, I didn't say that I agreed with what's going on, I'm just trying to explain it."

It looked for a moment as if she was going to attack him again but she abruptly paused then smiled. "I'm sorry. I get so angry . . . "

"So do I. Believe me, so do I."

The atmosphere lifted. "Perhaps I will have that drink."

"Of course. Tea? Coffee?"

"Have you any wine? It doesn't matter if you haven't, only I rather feel like something alcoholic."

"No problem." He opened a bottle from the wine rack in the kitchen and when he returned she seemed to have relaxed slightly.

"I've actually come over with an ulterior motive," she admitted. He raised his eyebrows and tried to balance interest and indifference.

"A friend of a friend got to hear about the Exner case, about what we did."

He smiled. "Not a lot, apparently."

She ignored him. "There's another case. Like this one, only already convicted. She denies she did it, but . . . "

"She?"

Helena nodded. "I haven't looked into the details yet but I'm told there are serious doubts about the conviction."

His first thoughts were a perfect blend of curiosity and refusal. To cover this he enquired, "Are you leaving divorce and conveyancing behind?"

A face of seriousness, she said, "If I can."

He smiled. "Can't say I blame you." To his relief she returned the smile. "I was wondering if you'd care to help me with it."

It was tempting but he had other considerations.

"I'm out of a job, Helena. I can't afford to work *pro bono,* even if you can."

"They'll pay." It occurred to him then that she was desperate for him to agree. "They're well off. They'll pay what's reasonable."

He considered. It would be more fun than five colorectal resections a day. "What about Bob?"

She frowned. "I talked to him. He doesn't know. His wife's ill and he's obviously preoccupied with her."

For a moment he wasn't sure, but then he caught her looking at him, a look almost of pleading. It was the nearest she'd ever come to affection for him.

He smiled, raised his glass and said, "Why not?"

They touched glasses, then drank and he saw how happy she was. Perhaps . . .

He suggested, "Do you remember we were about to set up a dinner date? Just before we were interrupted . . . ?"

Gravely she frowned in trying to recall the incident. "Ah, yes. Your girlfriend."

"Ex-girlfriend, Helena. Ex."

"Whatever." The tease was back. "Actually, I don't remember saying yes . . . "

He sat down next to her on the sofa. "Actually, I don't remember you saying no, either."

"True." She took a sip of wine, put the glass down. "I would only consider such a proposal if I were to choose the restaurant. And, Dr Eisenmenger, I think I should warn you, I have expensive tastes."

He put down his glass. He moved fractionally towards her and was relieved to see that she didn't move away. In fact . . .

He took her soft face in his hands and put his mouth to hers. The kiss tasted sweeter than heaven's nectar. Her hands came around his neck and when at last they broke, they rested cheek by cheek and she breathed in his ear, "I love – "

The telephone rang.

He sighed, hearing the fragments of the moment tinkling to the floor. They separated and he caught an exasperated smile on her lips. He picked up the receiver. "Yes?"

"It's Marie." She sounded dull and there was a tremor in her voice as if she was cold. The quality wasn't good and he realized from the background noise that she was on a mobile in the open air. Before he could say anything she continued, "I see you're with her."

That shut him up and into the silence she hissed, "*Miss Flemming.*"

"Look, Marie . . . "

He looked at Helena. She had heard him use the name and was looking at him intently.

"It's all right, John. I don't mind. I see now that she'll suffer in the same way that I did."

"Marie – "

"It suddenly came to me. Why you're such a bastard. You didn't love me, and you won't love her, will you?"

She sounded completely mad. From what she said, she was watching them. Perhaps she was even outside the floor now. Helena was still staring intently. He got up while he was talking. "Where are you, Marie? Why don't we talk things over?"

The curtains were drawn against the night. With one hand he pulled one aside. She was standing there in the middle of the well-lit car park, a mobile phone to her head. Her face was turned up to his window.

"You only ever loved one person, didn't you?"

Even from a distance he could see she was trembling. Helena came up behind him but stayed out of sight. "What do you mean?" he asked.

"You didn't think I knew, but I guessed that there was someone else, all along. Now I know who it is."

Helena said in an odd, puzzled voice, "She's standing in the middle of a puddle."

In his ear, Marie said, "She's the only one you've ever kept faith with."

"I don't know what you're talking about, Marie."

And Helena said, "It hasn't rained for days. Nowhere else is wet. Why's she in a puddle?"

Marie began to cry and the tremor in her voice became worse. "Of course you fucking do, you bastard! I'm talking about little Tamsin! She's the one you really care about! She's the only one for you!"

And Helena asked, "She looks wet, too."

For the first time he appreciated what she was saying and he looked anew at Marie just as she said, "I can't take her place, but I can join her, John. I'm going to make you love me, John."

She dropped the phone and suddenly he knew what was going on. He knew why she was wet and why she was standing in the middle of a puddle in a dust-dry car park.

And he screamed.

But as he screamed and his hands hit the double-glazed window, Marie brought out a small, silver cigarette lighter – a long-ago gift from her father – flicked it open, and exploded into a sphere of yellow-white, agonizing flame.